Fables for Children, Stories for
Children, Natural Science Stories,
Popular Education, Decembrists,
Moral Tales
Leo Tolstoy

Translator: Leo Wiener

# I. ÆSOP'S FABLES
## THE ANT AND THE DOVE

An Ant came down to the brook: he wanted to drink. A wave washed him down and almost drowned him. A Dove was carrying a branch; she saw the Ant was drowning, so she cast the branch down to him in the brook. The Ant got up on the branch and was saved. Then a hunter placed a snare for the Dove, and was on the point of drawing it in. The Ant crawled up to the hunter and bit him on the leg; the hunter groaned and dropped the snare. The Dove fluttered upwards and flew away.

## THE TURTLE AND THE EAGLE

A Turtle asked an Eagle to teach her how to fly. The Eagle advised her not to try, as she was not fit for it; but she insisted. The Eagle took her in his claws, raised her up, and dropped her: she fell on stones and broke to pieces.

## THE POLECAT

A Polecat entered a smithy and began to lick the filings. Blood began to flow from the Polecat's mouth, but he was glad and continued to lick; he thought that the|Pg 4| blood was coming from the iron, and lost his whole tongue.

## THE LION AND THE MOUSE

A Lion was sleeping. A Mouse ran over his body. He awoke and caught her. The Mouse besought him; she said:

"Let me go, and I will do you a favour!"

The Lion laughed at the Mouse for promising him a favour, and let her go.

Then the hunters caught the Lion and tied him with a rope to a tree. The Mouse heard the Lion's roar, ran up, gnawed the rope through, and said:

"Do you remember? You laughed, not thinking that I could repay, but now you see that a favour may come also from a Mouse."

## THE LIAR

A Boy was watching the sheep and, pretending that he saw a wolf, he began to cry:

"Help! A wolf! A wolf!"

The peasants came running up and saw that it was not so. After doing this for a second and a third time, it happened that a wolf came indeed. The Boy began to cry:

"Come, come, quickly, a wolf!"

The peasants thought that he was deceiving them as usual, and paid no attention to him. The wolf saw there was no reason to be afraid: he leisurely killed the whole flock.

## THE ASS AND THE HORSE

A man had an Ass and a Horse. They were walking on the road; the Ass said to the Horse:

"It is heavy for me.—I shall not be able to carry it all; take at least a part of my load."

|Pg 5|

The Horse paid no attention to him. The Ass fell down from overstraining himself, and died. When the master transferred the Ass's load on the Horse, and added the Ass's hide, the Horse began to complain:

"Oh, woe to me, poor one, woe to me, unfortunate Horse! I did not want to help him even a little, and now I have to carry everything, and his hide, too."

## THE JACKDAW AND THE DOVES

A Jackdaw saw that the Doves were well fed,—so she painted herself white and flew into the dove-cot. The Doves thought at first that she was a dove like them, and let her in. But the Jackdaw forgot herself and croaked in jackdaw fashion. Then the Doves began to pick at her and drove her away. The Jackdaw flew back to her friends, but the jackdaws were frightened at her, seeing her white, and themselves drove her away.

## THE WOMAN AND THE HEN

A Hen laid an egg each day. The Mistress thought that if she gave her more to eat, she would lay twice as much. So she did. The Hen grew fat and stopped laying.

## THE LION, THE BEAR, AND THE FOX

A Lion and a Bear procured some meat and began to fight for it. The Bear did not want to give in, nor did the Lion yield. They fought for so long a time that they both grew feeble and lay down. A Fox saw the meat between them; she grabbed it and ran away with it.

## THE DOG, THE COCK, AND THE FOX

A Dog and a Cock went to travel together. At night the Cock fell asleep in a tree, and the Dog fixed a place[Pg 6] for himself between the roots of that tree. When the time came, the Cock began to crow. A Fox heard the Cock, ran up to the tree, and began to beg the Cock to come down, as she wanted to give him her respects for such a fine voice.

The Cock said:

"You must first wake up the janitor,—he is sleeping between the roots. Let him open up, and I will come down."

The Fox began to look for the janitor, and started yelping. The Dog sprang out at once and killed the Fox.

## THE HORSE AND THE GROOM

A Groom stole the Horse's oats, and sold them, but he cleaned the Horse each day. Said the Horse:

"If you really wish me to be in good condition, do not sell my oats."

## THE FROG AND THE LION

A Lion heard a Frog croaking, and thought it was a large beast that was calling so loud. He walked up, and saw a Frog coming out of the swamp. The Lion crushed her with his paw and said:

"There is nothing to look at, and yet I was frightened."

## THE GRASSHOPPER AND THE ANTS

In the fall the wheat of the Ants got wet; they were drying it. A hungry Grasshopper asked them for something to eat. The Ants said:

"Why did you not gather food during the summer?"

She said:

"I had no time: I sang songs."

They laughed, and said:

"If you sang in the summer, dance in the winter!"

[Pg 7]

## THE HEN AND THE GOLDEN EGGS

A master had a Hen which laid golden eggs. He wanted more gold at once, and so killed the Hen (he thought that inside of her there was a large lump of gold), but she was just like any other hen.

## THE ASS IN THE LION'S SKIN

An Ass put on a lion's skin, and all thought it was a lion. Men and animals ran away from him. A wind sprang up, and the skin was blown aside, and the Ass could be seen. People ran up and beat the Ass.

## THE HEN AND THE SWALLOW

A Hen found some snake's eggs and began to sit on them. A Swallow saw it and said:

"Stupid one! You will hatch them out, and, when they grow up, you will be the first one to suffer from them."

## THE STAG AND THE FAWN

A Fawn once said to a Stag:

"Father, you are larger and fleeter than the dogs, and, besides, you have huge antlers for defence; why, then, are you so afraid of the dogs?"

The Stag laughed, and said:

"You speak the truth, my child. The trouble is,—the moment I hear the dogs bark, I run before I have time to think."

## THE FOX AND THE GRAPES

A Fox saw some ripe bunches of grapes hanging high, and tried to get at them, in order to eat them.

[Pg 8]

She tried hard, but could not get them. To drown her annoyance she said:

"They are still sour."

## THE MAIDS AND THE COCK

A mistress used to wake the Maids at night and, as soon as the cocks crowed, put them to work. The Maids found that hard, and decided to kill the Cock, so that the mistress should not be wakened. They killed him, but now they suffered more than ever: the mistress was afraid that she would sleep past the time and so began to wake the Maids earlier.

## THE FISHERMAN AND THE FISH

A Fisherman caught a Fish. Said the Fish:

"Fisherman, let me go into the water; you see I am small: you will have little profit of me. If you let me go, I shall grow up, and then you will catch me when it will be worth while."

But the Fisherman said:

"A fool would be he who should wait for greater profit, and let the lesser slip out of his hands."

## THE FOX AND THE GOAT

A Goat wanted to drink. He went down the incline to the well, drank his fill, and gained in weight. He started to get out, but could not do so. He began to bleat. A Fox saw him and said:

"That's it, stupid one! If you had as much sense in your head as there are hairs in your beard, you would have thought of how to get out before you climbed down."

## THE DOG AND HER SHADOW

A Dog was crossing the river over a plank, carrying a piece of meat in her teeth. She saw herself in the water|Pg 9| and thought that another dog was carrying a piece of meat. She dropped her piece and dashed forward to take away what the other dog had: the other meat was gone, and her own was carried away by the stream.

And thus the Dog was left without anything.

## THE CRANE AND THE STORK

A peasant put out his nets to catch the Cranes for tramping down his field. In the nets were caught the Cranes, and with them one Stork.

The Stork said to the peasant:

"Let me go! I am not a Crane, but a Stork; we are most honoured birds; I live on your father's house. You can see by my feathers that I am not a Crane."

The peasant said:

"With the Cranes I have caught you, and with them will I kill you."

## THE GARDENER AND HIS SONS

A Gardener wanted his Sons to get used to gardening. As he was dying, he called them up and said to them:

"Children, when I am dead, look for what is hidden in the vineyard."

The Sons thought that it was a treasure, and when their father died, they began to dig there, and dug up the whole ground. They did not find the treasure, but they ploughed the vineyard up so well that it brought forth more fruit than ever.

## THE WOLF AND THE CRANE

A Wolf had a bone stuck in his throat, and could not cough it up. He called the Crane, and said to him:

"Crane, you have a long neck. Thrust your head into my throat and draw out the bone! I will reward you."

|Pg 10|

The Crane stuck his head in, pulled out the bone, and said:

"Give me my reward!"

The Wolf gnashed his teeth and said:

"Is it not enough reward for you that I did not bite off your head when it was between my teeth?"

## THE HARES AND THE FROGS

The Hares once got together, and began to complain about their life:

"We perish from men, and from dogs, and from eagles, and from all the other beasts. It would be better to die at once than to live in fright and suffer. Come, let us drown ourselves!"

3

And the Hares raced away to drown themselves in a lake. The Frogs heard the Hares and plumped into the water. So one of the Hares said:

"Wait, boys! Let us put off the drowning! Evidently the Frogs are having a harder life than we: they are afraid even of us."

## THE FATHER AND HIS SONS

A Father told his Sons to live in peace: they paid no attention to him. So he told them to bring the bath broom, and said:

"Break it!"

No matter how much they tried, they could not break it. Then the Father unclosed the broom, and told them to break the rods singly. They broke it.

The Father said:

"So it is with you: if you live in peace, no one will overcome you; but if you quarrel, and are divided, any one will easily ruin you."

[Pg 11]

## THE FOX

A Fox got caught in a trap. She tore off her tail, and got away. She began to contrive how to cover up her shame. She called together the Foxes, and begged them to cut off their tails.

"A tail," she said, "is a useless thing. In vain do we drag along a dead weight."

One of the Foxes said:

"You would not be speaking thus, if you were not tailless!"

The tailless Fox grew silent and went away.

## THE WILD ASS AND THE TAME ASS

A Wild Ass saw a Tame Ass. The Wild Ass went up to him and began to praise his life, saying how smooth his body was, and what sweet feed he received. Later, when the Tame Ass was loaded down, and a driver began to goad him with a stick, the Wild Ass said:

"No, brother, I do not envy you: I see that your life is going hard with you."

## THE STAG

A Stag went to the brook to quench his thirst. He saw himself in the water, and began to admire his horns, seeing how large and branching they were; and he looked at his feet, and said: "But my feet are unseemly and thin."

Suddenly a Lion sprang out and made for the Stag. The Stag started to run over the open plain. He was getting away, but there came a forest, and his horns caught in the branches, and the lion caught him. As the Stag was dying, he said:

"How foolish I am! That which I thought to be unseemly and thin was saving me, and what I gloried in has been my ruin."

[Pg 12]

## THE DOG AND THE WOLF

A Dog fell asleep back of the yard. A Wolf ran up and wanted to eat him.

Said the Dog:

"Wolf, don't eat me yet: now I am lean and bony. Wait a little,—my master is going to celebrate a wedding; then I shall have plenty to eat; I shall grow fat. It will be better to eat me then."

The Wolf believed her, and went away. Then he came a second time, and saw the Dog lying on the roof. The Wolf said to her:

"Well, have they had the wedding?"

The Dog replied:

"Listen, Wolf! If you catch me again asleep in front of the yard, do not wait for the wedding."

## THE GNAT AND THE LION

A Gnat came to a Lion, and said:

"Do you think that you have more strength than I? You are mistaken! What does your strength consist in? Is it that you scratch with your claws, and gnaw with your teeth? That is the way the women quarrel with their husbands. I am stronger than you: if you wish let us fight!"

4

And the Gnat sounded his horn, and began to bite the Lion on his bare cheeks and his nose. The Lion struck his face with his paws and scratched it with his claws. He tore his face until the blood came, and gave up.

The Gnat trumpeted for joy, and flew away. Then he became entangled in a spider's web, and the spider began to suck him up. The Gnat said:

"I have vanquished the strong beast, the Lion, and now I perish from this nasty spider."

[Pg 13]

## THE HORSE AND HIS MASTERS

A gardener had a Horse. She had much to do, but little to eat; so she began to pray to God to get another master. And so it happened. The gardener sold the Horse to a potter. The Horse was glad, but the potter had even more work for her to do. And again the Horse complained of her lot, and began to pray that she might get a better master. And this prayer, too, was fulfilled. The potter sold the Horse to a tanner. When the Horse saw the skins of horses in the tanner's yard, she began to cry:

"Woe to me, wretched one! It would be better if I could stay with my old masters. It is evident they have sold me now not for work, but for my skin's sake."

## THE OLD MAN AND DEATH

An Old Man cut some wood, which he carried away. He had to carry it far. He grew tired, so he put down his bundle, and said:

"Oh, if Death would only come!"

Death came, and said:

"Here I am, what do you want?"

The Old Man was frightened, and said:

"Lift up my bundle!"

## THE LION AND THE FOX

A Lion, growing old, was unable to catch the animals, and so intended to live by cunning. He went into a den, lay down there, and pretended that he was sick. The animals came to see him, and he ate up those that went into his den. The Fox guessed the trick. She stood at the entrance of the den, and said:

"Well, Lion, how are you feeling?"

The Lion answered:

[Pg 14]

"Poorly. Why don't you come in?"

The Fox replied:

"I do not come in because I see by the tracks that many have entered, but none have come out."

## THE STAG AND THE VINEYARD

A Stag hid himself from the hunters in a vineyard. When the hunters missed him, the Stag began to nibble at the grape-vine leaves.

The hunters noticed that the leaves were moving, and so they thought, "There must be an animal under those leaves," and fired their guns, and wounded the Stag.

The Stag said, dying:

"It serves me right for wanting to eat the leaves that saved me."

## THE CAT AND THE MICE

A house was overrun with Mice. A Cat found his way into the house, and began to catch them. The Mice saw that matters were bad, and said:

"Mice, let us not come down from the ceiling! The Cat cannot get up there."

When the Mice stopped coming down, the Cat decided that he must catch them by a trick. He grasped the ceiling with one leg, hung down from it, and made believe that he was dead.

A Mouse looked out at him, but said:

"No, my friend! Even if you should turn into a bag, I would not go up to you."

## THE WOLF AND THE GOAT

A Wolf saw a Goat browsing on a rocky mountain, and he could not get at her; so he said to her:

"Come down lower! The place is more even, and the grass is much sweeter to feed on."

[Pg 15]

But the Goat answered:

"You are not calling me down for that, Wolf: you are troubling yourself not about my food, but about yours."

## THE REEDS AND THE OLIVE-TREE

The Olive-tree and the Reeds quarrelled about who was stronger and sounder. The Olive-tree laughed at the Reeds because they bent in every wind. The Reeds kept silence. A storm came: the Reeds swayed, tossed, bowed to the ground,—and remained unharmed. The Olive-tree strained her branches against the wind,—and broke.

## THE TWO COMPANIONS

Two Companions were walking through the forest when a Bear jumped out on them. One started to run, climbed a tree, and hid himself, but the other remained in the road. He had nothing to do, so he fell down on the ground and pretended that he was dead.

The Bear went up to him, and sniffed at him; but he had stopped breathing.

The Bear sniffed at his face; he thought that he was dead, and so went away.

When the Bear was gone, the Companion climbed down from the tree and laughing, said: "What did the Bear whisper in your ear?"

"He told me that those who in danger run away from their companions are bad people."

## THE WOLF AND THE LAMB

A Wolf saw a Lamb drinking at a river. The Wolf wanted to eat the Lamb, and so he began to annoy him. He said:

"You are muddling my water and do not let me drink."

[Pg 16]

The Lamb said:

"How can I muddle your water? I am standing downstream from you; besides, I drink with the tips of my lips."

And the Wolf said:

"Well, why did you call my father names last summer?"

The Lamb said:

"But, Wolf, I was not yet born last summer."

The Wolf got angry, and said:

"It is hard to get the best of you. Besides, my stomach is empty, so I will devour you."

## THE LION, THE WOLF, AND THE FOX

An old, sick Lion was lying in his den. All the animals came to see the king, but the Fox kept away. So the Wolf was glad of the chance, and began to slander the Fox before the Lion.

"She does not esteem you in the least," he said, "she has not come once to see the king."

The Fox happened to run by as he was saying these words. She heard what the Wolf had said, and thought:

"Wait, Wolf, I will get my revenge on you."

So the Lion began to roar at the Fox, but she said:

"Do not have me killed, but let me say a word! I did not come to see you because I had no time. And I had no time because I ran over the whole world to ask the doctors for a remedy for you. I have just got it, and so I have come to see you."

The Lion said:

"What is the remedy?"

"It is this: if you flay a live Wolf, and put his warm hide on you—"

When the Lion stretched out the Wolf, the Fox laughed, and said:

[Pg 17]

"That's it, my friend: masters ought to be led to do good, not evil."

## THE LION, THE ASS, AND THE FOX

6

The Lion, the Ass, and the Fox went out to hunt. They caught a large number of animals, and the Lion told the Ass to divide them up. The Ass divided them into three equal parts and said: "Now, take them!"

The Lion grew angry, ate up the Ass, and told the Fox to divide them up anew. The Fox collected them all into one heap, and left a small bit for herself. The Lion looked at it and said:

"Clever Fox! Who taught you to divide so well?"

She said:

"What about that Ass?"

## THE PEASANT AND THE WATER-SPRITE

A Peasant lost his axe in the river; he sat down on the bank in grief, and began to weep.

The Water-sprite heard the Peasant and took pity on him. He brought a gold axe out of the river, and said: "Is this your axe?"

The Peasant said: "No, it is not mine."

The Water-sprite brought another, a silver axe.

Again the Peasant said: "It is not my axe."

Then the Water-sprite brought out the real axe.

The Peasant said: "Now this is my axe."

The Water-sprite made the Peasant a present of all three axes, for having told the truth.

At home the Peasant showed his axes to his friends, and told them what had happened to him.

One of the peasants made up his mind to do the same: he went to the river, purposely threw his axe into the water, sat down on the bank, and began to weep.

[Pg 18]

The Water-sprite brought out a gold axe, and asked: "Is this your axe?"

The Peasant was glad, and called out: "It is mine, mine!"

The Water-sprite did not give him the gold axe, and did not bring him back his own either, because he had told an untruth.

## THE RAVEN AND THE FOX

A Raven got himself a piece of meat, and sat down on a tree. The Fox wanted to get it from him. She went up to him, and said:

"Oh, Raven, as I look at you,—from your size and beauty,—you ought to be a king! And you would certainly be a king, if you had a good voice."

The Raven opened his mouth wide, and began to croak with all his might and main. The meat fell down. The Fox caught it and said:

"Oh, Raven! If you had also sense, you would certainly be a king."

[Pg 19]

## II. ADAPTATIONS AND IMITATIONS OF HINDOO FABLES
### THE SNAKE'S HEAD AND TAIL

The Snake's Tail had a quarrel with the Snake's Head about who was to walk in front. The Head said:

"You cannot walk in front, because you have no eyes and no ears."

The Tail said:

"Yes, but I have strength, I move you; if I want to, I can wind myself around a tree, and you cannot get off the spot."

The Head said:

"Let us separate!"

And the Tail tore himself loose from the Head, and crept on; but the moment he got away from the Head, he fell into a hole and was lost.

### FINE THREAD

A Man ordered some fine thread from a Spinner. The Spinner spun it for him, but the Man said that the thread was not good, and that he wanted the finest thread he could get. The Spinner said:

"If this is not fine enough, take this!" and she pointed to an empty space.

He said that he did not see any. The Spinner said:

"You do not see it, because it is so fine. I do not see it myself."

The Fool was glad, and ordered some more thread of this kind, and paid her for what he got.

[Pg 20]

## THE PARTITION OF THE INHERITANCE

A Father had two Sons. He said to them: "When I die, divide everything into two equal parts."

When the Father died, the Sons could not divide without quarrelling. They went to a Neighbour to have him settle the matter. The Neighbour asked them how their Father had told them to divide. They said:

"He ordered us to divide everything into two equal parts."

The Neighbour said:

"If so, tear all your garments into two halves, break your dishes into two halves, and cut all your cattle into two halves!"

The Brothers obeyed their Neighbour, and lost everything.

## THE MONKEY

A Man went into the woods, cut down a tree, and began to saw it. He raised the end of the tree on a stump, sat astride over it, and began to saw. Then he drove a wedge into the split that he had sawed, and went on sawing; then he took out the wedge and drove it in farther down.

A Monkey was sitting on a tree and watching him. When the Man lay down to sleep, the Monkey seated herself astride the tree, and wanted to do the same; but when she took out the wedge, the tree sprang back and caught her tail. She began to tug and to cry. The Man woke up, beat the Monkey, and tied a rope to her.

## THE MONKEY AND THE PEASE

A Monkey was carrying both her hands full of pease. A pea dropped on the ground; the Monkey wanted to pick it up, and dropped twenty peas. She rushed to pick[Pg 21] them up and lost all the rest. Then she flew into a rage, swept away all the pease and ran off.

## THE MILCH COW

A Man had a Cow; she gave each day a pot full of milk. The Man invited a number of guests. To have as much milk as possible, he did not milk the Cow for ten days. He thought that on the tenth day the Cow would give him ten pitchers of milk.

But the Cow's milk went back, and she gave less milk than before.

## THE DUCK AND THE MOON

A Duck was swimming in the pond, trying to find some fish, but she did not find one in a whole day. When night came, she saw the Moon in the water; she thought that it was a fish, and plunged in to catch the Moon. The other ducks saw her do it and laughed at her.

That made the Duck feel so ashamed and bashful that when she saw a fish under the Water, she did not try to catch it, and so died of hunger.

## THE WOLF IN THE DUST

A Wolf wanted to pick a sheep out of a flock, and stepped into the wind, so that the dust of the flock might blow on him.

The Sheep Dog saw him, and said:

"There is no sense, Wolf, in your walking in the dust: it will make your eyes ache."

But the Wolf said:

"The trouble is, Doggy, that my eyes have been aching for quite awhile, and I have been told that the dust from a flock of sheep will cure the eyes."

[Pg 22]

## THE MOUSE UNDER THE GRANARY

A Mouse was living under the granary. In the floor of the granary there was a little hole, and the grain fell down through it. The Mouse had an easy life of it, but she wanted to brag of her ease: she gnawed a larger hole in the floor, and invited other mice.

"Come to a feast with me," said she; "there will be plenty to eat for everybody."

When she brought the mice, she saw there was no hole. The peasant had noticed the big hole in the floor, and had stopped it up.

## THE BEST PEARS

A master sent his Servant to buy the best-tasting pears. The Servant came to the shop and asked for pears. The dealer gave him some; but the Servant said:

"No, give me the best!"

The dealer said:

"Try one; you will see that they taste good."

"How shall I know," said the Servant, "that they all taste good, if I try one only?"

He bit off a piece from each pear, and brought them to his master. Then his master sent him away.

## THE FALCON AND THE COCK

The Falcon was used to the master, and came to his hand when he was called; the Cock ran away from his master and cried when people went up to him. So the Falcon said to the Cock:

"In you Cocks there is no gratitude; one can see that you are of a common breed. You go to your masters only when you are hungry. It is different with us wild birds. We have much strength, and we can fly faster than anybody; still we do not fly away from people, but[Pg 23] of our own accord go to their hands when we are called. We remember that they feed us."

Then the Cock said:

"You do not run away from people because you have never seen a roast Falcon, but we, you know, see roast Cocks."

## THE JACKALS AND THE ELEPHANT

The Jackals had eaten up all the carrion in the woods, and had nothing to eat. So an old Jackal was thinking how to find something to feed on. He went to an Elephant, and said:

"We had a king, but he became overweening: he told us to do things that nobody could do; we want to choose another king, and my people have sent me to ask you to be our king. You will have an easy life with us. Whatever you will order us to do, we will do, and we will honour you in everything. Come to our kingdom!"

The Elephant consented, and followed the Jackal. The Jackal brought him to a swamp. When the Elephant stuck fast in it, the Jackal said:

"Now command! Whatever you command, we will do."

The Elephant said:

"I command you to pull me out from here."

The Jackal began to laugh, and said:

"Take hold of my tail with your trunk, and I will pull you out at once."

The Elephant said:

"Can I be pulled out by a tail?"

But the Jackal said to him:

"Why, then, do you command us to do what is impossible? Did we not drive away our first king for telling us to do what could not be done?"

When the Elephant died in the swamp the Jackals came and ate him up.

[Pg 24]

## THE HERON, THE FISHES, AND THE CRAB

A Heron was living near a pond. She grew old, and had no strength left with which to catch the fish. She began to contrive how to live by cunning. So she said to the Fishes:

"You Fishes do not know that a calamity is in store for you: I have heard the people say that they are going to let off the pond, and catch every one of you. I know of a nice little pond back of the mountain. I should like to help you, but I am old, and it is hard for me to fly."

The Fishes begged the Heron to help them. So the Heron said:

9

"All right, I will do what I can for you, and will carry you over: only I cannot do it at once,—I will take you there one after another."

And the Fishes were happy; they kept begging her: "Carry me over! Carry me over!"

And the Heron started carrying them. She would take one up, would carry her into the field, and would eat her up. And thus she ate a large number of Fishes.

In the pond there lived an old Crab. When the Heron began to take out the Fishes, he saw what was up, and said:

"Now, Heron, take me to the new abode!"

The Heron took the Crab and carried him off. When she flew out on the field, she wanted to throw the Crab down. But the Crab saw the fish-bones on the ground, and so squeezed the Heron's neck with his claws, and choked her to death. Then he crawled back to the pond, and told the Fishes.

### THE WATER-SPRITE AND THE PEARL

A Man was rowing in a boat, and dropped a costly pearl into the sea. The Man returned to the shore, took[Pg 25] a pail, and began to draw up the water and to pour it out on the land. He drew the water and poured it out for three days without stopping.

On the fourth day the Water-sprite came out of the sea, and asked:

"Why are you drawing the water?"

The Man said:

"I am drawing it because I have dropped a pearl into it."

The Water-sprite asked him:

"Will you stop soon?"

The Man said:

"I will stop when I dry up the sea."

Then the Water-sprite returned to the sea, brought back that pearl, and gave it to the Man.

### THE BLIND MAN AND THE MILK

A Man born blind asked a Seeing Man:

"Of what colour is milk?"

The Seeing Man said: "The colour of milk is the same as that of white paper."

The Blind Man asked: "Well, does that colour rustle in your hands like paper?"

The Seeing Man said: "No, it is as white as white flour."

The Blind Man asked: "Well, is it as soft and as powdery as flour?"

The Seeing Man said: "No, it is simply as white as a white hare."

The Blind Man asked: "Well, is it as fluffy and soft as a hare?"

The Seeing Man said: "No, it is as white as snow."

The Blind Man asked: "Well, is it as cold as snow?"

And no matter how many examples the Seeing Man gave, the Blind Man was unable to understand what the white colour of milk was like.

[Pg 26]

### THE WOLF AND THE BOW

A hunter went out to hunt with bow and arrows. He killed a goat. He threw her on his shoulders and carried her along. On his way he saw a boar. He threw down the goat, and shot at the boar and wounded him. The boar rushed against the hunter and butted him to death, and himself died on the spot. A Wolf scented the blood, and came to the place where lay the goat, the boar, the man, and his bow. The Wolf was glad, and said:

"Now I shall have enough to eat for a long time; only I will not eat everything at once, but little by little, so that nothing may be lost: first I will eat the tougher things, and then I will lunch on what is soft and sweet."

The Wolf sniffed at the goat, the boar, and the man, and said:

"This is all soft food, so I will eat it later; let me first start on these sinews of the bow."

And he began to gnaw the sinews of the bow. When he bit through the string, the bow sprang back and hit him on his belly. He died on the spot, and other wolves ate up the man, the goat, the boar, and the Wolf.

### THE BIRDS IN THE NET

A Hunter set out a net near a lake and caught a number of birds. The birds were large, and they raised the net and flew away with it. The Hunter ran after them. A Peasant saw the Hunter running, and said:

"Where are you running? How can you catch up with the birds, while you are on foot?"

The Hunter said:

"If it were one bird, I should not catch it, but now I shall."

And so it happened. When evening came, the birds[Pg 27] began to pull for the night each in a different direction: one to the woods, another to the swamp, a third to the field; and all fell with the net to the ground, and the Hunter caught them.

## THE KING AND THE FALCON

A certain King let his favourite Falcon loose on a hare, and galloped after him.

The Falcon caught the hare. The King took him away, and began to look for some water to drink. The King found it on a knoll, but it came only drop by drop. The King fetched his cup from the saddle, and placed it under the water. The Water flowed in drops, and when the cup was filled, the King raised it to his mouth and wanted to drink it. Suddenly the Falcon fluttered on the King's arm and spilled the water. The King placed the cup once more under the drops. He waited for a long time for the cup to be filled even with the brim, and again, as he carried it to his mouth, the Falcon flapped his wings and spilled the water.

When the King filled his cup for the third time and began to carry it to his mouth, the Falcon again spilled it. The King flew into a rage and killed him by flinging him against a stone with all his force. Just then the King's servants rode up, and one of them ran up-hill to the spring, to find as much water as possible, and to fill the cup. But the servant did not bring the water; he returned with the empty cup, and said:

"You cannot drink that water; there is a snake in the spring, and she has let her venom into the water. It is fortunate that the Falcon has spilled the water. If you had drunk it, you would have died."

The King said:

"How badly I have repaid the Falcon! He has saved my life, and I killed him."
[Pg 28]

## THE KING AND THE ELEPHANTS

An Indian King ordered all the Blind People to be assembled, and when they came, he ordered that all the Elephants be shown to them. The Blind Men went to the stable and began to feel the Elephants. One felt a leg, another a tail, a third the stump of a tail, a fourth a belly, a fifth a back, a sixth the ears, a seventh the tusks, and an eighth a trunk.

Then the King called the Blind Men, and asked them: "What are my Elephants like?"

One Blind Man said: "Your Elephants are like posts." He had felt the legs.

Another Blind Man said: "They are like bath brooms." He had felt the end of the tail.

A third said: "They are like branches." He had felt the tail stump.

The one who had touched a belly said: "The Elephants are like a clod of earth."

The one who had touched the sides said: "They are like a wall."

The one who had touched a back said: "They are like a mound."

The one who had touched the ears said: "They are like a mortar."

The one who had touched the tusks said: "They are like horns."

The one who had touched the trunk said that they were like a stout rope.

And all the Blind Men began to dispute and to quarrel.

## WHY THERE IS EVIL IN THE WORLD

A Hermit was living in the forest, and the animals were not afraid of him. He and the animals talked together and understood each other.

Once the Hermit lay down under a tree, and a Raven[Pg 29] a Dove, a Stag, and a Snake gathered in the same place, to pass the night. The animals began to discuss why there was evil in the world.

The Raven said:

"All the evil in the world comes from hunger. When I eat my fill, I sit down on a branch and croak a little, and it is all jolly and good, and everything gives me pleasure; but let me just go without eating a day or two, and everything palls on me so that I do not feel like

11

looking at God's world. And something draws me on, and I fly from place to place, and have no rest. When I catch a glimpse of some meat, it makes me only feel sicker than ever, and I make for it without much thinking. At times they throw sticks and stones at me, and the wolves and dogs grab me, but I do not give in. Oh, how many of my brothers are perishing through hunger! All evil comes from hunger."

The Dove said:

"According to my opinion, the evil does not come from hunger, but from love. If we lived singly, the trouble would not be so bad. One head is not poor, and if it is, it is only one. But here we live in pairs. And you come to like your mate so much that you have no rest: you keep thinking of her all the time, wondering whether she has had enough to eat, and whether she is warm. And when your mate flies away from you, you feel entirely lost, and you keep thinking that a hawk may have carried her off, or men may have caught her; and you start out to find her, and fly to your ruin,—either into the hawk's claws, or into a snare. And when your mate is lost, nothing gives you any joy. You do not eat or drink, and all the time search and weep. Oh, so many of us perish in this way! All the evil is not from hunger, but from love."

The Snake said:

"No, the evil is not from hunger, nor from love, but[Pg 30] from rage. If we lived peacefully, without getting into a rage, everything would be nice for us. But, as it is, whenever a thing does not go exactly right, we get angry, and then nothing pleases us. All we think about is how to revenge ourselves on some one. Then we forget ourselves, and only hiss, and creep, and try to find some one to bite. And we do not spare a soul,—we even bite our own father and mother. We feel as though we could eat ourselves up. And we rage until we perish. All the evil in the World comes from rage."

The Stag said:

"No, not from rage, or from love, or from hunger does all the evil in the world come, but from terror. If it were possible not to be afraid, everything would be well. We have swift feet and much strength: against a small animal we defend ourselves with our horns, and from a large one we flee. But how can I help becoming frightened? Let a branch crackle in the forest, or a leaf rustle, and I am all atremble with fear, and my heart flutters as though it wanted to jump out, and I fly as fast as I can. Again, let a hare run by, or a bird flap its wings, or a dry twig break off, and you think that it is a beast, and you run straight up against him. Or you run away from a dog and run into the hands of a man. Frequently you get frightened and run, not knowing whither, and at full speed rush down a steep hill, and get killed. We have no rest. All the evil comes from terror."

Then the Hermit said:

"Not from hunger, not from love, not from rage, not from terror are all our sufferings, but from our bodies comes all the evil in the world. From them come hunger, and love, and rage, and terror."

## THE WOLF AND THE HUNTERS

A Wolf devoured a sheep. The Hunters caught the Wolf and began to beat him. The Wolf said:

[Pg 31]

"In vain do you beat me: it is not my fault that I am gray,—God has made me so."

But the Hunters said:

"We do not beat the Wolf for being gray, but for eating the sheep."

## THE TWO PEASANTS

Once upon a time two Peasants drove toward each other and caught in each other's sleighs. One cried:

"Get out of my way,—I am hurrying to town."

But the other said:

"Get out of my way, I am hurrying home."

They quarrelled for some time. A third Peasant saw them and said:

"If you are in a hurry, back up!"

## THE PEASANT AND THE HORSE

12

A Peasant went to town to fetch some oats for his Horse. He had barely left the village, when the Horse began to turn around, toward the house. The Peasant struck the Horse with his whip. She went on, and kept thinking about the Peasant:

"Whither is that fool driving me? He had better go home."

Before reaching town, the Peasant saw that the Horse trudged along through the mud with difficulty, so he turned her on the pavement; but the Horse began to turn back from the street. The Peasant gave the Horse the whip, and jerked at the reins; she went on the pavement, and thought:

"Why has he turned me on the pavement? It will only break my hoofs. It is rough underfoot."

The Peasant went to the shop, bought the oats, and drove home. When he came home, he gave the Horse some oats. The Horse ate them and thought:

|Pg 32|

"How stupid men are! They are fond of exercising their wits on us, but they have less sense than we. What did he trouble himself about? He drove me somewhere. No matter how far we went, we came home in the end. So it would have been better if we had remained at home from the start: he could have been sitting on the oven, and I eating oats."

### THE TWO HORSES

Two Horses were drawing their carts. The Front Horse pulled well, but the Hind Horse kept stopping all the time. The load of the Hind Horse was transferred to the front cart; when all was transferred, the Hind Horse went along with ease, and said to the Front Horse:

"Work hard and sweat! The more you try, the harder they will make you work."

When they arrived at the tavern, their master said:

"Why should I feed two Horses, and haul with one only? I shall do better to give one plenty to eat, and to kill the other: I shall at least have her hide."

So he did.

### THE AXE AND THE SAW

Two Peasants went to the forest to cut wood. One of them had an axe, and the other a saw. They picked out a tree, and began to dispute. One said that the tree had to be chopped, while the other said that it had to be sawed down.

A third Peasant said:

"I will easily make peace between you: if the axe is sharp, you had better chop it; but if the saw is sharp you had better saw it."

He took the axe, and began to chop it; but the axe was so dull that it was not possible to cut with it. Then he took the saw; the saw was worthless, and did not saw. So he said:

|Pg 33|

"Stop quarrelling awhile; the axe does not chop, and the saw does not saw. First grind your axe and file your saw, and then quarrel."

But the Peasants grew angrier still at one another, because one had a dull axe, and the other a dull saw. And they came to blows.

### THE DOGS AND THE COOK

A Cook was preparing a dinner. The Dogs were lying at the kitchen door. The Cook killed a calf and threw the guts out into the yard. The Dogs picked them up and ate them, and said:

"He is a good Cook: he cooks well."

After awhile the Cook began to clean pease, turnips, and onions, and threw out the refuse. The Dogs made for it; but they turned their noses up, and said:

"Our Cook has grown worse: he used to cook well, but now he is no longer any good."

But the Cook paid no attention to the Dogs, and continued to fix the dinner in his own way. The family, and not the Dogs, ate the dinner, and praised it.

### THE HARE AND THE HARRIER

A Hare once said to a Harrier:

"Why do you bark when you run after us? You would catch us easier, if you ran after us in silence. With your bark you only drive us against the hunter: he hears where we are running; and he rushes out with his gun and kills us, and does not give you anything."

The Harrier said:

"That is not the reason why I bark. I bark because, when I scent your odour, I am angry, and happy because I am about to catch you; I do not know why, but I cannot keep from barking."

[Pg 34]

## THE OAK AND THE HAZELBUSH

An old Oak dropped an acorn under a Hazelbush. The Hazelbush said to the Oak:

"Have you not enough space under your own branches? Drop your acorns in an open space. Here I am myself crowded by my shoots, and I do not drop my nuts to the ground, but give them to men."

"I have lived for two hundred years," said the Oak, "and the Oakling which will sprout from that acorn will live just as long."

Then the Hazelbush flew into a rage, and said:

"If so, I will choke your Oakling, and he will not live for three days."

The Oak made no reply, but told his son to sprout out of that acorn. The acorn got wet and burst, and clung to the ground with his crooked rootlet, and sent up a sprout.

The Hazelbush tried to choke him, and gave him no sun. But the Oakling spread upwards and grew stronger in the shade of the Hazelbush. A hundred years passed. The Hazelbush had long ago dried up, but the Oak from that acorn towered to the sky and spread his tent in all directions.

## THE HEN AND THE CHICKS

A Hen hatched some Chicks, but did not know how to take care of them. So she said to them:

"Creep back into your shells! When you are inside your shells, I will sit on you as before, and will take care of you."

The Chicks did as they were ordered and tried to creep into their shells, but were unable to do so, and only crushed their wings. Then one of the Chicks said to his mother:

"If we are to stay all the time in our shells, you ought never to have hatched us."

[Pg 35]

## THE CORN-CRAKE AND HIS MATE

A Corn-crake had made a nest in the meadow late in the year, and at mowing time his Mate was still sitting on her eggs. Early in the morning the peasants came to the meadow, took off the coats, whetted their scythes, and started one after another to mow down the grass and to put it down in rows. The Corn-crake flew up to see what the mowers were doing. When he saw a peasant swing his scythe and cut a snake in two, he rejoiced and flew back to his Mate and said:

"Don't fear the peasants! They have come to cut the snakes to pieces; they have given us no rest for quite awhile."

But his Mate said:

"The peasants are cutting the grass, and with the grass they are cutting everything which is in their way,—the snakes, and the Corn-crake's nest, and the Corn-crake's head. My heart forebodes nothing good: but I cannot carry away the eggs, nor fly from the nest, for fear of chilling them."

When the mowers came to the nest of the Corn-crake, one of the peasants swung his scythe and cut off the head of the Corn-crake's Mate, and put the eggs in his bosom and gave them to his children to play with.

## THE COW AND THE BILLY GOAT

An old woman had a Cow and a Billy Goat. The two pastured together. At milking the Cow was restless. The old woman brought out some bread and salt, and gave it to the Cow, and said:

"Stand still, motherkin; take it, take it! I will bring you some more, only stand still."

On the next evening the Goat came home from the field before the Cow, and spread his legs, and stood in front of the old woman. The old woman wanted to strike[Pg 36] him with the towel, but he stood still, and did not stir. He remembered that the woman had promised the Cow some bread if she would stand still. When the woman saw that he would not budge, she picked up a stick, and beat him with it.

When the Goat went away, the woman began once more to feed the Cow with bread, and to talk to her.

"There is no honesty in men," thought the Goat. "I stood still better than the Cow, and was beaten for it."

He stepped aside, took a run, hit against the milk-pail, spilled the milk, and hurt the old woman.

## THE FOX'S TAIL

A Man caught a Fox, and asked her:

"Who has taught you Foxes to cheat the dogs with your tails?"

The Fox asked: "How do you mean, to cheat? We do not cheat the dogs, but simply run from them as fast as we can."

The Man said:

"Yes, you do cheat them with your tails. When the dogs catch up with you and are about to clutch you, you turn your tails to one side; the dogs turn sharply after the tail, and then you run in the opposite direction."

The Fox laughed, and said:

"We do not do so in order to cheat the dogs, but in order to turn around; when a dog is after us, and we see that we cannot get away straight ahead, we turn to one side, and in order to do that suddenly, we have to swing the tail to the other side, just as you do with your arms, when you have to turn around. That is not our invention; God himself invented it when He created us, so that the dogs might not be able to catch all the Foxes."

[Pg 37]

## STORIES FOR CHILDREN
### 1869-1872

[Pg 38-39]

STORIES FOR CHILDREN
## THE FOUNDLING

A poor woman had a daughter by the name of Másha. Másha went in the morning to fetch water, and saw at the door something wrapped in rags. When she touched the rags, there came from it the sound of "Ooah, ooah, ooah!" Másha bent down and saw that it was a tiny, red-skinned baby. It was crying aloud: "Ooah, ooah!"

Másha took it into her arms and carried it into the house, and gave it milk with a spoon. Her mother said:

"What have you brought?"

"A baby. I found it at our door."

The mother said:

"We are poor as it is; we have nothing to feed the baby with; I will go to the chief and tell him to take the baby."

Másha began to cry, and said:

"Mother, the child will not eat much; leave it here! See what red, wrinkled little hands and fingers it has!"

Her mother looked at them, and she felt pity for the child. She did not take the baby away. Másha fed and swathed the child, and sang songs to it, when it went to sleep.

[Pg 40]

## THE PEASANT AND THE CUCUMBERS

A peasant once went to the gardener's, to steal cucumbers. He crept up to the cucumbers, and thought:

"I will carry off a bag of cucumbers, which I will sell; with the money I will buy a hen. The hen will lay eggs, hatch them, and raise a lot of chicks. I will feed the chicks and sell them; then I will buy me a young sow, and she will bear a lot of pigs. I will sell the pigs, and

15

buy me a mare; the mare will foal me some colts. I will raise the colts, and sell them. I will buy me a house, and start a garden. In the garden I will sow cucumbers, and will not let them be stolen, but will keep a sharp watch on them. I will hire watchmen, and put them in the cucumber patch, while I myself will come on them, unawares, and shout: 'Oh, there, keep a sharp lookout!'"

And this he shouted as loud as he could. The watchmen heard it, and they rushed out and beat the peasant.

[Pg 41]

## THE FIRE

During harvest-time the men and women went out to work. In the village were left only the old and the very young. In one hut there remained a grandmother with her three grandchildren.

The grandmother made a fire in the oven, and lay down to rest herself. Flies kept alighting on her and biting her. She covered her head with a towel and fell asleep. One of the grandchildren, Másha (she was three years old), opened the oven, scraped some coals into a potsherd, and went into the vestibule. In the vestibule lay sheaves: the women were getting them bound.

Másha brought the coals, put them under the sheaves, and began to blow. When the straw caught fire, she was glad; she went into the hut and took her brother Kiryúsha by the arm (he was a year and a half old, and had just learned to walk), and brought him out, and said to him:

"See, Kiryúsha, what a fire I have kindled."

The sheaves were already burning and crackling. When the vestibule was filled with smoke, Másha became frightened and ran back into the house. Kiryúsha fell over the threshold, hurt his nose, and began to cry; Másha pulled him into the house, and both hid under a bench.

The grandmother heard nothing, and did not wake. The elder boy, Ványa (he was eight years old), was in the street. When he saw the smoke rolling out of the vestibule, he ran to the door, made his way through the smoke into the house, and began to waken his grandmother; but she was dazed from her sleep, and, forgetting the[Pg 42] children, rushed out and ran to the farmyards to call the people.

In the meantime Másha was sitting under the bench and keeping quiet; but the little boy cried, because he had hurt his nose badly. Ványa heard his cry, looked under the bench, and called out to Másha:

"Run, you will burn!"

Másha ran to the vestibule, but could not pass for the smoke and fire. She turned back. Then Ványa raised a window and told her to climb through it. When she got through, Ványa picked up his brother and dragged him along. But the child was heavy and did not let his brother take him. He cried and pushed Ványa. Ványa fell down twice, and when he dragged him up to the window, the door of the hut was already burning. Ványa thrust the child's head through the window and wanted to push him through; but the child took hold of him with both his hands (he was very much frightened) and would not let them take him out. Then Ványa cried to Másha:

"Pull him by the head!" while he himself pushed him behind.

And thus they pulled him through the window and into the street.

[Pg 43]

## THE OLD HORSE

In our village there was an old, old man, Pímen Timoféich. He was ninety years old. He was living at the house of his grandson, doing no work. His back was bent: he walked with a cane and moved his feet slowly.

He had no teeth at all, and his face was wrinkled. His nether lip trembled; when he walked and when he talked, his lips smacked, and one could not understand what he was saying.

16

We were four brothers, and we were fond of riding. But we had no gentle riding-horses. We were allowed to ride only on one horse,—the name of that horse was Raven.

One day mamma allowed us to ride, and all of us went with the valet to the stable. The coachman saddled Raven for us, and my eldest brother was the first to take a ride. He rode for a long time; he rode to the threshing-floor and around the garden, and when he came back, we shouted:

"Now gallop past us!"

My elder brother began to strike Raven with his feet and with the whip, and Raven galloped past us.

After him, my second brother mounted the horse. He, too, rode for quite awhile, and he, too, urged Raven on with the whip and galloped up the hill. He wanted to ride longer, but my third brother begged him to let him ride at once.

My third brother rode to the threshing-floor, and around the garden, and down the village, and raced up-hill to the[Pg 44] stable. When he rode up to us Raven was panting, and his neck and shoulders were dark from sweat.

When my turn came, I wanted to surprise my brothers and to show them how well I could ride, so I began to drive Raven with all my might, but he did not want to get away from the stable. And no matter how much I beat him, he would not run, but only shied and turned back. I grew angry at the horse, and struck him as hard as I could with my feet and with the whip. I tried to strike him in places where it would hurt most; I broke the whip and began to strike his head with what was left of the whip. But Raven would not run. Then I turned back, rode up to the valet, and asked him for a stout switch. But the valet said to me:

"Don't ride any more, sir! Get down! What use is there in torturing the horse?"

I felt offended, and said:

"But I have not had a ride yet. Just watch me gallop! Please, give me a good-sized switch! I will heat him up."

Then the valet shook his head, and said:

"Oh, sir, you have no pity; why should you heat him up? He is twenty years old. The horse is worn out; he can barely breathe, and is old. He is so very old! Just like Pímen Timoféich. You might just as well sit down on Timoféich's back and urge him on with a switch. Well, would you not pity him?"

I thought of Pímen, and listened to the valet's words. I climbed down from the horse and, when I saw how his sweaty sides hung down, how he breathed heavily through his nostrils, and how he switched his bald tail, I understood that it was hard for the horse. Before that I used to think that it was as much fun for him as for me. I felt so sorry for Raven that I began to kiss his sweaty neck and to beg his forgiveness for having beaten him.

[Pg 45]

Since then I have grown to be a big man, and I always am careful with the horses, and always think of Raven and of Pímen Timoféitch whenever I see anybody torture a horse.

[Pg 46]

### HOW I LEARNED TO RIDE

When I was a little fellow, we used to study every day, and only on Sundays and holidays went out and played with our brothers. Once my father said:

"The children must learn to ride. Send them to the riding-school!"

I was the youngest of the brothers, and I asked:

"May I, too, learn to ride?"

My father said:

"You will fall down."

I began to beg him to let me learn, and almost cried. My father said:

"All right, you may go, too. Only look out! Don't cry when you fall off. He who does not once fall down from a horse will not learn to ride."

When Wednesday came, all three of us were taken to the riding-school. We entered by a large porch, and from the large porch went to a smaller one. Beyond the porch was a very large room: instead of a floor it had sand. And in this room were gentlemen and ladies

17

and just such boys as we. That was the riding-school. The riding-school was not very light, and there was a smell of horses, and you could hear them snap whips and call to the horses, and the horses strike their hoofs against the wooden walls. At first I was frightened and could not see things well. Then our valet called the riding-master, and said:

"Give these boys some horses: they are going to learn how to ride."

The master said:

[Pg 47]

"All right!"

Then he looked at me, and said:

"He is very small, yet."

But the valet said:

"He promised not to cry when he falls down."

The master laughed and went away.

Then they brought three saddled horses, and we took off our cloaks and walked down a staircase to the riding-school. The master was holding a horse by a cord, and my brothers rode around him. At first they rode at a slow pace, and later at a trot. Then they brought a pony. It was a red horse, and his tail was cut off. He was called Ruddy. The master laughed, and said to me:

"Well, young gentleman, get on your horse!"

I was both happy and afraid, and tried to act in such a manner as not to be noticed by anybody. For a long time I tried to get my foot into the stirrup, but could not do it because I was too small. Then the master raised me up in his hands and put me on the saddle. He said:

"The young master is not heavy,—about two pounds in weight, that is all."

At first he held me by my hand, but I saw that my brothers were not held, and so I begged him to let go of me. He said:

"Are you not afraid?"

I was very much afraid, but I said that I was not. I was so much afraid because Ruddy kept dropping his ears. I thought he was angry at me. The master said:

"Look out, don't fall down!" and let go of me. At first Ruddy went at a slow pace, and I sat up straight. But the saddle was sleek, and I was afraid I would slip off. The master asked me:

"Well, are you fast in the saddle?"

I said:

"Yes, I am."

[Pg 48]

"If so, go at a slow trot!" and the master clicked his tongue.

Ruddy started at a slow trot, and began to jog me. But I kept silent, and tried not to slip to one side. The master praised me:

"Oh, a fine young gentleman, indeed!"

I was very glad to hear it.

Just then the master's friend went up to him and began to talk with him, and the master stopped looking at me.

Suddenly I felt that I had slipped a little to one side on my saddle. I wanted to straighten myself up, but was unable to do so. I wanted to call out to the master to stop the horse, but I thought it would be a disgrace if I did it, and so kept silence. The master was not looking at me and Ruddy ran at a trot, and I slipped still more to one side. I looked at the master and thought that he would help me, but he was still talking with his friend, and without looking at me kept repeating:

"Well done, young gentleman!"

I was now altogether to one side, and was very much frightened. I thought that I was lost; but I felt ashamed to cry. Ruddy shook me up once more, and I slipped off entirely and fell to the ground. Then Ruddy stopped, and the master looked at the horse and saw that I was not on him. He said:

"I declare, my young gentleman has dropped off!" and walked over to me.

When I told him that I was not hurt, he laughed and said:

"A child's body is soft."

I felt like crying. I asked him to put me again on the horse, and I was lifted on the horse. After that I did not fall down again.

Thus we rode twice a week in the riding-school, and I soon learned to ride well, and was not afraid of anything.

[Pg 49]

## THE WILLOW

During Easter week a peasant went out to see whether the ground was all thawed out.

He went into the garden and touched the soil with a stick. The earth was soft. The peasant went into the woods; here the catkins were already swelling on the willows. The peasant thought:

"I will fence my garden with willows; they will grow up and will make a good hedge!"

He took his axe, cut down a dozen willows, sharpened them at the end, and stuck them in the ground.

All the willows sent up sprouts with leaves, and underground let out just such sprouts for roots; and some of them took hold of the ground and grew, and others did not hold well to the ground with their roots, and died and fell down.

In the fall the peasant was glad at the sight of his willows: six of them had taken root. The following spring the sheep killed two willows by gnawing at them, and only two were left. Next spring the sheep nibbled at these also. One of them was completely ruined, and the other came to, took root, and grew to be a tree. In the spring the bees just buzzed in the willow. In swarming time the swarms were often put out on the willow, and the peasants brushed them in. The men and women frequently ate and slept under the willow, and the children climbed on it and broke off rods from it.

The peasant that had set out the willow was long dead, and still it grew. His eldest son twice cut down its branches and used them for fire-wood. The willow kept[Pg 50] growing. They trimmed it all around, and cut it down to a stump, but in the spring it again sent out twigs, thinner ones than before, but twice as many as ever, as is the case with a colt's forelock.

And the eldest son quit farming, and the village was given up, but the willow grew in the open field. Other peasants came there, and chopped the willow, but still it grew. The lightning struck it; but it sent forth side branches, and it grew and blossomed. A peasant wanted to cut it down for a block, but he gave it up, it was too rotten. It leaned sidewise, and held on with one side only; and still it grew, and every year the bees came there to gather the pollen.

One day, early in the spring, the boys gathered under the willow, to watch the horses. They felt cold, so they started a fire. They gathered stubbles, wormwood, and sticks. One of them climbed on the willow and broke off a lot of twigs. They put it all in the hollow of the willow and set fire to it. The tree began to hiss and its sap to boil, and the smoke rose and the tree burned; its whole inside was smudged. The young shoots dried up, the blossoms withered.

The children drove the horses home. The scorched willow was left all alone in the field. A black raven flew by, and he sat down on it, and cried:

"So you are dead, old smudge! You ought to have died long ago!"

[Pg 51]

## BÚLKA

I had a small bulldog. He was called Búlka. He was black; only the tips of his front feet were white. All bulldogs have their lower jaws longer than the upper, and the upper teeth come down behind the nether teeth, but Búlka's lower jaw protruded so much that I could put my finger between the two rows of teeth. His face was broad, his eyes large, black, and sparkling; and his teeth and incisors stood out prominently. He was as black as a negro. He was gentle and did not bite, but he was strong and stubborn. If he took hold of a thing, he clenched his teeth and clung to it like a rag, and it was not possible to tear him off, any more than as though he were a lobster.

19

Once he was let loose on a bear, and he got hold of the bear's ear and stuck to him like a leech. The bear struck him with his paws and squeezed him, and shook him from side to side, but could not tear himself loose from him, and so he fell down on his head, in order to crush Búlka; but Búlka held on to him until they poured cold water over him.

I got him as a puppy, and raised him myself. When I went to the Caucasus, I did not want to take him along, and so went away from him quietly, ordering him to be shut up. At the first station I was about to change the relay, when suddenly I saw something black and shining coming down the road. It was Búlka in his brass collar. He was flying at full speed toward the station. He rushed up to me, licked my hand, and stretched himself out in the shade under the cart. His tongue stuck out a[Pg 52] whole hand's length. He now drew it in to swallow the spittle, and now stuck it out again a whole hand's length. He tried to breathe fast, but could not do so, and his sides just shook. He turned from one side to the other, and struck his tail against the ground.

I learned later that after I had left he had broken a pane, jumped out of the window, and followed my track along the road, and thus raced twenty versts through the greatest heat.

[Pg 53]
## BÚLKA AND THE WILD BOAR

Once we went into the Caucasus to hunt the wild boar, and Búlka went with me. The moment the hounds started, Búlka rushed after them, following their sound, and disappeared in the forest. That was in the month of November; the boars and sows are then very fat.

In the Caucasus there are many edible fruits in the forests where the boars live: wild grapes, cones, apples, pears, blackberries, acorns, wild plums. And when all these fruits get ripe and are touched by the frost, the boars eat them and grow fat.

At that time a boar gets so fat that he cannot run from the dogs. When they chase him for about two hours, he makes for the thicket and there stops. Then the hunters run up to the place where he stands, and shoot him. They can tell by the bark of the hounds whether the boar has stopped, or is running. If he is running, the hounds yelp, as though they were beaten; but when he stops, they bark as though at a man, with a howling sound.

During that chase I ran for a long time through the forest, but not once did I cross a boar track. Finally I heard the long-drawn bark and howl of the hounds, and ran up to that place. I was already near the boar. I could hear the crashing in the thicket. The boar was turning around on the dogs, but I could not tell by the bark that they were not catching him, but only circling around him. Suddenly I heard something rustle behind me, and I saw that it was Búlka. He had evidently strayed from the hounds in the forest and had lost his way, and now was hearing their barking and making for[Pg 54] them, like me, as fast as he could. He ran across a clearing through the high grass, and all I could see of him was his black head and his tongue clinched between his white teeth. I called him back, but he did not look around, and ran past me and disappeared in the thicket. I ran after him, but the farther I went, the more and more dense did the forest grow. The branches kept knocking off my cap and struck me in the face, and the thorns caught in my garments. I was near to the barking, but could not see anything.

Suddenly I heard the dogs bark louder, and something crashed loudly, and the boar began to puff and snort. I immediately made up my mind that Búlka had got up to him and was busy with him. I ran with all my might through the thicket to that place. In the densest part of the thicket I saw a dappled hound. She was barking and howling in one spot, and within three steps from her something black could be seen moving around.

When I came nearer, I could make out the boar, and I heard Búlka whining shrilly. The boar grunted and made for the hound; the hound took her tail between her legs and leaped away. I could see the boar's side and head. I aimed at his side and fired. I saw that I had hit him. The boar grunted and crashed through the thicket away from me. The dogs whimpered and barked in his track; I tried to follow them through the undergrowth. Suddenly I saw and heard something almost under my feet. It was Búlka. He was lying on his side and whining. Under him there was a puddle of blood. I thought the dog was lost; but I had no time to look after him, I continued to make my way through the thicket. Soon I saw the boar. The dogs were trying to catch him from behind, and he kept turning, now to one side, and now to another. When the boar saw me, he moved toward me. I fired a second time, almost resting the barrel against him, so that his bristles caught fire, and the boar groaned[Pg 55] and tottered, and with his whole cadaver dropped heavily on the ground.

When I came up, the boar was dead, and only here and there did his body jerk and twitch. Some of the dogs, with bristling hair, were tearing his belly and legs, while the others were lapping the blood from his wound.

Then I thought of Búlka, and went back to find him. He was crawling toward me and groaning. I went up to him and looked at his wound. His belly was ripped open, and a whole piece of his guts was sticking out of his body and dragging on the dry leaves. When my companions came up to me, we put the guts back and sewed up his belly. While we were sewing him up and sticking the needle through his skin, he kept licking my hand.

The boar was tied up to the horse's tail, to pull him out of the forest, and Búlka was put on the horse, and thus taken home. Búlka was sick for about six weeks, and got well again.

[Pg 56]

## PHEASANTS

Wild fowls are called pheasants in the Caucasus. There are so many of them that they are cheaper there than tame chickens. Pheasants are hunted with the "hobby," by scaring up, and from under dogs. This is the way they are hunted with the "hobby." They take a piece of canvas and stretch it over a frame, and in the middle of the frame they make a cross piece. They cut a hole in the canvas. This frame with the canvas is called a hobby. With this hobby and with the gun they start out at dawn to the forest. The hobby is carried in front, and through the hole they look out for the pheasants. The pheasants feed at daybreak in the clearings. At times it is a whole brood,—a hen with all her chicks, and at others a cock with his hen, or several cocks together.

The pheasants do not see the man, and they are not afraid of the canvas and let the hunter come close to them. Then the hunter puts down the hobby, sticks his gun through the rent, and shoots at whichever bird he pleases.

This is the way they hunt by scaring up. They let a watch-dog into the forest and follow him. When the dog finds a pheasant, he rushes for it. The pheasant flies on a tree, and then the dog begins to bark at it. The hunter follows up the barking and shoots the pheasant in the tree. This chase would be easy, if the pheasant alighted on a tree in an open place, or if it sat still, so that it might be seen. But they always alight on dense trees, in the thicket, and when they see the hunter they hide themselves in the branches. And it is hard to make one's[Pg 57] way through the thicket to the tree on which a pheasant is sitting, and hard to see it. So long as the dog alone barks at it, it is not afraid: it sits on a branch and preens and flaps its wings at the dog. But the moment it sees a man, it immediately stretches itself out along a bough, so that only an experienced hunter can tell it, while an inexperienced one will stand near by and see nothing.

When the Cossacks steal up to the pheasants, they pull their caps over their faces and do not look up, because a pheasant is afraid of a man with his gun, but more still of his eyes.

This is the way they hunt from under dogs. They take a setter and follow him to the forest. The dog scents the place where the pheasants have been feeding at daybreak, and begins to make out their tracks. No matter how the pheasants may have mixed them up, a good dog will always find the last track, that takes them out from the spot where they have been feeding. The farther the dog follows the track, the stronger will the scent be, and thus he will reach the place where the pheasant sits or walks about in the grass in the daytime. When he comes near to where the bird is, he thinks that it is right before him, and starts walking more cautiously so as not to frighten it, and will stop now and then, ready to jump and catch it. When the dog comes up very near to the pheasant, it flies up, and the hunter shoots it.

21

## MILTON AND BÚLKA

I bought me a setter to hunt pheasants with. The name of the dog was Milton. He was a big, thin, gray, spotted dog, with long lips and ears, and he was very strong and intelligent. He did not fight with Búlka. No dog ever tried to get into a fight with Búlka. He needed only to show his teeth, and the dogs would take their tails between their legs and slink away.

Once I went with Milton to hunt pheasants. Suddenly Búlka ran after me to the forest. I wanted to drive him back, but could not do so; and it was too far for me to take him home. I thought he would not be in my way, and so walked on; but the moment Milton scented a pheasant in the grass and began to search for it, Búlka rushed forward and tossed from side to side. He tried to scare up the pheasant before Milton. He heard something in the grass, and jumped and whirled around; but he had a poor scent and could not find the track himself, but watched Milton, to see where he was running. The moment Milton started on the trail, Búlka ran ahead of him. I called Búlka back and beat him, but could not do a thing with him. The moment Milton began to search, he darted forward and interfered with him.

I was already on the point of going home, because I thought that the chase was spoiled; but Milton found a better way of cheating Búlka. This is what he did: the moment Búlka rushed ahead of him, he gave up the trail and turned in another direction, pretending that he was searching there. Búlka rushed there where Milton was, and Milton looked at me and wagged his tail and went[Pg 59]back to the right trail. Búlka again ran up to Milton and rushed past him, and again Milton took some ten steps to one side and cheated Búlka, and again led me straight; and so he cheated Búlka all the way and did not let him spoil the chase.

## THE TURTLE

Once I went with Milton to the chase. Near the forest he began to search. He straightened out his tail, pricked his ears, and began to sniff. I fixed the gun and followed him. I thought that he was looking for a partridge, hare, or pheasant. But Milton did not make for the forest, but for the field. I followed him and looked ahead of me. Suddenly I saw what he was searching for. In front of him was running a small turtle, of the size of a cap. Its bare, dark gray head on a long neck was stretched out like a pestle; the turtle in walking stretched its bare legs far out, and its back was all covered with bark.

When it saw the dog, it hid its legs and head and let itself down on the grass so that only its shell could be seen. Milton grabbed it and began to bite at it, but could not bite through it, because the turtle has just such a shell on its belly as it has on its back, and has only openings in front, at the back, and at the sides, where it puts forth its head, its legs, and its tail.

I took the turtle away from Milton, and tried to see how its back was painted, and what kind of a shell it had, and how it hid itself. When you hold it in your hands and look between the shell, you can see something black and alive inside, as though in a cellar. I threw away the turtle, and walked on, but Milton would not leave it, and carried it in his teeth behind me. Suddenly Milton whimpered and dropped it. The turtle had put forth its foot inside of his mouth, and had scratched it. That made him so angry that he began to bark; he grasped it once more and carried it behind me. I ordered Milton to[Pg 61] throw it away, but he paid no attention to me. Then I took the turtle from him and threw it away. But he did not leave it. He hurriedly dug a hole near it; when the hole was dug, he threw the turtle into it and covered it up with dirt.

The turtles live on land and in the water, like snakes and frogs. They breed their young from eggs. These eggs they lay on the ground, and they do not hatch them, but the eggs burst themselves, like fish spawn, and the turtles crawl out of them. There are small turtles, not larger than a saucer, and large ones, seven feet in length and weighing seven hundredweights. The large turtles live in the sea.

One turtle lays in the spring hundreds of eggs. The turtle's shells are its ribs. Men and other animals have each rib separate, while the turtle's ribs are all grown together into a shell. But the main thing is that with all the animals the ribs are inside the flesh, while the turtle has the ribs on the outside, and the flesh beneath them.

[Pg 62]

## BÚLKA AND THE WOLF

When I left the Caucasus, they were still fighting there, and in the night it was dangerous to travel without a guard.

I wanted to leave as early as possible, and so did not lie down to sleep.

My friend came to see me off, and we sat the whole evening and night in the village street, in front of my cabin.

It was a moonlit night with a mist, and so bright that one could read, though the moon was not to be seen.

In the middle of the night we suddenly heard a pig squealing in the yard across the street. One of us cried: "A wolf is choking the pig!"

I ran into the house, grasped a loaded gun, and ran into the street. They were all standing at the gate of the yard where the pig was squealing, and cried to me: "Here!" Milton rushed after me,—no doubt he thought that I was going out to hunt with the gun; but Búlka pricked his short ears, and tossed from side to side, as though to ask me whom he was to clutch. When I ran up to the wicker fence, I saw a beast running straight toward me from the other side of the yard. That was the wolf. He ran up to the fence and jumped on it. I stepped aside and fixed my gun. The moment the wolf jumped down from the fence to my side, I aimed, almost touching him with the gun, and pulled the trigger; but my gun made "Click" and did not go off. The Wolf did not stop, but ran across the street.

[Pg 63]

Milton and Búlka made for him. Milton was near to the wolf, but was afraid to take hold of him; and no matter how fast Búlka ran on his short legs, he could not keep up with him. We ran as fast as we could after the wolf, but both the wolf and the dogs disappeared from sight. Only at the ditch, at the end of the village, did we hear a low barking and whimpering, and saw the dust rise in the mist of the moon and the dogs busy with the wolf. When we ran up to the ditch, the wolf was no longer there, and both dogs returned to us with raised tails and angry faces. Búlka snarled and pushed me with his head: evidently he wanted to tell me something, but did not know how.

We examined the dogs, and found a small wound on Búlka's head. He had evidently caught up with the wolf before he got to the ditch, but had not had a chance to get hold of him, while the wolf snapped at him and ran away. It was a small wound, so there was no danger.

We returned to the cabin, and sat down and talked about what had happened. I was angry because the gun had missed fire, and thought of how the wolf would have remained on the spot, if the gun had shot. My friend wondered how the wolf could have crept into the yard. An old Cossack said that there was nothing remarkable about it, because that was not a wolf, but a witch who had charmed my gun. Thus we sat and kept talking. Suddenly the dogs darted off, and we saw the same wolf in the middle of the street; but this time he ran so fast when he heard our shout that the dogs could not catch up with him.

After that the old Cossack was fully convinced that it was not a wolf, but a witch; but I thought that it was a mad wolf, because I had never seen or heard of such a thing as a wolf's coming back toward the people, after it had been driven away.

In any case I poured some powder on Búlka's wound, [Pg 64] and set it on fire. The powder flashed up and burned out the sore spot.

I burned out the sore with powder, in order to burn away the poisonous saliva, if it had not yet entered the blood. But if the saliva had already entered the blood, I knew that the blood would carry it through the whole body, and then it would not be possible to cure him.

# WHAT HAPPENED TO BÚLKA IN PYATIGÓRSK

From the Cossack village I did not travel directly to Russia, but first to Pyatigórsk, where I stayed two months. Milton I gave away to a Cossack hunter, and Búlka I took along with me to Pyatigórsk.

Pyatigórsk [in English, Five-Mountains] is called so because it is situated on Mount Besh-tau. And besh means in Tartar "five," and tau "mountain." From this mountain flows a hot sulphur stream. It is as hot as boiling water, and over the spot where the water flows from the mountain there is always a steam as from a samovár.

The whole place, on which the city stands, is very cheerful. From the mountain flow the hot springs, and at the foot of the mountain is the river Podkúmok. On the slopes of the mountain are forests; all around the city are fields, and in the distance are seen the mountains of the Caucasus. On these the snow never melts, and they are always as white as sugar. One large mountain, Elbrus, is like a white loaf of sugar; it can be seen from everywhere when the weather is clear. People come to the hot springs to be cured, and over them there are arbours and awnings, and all around them are gardens with walks. In the morning the music plays, and people drink the water, or bathe, or stroll about.

The city itself is on the mountain, but at the foot of it there is a suburb. I lived in that suburb in a small house. The house stood in a yard, and before the windows was a small garden, and in the garden stood the landlord's beehives, not in hollow stems, as in Russia, but[Pg 66] in round, plaited baskets. The bees are there so gentle that in the morning I used to sit with Búlka in that garden, amongst the beehives.

Búlka walked about between the hives, and sniffed, and listened to the bees' buzzing; he walked so softly among them that he did not interfere with them, and they did not bother him.

One morning I returned home from the waters, and sat down in the garden to drink coffee. Búlka began to scratch himself behind his ears, and made a grating noise with his collar. The noise worried the bees, and so I took the collar off. A little while later I heard a strange and terrible noise coming from the city. The dogs barked, howled, and whimpered, people shouted, and the noise descended lower from the mountain and came nearer and nearer to our suburb.

Búlka stopped scratching himself, put his broad head with its white teeth between his fore legs, stuck out his tongue as he wished, and lay quietly by my side. When he heard the noise he seemed to understand what it was. He pricked his ears, showed his teeth, jumped up, and began to snarl. The noise came nearer. It sounded as though all the dogs of the city were howling, whimpering, and barking. I went to the gate to see what it was, and my landlady came out, too. I asked her:

"What is this?"

She said:

"The prisoners of the jail are coming down to kill the dogs. The dogs have been breeding so much that the city authorities have ordered all the dogs in the city to be killed."

"So they would kill Búlka, too, if they caught him?"

"No, they are not allowed to kill dogs with collars."

Just as I was speaking, the prisoners were coming up to our house. In front walked the soldiers, and behind them four prisoners in chains. Two of the prisoners had[Pg 67] in their hands long iron hooks, and two had clubs. In front of our house, one of the prisoners caught a watch-dog with his hook and pulled it up to the middle of the street, and another began to strike it with the club.

The little dog whined dreadfully, but the prisoners shouted and laughed. The prisoner with the hook turned over the dog, and when he saw that it was dead, he pulled out the hook and looked around for other dogs.

Just then Búlka rushed headlong at that prisoner, as though he were a bear. I happened to think that he was without his collar, so I shouted: "Búlka, back!" and told the prisoners not to strike the dog. But the prisoner laughed when he saw Búlka, and with his hook nimbly struck him and caught him by his thigh. Búlka tried to get away; but the prisoner pulled him up toward him and told the other prisoner to strike him. The other raised his club, and Búlka would have been killed, but he jerked, and broke the skin at the thigh and, taking his tail between his legs, flew, with the red sore on his body, through the gate and into the house, and hid himself under my bed.

He was saved because the skin had broken in the spot where the hook was.

[Pg 68]

## BÚLKA'S AND MILTON'S END

Búlka and Milton died at the same time. The old Cossack did not know how to get along with Milton. Instead of taking him out only for birds, he went with him to hunt wild boars. And that same fall a tusky boar ripped him open. Nobody knew how to sew him up, and so he died.

Búlka, too, did not live long after the prisoners had caught him. Soon after his salvation from the prisoners he began to feel unhappy, and started to lick everything that he saw. He licked my hands, but not as formerly when he fawned. He licked for a long time, and pressed his tongue against me, and then began to snap. Evidently he felt like biting my hand, but did not want to do so. I did not give him my hand. Then he licked my boot and the foot of a table, and then he began to snap at these things. That lasted about two days, and on the third he disappeared, and no one saw him or heard of him.

He could not have been stolen or run away from me. This happened six weeks after the wolf had bitten him. Evidently the wolf had been mad. Búlka had gone mad, and so went away. He had what hunters call the rabies. They say that this madness consists in this, that the mad animal gets cramps in its throat. It wants to drink and cannot, because the water makes the cramps worse. And so it gets beside itself from pain and thirst, and begins to bite. Evidently Búlka was beginning to have these cramps when he started to lick and then to bite my hand and the foot of the table.

[Pg 69]

I went everywhere in the neighbourhood and asked about Búlka, but could not find out what had become of him, or how he had died. If he had been running about and biting, as mad dogs do, I should have heard of him. No doubt he ran somewhere into a thicket and there died by himself.

The hunters say that when an intelligent dog gets the rabies, he runs to the fields and forests, and there tries to find the herb which he needs, and rolls in the dew, and gets cured. Evidently Búlka never got cured. He never came back.

[Pg 70]

## THE GRAY HARE

A gray hare was living in the winter near the village. When night came, he pricked one ear and listened; then he pricked his second ear, moved his whiskers, sniffed, and sat down on his hind legs. Then he took a leap or two over the deep snow, and again sat down on his hind legs, and looked around him. Nothing could be seen but snow. The snow lay in waves and glistened like sugar. Over the hare's head hovered a frost vapour, and through this vapour could be seen the large, bright stars.

The hare had to cross the highway, in order to come to a threshing-floor he knew of. On the highway the runners could be heard squeaking, and the horses snorting, and seats creaking in the sleighs.

The hare again stopped near the road. Peasants were walking beside the sleighs, and the collars of their caftans were raised. Their faces were scarcely visible. Their beards, moustaches, and eyelashes were white. Steam rose from their mouths and noses. Their horses were sweaty, and the hoarfrost clung to the sweat. The horses jostled under their arches, and dived in and out of snow-drifts. The peasants ran behind the horses and in front of them, and beat them with their whips. Two peasants walked beside each other, and one of them told the other how a horse of his had once been stolen.

When the carts passed by, the hare leaped across the road and softly made for the threshing-floor. A dog saw the hare from a cart. He began to bark and darted after the hare. The hare leaped toward the threshing-floor over the snow-drifts, which held him back; but

25

the dog[Pg 71] stuck fast in the snow after the tenth leap, and stopped. Then the hare, too, stopped and sat up on his hind legs, and then softly went on to the threshing-floor.

On his way he met two other hares on the sowed winter field. They were feeding and playing. The hare played awhile with his companions, dug away the frosty snow with them, ate the wintergreen, and went on.

In the village everything was quiet; the fires were out. All one could hear was a baby's cry in a hut and the crackling of the frost in the logs of the cabins. The hare went to the threshing-floor, and there found some companions. He played awhile with them on the cleared floor, ate some oats from the open granary, climbed on the kiln over the snow-covered roof, and across the wicker fence started back to his ravine.

The dawn was glimmering in the east; the stars grew less, and the frost vapours rose more densely from the earth. In the near-by village the women got up, and went to fetch water; the peasants brought the feed from the barn; the children shouted and cried. There were still more carts going down the road, and the peasants talked aloud to each other.

The hare leaped across the road, went up to his old lair, picked out a high place, dug away the snow, lay with his back in his new lair, dropped his ears on his back, and fell asleep with open eyes.

[Pg 72]
## GOD SEES THE TRUTH, BUT DOES NOT TELL AT ONCE
In the city of Vladímir there lived a young merchant, Aksénov by name. He had two shops and a house.

Aksénov was a light-complexioned, curly-headed, fine-looking man and a very jolly fellow and good singer. In his youth Aksénov had drunk much, and when he was drunk he used to become riotous, but when he married he gave up drinking, and that now happened very rarely with him.

One day in the summer Aksénov went to the Nízhni-Nóvgorod fair. As he bade his family good-bye, his wife said to him:

"Iván Dmítrievich, do not start to-day! I have had a bad dream about you."

Aksénov laughed, and said:

"Are you afraid that I might go on a spree at the fair?"

His wife said:

"I do not know what I am afraid of, but I had a bad dream: I dreamed that you came to town, and when you took off your cap I saw that your head was all gray."

Aksénov laughed.

"That means that I shall make some profit. If I strike a good bargain, you will see me bring you some costly presents."

And he bade his family farewell, and started.

In the middle of his journey he met a merchant whom he knew, and they stopped together in a hostelry for the night. They drank their tea together, and lay down to [Pg 73]sleep in two adjoining rooms. Aksénov did not like to sleep long; he awoke in the middle of the night and, as it was easier to travel when it was cool, wakened his driver and told him to hitch the horses. Then he went to the "black" hut, paid his bill, and went away.

**"'Whose knife is this?'"**

*Photogravure from Painting by A. Kívshénko*

When he had gone about forty versts, he again stopped to feed the horses and to rest in the vestibule of a hostelry. At dinner-time he came out on the porch, and ordered the samovár to be prepared for him. He took out his guitar and began to play. Suddenly a tróyka with bells drove up to the hostelry, and from the cart leaped an officer with two soldiers, and he went up to Aksénov, and asked him who he was and where he came from.

Aksénov told him everything as it was, and said:

"Would you not like to drink tea with me?"

But the officer kept asking him questions:

"Where did you stay last night? Were you alone, or with a merchant? Did you see the merchant in the morning? Why did you leave so early in the morning?"

Aksénov wondered why they asked him about all that; he told them everything as it was, and said:

"Why do you ask me this? I am not a thief, nor a robber. I am travelling on business of my own, and you have nothing to ask me about."

Then the officer called the soldiers, and said:

"I am the chief of the rural police, and I ask you this, because the merchant with whom you passed last night has been found with his throat cut. Show me your things, and you look through them!"

They entered the house, took his valise and bag, and opened them and began to look through them. Suddenly the chief took a knife out of the bag, and cried out:

"Whose knife is this?"

Aksénov looked, and saw that they had taken out a blood-stained knife from his bag, and he was frightened[Pg 74] "How did the blood get on the knife?"

Aksénov wanted to answer, but could not pronounce a word.

"I—I do not know—I—the knife—is not mine!"

Then the chief said:

"In the morning the merchant was found in his bed with his throat cut. No one but you could have done it. The house was locked from within, and there was no one in the house but you. Here is the bloody knife in your bag, and your face shows your guilt. Tell me, how did you kill him, and how much money did you rob him of?"

Aksénov swore that he had not done it; that he had not seen the merchant after drinking tea with him; that he had with him his own eight thousand; that the knife was not his. But his voice faltered, his face was pale, and he trembled from fear, as though he were guilty.

The chief called in the soldiers, told them to bind him and to take him to the cart. When he was rolled into the cart with his legs tied, he made the sign of the cross and began to cry. They took away his money and things, and sent him to jail to the nearest town. They sent to Vladímir to find out what kind of a man Aksénov was, and all the merchants and inhabitants of Vladímir testified to the fact that Aksénov had drunk and caroused when he was young, but that he was a good man. Then they began to try him. He was tried for having killed the Ryazán merchant and having robbed him of twenty thousand roubles.

The wife was grieving for her husband and did not know what to think. Her children were still young, and one was still at the breast. She took them all and went with them to the town where her husband was kept in prison. At first she was not admitted, but later she implored the authorities, and she was taken to her husband. When she saw him in prison garb and in chains, together[Pg 75] with murderers, she fell to the ground and could not come to for a long time. Then she placed her children about her, sat down beside him, and began to tell him about house matters, and to ask him about everything which had happened. He told her everything. She said:

"What shall I do?"

He said:

"We must petition the Tsar. An innocent man cannot be allowed to perish."

His wife said that she had already petitioned the Tsar, but that the petition had not reached him. Aksénov said nothing, and only lowered his head. Then his wife said:

"You remember the dream I had about your getting gray. Indeed, you have grown gray from sorrow. If you had only not started then!"

And she looked over his hair, and said:

"Iván, my darling, tell your wife the truth: did you not do it?"

Aksénov said, "And you, too, suspect me!" and covered his face with his hands, and began to weep.

Then a soldier came, and told his wife that she must leave with her children. And Aksénov for the last time bade his family farewell.

When his wife had left, Aksénov thought about what they had been talking of. When he recalled that his wife had also suspected him and had asked him whether he had killed the merchant, he said to himself: "Evidently none but God can know the truth, and He alone

27

must be asked, and from Him alone can I expect mercy." And from that time on Aksénov no longer handed in petitions and stopped hoping, but only prayed to God.

Aksénov was sentenced to be beaten with the knout, and to be sent to hard labour. And it was done.

He was beaten with the knout, and later, when the knout sores healed over, he was driven with other convicts to Siberia.

[Pg 76]

In Siberia, Aksénov passed twenty-six years at hard labour. His hair turned white like snow, and his beard grew long, narrow, and gray. All his mirth went away. He stooped, began to walk softly, spoke little, never laughed, and frequently prayed to God.

In the prison Aksénov learned to make boots, and with the money which he earned he bought himself the "Legends of the Holy Martyrs," and read them while it was light in the prison; on holidays he went to the prison church and read the Epistles, and sang in the choir,—his voice was still good. The authorities were fond of Aksénov for his gentleness, and his prison comrades respected him and called him "grandfather" and "God's man." When there were any requests to be made of the authorities, his comrades always sent him to speak for them, and when the convicts had any disputes between themselves, they came to Aksénov to settle them.

No one wrote Aksénov letters from his home, and he did not know whether his wife and children were alive, or not.

Once they brought some new prisoners to the prison. In the evening the old prisoners gathered around the new men, and asked them from what town they came, or from what village, and for what acts they had been sent up. Aksénov, too, sat down on the bed-boards near the new prisoners and, lowering his head, listened to what they were saying. One of the new prisoners was a tall, sound-looking old man of about sixty years of age, with a gray, clipped beard. He was telling them what he had been sent up for:

"Yes, brothers, I have come here for no crime at all. I had unhitched a driver's horse from the sleigh. I was caught. They said, 'You stole it.' And I said, 'I only wanted to get home quickly, for I let the horse go. Besides, the driver is a friend of mine. I am telling you the truth.'—'No,' they said, 'you have stolen it.' But they did not know what I had been stealing, or where I had[Pg 77] been stealing. There were crimes for which I ought to have been sent up long ago, but they could not convict me, and now I am here contrary to the law. 'You are lying,—you have been in Siberia, but you did not make a long visit there—'"

"Where do you come from?" asked one of the prisoners.

"I am from the city of Vladímir, a burgher of that place. My name is Makár, and by my father Seménovich."

Aksénov raised his head, and asked:

"Seménovich, have you not heard in Vladímir about the family of Merchant Aksénov? Are they alive?"

"Yes, I have heard about them! They are rich merchants, even though their father is in Siberia. He is as much a sinner as I, I think. And you, grandfather, what are you here for?"

Aksénov did not like to talk of his misfortune. He sighed, and said:

"For my sins have I passed twenty-six years at hard labour."

Makár Seménovich said:

"For what sins?"

Aksénov said, "No doubt, I deserved it," and did not wish to tell him any more; but the other prison people told the new man how Aksénov had come to be in Siberia. They told him how on the road some one had killed a merchant and had put the knife into his bag, and he thus was sentenced though he was innocent.

When Makár Seménovich heard that, he looked at Aksénov, clapped his knees with his hands, and said:

"What a marvel! What a marvel! But you have grown old, grandfather!"

He was asked what he was marvelling at, and where he had seen Aksénov, but Makár Seménovich made no reply, and only said:

"It is wonderful, boys, where we were fated to meet!"

[Pg 78]

And these words made Aksénov think that this man might know something about who had killed the merchant. He said:

"Seménovich, have you heard before this about that matter, or have we met before?"

"Of course I have heard. The earth is full of rumours. That happened a long time ago: I have forgotten what I heard," said Makár Seménovich.

"Maybe you have heard who killed the merchant?" asked Aksénov.

Makár Seménovich laughed and said:

"I suppose he was killed by the man in whose bag the knife was found. Even if somebody stuck that knife into that bag, he was not caught, so he is no thief. And how could the knife have been put in? Was not the bag under your head? You would have heard him."

The moment Aksénov heard these words, he thought that that was the man who had killed the merchant. He got up and walked away. All that night Aksénov could not fall asleep. He felt sad, and had visions: now he saw his wife such as she had been when she bade him farewell for the last time, as he went to the fair. He saw her, as though she was alive, and he saw her face and eyes, and heard her speak to him and laugh. Then he saw his children such as they had been then,—just as little,—one of them in a fur coat, the other at the breast. And he thought of himself, such as he had been then,—gay and young; he recalled how he had been sitting on the porch of the hostelry, where he was arrested, and had been playing the guitar, and how light his heart had been then. And he recalled the pillory, where he had been whipped, and the executioner, and the people all around, and the chains, and the prisoners, and his prison life of the last twenty-six years, and his old age. And such gloom came over him that he felt like laying hands on himself.

[Pg 79]

"And all that on account of that evil-doer!" thought Aksénov.

And such a rage fell upon him against Makár Seménovich, that he wanted to have his revenge upon him, even if he himself were to be ruined by it. He said his prayers all night long, but could not calm himself. In the daytime he did not walk over to Makár Seménovich, and did not look at him.

Thus two weeks passed. At night Aksénov could not sleep, and he felt so sad that he did not know what to do with himself.

Once, in the night, he walked all over the prison, and saw dirt falling from underneath one bedplace. He stopped to see what it was. Suddenly Makár Seménovich jumped up from under the bed and looked at Aksénov with a frightened face. Aksénov wanted to pass on, so as not to see him; but Makár took him by his arm, and told him that he had dug a passage way under the wall, and that he each day carried the dirt away in his boot-legs and poured it out in the open, whenever they took the convicts out to work. He said:

"Keep quiet, old man,—I will take you out, too. And if you tell, they will whip me, and I will not forgive you,—I will kill you."

When Aksénov saw the one who had done him evil, he trembled in his rage, and pulled away his arm, and said:

"I have no reason to get away from here, and there is no sense in killing me,—you killed me long ago. And whether I will tell on you or not depends on what God will put into my soul."

On the following day, when the convicts were taken out to work, the soldiers noticed that Makár Seménovich was pouring out the dirt, and so they began to search in the prison, and found the hole. The chief came to the prison and began to ask all who had dug the hole. Everybody denied it. Those who knew had not seen Makár[Pg 80] Seménovich, because they knew that for this act he would be whipped half-dead. Then the chief turned to Aksénov. He knew that Aksénov was a just man, and said:

"Old man, you are a truthful man, tell me before God who has done that."

Makár Seménovich stood as though nothing had happened and looked at the chief, and did not glance at Aksénov. Aksénov's arms and lips trembled, and he could not utter a word for long time. He thought: "If I protect him, why should I forgive him, since he has ruined me? Let him suffer for my torments! And if I tell on him, they will indeed whip him to death. And suppose that I have a wrong suspicion against him. Will that make it easier for me?"

The chief said once more:

"Well, old man, speak, tell the truth! Who has been digging it?"

Aksénov looked at Makár Seménovich, and said:

"I cannot tell, your Honour. God orders me not to tell. And I will not tell. Do with me as you please,—you have the power."

No matter how much the chief tried, Aksénov would not say anything more. And so they did not find out who had done the digging.

On the following night, as Aksénov lay down on the bed-boards and was just falling asleep, he heard somebody come up to him and sit down at his feet. He looked in the darkness and recognized Makár. Aksénov said:

"What more do you want of me? What are you doing here?"

Makár Seménovich was silent. Aksénov raised himself, and said:

"What do you want? Go away, or I will call the soldier."

Makár bent down close to Aksénov, and said to him in a whisper:

**"'God will forgive you'"**

*Photogravure from Painting by A. Kivshénko*

[Pg 81]

"Iván Dmítrievich, forgive me!"

Aksénov said:

"For what shall I forgive you?"

"It was I who killed the merchant and put the knife into your bag. I wanted to kill you, too, but they made a noise in the yard, so I put the knife into your bag and climbed through the window."

Aksénov was silent and did not know what to say. Makár Seménovich slipped down from the bed, made a low obeisance, and said:

"Iván Dmítrievich, forgive me, forgive me for God's sake! I will declare that it was I who killed the merchant,—you will be forgiven. You will return home."

Aksénov said:

"It is easy for you to speak so, but see how I have suffered! Where shall I go now? My wife has died, my children have forgotten me. I have no place to go to—"

Makár Seménovich did not get up from the floor. He struck his head against the earth, and said:

"Iván Dmítrievich, forgive me! When they whipped me with the knout I felt better than now that I am looking at you. You pitied me, and did not tell on me. Forgive me, for Christ's sake! Forgive me, the accursed evil-doer!" And he burst out into tears.

When Aksénov heard Makár Seménovich crying, he began to weep himself, and said:

"God will forgive you. Maybe I am a hundred times worse than you!"

And suddenly a load fell off from his soul. And he no longer pined for his home, and did not wish to leave the prison, but only thought of his last hour.

Makár Seménovich did not listen to Aksénov, but declared his guilt. When the decision came for Aksénov to leave,—he was dead.

[Pg 82]

## HUNTING WORSE THAN SLAVERY

We were hunting bears. My companion had a chance to shoot at a bear: he wounded him, but only in a soft spot. A little blood was left on the snow, but the bear got away.

We met in the forest and began to discuss what to do: whether to go and find that bear, or to wait two or three days until the bear should lie down again.

We asked the peasant bear drivers whether we could now surround the bear. An old bear driver said:

"No, we must give the bear a chance to calm himself. In about five days it will be possible to surround him, but if we go after him now he will only be frightened and will not lie down."

But a young bear driver disputed with the old man, and said that he could surround him now.

"Over this snow," he said, "the bear cannot get away far,—he is fat. He will lie down to-day again. And if he does not, I will overtake him on snow-shoes."

My companion, too, did not want to surround the bear now, and advised waiting. But I said:

"What is the use of discussing the matter? Do as you please, but I will go with Demyán along the track. If we overtake him, so much is gained; if not,—I have nothing else to do to-day anyway, and it is not yet late."

And so we did.

My companions went to the sleigh, and back to the village, but Demyán and I took bread with us, and remained in the woods.

[Pg 83]

When all had left us, Demyán and I examined our guns, tucked our fur coats over our belts, and followed the track.

It was fine weather, chilly and calm. But walking on snow-shoes was a hard matter: the snow was deep and powdery.

The snow had not settled in the forest, and, besides, fresh snow had fallen on the day before, so that the snow-shoes sunk half a foot in the snow, and in places even deeper.

The bear track could be seen a distance away. We could see the way the bear had walked, for in spots he had fallen in the snow to his belly and had swept the snow aside. At first we walked in plain sight of the track, through a forest of large trees; then, when the track went into a small pine wood, Demyán stopped.

"We must now give up the track," he said. "He will, no doubt, lie down here. He has been sitting on his haunches,—you can see it by the snow. Let us go away from the track, and make a circle around him. But we must walk softly and make no noise, not even cough, or we shall scare him."

We went away from the track, to the left. We walked about five hundred steps and there we again saw the track before us. We again followed the track, and this took us to the road. We stopped on the road and began to look around, to see in what direction the bear had gone. Here and there on the road we could see the bear's paws with all the toes printed on the snow, while in others we could see the tracks of a peasant's bast shoes. He had, evidently, gone to the village.

We walked along the road. Demyán said to me:

"We need not watch the road; somewhere he will turn off the road, to the right or to the left,—we shall see in the snow. Somewhere he will turn off,—he will not go to the village."

[Pg 84]

We walked thus about a mile along the road; suddenly we saw the track turn off from the road. We looked at it, and see the wonder! It was a bear's track, but leading not from the road to the woods, but from the woods to the road: the toes were turned to the road. I said:

"That is another bear."

Demyán looked at it, and thought awhile.

"No," he said, "that is the same bear, only he has begun to cheat. He left the road backwards."

We followed the track, and so it was. The bear had evidently walked about ten steps backwards from the road, until he got beyond a fir-tree, and then he had turned and gone on straight ahead. Demyán stopped, and said:

"Now we shall certainly fall in with him. He has no place but this swamp to lie down in. Let us surround him."

We started to surround him, going through the dense pine forest. I was getting tired, and it was now much harder to travel. Now I would strike against a juniper-bush, and get caught in it; or a small pine-tree would get under my feet; or the snow-shoes would twist, as I was not used to them; or I would strike a stump or a block under the snow. I was beginning to be worn out. I took off my fur coat, and the sweat was just pouring down from me. But Demyán sailed along as in a boat. It looked as though the snow-shoes walked under him of their own accord. He neither caught in anything, nor did his shoes turn on him.

And he even threw my fur coat over his shoulders, and kept urging me on.

We made about three versts in a circle, and walked past the swamp. Demyán suddenly stopped in front of me, and waved his hand. I walked over to him. Demyán bent down, and pointed with his hand, and whispered to me:

[Pg 85]

"Do you see, a magpie is chattering on a windfall: the bird is scenting the bear from a distance. It is he."

We walked to one side, made another verst, and again hit the old trail. Thus we had made a circle around the bear, and he was inside of it. We stopped. I took off my hat and loosened my wraps: I felt as hot as in a bath, and was as wet as a mouse. Demyán, too, was all red, and he wiped his face with his sleeve.

"Well," he said, "we have done our work, sir, so we may take a rest."

The evening glow could be seen through the forest. We sat down on the snow-shoes to rest ourselves. We took the bread and salt out of the bags; first I ate a little snow, and then the bread. The bread tasted to me better than any I had eaten in all my life. We sat awhile; it began to grow dark. I asked Demyán how far it was to the village.

"About twelve versts. We shall reach it in the night; but now we must rest. Put on your fur coat, sir, or you will catch a cold."

Demyán broke off some pine branches, knocked down the snow, made a bed, and we lay down beside each other, with our arms under our heads. I do not remember how I fell asleep. I awoke about two hours later. Something crashed.

I had been sleeping so soundly that I forgot where I was. I looked around me: what marvel was that? Where was I? Above me were some white chambers, and white posts, and on everything glistened white tinsel. I looked up: there was a white, checkered cloth, and between the checks was a black vault in which burned fires of all colours. I looked around, and I recalled that we were in the forest, and that the snow-covered trees had appeared to me as chambers, and that the fires were nothing but the stars that flickered between the branches.

In the night a hoarfrost had fallen, and there was hoarfrost[Pg 86] on the branches, and on my fur coat, and Demyán was all covered with hoarfrost, and hoarfrost fell from above. I awoke Demyán. We got up on our snow-shoes and started. The forest was quiet. All that could be heard was the sound we made as we slid on our snow-shoes over the soft snow, or when a tree would crackle from the frost, and a hollow sound would pass through the whole woods. Only once did something living stir close to us and run away again. I thought it was the bear. We walked over to the place from where the noise had come, and we saw hare tracks. The young aspens were nibbled down. The hares had been feeding on them.

We came out to the road, tied the snow-shoes behind us, and walked down the road. It was easy to walk. The snow-shoes rattled and rumbled over the beaten road; the snow creaked under our boots; the cold hoarfrost stuck to our faces like down. And the stars seemed to run toward us along the branches: they would flash, and go out again,—just as though the sky were walking round and round.

My companion was asleep,—I awoke him. We told him how we had made a circle around the bear, and told the landlord to collect the drivers for the morning. We ate our supper and lay down to sleep.

I was so tired that I could have slept until dinner, but my companion woke me. I jumped up and saw that my companion was all dressed and busy with his gun.

"Where is Demyán?"

"He has been in the forest for quite awhile. He has investigated the circle, and has been back to take the drivers out."

I washed myself, put on my clothes, and loaded my guns. We seated ourselves in the sleigh, and started.

There was a severe frost, the air was calm, and the sun could not be seen: there was a mist above, and the hoarfrost was settling.

[Pg 87]

We travelled about three versts by the road, and reached the forest. We saw a blue smoke in a hollow, and peasants, men and women, were there with clubs.

32

We climbed out of the sleigh and went up to the people. The peasants were sitting and baking potatoes, and joking with the women.

Demyán was with them. The people got up, and Demyán took them away to place them in our last night's circuit. The men and women stretched themselves out in single file,—there were thirty of them and they could be seen only from the belt up,—and went into the woods; then my companion and I followed their tracks.

Though they had made a path, it was hard to walk; still, we could not fall, for it was like walking between two walls.

Thus we walked for half a verst. I looked up, and there was Demyán running to us from the other side on snow-shoes, and waving his hand for us to come to him.

We went up to him, and he showed us where to stand. I took up my position and looked around.

To the left of me was a tall pine forest. I could see far through it, and beyond the trees I saw the black spot of a peasant driver. Opposite me was a young pine growth, as tall as a man's stature. In this pine growth the branches were hanging down and stuck together from the snow. The path through the middle of the pine grove was covered with snow. This path was leading toward me. To the right of me was a dense pine forest, and beyond the pine grove there was a clearing. And on this clearing I saw Demyán place my companion.

I examined my two guns and cocked them, and began to think where to take up a stand. Behind me, about three steps from me, there was a pine-tree. "I will stand by that pine, and will lean the other gun against it." I made my way to that pine, walking knee-deep in snow. I tramped down a space of about four feet each way, and[Pg 88] there took my stand. One gun I took into my hands, and the other, with hammers raised, I placed against the tree. I unsheathed my dagger and put it back in the scabbard, to be sure that in case of need it would come out easily.

I had hardly fixed myself, when Demyán shouted from the woods:

"Start it now, start it!"

And as Demyán shouted this, the peasants in the circuit cried, each with a different tone of voice: "Come now! OO-oo-oo!" and the women cried, in their thin voices: "Ai! Eekh!"

The bear was in the circle. Demyán was driving him. In the circuit the people shouted, and only my companion and I stood still, did not speak or move, and waited for the bear. I stood, and looked, and listened, and my heart went pitapat. I was clutching my gun and trembling. Now, now he will jump out, I thought, and I will aim and shoot, and he will fall— Suddenly I heard to the left something tumbling through the snow, only it was far away. I looked into the tall pine forest: about fifty steps from me, behind the trees, stood something large and black. I aimed and waited. I thought it might come nearer. I saw it move its ears and turn around. Now I could see the whole of him from the side. It was a huge beast. I aimed hastily. Bang! I heard the bullet strike the tree. Through the smoke I saw the bear make back for the cover and disappear in the forest. "Well," I thought, "my business is spoiled: he will not run up to me again; either my companion will have a chance to shoot at him, or he will go through between the peasants, but never again toward me." I reloaded the gun, and stood and listened. The peasants were shouting on all sides, but on the right, not far from my companion, I heard a woman yell, "Here he is! Here he is! Here he is! This way! This way! Oi, oi, oi! Ai, ai, ai!"

There was the bear, in full sight. I was no longer expecting[Pg 89] the bear to come toward me, and so looked to the right toward my companion. I saw Demyán running without the snow-shoes along the path, with a stick in his hand, and going up to my companion, sitting down near him, and pointing with the stick at something, as though he were aiming. I saw my companion raise his gun and aim at where Demyán was pointing. Bang! he fired it off.

"Well," I thought, "he has killed him." But I saw that my companion was not running toward the bear. "Evidently he missed him, or did not strike him right. He will get away," I thought, "but he will not come toward me."

What was that? Suddenly I heard something in front of me: somebody was flying like a whirlwind, and scattering the snow near by, and panting. I looked ahead of me, but he was

33

making headlong toward me along the path through the dense pine growth. I could see that he was beside himself with fear. When he was within five steps of me I could see the whole of him: his chest was black and his head was enormous, and of a reddish colour. He was flying straight toward me, and scattering the snow in all directions. I could see by the bear's eyes that he did not see me and in his fright was rushing headlong. He was making straight for the pine where I was standing. I raised my gun, and shot, but he came still nearer. I saw that I had not hit him: the bullet was carried past him. He heard nothing, plunged onward, and did not see me. I bent down the gun, almost rested it against his head. Bang! This time I hit him, but did not kill him.

He raised his head, dropped his ears, showed his teeth,—and straight toward me. I grasped the other gun; but before I had it in my hand, he was already on me, knocked me down, and flew over me. "Well," I thought, "that is good, he will not touch me." I was just getting up, when[Pg 90] I felt something pressing against me and holding me down. In his onrush he ran past me, but he turned around and rushed against me with his whole breast. I felt something heavy upon me, something warm over my face, and I felt him taking my face into his jaws. My nose was already in his mouth, and I felt hot, and smelled his blood. He pressed my shoulders with his paws, and I could not stir. All I could do was to pull my head out of his jaws and press it against my breast, and I turned my nose and eyes away. But he was trying to get at my eyes and nose. I felt him strike the teeth of his upper jaw into my forehead, right below the hair, and the lower jaw into the cheek-bones below the eyes, and he began to crush me. It was as though my head were cut with knives. I jerked and pulled out my head, but he chawed and chawed and snapped at me like a dog. I would turn my head away, and he would catch it again. "Well," I thought, "my end has come." Suddenly I felt lighter. I looked up, and he was gone: he had jumped away from me, and was running now.

When my companion and Demyán saw that the bear had knocked me into the snow, they dashed for me. My companion wanted to get there as fast as possible, but lost his way; instead of running on the trodden path, he ran straight ahead, and fell down. While he was trying to get out of the snow, the bear was gnawing at me. Demyán ran up to me along the path, without a gun, just with the stick which he had in his hands, and he shouted, "He is eating up the gentleman! He is eating up the gentleman!" And he kept running and shouting, "Oh, you wretched beast! What are you doing? Stop! Stop!"

The bear listened to him, stopped, and ran away. When I got up, there was much blood on the snow, just as though a sheep had been killed, and over my eyes the flesh hung in rags. While the wound was fresh I felt no pain.

[Pg 91]

My companion ran up to me, and the peasants gathered around me. They looked at my wounds, and washed them with snow. I had entirely forgotten about the wounds, and only asked, "Where is the bear? Where has he gone?"

Suddenly we heard, "Here he is! Here he is!" We saw the bear running once more against us. We grasped our guns, but before we fired he ran past us. The bear was mad: he wanted to bite me again, but when he saw so many people he became frightened. We saw by the track that the bear was bleeding from the head. We wanted to follow him up, but my head hurt me, and so we drove to town to see a doctor.

The doctor sewed up my wounds with silk, and they began to heal.

A month later we went out again to hunt that bear; but I did not get the chance to kill him. The bear would not leave the cover, and kept walking around and around and roaring terribly. Demyán killed him. My shot had crushed his lower jaw and knocked out a tooth.

This bear was very large, and he had beautiful black fur. I had the skin stuffed, and it is lying now in my room. The wounds on my head have healed, so that one can scarcely see where they were.

[Pg 92]

## A PRISONER OF THE CAUCASUS
### I.

34

A certain gentleman was serving as an officer in the Caucasus. His name was Zhilín. One day he received a letter from home. His old mother wrote to him:

"I have grown old, and I should like to see my darling son before my death. Come to bid me farewell and bury me, and then, with God's aid, return to the service. I have also found a bride for you: she is bright and pretty and has property. If you take a liking to her, you can marry her, and stay here for good."

Zhilín reflected: "Indeed, my old mother has grown feeble; perhaps I shall never see her again. I must go; and if the bride is a good girl, I may marry her."

He went to the colonel, got a furlough, bade his companions good-bye, treated his soldiers to four buckets of vódka, and got himself ready to go.

At that time there was a war in the Caucasus. Neither in the daytime, nor at night, was it safe to travel on the roads. The moment a Russian walked or drove away from a fortress, the Tartars either killed him or took him as a prisoner to the mountains. It was a rule that a guard of soldiers should go twice a week from fortress to fortress. In front and in the rear walked soldiers, and between them were other people.

It was in the summer. The carts gathered at daybreak outside the fortress, and the soldiers of the convoy came[Pg 93] out, and all started. Zhilín rode on horseback, and his cart with his things went with the caravan.

They had to travel twenty-five versts. The caravan proceeded slowly; now the soldiers stopped, and now a wheel came off a cart, or a horse stopped, and all had to stand still and wait.

The sun had already passed midday, but the caravan had made only half the distance. It was dusty and hot; the sun just roasted them, and there was no shelter: it was a barren plain, with neither tree nor bush along the road.

Zhilín rode out ahead. He stopped and waited for the caravan to catch up with him. He heard them blow the signal-horn behind: they had stopped again.

Zhilín thought: "Why can't I ride on, without the soldiers? I have a good horse under me, and if I run against Tartars, I will gallop away. Or had I better not go?"

He stopped to think it over. There rode up to him another officer, Kostylín, with a gun, and said:

"Let us ride by ourselves, Zhilín! I cannot stand it any longer: I am hungry, and it is so hot. My shirt is dripping wet."

Kostylín was a heavy, stout man, with a red face, and the perspiration was just rolling down his face. Zhilín thought awhile and said:

"Is your gun loaded?"

"It is."

"Well, then, we will go, but on one condition, that we do not separate."

And so they rode ahead on the highway. They rode through the steppe, and talked, and looked about them. They could see a long way off.

When the steppe came to an end, the road entered a cleft between two mountains. So Zhilín said:

"We ought to ride up the mountain to take a look;[Pg 94] for here they may leap out on us from the mountain without our seeing them."

But Kostylín said:

"What is the use of looking? Let us ride on!"

Zhilín paid no attention to him.

"No," he said, "you wait here below, and I will take a look up there."

And he turned his horse to the left, up-hill. The horse under Zhilín was a thoroughbred (he had paid a hundred roubles for it when it was a colt, and had himself trained it), and it carried him up the slope as though on wings. The moment he reached the summit, he saw before him a number of Tartars on horseback, about eighty fathoms away. There were about thirty of them. When he saw them, he began to turn back; and the Tartars saw him, and galloped toward him, and on the ride took their guns out of the covers. Zhilín urged his horse down-hill as fast as its legs would carry him, and he shouted to Kostylín:

"Take out the gun!" and he himself thought about his horse: "Darling, take me away from here! Don't stumble! If you do, I am lost. If I get to the gun, they shall not catch me."

35

But Kostylín, instead of waiting, galloped at full speed toward the fortress, the moment he saw the Tartars. He urged the horse on with the whip, now on one side, and now on the other. One could see through the dust only the horse switching her tail.

Zhilín saw that things were bad. The gun had disappeared, and he could do nothing with a sword. He turned his horse back to the soldiers, thinking that he might get away. He saw six men crossing his path. He had a good horse under him, but theirs were better still, and they crossed his path. He began to check his horse: he wanted to turn around; but the horse was running at full speed and could not be stopped, and he flew straight[Pg 95] toward them. He saw a red-bearded Tartar on a gray horse, who was coming near to him. He howled and showed his teeth, and his gun was against his shoulder.

"Well," thought Zhilín, "I know you devils. When you take one alive, you put him in a hole and beat him with a whip. I will not fall into your hands alive——"

Though Zhilín was not tall, he was brave. He drew his sword, turned his horse straight against the Tartar, and thought:

"Either I will knock his horse off its feet, or I will strike the Tartar with my sword."

Zhilín got within a horse's length from him, when they shot at him from behind and hit the horse. The horse dropped on the ground while going at full speed, and fell on Zhilín's leg.

He wanted to get up, but two stinking Tartars were already astride of him. He tugged and knocked down the two Tartars, but three more jumped down from their horses and began to strike him with the butts of their guns. Things grew dim before his eyes, and he tottered. The Tartars took hold of him, took from their saddles some reserve straps, twisted his arms behind his back, tied them with a Tartar knot, and fastened him to the saddle. They knocked down his hat, pulled off his boots, rummaged all over him, and took away his money and his watch, and tore all his clothes.

Zhilín looked back at his horse. The dear animal was lying just as it had fallen down, and only twitched its legs and did not reach the ground with them; in its head there was a hole, and from it the black blood gushed and wet the dust for an ell around.

A Tartar went up to the horse, to pull off the saddle. The horse was struggling still, and so he took out his dagger and cut its throat. A whistling sound came from the throat, and the horse twitched, and was dead.

The Tartars took off the saddle and the trappings.[Pg 96] The red-bearded Tartar mounted his horse, and the others seated Zhilín behind him. To prevent his falling off, they attached him by a strap to the Tartar's belt, and they rode off to the mountains.

Zhilín was sitting back of the Tartar, and shaking and striking with his face against the stinking Tartar's back. All he saw before him was the mighty back, and the muscular neck, and the livid, shaved nape of his head underneath his cap. Zhilín's head was bruised, and the blood was clotted under his eyes. And he could not straighten himself on the saddle, nor wipe off his blood. His arms were twisted so badly that his shoulder bones pained him.

They rode for a long time from one mountain to another, and forded a river, and came out on a path, where they rode through a ravine.

Zhilín wanted to take note of the road on which they were travelling, but his eyes were smeared with blood, and he could not turn around.

It was getting dark. They crossed another stream and rode up a rocky mountain. There was an odour of smoke, and the dogs began to bark. They had come to a native village. The Tartars got down from their horses; the Tartar children gathered around Zhilín, and screamed, and rejoiced, and aimed stones at him.

The Tartar drove the boys away, took Zhilín down from his horse, and called a labourer. There came a Nogay, with large cheek-bones; he wore nothing but a shirt. The shirt was torn and left his breast bare. The Tartar gave him a command. The labourer brought the stocks,—two oak planks drawn through iron rings, and one of these rings with a clasp and lock.

They untied Zhilín's hands, put the stocks on him, and led him into a shed: they pushed him in and locked the door. Zhilín fell on the manure pile. He felt around in the darkness for a soft spot, and lay down there.

36

[Pg 97]

## II.

Zhilín lay awake nearly the whole night. The nights were short. He saw through a chink that it was getting light. He got up, made the chink larger, and looked out.

Through the chink Zhilín saw the road: it went down-hill; on the right was a Tartar cabin, and near it two trees. A black dog lay on the threshold, and a goat strutted about with her kids, which were jerking their little tails. He saw a young Tartar woman coming up the hill; she wore a loose coloured shirt and pantaloons and boots, and her head was covered with a caftan, and on her head there was a large tin pitcher with water. She walked along, jerking her back, and bending over, and by the hand she led a young shaven Tartar boy in nothing but his shirt. The Tartar woman went into the cabin with the water, and out came the Tartar of the day before, with the red beard, wearing a silk half-coat, a silver dagger on a strap, and shoes on his bare feet. On his head there was a tall, black sheepskin hat, tilted backwards. He came out, and he stretched himself and smoothed his red beard. He stood awhile, gave the labourer an order, and went away.

Then two boys rode by, taking the horses to water. The muzzles of the horses were wet. Then there ran out some other shaven boys, in nothing but their shirts, with no trousers; they gathered in a crowd, walked over to the shed, picked up a stick, and began to poke it through the chink. When Zhilín shouted at the children, they screamed and started to run back, so that their bare knees glistened in the sun.

Zhilín wanted to drink,—his throat was all dried up. He thought: "If they would only come to see me!" He heard them open the shed. The red Tartar came in, and with him another, black-looking fellow, of smaller stature.[Pg 98] His eyes were black and bright, his cheeks ruddy, his small beard clipped; his face looked jolly, and he kept laughing all the time. This swarthy fellow was dressed even better: he had on a silk half-coat, of a blue colour, embroidered with galloons. In his belt there was a large silver dagger; his slippers were of red morocco and also embroidered with silver. Over his thin slippers he wore heavier shoes. His cap was tall, of white astrakhan.

The red Tartar came in. He said something, as though scolding, and stopped. He leaned against the door-post, dangled his dagger, and like a wolf looked furtively at Zhilín. But the swarthy fellow—swift, lively, walking around as though on springs—went up straight to Zhilín, squatted down, showed his teeth, slapped him on the shoulder, began to rattle off something in his language, winked with his eyes, clicked his tongue, and kept repeating: "Goot Uruss! Goot Uruss!"

Zhilín did not understand a thing and said:

"Give me to drink, give me water to drink!"

The swarthy fellow laughed. "Goot Uruss!" he kept rattling off.

Zhilín showed with his lips and hands that he wanted something to drink.

The swarthy fellow understood what he wanted, laughed out, looked through the door, and called some one: "Dina!"

In came a thin, slender little girl, of about thirteen years of age, who resembled the swarthy man very much. Evidently she was his daughter. Her eyes, too, were black and bright, and her face was pretty. She wore a long blue shirt, with broad sleeves and without a belt. The skirt, the breast, and the sleeves were trimmed with red. On her legs were pantaloons, and on her feet slippers, with high-heeled shoes over them; on her neck she wore a necklace of Russian half-roubles. Her head was uncovered; her braid was black, with a ribbon[Pg 99] through it, and from the ribbon hung small plates and a Russian rouble.

Her father gave her a command. She ran away, and came back and brought a small tin pitcher. She gave him the water, and herself squatted down, bending up in such a way that her shoulders were below her knees. She sat there, and opened her eyes, and looked at Zhilín drinking, as though he were some animal.

Zhilín handed her back the pitcher. She jumped away like a wild goat. Even her father laughed. He sent her somewhere else. She took the pitcher and ran away; she brought some fresh bread on a round board, and again sat down, bent over, riveted her eyes on him, and kept looking.

The Tartars went away and locked the door.

After awhile the Nogay came to Zhilín, and said:

"Ai-da, master, ai-da!"

He did not know any Russian, either. All Zhilín could make out was that he should follow him.

Zhilín started with the stocks, and he limped and could not walk, so much did the stocks pull his legs aside. Zhilín went out with the Nogay. He saw a Tartar village of about ten houses, and a church of theirs, with a small tower. Near one house stood three horses, all saddled. Boys were holding the reins. From the house sprang the swarthy Tartar, and he waved his hand for Zhilín to come up. He laughed all the while, and talked in his language, and disappeared through the door.

Zhilín entered the house. It was a good living-room,—the walls were plastered smooth with clay. Along the front wall lay coloured cushions, and at the sides hung costly rugs; on the rugs were guns, pistols, swords,—all in silver. By one wall there was a small stove, on a level with the floor. The floor was of dirt and as clean as a threshing-floor, and the whole front corner was carpeted with felt; and over the felt lay rugs, and on[Pg 100] the rugs cushions. On these rugs sat the Tartars, in their slippers without their outer shoes: there were the swarthy fellow, the red Tartar, and three guests. At their backs were feather cushions, and before them, on a round board, were millet cakes and melted butter in a bowl, and Tartar beer, "buza," in a small pitcher. They were eating with their hands, and their hands were all greasy from the butter.

The swarthy man jumped up and ordered Zhilín to be placed to one side, not on a rug, but on the bare floor; he went back to his rug, and treated his guests to millet cakes and buza. The labourer placed Zhilín where he had been ordered, himself took off his outer shoes, put them at the door, where stood the other shoes, and sat down on the felt next to the masters. He looked at them as they ate, and wiped off his spittle.

The Tartars ate the cakes. Then there came a Tartar woman, in a shirt like the one the girl had on, and in pantaloons, and with a kerchief over her head. She carried away the butter and the cakes, and brought a small wash-basin of a pretty shape, and a pitcher with a narrow neck. The Tartars washed their hands, then folded them, knelt down, blew in every direction, and said their prayers. Then one of the Tartar guests turned to Zhilín, and began to speak in Russian:

"You," he said, "were taken by Kazi-Muhammed," and he pointed to the red Tartar, "and he gave you to Abdul-Murat." He pointed to the swarthy man. "Abdul-Murat is now your master."

Zhilín kept silence. Then Abdul-Murat began to speak. He pointed to Zhilín, and laughed, and kept repeating:

"Soldier Uruss! Goot Uruss!"

The interpreter said:

"He wants you to write a letter home that they may send a ransom for you. When they send it, you will be set free."

[Pg 101]

Zhilín thought awhile and said:

"How much ransom does he want?"

The Tartars talked together; then the interpreter said:

"Three thousand in silver."

"No," said Zhilín, "I cannot pay that."

Abdul jumped up, began to wave his hands and to talk to Zhilín, thinking that he would understand him. The interpreter translated. He said:

"How much will you give?"

Zhilín thought awhile, and said:

"Five hundred roubles."

Then the Tartars began to talk a great deal, all at the same time. Abdul shouted at the red Tartar. He was so excited that the spittle just spirted from his mouth.

But the red Tartar only scowled and clicked his tongue.

They grew silent, and the interpreter said:

"The master is not satisfied with five hundred roubles. He has himself paid two hundred for you. Kazi-Muhammed owed him a debt. He took you for that debt. Three thousand roubles, nothing less will do. And if you do not write, you will be put in a hole and beaten with a whip."

"Oh," thought Zhilín, "it will not do to show that I am frightened; that will only be worse." He leaped to his feet, and said:

"Tell that dog that if he is going to frighten me, I will not give him a penny, and I will refuse to write. I have never been afraid of you dogs, and I never will be."

The interpreter translated, and all began to speak at the same time.

They babbled for a long time; then the swarthy Tartar jumped up and walked over to Zhilín:

"Uruss," he said, "dzhigit, dzhigit Uruss!"

|Pg 102|

Dzhigit in their language means a "brave." And he laughed; he said something to the interpreter, and the interpreter said:

"Give one thousand roubles!"

Zhilín stuck to what he had said:

"I will not give more than five hundred. And if you kill me, you will get nothing."

The Tartars talked awhile and sent the labourer somewhere, and themselves kept looking now at Zhilín and now at the door. The labourer came, and behind him walked a fat man; he was barefoot and tattered; he, too, had on the stocks.

Zhilín just shouted, for he recognized Kostylín. He, too, had been caught. They were placed beside each other. They began to talk to each other, and the Tartars kept silence and looked at them. Zhilín told what had happened to him; and Kostylín told him that his horse had stopped and his gun had missed fire, and that the same Abdul had overtaken and captured him.

Abdul jumped up, and pointed to Kostylín, and said something. The interpreter translated it, and said that both of them belonged to the same master, and that the one who would first furnish the money would be the first to be released.

"Now you," he said, "are a cross fellow, but your friend is meek; he has written a letter home, and they will send five thousand roubles. He will be fed well, and will not be insulted."

So Zhilín said:

"My friend may do as he pleases; maybe he is rich, but I am not. As I have said, so will it be. If you want to, kill me,—you will not gain by it,—but more than five hundred will I not give."

They were silent for awhile. Suddenly Abdul jumped up, fetched a small box, took out a pen, a piece of paper, and some ink, put it all before Zhilín, slapped him on the|Pg 103| shoulder, and motioned for him to write. He agreed to the five hundred.

"Wait awhile," Zhilín said to the interpreter. "Tell him that he has to feed us well, and give us the proper clothes and shoes, and keep us together,—it will be jollier for us,—and take off the stocks." He looked at the master and laughed. The master himself laughed. He listened to the interpreter, and said:

"I will give you the best of clothes,—a Circassian mantle and boots,—you will be fit to marry. We will feed you like princes. And if you want to stay together, you may live in the shed. But the stocks cannot be taken off, for you will run away. For the night we will take them off."

He ran up to Zhilín, and tapped him on the shoulder:

"You goot, me goot!"

Zhilín wrote the letter, but he did not address it right. He thought he would run away.

Zhilín and Kostylín were taken back to the shed. They brought for them maize straw, water in a pitcher, bread, two old mantles, and worn soldier boots. They had evidently been pulled off dead soldiers. For the night the stocks were taken off, and they were locked in the barn.

39

# III.

Zhilín and his companion lived thus for a whole month. Their master kept laughing.

"You, Iván, goot, me, Abdul, goot!"

But he did not feed them well. All he gave them to eat was unsalted millet bread, baked like pones, or entirely unbaked dough.

Kostylín wrote home a second letter. He was waiting for the money to come, and felt lonesome. He sat for days at a time in the shed counting the days before the letter would come, or he slept. But Zhilín knew that[Pg 104] his letter would not reach any one, and so he did not write another.

"Where," he thought, "is my mother to get so much money? As it is, she lived mainly by what I sent her. If she should collect five hundred roubles, she would be ruined in the end. If God grants it, I will manage to get away from here."

And he watched and thought of how to get away.

He walked through the village and whistled, or he sat down somewhere to work with his hands, either making a doll from clay, or weaving a fence from twigs. Zhilín was a great hand at all kinds of such work.

One day he made a doll, with a nose, and hands, and legs, in a Tartar shirt, and put the doll on the roof. The Tartar maidens were going for water. His master's daughter, Dina, saw the doll, and she called up the Tartar girls. They put down their pitchers, and looked, and laughed. Zhilín took down the doll and gave it to them. They laughed, and did not dare take it. He left the doll, and went back to the shed to see what they would do.

Dina ran up, looked around, grasped the doll, and ran away with it.

In the morning, at daybreak, he saw Dina coming out with the doll in front of the house. The doll was all dressed up in red rags, and she was rocking the doll and singing to it in her fashion. The old woman came out. She scolded her, took the doll away from her and broke it, and sent Dina to work.

Zhilín made another doll, a better one than before, and he gave it to Dina. One day Dina brought him a small pitcher. She put it down, herself sat down and looked at him, and laughed, as she pointed to the pitcher.

"What is she so happy about?" thought Zhilín.

He took the pitcher and began to drink. He thought it was water, but, behold, it was milk. He drank the milk, and said:

[Pg 105]

"It is good!"

Dina was very happy.

"Good, Iván, good!" and she jumped up, clapped her hands, took away the pitcher, and ran off.

From that time she brought him milk every day on the sly. The Tartars make cheese-cakes from goat milk, and dry them on the roofs,—and so she brought him those cakes also. One day the master killed a sheep, so she brought him a piece of mutton in her sleeve. She would throw it down and run away.

One day there was a severe storm, and for an hour the rain fell as though from a pail. All the streams became turbid. Where there was a ford, the water was now eight feet deep, and stones were borne down. Torrents were running everywhere, and there was a roar in the mountains. When the storm was over, streams were coming down the village in every direction. Zhilín asked his master to let him have a penknife, and with it he cut out a small axle and little boards, and made a wheel, and to each end of the wheel he attached a doll.

The girls brought him pieces of material, and he dressed the dolls: one a man, the other a woman. He fixed them firmly, and placed the wheel over a brook. The wheel began to turn, and the dolls to jump.

The whole village gathered around it; boys, girls, women, and men came, and they clicked with their tongues:

"Ai, Uruss! Ai, Iván!"

Abdul had a Russian watch, but it was broken. He called Zhilín, showed it to him, and clicked his tongue. Zhilín said:

"Let me have it! I will fix it!"

40

He took it to pieces with a penknife; then he put it together, and gave it back to him. The watch was running now.

The master was delighted. He brought his old half-coat,—it[Pg 106] was all in rags,—and made him a present of it. What could he do but take it? He thought it would be good enough to cover himself with in the night.

After that the rumour went abroad that Zhilín was a great master. They began to come to him from distant villages: one, to have him fix a gun-lock or a pistol, another, to set a clock a-going. His master brought him tools,—pinchers, gimlets, and files.

One day a Tartar became sick: they sent to Zhilín, and said, "Go and cure him!" Zhilín did not know anything about medicine. He went, took a look at him, and thought, "Maybe he will get well by himself." He went to the barn, took some water and sand, and mixed it. In the presence of the Tartars he said a charm over the water, and gave it to him to drink. Luckily for him, the Tartar got well.

Zhilín began to understand their language. Some of the Tartars got used to him. When they needed him, they called, "Iván, Iván!" but others looked at him awry, as at an animal.

The red Tartar did not like Zhilín. Whenever he saw him, he frowned and turned away, or called him names. There was also an old man; he did not live in the village, but came from farther down the mountain. Zhilín saw him only when he came to the mosque, to pray to God. He was a small man; his cap was wrapped with a white towel. His beard and moustache were clipped, and they were as white as down; his face was wrinkled and as red as a brick. His nose was hooked, like a hawk's beak, and his eyes were gray and mean-looking; of teeth he had only two tusks. He used to walk in his turban, leaning on a crutch, and looking around him like a wolf. Whenever he saw Zhilín, he grunted and turned away.

One day Zhilín went down-hill, to see where the old man was living. He walked down the road, and saw a little garden, with a stone fence, and inside the fence were[Pg 107] cherry and apricot trees, and stood a hut with a flat roof. He came closer to it, and he saw beehives woven from straw, and bees were swarming around and buzzing. The old man was kneeling, and doing something to a hive. Zhilín got up higher, to get a good look, and made a noise with his stocks. The old man looked around and shrieked; he pulled the pistol out from his belt and fired at Zhilín. He had just time to hide behind a rock.

The old man went to the master to complain about Zhilín. The master called up Zhilín, and laughed, and asked:

"Why did you go to the old man?"

"I have not done him any harm," he said. "I just wanted to see how he lives."

The master told the old man that. But the old man was angry, and hissed, and rattled something off; he showed his teeth and waved his hand threateningly at Zhilín.

Zhilín did not understand it all; but he understood that the old man was telling his master to kill all the Russians, and not to keep them in the village. The old man went away.

Zhilín asked his master what kind of a man that old Tartar was. The master said:

"He is a big man! He used to be the first dzhigit: he killed a lot of Russians, and he was rich. He had three wives and eight sons. All of them lived in the same village. The Russians came, destroyed the village, and killed seven of his sons. One son was left alive, and he surrendered himself to the Russians. The old man went and surrendered himself, too, to the Russians. He stayed with them three months, found his son there, and killed him, and then he ran away. Since then he has stopped fighting. He has been to Mecca, to pray to God, and that is why he wears the turban. He who has been to Mecca is called a Hadji and puts on a turban. He has no use[Pg 108] for you fellows. He tells me to kill you; but I cannot kill you,—I have paid for you; and then, Iván, I like you. I not only have no intention of killing you, but I would not let you go back, if I had not given my word to you." He laughed as he said that, and added in Russian: "You, Iván, good, me, Abdul, good!"

## IV.

Zhilín lived thus for a month. In the daytime he walked around the village and made things with his hands, and when night came, and all was quiet in the village, he began to dig in the shed. It was difficult to dig on account of the rocks, but he sawed the stones with the file, and made a hole through which he meant to crawl later. "First I must find out what direction to go in," he thought; "but the Tartars will not tell me anything."

So he chose a time when his master was away; he went after dinner back of the village, up-hill, where he could see the place. But when his master went away, he told his little boy to keep an eye on Zhilín and to follow him everywhere. So the boy ran after Zhilín, and said:

"Don't go! Father said that you should not go there. I will call the people!"

Zhilín began to persuade him.

"I do not want to go far," he said; "I just want to walk up the mountain: I want to find an herb with which to cure you people. Come with me; I cannot run away with the stocks. To-morrow I will make you a bow and arrows."

He persuaded the boy, and they went together. As he looked up the mountain, it looked near, but with the stocks it was hard to walk; he walked and walked, and climbed the mountain with difficulty. Zhilín sat down and began to look at the place. To the south of the shed[Pg 109] there was a ravine, and there a herd of horses was grazing, and in a hollow could be seen another village. At that village began a steeper mountain, and beyond that mountain there was another mountain. Between the mountains could be seen a forest, and beyond it again the mountains, rising higher and higher. Highest of all, there were white mountains, capped with snow, just like sugar loaves. And one snow mountain stood with its cap above all the rest. To the east and the west there were just such mountains; here and there smoke rose from villages in the clefts.

"Well," he thought, "that is all their side."

He began to look to the Russian side. At his feet was a brook and his village, and all around were little gardens. At the brook women were sitting,—they looked as small as dolls,—and washing the linen. Beyond the village and below it there was a mountain, and beyond that, two other mountains, covered with forests; between the two mountains could be seen an even spot, and on that plain, far, far away, it looked as though smoke were settling. Zhilín recalled where the sun used to rise and set when he was at home in the fortress. He looked down there,—sure enough, that was the valley where the Russian fortress ought to be. There, then, between those two mountains, he had to run.

The sun was beginning to go down. The snow-capped mountains changed from white to violet; it grew dark in the black mountains; vapour arose from the clefts, and the valley, where our fortress no doubt was, gleamed in the sunset as though on fire. Zhilín began to look sharply,—something was quivering in the valley, like smoke rising from chimneys. He was sure now that it must be the Russian fortress.

It grew late; he could hear the mullah call; the flock was being driven, and the cows lowed. The boy said to him, "Come!" but Zhilín did not feel like leaving.

[Pg 110]

They returned home. "Well," thought Zhilín, "now I know the place, and I must run." He wanted to run that same night. The nights were dark,—the moon was on the wane. Unfortunately the Tartars returned toward evening. At other times they returned driving cattle before them, and then they were jolly. But this time they did not drive home anything, but brought back a dead Tartar, a red-haired companion of theirs. They came back angry, and all gathered to bury him. Zhilín, too, went out to see. They wrapped the dead man in linen, without putting him in a coffin, and carried him under the plane-trees beyond the village, and placed him on the grass. The mullah came, and the old men gathered around him, their caps wrapped with towels, and took off their shoes and seated themselves in a row on their heels, in front of the dead man.

At their head was the mullah, and then three old men in turbans, sitting in a row, and behind them other Tartars. They sat, and bent their heads, and kept silence. They were silent for quite awhile. Then the mullah raised his head, and said:

"Allah!" (That means "God.") He said that one word, and again they lowered their heads and kept silence for a long time; they sat without stirring. Again the mullah raised his head:

"Allah!" and all repeated, "Allah!" and again they were silent. The dead man lay on the grass, and did not stir, and they sat about him like the dead. Not one of them stirred. One could hear only the leaves on the plane-tree rustling in the breeze. Then the mullah said a prayer, and all got up, lifted the dead body, and carried it away. They took it to a grave,—not a simple grave, but dug under like a cave. They took the dead man under his arms and by his legs, bent him over, let him down softly, pushed him under in a sitting posture, and fixed his arms on his body.

[Pg 111]

A Nogay dragged up a lot of green reeds; they bedded the grave with it, then quickly filled it with dirt, levelled it up, and put a stone up straight at the head of it. They tramped down the earth, and again sat down in a row near the grave. They were silent for a long time.

"Allah, Allah, Allah!" They sighed and got up.

A red-haired Tartar distributed money to the old men; then he got up, took a whip, struck himself three times on his forehead, and went home.

Next morning Zhilín saw the red Tartar take a mare out of the village, and three Tartars followed him. They went outside the village; then the red-haired Tartar took off his coat, rolled up his sleeves,—he had immense arms,—and took out his dagger and whetted it on a steel. The Tartars jerked up the mare's head, and the red-haired man walked over to her, cut her throat, threw her down, and began to flay her,—to rip the skin open with his fists. Then came women and girls, and they began to wash the inside and the entrails. Then they chopped up the mare and dragged the flesh to the house. And the whole village gathered at the house of the red-haired Tartar to celebrate the dead man's wake.

For three days did they eat the horse-flesh, drink buza, and remember the dead man. On the fourth day Zhilín saw them get ready to go somewhere for a dinner. They brought horses, dressed themselves up, and went away,—about ten men, and the red Tartar with them; Abdul was the only one who was left at home. The moon was just beginning to increase, and the nights were still dark.

"Well," thought Zhilín, "to-night I must run," and he told Kostylín so. But Kostylín was timid.

"How can we run? We do not know the road."

"I know it."

"But we cannot reach it in the night."

"If we do not, we shall stay for the night in the woods. I have a lot of cakes with me. You certainly do not mean[Pg 112] to stay. It would be all right if they sent the money; but suppose they cannot get together so much. The Tartars are mean now, because the Russians have killed one of theirs. I understand they want to kill us now."

Kostylín thought awhile:

"Well, let us go!"

V.

Zhilín crept into the hole and dug it wider, so that Kostylín could get through; and then they sat still and waited for everything to quiet down in the village.

When all grew quiet, Zhilín crawled through the hole and got out. He whispered to Kostylín to crawl out. Kostylín started to come out, but he caught a stone with his foot, and it made a noise. Now their master had a dappled watch-dog, and he was dreadfully mean; his name was Ulyashin. Zhilín had been feeding him before. When Ulyashin heard the voice, he began to bark and rushed forward, and with him other dogs. Zhilín gave a low whistle and threw a piece of cake to the dog, and the dog recognized him and wagged his tail and stopped barking.

The master heard it, and he called out from the hut, "Hait, hait, Ulyashin!"

But Zhilín was scratching Ulyashin behind his ears; so the dog was silent and rubbed against his legs and wagged his tail.

They sat awhile around the corner. All was silent; nothing could be heard but the sheep coughing in the hut corner, and the water rippling down the pebbles. It was dark; the stars stood high in the heaven; the young moon shone red above the mountain, and its horns were turned upward. In the clefts the mist looked as white as milk.

Zhilín got up and said to his companion:

"Now, my friend, let us start!"

They started. They had made but a few steps, when[Pg 113] they heard the mullah sing out on the roof: "Allah besmillah! Ilrakhman!" That meant that the people were going to the mosque. They sat down again, hiding behind a wall. They sat for a long time, waiting for the people to pass by. Again everything was quiet.

"Well, with God's aid!" They made the sign of the cross, and started. They crossed the yard and went down-hill to the brook; they crossed the brook and walked down the ravine. The mist was dense and low on the ground, and overhead the stars were, oh, so visible. Zhilín saw by the stars in what direction they had to go. In the mist it felt fresh, and it was easy to walk, only the boots were awkward, they had worn down so much. Zhilín took off his boots and threw them away, and marched on barefoot. He leaped from stone to stone, and kept watching the stars. Kostylín began to fall behind.

"Walk slower," he said. "The accursed boots,—they have chafed my feet."

"Take them off! You will find it easier without them."

Kostylín walked barefoot after that; but it was only worse: he cut his feet on the rocks, and kept falling behind. Zhilín said to him:

"If you bruise your feet, they will heal up; but if they catch you; they will kill you,—so it will be worse."

Kostylín said nothing, but he groaned as he walked. They walked for a long time through a ravine. Suddenly they heard dogs barking. Zhilín stopped and looked around; he groped with his hands and climbed a hill.

"Oh," he said, "we have made a mistake,—we have borne too much to the right. Here is a village,—I saw it from the mountain; we must go back and to the left, and up the mountain. There must be a forest here."

But Kostylín said:

"Wait at least awhile! Let me rest: my feet are all blood-stained."

[Pg 114]

"Never mind, friend, they will heal up! Jump more lightly,—like this!"

And Zhilín ran back, and to the left, up the mountain into the forest. Kostylín kept falling behind and groaning. Zhilín hushed him, and walked on.

They got up the mountain, and there, indeed, was a forest. They went into the forest, and tore all the clothes they had against the thorns. They struck a path in the forest, and followed it.

"Stop!" Hoofs were heard tramping on the path. They stopped to listen. It was the sound of a horse's hoofs. They started, and again it began to thud. They stopped, and it, too, stopped. Zhilín crawled up to it, and saw something standing in the light on the road. It was not exactly a horse, and again it was like a horse with something strange above it, and certainly not a man. He heard it snort. "What in the world is it?" Zhilín gave a light whistle, and it bolted away from the path, so that he could hear it crash through the woods: the branches broke off, as though a storm went through them.

Kostylín fell down in fright. But Zhilín laughed and said:

"That is a stag. Do you hear him break the branches with his horns? We are afraid of him, and he is afraid of us."

They walked on. The Pleiades were beginning to settle,—it was not far from morning. They did not know whether they were going right, or not. Zhilín thought that that was the path over which they had taken him, and that he was about ten versts from his own people; still there were no certain signs, and, besides, in the night nothing could be made out. They came out on a clearing. Kostylín sat down, and said:

"Do as you please, but I will not go any farther! My feet refuse to move."

Zhilín begged him to go on.

[Pg 115]

"No," he said, "I cannot walk on."

Zhilín got angry, spit out in disgust, and scolded him.

"Then I will go by myself,—good-bye!"

Kostylín got up and walked on. They walked about four versts. The mist grew denser in the forest, and nothing could be seen in front of them, and the stars were quite dim.

44

Suddenly they heard a horse tramping in front of them. They could hear the horse catch with its hoofs in the stones. Zhilín lay down on his belly, and put his ear to the ground to listen.

"So it is, a rider is coming this way!"

They ran off the road, sat down in the bushes, and waited. Zhilín crept up to the road, and saw a Tartar on horseback, driving a cow before him, and mumbling something to himself. The Tartar passed by them. Zhilín went back to Kostylín.

"Well, with God's help, he is gone. Get up, and let us go!"

Kostylín tried to get up, but fell down.

"I cannot, upon my word, I cannot. I have no strength."

The heavy, puffed-up man was in a perspiration, and as the cold mist in the forest went through him and his feet were all torn, he went all to pieces. Zhilín tried to get him up, but Kostylín cried:

"Oh, it hurts!"

Zhilín was frightened.

"Don't shout so! You know that the Tartar is not far off,—he will hear you." But he thought: "He is, indeed, weak, so what shall I do with him? It will not do to abandon my companion."

"Well," he said, "get up, get on my back, and I will carry you, if you cannot walk."

He took Kostylín on his back, put his hands on Kostylín's legs, walked out on the road, and walked on.

[Pg 116]

"Only be sure," he said, "and do not choke me with your hands, for Christ's sake. Hold on to my shoulders!"

It was hard for Zhilín: his feet, too, were blood-stained, and he was worn out. He kept bending down, straightening up Kostylín, and throwing him up, so that he might sit higher, and dragged him along the road.

Evidently the Tartar had heard Kostylín's shout. Zhilín heard some one riding from behind and calling in his language. Zhilín made for the brush. The Tartar pulled out his gun and fired; he screeched in his fashion, and rode back along the road.

"Well," said Zhilín, "we are lost, my friend! That dog will collect the Tartars and they will start after us. If we cannot make another three versts, we are lost." But he thought about Kostylín: "The devil has tempted me to take this log along. If I had been alone, I should have escaped long ago."

Kostylín said:

"Go yourself! Why should you perish for my sake?"

"No, I will not go,—it will not do to leave a comrade."

He took him once more on his shoulders, and held on to him. Thus they walked another verst. The woods extended everywhere, and no end was to be seen. The mist was beginning to lift, and rose in the air like little clouds, and the stars could not be seen. Zhilín was worn out.

They came to a little spring by the road; it was lined with stones. Zhilín stopped and put down Kostylín.

"Let me rest," he said, "and get a drink! We will eat our cakes. It cannot be far now."

He had just got down to drink, when he heard the tramping of horses behind them. Again they rushed to the right, into the bushes, down an incline, and lay down.

They could hear Tartar voices. The Tartars stopped at the very spot where they had left the road. They[Pg 117] talked awhile, then they made a sound, as though sicking dogs. Something crashed through the bushes, and a strange dog made straight for them. It stopped and began to bark.

Then the Tartars came down,—they, too, were strangers. They took them, bound them, put them on their horses, and carried them off.

They travelled about three versts, when they were met by Abdul, the prisoners' master, and two more Tartars. They talked with each other, and the prisoners were put on the other horses and taken back to the village.

Abdul no longer laughed, and did not speak one word with them.

They were brought to the village at daybreak, and were placed in the street. The children ran up and beat them with stones and sticks, and screamed.

The Tartars gathered in a circle, and the old man from down-hill came, too. They talked together. Zhilín saw that they were sitting in judgment on them, discussing what to do with them. Some said that they ought to be sent farther into the mountains, but the old man said that they should be killed. Abdul disputed with them and said:

"I have paid money for them, and I will get a ransom for them."

But the old man said:

"They will not pay us anything; they will only give us trouble. It is a sin to feed Russians. Kill them, and that will be the end of it."

They all went their way. The master walked over to Zhilín and said:

"If the ransom does not come in two weeks, I will beat you to death. And if you try to run again I will kill you like a dog. Write a letter, and write it well!"

Paper was brought to them, and they wrote the letters. The stocks were put on them, and they were taken back[Pg 118] of the mosque. There was a ditch there, about twelve feet in depth,—and into this ditch they were let down.

## VI.

They now led a very hard life. The stocks were not taken off, and they were not let out into the wide world. Unbaked dough was thrown down to them, as to dogs, and water was let down to them in a pitcher. There was a stench in the ditch, and it was close and damp. Kostylín grew very ill, and swelled, and had a breaking out on his whole body; and he kept groaning all the time, or he slept. Zhilín was discouraged: he saw that the situation was desperate. He did not know how to get out of it.

He began to dig, but there was no place to throw the dirt in; the master saw it, and threatened to kill him.

One day he was squatting in the ditch, and thinking of the free world, and he felt pretty bad. Suddenly a cake fell down on his knees, and a second, and some cherries. He looked up,—it was Dina. She looked at him, laughed, and ran away. Zhilín thought: "Maybe Dina will help me."

He cleaned up a place in the ditch, scraped up some clay, and began to make dolls. He made men, horses, and dogs. He thought: "When Dina comes I will throw them to her."

But on the next day Dina did not come. Zhilín heard the tramping of horses; somebody rode by, and the Tartars gathered at the mosque; they quarrelled and shouted, and talked about the Russians. And he heard the old man's voice. He could not make out exactly what it was, but he guessed that the Russians had come close to the village, and that the Tartars were afraid that they might come to the village, and they did not know what to do with the prisoners.

They talked awhile and went away. Suddenly he heard[Pg 119] something rustle above him. He looked up; Dina was squatting down, and her knees towered above her head; she leaned over, and her necklace hung down and dangled over the ditch. Her little eyes glistened like stars. She took two cheese-cakes out of her sleeve and threw them down to him. Zhilín said to her:

"Why have you not been here for so long? I have made you some toys. Here they are!"

He began to throw one after the other to her, but she shook her head, and did not look at them.

"I do not want them," she said. She sat awhile in silence, and said; "Iván, they want to kill you!" She pointed with her hand to her neck.

"Who wants to kill me?"

"My father,—the old men tell him to. I am sorry for you."

So Zhilín said:

"If you pity me, bring me a long stick!"

She shook her head, to say that she could not. He folded his hands, and began to beg her:

"Dina, if you please! Dear Dina, bring it to me!"

"I cannot," she said. "The people are at home, and they would see me."

And she went away.

Zhilín was sitting there in the evening, and thinking what would happen. He kept looking up. The stars could be seen, and the moon was not yet up. The mullah called, and all grew quiet. Zhilín was beginning to fall asleep; he thought the girl would be afraid.

Suddenly some clay fell on his head. He looked up and saw a long pole coming down at the end of the ditch. It tumbled, and descended, and came down into the ditch. Zhilín was happy; he took hold of it and let it down,—it was a stout pole. He had seen it before on his master's roof.

He looked up: the stars were shining high in the[Pg 120] heavens, and over the very ditch Dina's eyes glistened in the darkness. She bent her face over the edge of the ditch, and whispered: "Iván, Iván!" and waved her hands in front of her face, as much as to say: "Speak softly!"

"What is it?" asked Zhilín.

"They are all gone. There are two only at the house."

So Zhilín said:

"Kostylín, come, let us try for the last time; I will give you a lift."

Kostylín would not even listen.

"No," he said, "I shall never get away from here. Where should I go, since I have no strength to turn around?"

"If so, good-bye! Do not think ill of me!"

He kissed Kostylín.

He took hold of the pole, told Dina to hold on to it, and climbed up. Two or three times he slipped down: the stocks were in his way. Kostylín held him up, and he managed to get on. Dina pulled him by the shirt with all her might, and laughed.

Zhilín took the pole, and said:

"Take it to where you found it, for if they see it, they will beat you."

She dragged the pole away, and Zhilín went down-hill. He crawled down an incline, took a sharp stone, and tried to break the lock of the stocks. But the lock was a strong one, and he could not break it. He heard some one running down the hill, leaping lightly. He thought it was Dina. Dina ran up, took a stone, and said:

"Let me do it!"

She knelt down and tried to break it; but her arms were as thin as rods,—there was no strength in them. She threw away the stone, and began to weep. Zhilín again worked on the lock, and Dina squatted near him, and held on to his shoulder. Zhilín looked around; on[Pg 121] the left, beyond the mountain, he saw a red glow,—the moon was rising.

"Well," he thought, "before the moon is up I must cross the ravine and get to the forest."

He got up, threw away the stone, and, though in the stocks, started to go.

"Good-bye, Dina dear! I will remember you all my life."

Dina took hold of him; she groped all over him, trying to find a place to put the cakes. He took them from her.

"Thank you," he said, "you are a clever girl. Who will make dolls for you without me?" And he patted her on the head.

Dina began to cry. She covered her eyes with her hands, and ran up-hill like a kid. In the darkness he could hear the ornaments in the braid striking against her shoulders.

Zhilín made the sign of the cross, took the lock of his fetters in his hand, that it might not clank, and started down the road, dragging his feet along, and looking at the glow, where the moon was rising. He recognized the road. By the straight road it would be about eight versts. If he only could get to the woods before the moon was entirely out! He crossed a brook,—and it was getting light beyond the mountain. He walked through the ravine; he walked and looked, but the moon was not yet to be seen. It was getting brighter, and on one side of the ravine everything could be seen more and more clearly. The shadow was creeping down the mountain, up toward him.

Zhilín walked and kept in the shade. He hurried on, but the moon was coming out faster still; the tops of the trees on the right side were now in the light. As he came up to the woods, the moon came out entirely from behind the mountains, and it grew bright and white as in the daytime. All the leaves could be seen on the trees.[Pg 122] The mountains were calm and bright; it was as though everything were dead. All that could be heard was the rippling of a brook below.

He reached the forest,—he came across no men. Zhilín found a dark spot in the woods and sat down to rest himself.

He rested, and ate a cake. He found a stone, and began once more to break down the lock. He bruised his hands, but did not break the lock. He got up, and walked on. He marched about a verst, but his strength gave out,—his feet hurt him so. He would make ten steps and then stop. "What is to be done?" he thought. "I will drag myself along until my strength gives out entirely. If I sit down, I shall not be able to get up. I cannot reach the fortress, so, when day breaks, I will lie down in the forest for the day, and at night I will move on."

He walked the whole night. He came across two Tartars only, but he heard them from afar, and so hid behind a tree.

The moon was beginning to pale, and Zhilín had not yet reached the edge of the forest.

"Well," he thought, "I will take another thirty steps, after which I will turn into the forest, where I will sit down."

He took the thirty steps, and there he saw that the forest came to an end. He went to the edge of it, and there it was quite light. Before him lay the steppe and the fortress, as in the palm of the hand, and to the left, close by at the foot of the mountain, fires were burning and going out, and the smoke was spreading, and men were near the camp-fires.

He took a sharp look at them: the guns were glistening,—those were Cossacks and soldiers.

Zhilín was happy. He collected his last strength and walked down-hill. And he thought: "God forfend that[Pg 123] a Tartar rider should see me in the open! Though it is not far off, I should not get away."

No sooner had he thought so, when, behold, on a mound stood three Tartars, not more than 150 fathoms away. They saw him, and darted toward him. His heart just sank in him. He waved his arms and shouted as loud as he could:

"Brothers! Help, brothers!"

Our men heard him, and away flew the mounted Cossacks. They started toward him, to cut off the Tartars.

The Cossacks had far to go, but the Tartars were near. And Zhilín collected his last strength, took the stocks in his hand, and ran toward the Cossacks. He was beside himself, and he made the sign of the cross, and shouted:

"Brothers! Brothers! Brothers!"

There were about fifteen Cossacks.

The Tartars were frightened, and they stopped before they reached him. And Zhilín ran up to the Cossacks.

The Cossacks surrounded him, and asked:

"Who are you? Where do you come from?"

But Zhilín was beside himself, and he wept, and muttered:

"Brothers! Brothers!"

The soldiers ran out, and surrounded Zhilín: one gave him bread, another gruel, a third vódka; one covered him with a cloak, another broke off the lock.

The officers heard of it, and took him to the fortress. The soldiers were happy, and his companions came to see him.

Zhilín told them what had happened, and said:

"So I have been home, and got married! No, evidently that is not my fate."

And he remained in the service in the Caucasus. Not till a month later was Kostylín ransomed for five thousand. He was brought back more dead than alive.

[Pg 124]

## ERMÁK

48

In the reign of Iván Vasílevich the Terrible there were the rich merchants, the Stroganóvs, and they lived in Perm, on the river Káma. They heard that along the river Káma, in a circle of 140 versts, there was good land: the soil had not been ploughed for centuries, the forests had not been cut down for centuries. In the forests were many wild animals, and along the river fish lakes, and no one was living on that land, but only Tartars passed through it.

The Stroganóvs wrote a letter to the Tsar:

"Give us this land, and we will ourselves build towns there and gather people and settle them there, and will not allow the Tartars to pass through it."

The Tsar agreed to it, and gave them the land. The Stroganóvs sent out clerks to gather people. And there came to them a large number of roving people. Whoever came received from the Stroganóvs land, forest, and cattle, and no tenant pay was collected. All they had to do was to live and, in case of need, to go out in mass to fight the Tartars. Thus the land was settled by the Russian people.

About twenty years passed. The Stroganóvs grew richer yet, and that land, 140 versts around, was not enough for them. They wanted to have more land still. About one hundred versts from them were high mountains, the Ural Mountains, and beyond them, they had heard, there was good land, and to that land there was no end. This land was ruled by a small Siberian prince, Kuchum by name. In former days Kuchum had sworn allegiance to[Pg 125] the Russian Tsar, but later he began to rebel, and he threatened to destroy Stroganóv's towns.

So the Stroganóvs wrote to the Tsar:

"You have given us land, and we have conquered it and turned it over to you; now the thievish Tsarling Kuchum is rebelling against you, and wants to take that land away and ruin us. Command us to take possession of the land beyond the Ural Mountains; we will conquer Kuchum, and will bring all his land under your rule."

The Tsar assented, and wrote back:

"If you have sufficient force, take the land away from Kuchum. Only do not entice many people away from Russia."

When the Stroganóvs got that letter from the Tsar, they sent out clerks to collect more people. And they ordered them to persuade mostly the Cossacks from the Vólga and the Don to come. At that time many Cossacks were roving along the Vólga and the Don. They used to gather in bands of two, three, or six hundred men, and to select an atamán, and to row down in barges, to capture ships and rob them, and for the winter they stayed in little towns on the shore.

The clerks arrived at the Vólga, and there they asked who the famous Cossacks of that region were. They were told:

"There are many Cossacks. It is impossible to live for them. There is Míshka Cherkáshenin, and Sarý-Azmán; but there is no fiercer one than Ermák Timoféich, the atamán. He has a thousand men, and not only the merchants and the people are afraid of him, but even the Tsarian army does not dare to cope with him."

And the clerks went to Ermák the atamán, and began to persuade him to go to the Stroganóvs. Ermák received the clerks, listened to their speeches, and promised to come with his people about the time of the Assumption of the Blessed Virgin.

[Pg 126]

Near the holiday of the Assumption there came to the Stroganóvs six hundred Cossacks, with their atamán, Ermák Timoféich. At first Stroganóv sent them against the neighbouring Tartars. The Cossacks annihilated them. Then, when nothing was doing, the Cossacks roved in the neighbourhood and robbed.

So Stroganóv sent for Ermák, and said:

"I will not keep you any longer, if you are going to be so wanton."

But Ermák said:

"I do not like it myself, but I cannot control my people, they are spoiled. Give us work to do!"

So Stroganóv said:

"Go beyond the Ural and fight Kuchum, and take possession of his land. The Tsar will reward you for it."

And he showed the Tsar's letter to Ermák. Ermák rejoiced, and collected his men, and said:

"You are shaming me before my master,—you are robbing without reason. If you do not stop, he will drive you away, and where will you go then? At the Vólga there is a large Tsarian army; we shall be caught, and then we shall suffer for our old misdeeds. But if you feel lonesome, here is work for you."

And he showed them the Tsar's letter, in which it said that Stroganóv had been permitted to conquer land beyond the Ural. The Cossacks had a consultation, and agreed to go. Ermák went to Stroganóv, and they began to deliberate how they had best go.

They discussed how many barges they needed, how much grain, cattle, guns, powder, lead, how many captive Tartar interpreters, and how many foreigners as masters of gunnery.

Stroganóv thought:

"Though it may cost me much, I must give them everything or else they will stay here and will ruin me."

[Pg 127]

Stroganóv agreed to everything, gathered what was needed, and fitted out Ermák and the Cossacks.

On the 1st of September the Cossacks rowed with Ermák up the river Chúsovaya on thirty-two barges, with twelve men in each. For four days they rowed up the river, and then they turned into Serébryanaya River. Beyond that point it was impossible to navigate. They asked the guides, and learned that from there they had to cross the mountains and walk overland about two hundred versts, and then the rivers would begin again. The Cossacks stopped, built a town, and unloaded all their equipment; they abandoned the boats, made carts, put everything upon them, and started overland, across the mountains. All those places were covered with forest, and nobody was living there. They marched for about ten days, and struck the river Zharóvnya. Here they stopped again, and made themselves boats. They loaded them, and rowed down the river. They rowed five days, and then came more cheerful places,—meadows, forests, lakes. There was a plenty of fish and of animals, and animals that had not been scared by hunters. They rowed another day, and sailed into the river Túra. Along the Túra they came on Tartar people and towns.

Ermák sent some Cossacks to take a look at a town, to see what it was like, and whether there was any considerable force in it. Twenty Cossacks went there, and they frightened all the Tartars, and seized the whole town, and captured all the cattle. Some of the Tartars they killed, and others they brought back alive.

Ermák asked the Tartars through his interpreters what kind of people they were, and under whose rule they were living. The Tartars said that they were in the Siberian kingdom, and that their king was Kuchum.

Ermák let the Tartars go, but three of the more intelligent he took with him, to show him the road.

They rowed on. The farther they rowed, the larger[Pg 128] did the river grow; and the farther they went, the better did the places become.

They met more and more people; only they were not strong men. And all the towns that were near the river the Cossacks conquered.

In one town they captured a large number of Tartars and one old man who was held in respect. They asked him what kind of a man he was. He said:

"I am Tauzik, a servant of my king, Kuchum, who has made me a commander in this town."

Ermák asked Tauzik about his king; how far his city of Sibír was; whether Kuchum had a large force; whether he had much wealth. Tauzik told him everything. He said:

"Kuchum is the first king in the world. His city of Sibír is the largest city in the world. In that city," he said, "there are as many people and as many cattle as there are stars in the heaven. There is no counting his force, and not all the kings of the world can conquer him."

But Ermák said:

50

"We Russians have come here to conquer your king and to take his city, and to put it into the hands of the Russian Tsar. We have a large force. Those who have come with me are only the advance-guard; those that are rowing down behind us in barges are numberless, and all of them have guns. Our guns pierce trees, not like your bows and arrows. Just look!"

And Ermák fired at a tree, and pierced it, and the Cossacks began to shoot on all sides. Tauzik in fright fell on his knees. Ermák said to him:

"Go to your King Kuchum and tell him what you have seen! Let him surrender, and if he does not, we will destroy him."

And he dismissed Tauzik.

The Cossacks rowed on. They sailed into the river[Pg 129] Toból, and were getting nearer to the city of Sibír. They sailed up to the small river Babasán, and there they saw a small town on its bank, and around the town a large number of Tartars.

They sent an interpreter to the Tartars, to find out what kind of people they were. The interpreter returned, and said:

"That is Kuchum's army that has gathered there. The leader of that army is Kuchum's own son-in-law, Mametkul. He has commanded me to tell you that you must return, or else he will destroy you."

Ermák gathered his Cossacks, landed on the bank, and began to shoot at the Tartars. The moment the Tartars heard the shooting, they began to run. The Cossacks ran after them, and killed some, and captured others. Mametkul barely escaped.

The Cossacks sailed on. They sailed into a broad, rapid river, the Irtýsh. Down Irtýsh River they sailed for a day, and came to a fair town, and there they stopped. The Cossacks went to the town. As they were coming near, the Tartars began to shoot their arrows, and they wounded three Cossacks. Then Ermák sent an interpreter to tell the Tartars that they must surrender the town, or else they would all be killed. The interpreter went, and he returned, and said:

"Here lives Kuchum's servant, Atik Murza Kachara. He has a large force, and he says that he will not surrender the town."

Ermák gathered the Cossacks, and said:

"Boys, if we do not take this town, the Tartars will rejoice, and will not let us pass on. The more we strike them with terror, the easier will it be. Land all, and attack them all at once!"

So they did. There were many Tartars there, and they were brave.

When the Cossacks rushed at them, the Tartars began[Pg 130] to shoot their arrows. They covered the Cossacks with them. Some were killed, and some wounded.

The Cossacks became enraged, and when they got to the Tartars, they killed all they could lay their hands on.

In this town the Cossacks found much property,—cattle, rugs, furs, and honey. They buried the dead, rested themselves, took away much property, and sailed on. They did not sail far, when they saw on the shore, like a city, an endless number of troops, and the whole army surrounded by a ditch and the ditch protected by timber. The Cossacks stopped. They deliberated. Ermák gathered a circle about him.

"Well, boys, what shall we do?"

The Cossacks were frightened. Some said that they ought to sail past, while others said that they ought to go back.

And they looked gloomy and began to scold Ermák. They said:

"Why did you bring us here? Already a few of ours have been killed, and many have been wounded; and all of us will perish here."

They began to weep.

But Ermák said to his sub-atamán, Iván Koltsó:

"Well, Ványa, what do you think?"

And Koltsó said:

"What do I think? If they do not kill us to-day, they will to-morrow; and if not to-morrow, we shall die anyway on the oven. In my opinion, we ought to go out on the shore and rush in a body against the Tartars. Maybe God will give us victory."

Ermák said:

"You are a brave man, Ványa! That is what must be done. Oh, you boys! You are not Cossacks, but old women. All you are good for is to catch sturgeon and frighten Tartar women. Can't you see for yourselves? If we turn back we shall be destroyed; and if we stay here,[Pg 131] they will destroy us. How can we go back? After a little work, it will come easier. Listen, boys! My father had a strong mare. Down-hill she would pull and on an even place she would pull. But when it came to going up-hill, she became stubborn and turned back, thinking that it would be easier. But my father took a club and belaboured her with it. She twisted and tugged and broke the whole cart. My father unhitched her from the cart and gave her a terrible whacking. If she had pulled the cart, she would have suffered no torment. So it is with us, boys. There is only one thing left for us to do, and that is to make straight for the Tartars."

The Cossacks laughed, and said:

"Timoféich, you are evidently more clever than we are. You have no business to ask us fools. Take us where you please. A man does not die twice, and one death cannot be escaped."

And Ermák said:

"Listen, boys! This is what we shall do. They have not yet seen us all. Let us divide into three parts. Those in the middle will march straight against them, and the other two divisions will surround them on the right and on the left. When the middle detachment begins to walk toward them, they will think that we are all there, and so they will leap forward. Then we will strike them from the sides. That's the way, boys! If we beat these, we shall not have to be afraid of anybody. We shall ourselves be kings."

And so they did. When the middle detachment with Ermák advanced, the Tartars screamed and leaped forward; then they were attacked by Iván Koltsó on the right, and by Meshcheryákov the atamán on the left. The Tartars were frightened, and ran. The Cossacks killed a great many of them. After that nobody dared to oppose Ermák. And thus he entered the very city of Sibír. And there Ermák settled down as though he were a king.

[Pg 132]

Then kinglets came to see Ermák, to bow to him. Tartars began to settle down in Sibír, and Kuchum and his son-in-law Mametkul were afraid to go straight at him, but kept going around in a circle, wondering how they might destroy him.

In the spring, during high water, the Tartars came running to Ermák, and said:

"Mametkul is again going against you: he has gathered a large army, and is making a stand near the river Vagáy."

Ermák made his way over rivers, swamps, brooks, and forests, stole up with his Cossacks, rushed against Mametkul, killed a large number of Tartars, and took Mametkul alive and brought him to Sibír. After that there were only a few unruly Tartars left, and Ermák went that summer against those that had not yet surrendered; and along the Irtýsh and the Ob Ermák conquered so much land that one could not march around it in two months.

When Ermák had conquered all that land, he sent a messenger to the Stroganóvs, and a letter:

"I have taken Kuchum's city," he said, "and have captured Mametkul, and have brought all the people here under my rule. Only I have lost many Cossacks. Send people to us that we may feel more cheerful. There is no end to the wealth in this country."

He sent to them many costly furs,—fox, marten, and sable furs.

Two years passed after that. Ermák was still holding Sibír, but no aid came from Russia, and few Russians were left with Ermák.

One day the Tartar Karacha sent a messenger to Ermák, saying:

"We have surrendered to you, but now the Nogays are oppressing us. Send your brave men to aid us! We shall together conquer the Nogays. And we swear to you that we shall not insult your brave men."

Ermák believed their oath, and sent forty men under[Pg 133] Iván Koltsó. When these forty men came there, the Tartars rushed against them and killed them, so there were still fewer Cossacks left.

52

Another time some Bukhara merchants sent word to Ermák that they were on their way to the city of Sibír with goods, but that Kuchum had taken his stand with an army and would not let them pass through.

Ermák took with him fifty men and went out to clear the road for the Bukhara merchants. He came to the Irtýsh River, but did not find the Bukharans. He remained there over night. It was a dark night, and it rained. The Cossacks had just lain down to sleep, when suddenly the Tartars rushed out and threw themselves on the sleepy men and began to strike them down. Ermák jumped up and began to fight. He was wounded in the hand. He ran toward the river. The Tartars after him. He threw himself into the river. That was the last time he was seen. His body was not recovered, and no one found out how he died.

The following year came the Tsar's army, and the Tartars were pacified.

[Pg 134]
[Pg 135]

# NATURAL SCIENCE STORIES
## 1869-1872

[Pg 136]
[Pg 137]

NATURAL SCIENCE STORIES
## STORIES FROM PHYSICS
## THE MAGNET
### I.

In olden days there was a shepherd whose name was Magnes. Magnes lost a sheep. He went to the mountains to find it. He came to a place where there were barren rocks. He walked over these rocks, and felt that his boots were sticking to them. He touched them with his hand, but they were dry and did not stick to his hand. He started to walk again, and again his boots stuck to the rocks. He sat down, took off one of his boots, took it into his hand, and touched the rocks with it.

Whenever he touched them with his skin, or with the sole of his boot, they did not stick; but when he touched them with the nails, they did stick.

Magnes had a cane with an iron point.

He touched a rock with the wood; it did not stick; he touched it with the iron end, and it stuck so that he could not pull it off.

Magnes looked at the stone, and he saw that it looked like iron, and he took pieces of that stone home with him. Since then that rock has been known, and has been called Magnet.

[Pg 138]

### II.

Magnet is found in the earth with iron ore. Where there is magnet in the ore, the iron is of the best quality. The magnet resembles iron.

If you put a piece of iron on a magnet, the iron itself begins to attract other iron. And if you put a steel needle on a magnet, and hold it thus for awhile, the needle will become a magnet, and will attract iron. If two magnets are brought together at their ends, one side will turn away from the other, while the other sides will be attracted.

If a magnetic rod is broken in two, each half will attract at one end, and will turn away at the other end. Cut it again, and the same will happen; cut it again, as often as you please, and still the same will happen: equal ends will turn away from each other, while opposite ends will be attracted, as though the magnet were pushing away at one end, and pulling in at the other. No matter how you may break it, it will be as though there were a bump at one end, and a saucer at the other. Whichever way you put them together,—a bump and a saucer will meet, but a bump and a bump, or a saucer and a saucer will not.

### III.

If you magnetize a needle (holding it for awhile over a magnet), and attach it in the middle to a pivot in such a way that it can move freely around, and let it loose, it will turn with one end toward midday (south), and with the other toward midnight (north).

When the magnet was not known, people did not sail far out to sea. When they went out far into the sea, so that land was not to be seen, they could tell only by the stars and the

53

sun where they had to sail. But when it was dark, and the sun or stars could not be seen, they did[Pg 139] not know which way to sail. And a ship was borne by the winds and carried on rocks and wrecked.

So long as the magnet was not known, they did not sail far from the shore; but when the magnet was discovered, they made a magnetic needle on a pivot, so that it should move around freely. By this needle they could tell in which direction to sail. With the magnetic needle they began to sail farther away from the shores, and since then they have discovered many new seas.

On ships there is always a magnetic needle (compass), and there is a measuring-rope with knots at the stern of a ship. This rope is fixed in such a way that when it unrolls, they can tell how far the ship has travelled. And thus, in sailing in a boat, they always know in what spot it is, whether far from the shore, and in what direction it is sailing.

[Pg 140]

## MOISTURE
### I.

Why does a spider sometimes make a close cobweb, and sit in the very middle of its nest, and at other times leave its nest and start a new spider-web?

The spider makes its cobweb according to the weather, both the present and the future weather. Looking at a spider, you can tell what kind of weather it is going to be: if it sits tightly in the middle of the cobweb and does not come out, it means that it is going to rain. If it leaves the nest and makes new cobwebs, it is going to clear off.

How can the spider know in advance what weather it is going to be?

The spider's senses are so fine that as soon as the moisture begins to gather in the air,—though we do not yet feel it, and for us the weather is clear,—for the spider it is already raining.

Just as a naked man will feel the moisture, when a man in his clothes does not, so it is already raining for a spider, while for us it is only getting ready to rain.

### II.

Why do the doors swell in the winter and close badly, while in the summer they shrink and close well?

Because in the fall and winter the wood is saturated with water, like a sponge, and spreads out, while in the[Pg 141] summer the water comes out as a vapour, and the wood shrinks.

Why does soft wood, like aspen, swell more, and oak less?

Because in the hard wood, in the oak, the empty places are smaller, and the water cannot gather there, while in the soft wood in the aspen, there are larger empty places, and the water can gather there. In rotten wood these empty places are still larger, and so rotten wood swells most and shrinks most.

Beehives are made out of the softest and rottenest wood; the very best are made from rotten willow wood. Why? Because the air passes through the rotten wood, and in such a hive the bees feel better.

Why do boards warp?

Because they dry unevenly. If you place a damp board with one side toward the stove, the water will leave it, and the board will contract on that side and will pull the other side along; but the damp side cannot contract, because it is full of water, and so the whole board will be bent.

To keep the floors from warping, the dry boards are cut into small pieces, and these pieces are boiled in water. When all the water is boiled out of them, they are glued together, and then they never warp (parquetry).

[Pg 142]

## THE DIFFERENT CONNECTION OF PARTICLES

Why are cart bolsters cut and wheel naves turned not from oak, but from birch? Bolsters and naves have to be strong, and oak is not more expensive than birch.

Because oak splits lengthwise, and birch does not split, but ravels out.

Because, though oak is more firmly connected than birch, it is connected in such a way that it splits lengthwise, while birch does not.

Why are wheels and runners bent from oak and elm, and not from birch and linden?

Because, when oak and elm are steamed in a bath, they bend and do not break, while birch and linden ravel in every direction.

This is again for the same reason, that is, that the particles of the wood in the oak and in the birch are differently connected.

|Pg 143|

## CRYSTALS

If you pour salt into water and stir it, the salt will begin to melt and will entirely disappear; but if you pour more and still more salt into it, the salt will in the end not dissolve, and no matter how much you may stir after that, the salt will remain as a white powder. The water is saturated with the salt and cannot receive any more. But heat the water and it will receive more; and the salt which did not dissolve in the cold water, will melt in hot water. But pour in more salt, even the hot water will not receive it. And if you heat the water still more, the water will pass away in steam, and more of the salt will be left.

Thus, for everything which dissolves in the water there is a measure after which the water will not dissolve any more. Of anything, more will be dissolved in hot than in cold water, and in each case, when it is saturated, it will not receive any more. The thing will be left, but the water will go away in steam.

If the water is saturated with saltpetre powder, and then more saltpetre is added, and all is heated and is allowed to cool off without being stirred, the superfluous saltpetre will not settle as a powder at the bottom of the water, but will all gather in little six-edged columns, and will settle at the bottom and at the sides, one column near another. If the water is saturated with saltpetre powder and is put in a warm place, the water will go away in vapours, and the superfluous saltpetre will again gather in six-edged columns.

If water is saturated with simple salt and heated, and|Pg 144| is allowed to pass away in vapour, the superfluous salt will not settle as powder, but as little cubes. If the water is saturated both with salt and saltpetre, the superfluous salt and saltpetre will not mix, but will settle each in its own way: the saltpetre in columns, and the salt in cubes.

If water is saturated with lime, or with some other salt, and anything else, each thing will settle in its own way, when the water passes away in vapour: one in three-edged columns, another in eight-edged columns, a third in bricks, a fourth in little stars,—each in its own way. These figures are different in each solid thing. At times these forms are as large as a hand,—such stones are found in the ground. At times these forms are so small that they cannot be made out with the naked eye; but in each thing there is its own form.

If, when the water is saturated with saltpetre, and little figures are forming in it, a corner be broken off one of these little figures with a needle, new pieces of saltpetre will come up and will fix the broken end as it ought to be,—into a six-edged column. The same will happen to salt and to any other thing. All the tiny particles turn around and attach themselves with the right side to each other.

When ice freezes, the same takes place.

A snowflake flies, and no figure is seen in it; but the moment it settles on anything dark and cold, on cloth, on fur,—you can make out its figure; you will see a little star, or a six-cornered little board. On the windows the steam does not freeze in any form whatever, but always as a star.

What is ice? It is cold, solid water. When liquid water becomes solid, it forms itself into figures and the heat leaves it. The same takes place with saltpetre: when it changes from a liquid into solid figures, the heat leaves it. The same is true of salt, of melted cast-iron, when it changes from a liquid into a solid. Whenever a|Pg 145| thing changes from a liquid into a solid, heat leaves it, and it forms figures. And when it changes from a solid to a liquid it takes up heat, and the cold leaves it, and its figures are dissolved.

Bring in melted iron and let it cool off; bring in hot dough and let it cool off; bring in slacked lime and let it cool off,—and it will be warm. Bring in ice and let it melt,—and it will grow cold. Bring in saltpetre, salt, or any other thing that dissolves in the water, and melt it in the water, and it will grow cold. In order to freeze ice-cream, they put salt in the water.

[Pg 146]

## INJURIOUS AIR

In the village of Nikólskoe, the people went on a holiday to mass. In the manor yard were left the cow-tender, the elder, and the groom. The cow-tender went to the well for water. The well was in the yard itself. She pulled out the bucket, but could not hold it. The bucket pulled away from her, struck the side of the well, and tore the rope. The cow-tender returned to the hut and said to the elder:

"Aleksándr! Climb down into the well,—I have dropped the bucket into it."

Aleksándr said:

"You have dropped it, so climb down yourself."

The cow-tender said that she did not mind fetching it herself, if he would let her down.

The elder laughed at her, and said:

"Well, let us go! You have an empty stomach now, so I shall be able to hold you up, for after dinner I could not do it."

The elder tied a stick to a rope, and the woman sat astride it, took hold of the rope, and began to climb down into the well, while the elder turned the well-wheel. The well was about twenty feet deep, and there was less than three feet of water in it. The elder let her down slowly, and kept asking:

"A little more?"

And the cow-tender cried from below:

"Just a little more!"

Suddenly the elder felt the rope give way: he called the cow-tender, but she did not answer. The elder looked[Pg 147] into the well, and saw the cow-tender lying with her head in the water, and with her feet in the air. The elder called for help, but there was nobody near by; only the groom came. The elder told him to hold the wheel, and he himself pulled out the rope, sat down on the stick, and went down into the well.

The moment the groom let the elder down to the water, the same thing happened to the elder. He let go of the rope and fell head foremost upon the woman. The groom began to cry, and ran to church to call the people. Mass was over, and people were walking home. All the men and women rushed to the well. They gathered around it, and everybody holloaed, but nobody knew what to do. The young carpenter Iván made his way through the crowd, took hold of the rope, sat down on the stick, and told them to let him down. Iván tied himself to the rope with his belt. Two men let him down, and the rest looked into the well, to see what would become of Iván. Just as he was getting near the water, he dropped his hands from the rope, and would have fallen down head foremost, if the belt had not held him. All shouted, "Pull him out!" and Iván was pulled out.

He hung like dead down from the belt, and his head was drooping and beating against the sides of the well. His face was livid. They took him off the rope and put him down on the ground. They thought that he was dead; but he suddenly drew a deep breath, began to rattle, and soon revived.

Others wanted to climb down, but an old peasant said that they could not go down because there was bad air in the well, and that that bad air killed people. Then the peasants ran for hooks and began to pull out the elder and the woman. The elder's mother and wife cried at the well, and others tried to quiet them; in the meantime the peasants put down the hooks and tried to get out the dead people. Twice they got the elder half-way up by[Pg 148] his clothes; but he was heavy, and his clothes tore and he fell down. Finally they stuck two hooks into him and pulled him out. Then they pulled out the cow-tender. Both were dead and did not revive.

56

Then, when they examined the well, they found that indeed there was bad air down in the well.

This air is so heavy that neither man nor any animal can live in it. They let down a cat into the well, and the moment she reached the place where the bad air was, she died. Not only can no animal live there, even no candle will burn in it. They let down a candle, and the moment it reached that spot, it went out.

There are places underground where that air gathers, and when a person gets into one of those places, he dies at once. For this purpose they have lamps in the mines, and before a man goes down to such a place, they let down the lamp. If it goes out, no man can go there; then they let down fresh air until the lamp will burn.

Near the city of Naples there is one such cave. There is always about three feet of bad air in it on the ground, but above it the air is good. A man can walk through the cave, and nothing will happen to him, but a dog will die the moment it enters.

Where does this bad air come from? It is made of the same good air that we breathe. If you gather a lot of people in one place, and close all the doors and windows, so that no fresh air can get in, you will get the same kind of an air as in the well, and people will die.

One hundred years ago, during a war, the Hindoos captured 146 Englishmen and shut them up in a cave underground, where the air could not get in.

After the captured Englishmen had been there a few hours they began to die, and toward the end of the night 123 had died, and the rest came out more dead than alive, and ailing. At first the air had been good in the cave; but when the captives had inhaled all the good air,[Pg 149] and no fresh air came in, it became bad, just like what was in the well, and they died.

Why does the good air become bad when many people come together?

Because, when people breathe, they take in good air and breathe out bad air.

[Pg 150]

## HOW BALLOONS ARE MADE

If you take a blown-up bladder under water and let go of it, it will fly up to the surface of the water and will swim on it. Just so, when water is boiled in a pot, it becomes light at the bottom, over the fire,—it is turned into a gas; and when a little of that water-gas is collected it goes up as a bubble. First comes up one bubble, then another, and when the whole water is heated, the bubbles come up without stopping. Then the water boils.

Just as the bubbles leap to the surface, full of vapoury water, because they are lighter than water, just so will a bladder which is filled with hydrogen, or with hot air, rise, because hot air is lighter than cold air, and hydrogen is lighter than any other gases.

Balloons are made with hydrogen or with hot air. With hydrogen they are made as follows: They make a large bladder, attach it by ropes to posts, and fill it with hydrogen. The moment the ropes are untied, the balloon flies up in the air, and keeps flying up until it gets beyond the air which is heavier than hydrogen. When it gets up into the light air, it begins to swim in it like a bladder on the surface of the water.

With hot air balloons are made like this: They make a large empty ball, with a neck below, like an upturned pitcher, and to the mouth of it they attach a bunch of cotton, and that cotton is soaked with spirits, and lighted. The fire heats the air in the balloon, and makes it lighter than the cold air, and the balloon is drawn upward, like the bladder in the water. And the balloon will fly up[Pg 151]until it comes to the air which is lighter than the hot air in the balloon.

Nearly one hundred years ago two Frenchmen, the brothers Montgolfier, invented the air balloons. They made a balloon of canvas and paper and filled it with hot air,—the balloon flew. Then they made another, a larger balloon, and tied under the balloon a sheep, a cock, and a duck, and let it off. The balloon rose and came down safely. Then they attached a little basket under the balloon, and a man seated himself in it. The balloon flew so high that it disappeared from view; it flew away, and came down safely. Then they thought of filling a balloon with hydrogen, and began to fly higher and faster.

57

In order to fly with a balloon, they attach a basket under the balloon, and in this basket two, three, and even eight persons are seated, and they take with them food and drink.

In order to rise and come down as one pleases, there is a valve in the balloon, and the man who is flying with it can pull a rope and open or close the valve. If the balloon rises too high, and the man who is flying wants to come down, he opens the valve,—the gas escapes, the balloon is compressed, and begins to come down. Then there are always bags with sand in the balloon. When a bag with sand is thrown out, the balloon gets lighter, and it flies up. If the one who is flying wants to get down, but sees that it is not what he wants below him,—either a river or a forest,—he throws out the sand from the bags, and the balloon grows lighter and rises again.

[Pg 152]

## GALVANISM

There was once a learned Italian, Galvani. He had an electric machine, and he showed his students what electricity was. He rubbed the glass hard with silk with something smeared over it, and then he approached to the glass a brass knob which was attached to the glass, and a spark flew across from the glass to the brass knob. He explained to them that the same kind of a spark came from sealing-wax and amber. He showed them that feathers and bits of paper were now attracted, and now repelled, by electricity, and explained to them the reason of it. He did all kinds of experiments with electricity, and showed them all to his students.

Once his wife grew ill. He called a doctor and asked him how to cure her. The doctor told him to prepare a frog soup for her. Galvani gave order to have edible frogs caught. They caught them for him, killed them, and left them on his table.

Before the cook came after the frogs, Galvani kept on showing the electric machine to his students, and sending sparks through it.

Suddenly he saw the dead frogs jerk their legs on the table. He watched them, and saw that every time when he sent a spark through the machine, the frogs jerked their legs. Galvani collected more frogs, and began to experiment with them. And every time he sent a spark through the machine, the dead frogs moved their legs as though they were alive.

It occurred to Galvani that live frogs moved their legs because electricity passed through them. Galvani knew[Pg 153] that there was electricity in the air; that it was more noticeable in the amber and glass, but that it was also in the air, and that thunder and lightning came from the electricity in the air.

So he tried to discover whether the dead frogs would not move their legs from the electricity in the air. For this purpose he took the frogs, skinned them, chopped off their heads, and hung them on brass hooks on the roof, beneath an iron gutter. He thought that as soon as there should be a storm, and the air should be filled with electricity, it would pass by the brass rod to the frogs, and they would begin to move.

But the storm passed several times, and the frogs did not move. Galvani was just taking them down, and as he did so a frog's leg touched the iron gutter, and it jerked. Galvani took down the frogs and made the following experiment: he tied to the brass hook an iron wire, and touched the leg with the wire, and it jerked.

So Galvani decided that the animals lived because there was electricity in them, and that the electricity jumped from the brain to the flesh, and that made the animals move. Nobody had at that time tried this matter and they did not know any better, and so they all believed Galvani. But at that time another learned man, Volta, experimented in his own way, and proved to everybody that Galvani was mistaken. He tried touching the frog differently from what Galvani had done, not with a copper hook with an iron wire, but either with a copper hook and a copper wire, or an iron hook and an iron wire,—and the frogs did not move. The frogs moved only when Volta touched them with an iron wire that was connected with a copper wire.

Volta thought that the electricity was not in the dead frog but in the iron and copper. He experimented and found it to be so: whenever he brought together the iron and the copper, there was electricity; and this electricity[Pg 154] made the dead frogs jerk their legs.

Volta tried to produce electricity differently from what it had been produced before. Before that they used to get electricity by rubbing glass or sealing-wax. But Volta got electricity by uniting iron and copper. He tried to connect iron and copper and other metals, and by the mere combination of metals, silver, platinum, zinc, lead, iron, he produced electric sparks.

After Volta they tried to increase electricity by pouring all kinds of liquids—water and acids—between the metals. These liquids made the electricity more powerful, so that it was no longer necessary, as before, to rub in order to produce it; it is enough to put pieces of several metals in a bowl and fill it with a liquid, and there will be electricity in that bowl, and the sparks will come from the wires.

When this kind of electricity was discovered, people began to apply it: they invented a way of gold and silver plating by means of electricity, and electric light, and a way to transmit signs from place to place over a long distance by means of electricity.

For this purpose pieces of different metals are placed in jars, and liquids are poured into them. Electricity is collected in these jars, and is transferred by means of wires to the place where it is wanted, and from that place the wire is put into the ground. The electricity runs through the ground back to the jars, and rises from the earth by means of the other wire; thus the electricity keeps going around and around, as in a ring,—from the wire into the ground, and along the ground, and up the wire, and again through the earth. Electricity can travel in either direction, just as one wants to send it: it can first go along the wire and return through the earth, or first go through the earth, and then return through the wire. Above the wire, in the place where the signs are given, there is attached a magnetic hand, and that hand[Pg 155] turns in one direction, when the electricity is allowed to pass through the wire and back through the earth, and in another direction, when the electricity is sent through the earth and back through the wire. Along this hand there are certain signs, and by means of these signs they write from one place to another on the telegraph.

[Pg 156]

## THE SUN'S HEAT

Go out in the winter on a calm, frosty day into the field, or into the woods, and look about you and listen: all around you is snow, the rivers are frozen, dry grass blades stick out of the grass, the trees are bare,—nothing is moving.

Look in the summer: the rivers are running and rippling, in every puddle the frogs croak and plunge in; the birds fly from place to place, and whistle, and sing; the flies and the gnats whirl around and buzz; the trees and the grass grow and wave to and fro.

Freeze a pot with water, and it will become as hard as a rock. Put the frozen pot on the fire: the ice will begin to break, and melt, and move; the water will begin to stir, and bubbles will rise; then, when it begins to boil, it whirls about and makes a noise. The same happens in the world from the heat. Without heat everything is dead; with the heat everything moves and lives. If there is little heat, there is little motion; with more heat, there is more motion; with much heat, there is much motion; with very much heat, there is also very much motion.

Where does the heat in the world come from? The heat comes from the sun.

In winter the sun travels low, to one side, and its beams do not fall straight upon the earth, and nothing moves. The sun begins to travel higher above our heads, and begins to shine straight down upon the earth, and everything is warmed up in the world, and begins to stir.

The snow settles down; the ice begins to melt on the[Pg 157] rivers; the water comes down from the mountains; the vapours rise from the water to the clouds, and rain begins to fall. Who does it all?—The sun. The seeds swell, and let out rootlets; the rootlets take hold of the ground; old roots send up new shoots, and the trees and the grass begin to grow. Who has done that?—The sun.

The bears and moles get up; the flies and bees awaken; the gnats are hatched, and the fish come out from their eggs, when it is warm. Who has done it all?—The sun.

The air gets warmed up in one place, and rises, and in its place comes colder air,— and there is a wind. Who has done that?—The sun.

59

The clouds rise and begin to gather and to scatter,—and the lightning flashes. Who has made that fire?—The sun.

The grass, the grain, the fruits, the trees grow up; animals find their food, men eat their fill, and gather food and fuel for the winter; they build themselves houses, railways, cities. Who has prepared it all?—The sun.

A man has built himself a house. What has he made it of? Of timbers. The timbers were cut out of trees, but the trees are made to grow by the sun.

The stove is heated with wood. Who has made the wood to grow?—The sun.

Man eats bread, or potatoes. Who has made them grow?—The sun. Man eats meat. Who has made the animals, the birds to grow?—The grass. But the grass is made to grow by the sun.

A man builds himself a house from brick and lime. The bricks and the lime are burnt by wood. The wood has been prepared by the sun.

Everything that men need, that is for their use,—all that is prepared by the sun, and on all that goes much sun's heat. The reason that men need bread is because the sun has produced it, and because there is much sun's heat in it. Bread warms him who eats it.

[Pg 158]

The reason that wood and logs are needed is because there is much heat in them. He who buys wood for the winter, buys sun's heat; and in the winter he burns the wood whenever he wants it, and lets the sun's heat into his room.

When there is heat, there is motion. No matter what motion it may be,—it all comes from heat, either directly from the sun's heat, or from the heat which the sun has prepared in the coal, the wood, the bread, and the grass.

Horses and oxen pull, men work,—who moves them?—Heat. Where does the heat come from?—From the food. And the food has been prepared by the sun.

Watermills and windmills turn around and grind. Who moves them?—Wind and water. And who drives the wind?—Heat. And who drives the water?—Again heat. Heat raises the water in the shape of vapour, and without this the water would not be falling down. A machine works,—it is moved by steam. And who makes steam?—Wood. And in the wood is the sun's heat.

Heat makes motion, and motion makes heat. And both heat and motion are from the sun.

[Pg 159]

## STORIES FROM ZOOLOGY
## THE OWL AND THE HARE

It was dusk. The owls began to fly through the forest to find some prey.

A large hare leaped out on a clearing and began to smooth out his fur. An old owl looked at the hare, and seated himself on a branch; but a young owl said to him:

"Why do you not catch the hare?"

The old owl said:

"He is too much for me: if I get caught in him, he will drag me into the woods."

But the young owl said:

"I will stick one claw into his body, and with the other I will clutch a tree."

The young owl made for the hare, and stuck one claw into his back so that all his talons entered the flesh, and the other claw it got ready to push into the tree. The hare yanked the owl, while the owl held on to the tree, and thought, "He will not get away." The hare darted forward and tore the owl. One claw was left in the tree, and the other in the hare's back.

The next year a hunter killed that hare, and wondered how the owl's talons had grown into the hare's back.

[Pg 160]

## HOW THE WOLVES TEACH THEIR WHELPS

60

I was walking along the road, and heard a shout behind me. It was the shepherd boy who was shouting. He was running through the field, and pointing to something.

I looked, and saw two wolves running through the field: one was full-grown, and the other a whelp. The whelp was carrying a dead lamb on his shoulders, and holding on to one of its legs with its teeth. The old wolf was running behind. When I saw the wolves, I ran after them with the shepherd, and we began to shout. In response to our cries came peasants with dogs.

The moment the old wolf saw the dogs and the people, he ran up to the whelp, took the lamb away from him, threw it over his back, and both wolves ran as fast as they could, and disappeared from view.

Then the boy told what had happened: the large wolf had leaped out from the ravine, had seized the lamb, killed it, and carried it off.

The whelp ran up to him and grasped the lamb. The old wolf let the whelp carry the lamb, while he himself ran slowly beside him.

Only when there was danger, did the old wolf stop his teaching and himself take the lamb.

[Pg 161]

## HARES AND WOLVES

The hares feed at night on tree bark; the field hares eat the winter rye and the grass, and the threshing-floor hares eat the grain in the granary. Through the night the hares make a deep, visible track through the snow. The hares are hunted by men, and dogs, and wolves, and foxes, and ravens, and eagles. If a hare walked straight ahead, he would be easily caught in the morning by his tracks; but God has made a hare timid, and his timidity saves him.

A hare goes at night fearlessly through the forests and fields, making straight tracks; but as soon as morning comes and his enemies wake up, and he hears the bark of dogs, or the squeak of sleighs, or the voice of peasants, or the crashing of a wolf through the forest, he begins to toss from side to side in his fear. He jumps forward, gets frightened at something, and runs back on his track. He hears something again, and he leaps at full speed to one side and runs away from his old track. Again something makes a noise, and the hare turns back, and again leaps to one side. When it is daylight, he lies down.

In the morning the hunters try to follow the hare tracks, and they get mixed up on the double tracks and long leaps, and marvel at the hare's cunning. But the hare did not mean to be cunning. He is merely afraid of everything.

[Pg 162]

## THE SCENT

Man sees with his eyes, hears with his ears, smells with his nose, tastes with his mouth, and feels with his fingers. One man's eyes see better, another man's see worse. One hears from a distance, and another is deaf. One has keen senses and smells a thing from a distance, while another smells at a rotten egg and does not perceive it. One can tell a thing by the touch, and another cannot tell by touch what is wood and what paper. One will take a substance in his mouth and will find it sweet, while another will swallow it without making out whether it is bitter or sweet.

Just so the different senses differ in strength in the animals. But with all the animals the sense of smell is stronger than in man.

When a man wants to recognize a thing, he looks at it, listens to the noise that it makes, now and then smells at it, or tastes it; but, above all, a man has to feel a thing, to recognize it.

But nearly all animals more than anything else need to smell a thing. A horse, a wolf, a dog, a cow, a bear do not know a thing until they smell it.

When a horse is afraid of anything, it snorts,—it clears its nose so as to scent better, and does not stop being afraid until it has smelled the object well.

61

A dog frequently follows its master's track, but when it sees him, it does not recognize him and begins to bark, until it smells him and finds out that that which has looked so terrible is its master.

Oxen see other oxen stricken down, and hear them roar[Pg 163] in the slaughter-house, but still do not understand what is going on. But an ox or a cow need only find a spot where there is ox blood, and smell it, and it will understand and will roar and strike with its feet, and cannot be driven off the spot.

An old man's wife had fallen ill; he went himself to milk the cow. The cow snorted,—she discovered that it was not her mistress, and would not give him any milk. The mistress told her husband to put on her fur coat and kerchief,—and the cow gave milk; but the old man threw open the coat, and the cow scented him, and stopped giving milk.

When hounds follow an animal's trail, they never run on the track itself, but to one side, about twenty paces from it. When an inexperienced hunter wants to show the dog the scent, and sticks its nose on the track, it will always jump to one side. The track itself smells so strong to the dog that it cannot make out on the track whether the animal has run ahead or backward. It runs to one side, and then only discovers in what direction the scent grows stronger, and so follows the animal. The dog does precisely what we do when somebody speaks very loud in our ears; we step a distance away, and only then do we make out what is being said. Or, if anything we are looking at is too close, we step back and only then make it out.

Dogs recognize each other and make signs to each other by means of their scent.

The scent is more delicate still in insects. A bee flies directly to the flower that it wants to reach; a worm crawls to its leaf; a bedbug, a flea, a mosquito scents a man a hundred thousand of its steps away.

If the particles which separate from a substance and enter our noses are small, how small must be those particles that reach the organ of smell of the insects!

[Pg 164]

## TOUCH AND SIGHT

Twist the forefinger over the middle finger and touch a small ball with them, so that it may roll between the two fingers, and shut your eyes. You will think that there are two balls. Open your eyes,—and you will see that it is one ball. The fingers have deceived you, but the eyes correct you.

Look (best of all sidewise) at a good, clean mirror,—you will think that it is a window or a door, and that there is something behind it. Touch it with a finger,—and you will see that it is a mirror. The eyes have deceived you, but the fingers correct you.

[Pg 165]

## THE SILKWORM

I had some old mulberry-trees in my garden. My grandfather had planted them. In the fall I was given a dram of silkworm eggs, and was advised to hatch them and raise silkworms. These eggs are dark gray and so small that in that dram I counted 5,835 of them. They are smaller than the tiniest pin-head. They are quite dead; only when you crush them do they crack.

The eggs had been lying around on my table, and I had almost forgotten about them.

One day, in the spring, I went into the orchard and noticed the buds swelling on the mulberry-trees, and where the sun beat down, the leaves were out. I thought of the silkworm eggs, and took them apart at home and gave them more room. The majority of the eggs were no longer dark gray, as before, but some were light gray, while others were lighter still, with a milky shade.

The next morning, I looked at the eggs, and saw that some of the worms had hatched out, while other eggs were quite swollen. Evidently they felt in their shells that their food was ripening.

The worms were black and shaggy, and so small that it was hard to see them. I looked at them through a magnifying-glass, and saw that in the eggs they lay curled up in rings, and when they came out they straightened themselves out. I went to the garden for some mulberry leaves; I got about three handfuls of leaves, which I put on my table, and began to fix a place for the worms, as I had been taught to do.

While I was fixing the paper, the worms smelled[Pg 166] their food and started to crawl toward it. I pushed it away, and began to entice the worms to a leaf, and they made for it, as dogs make for a piece of meat, crawling after the leaf over the cloth of the table and across pencils, scissors, and papers. Then I cut off a piece of paper, stuck holes through it with a penknife, placed the leaf on top of it, and with the leaf put it down on the worms. The worms crawled through the holes, climbed on the leaf, and started to eat.

When the other worms hatched out, I again put a piece of paper with a leaf on them, and all crawled through the holes and began to eat. The worms gathered on each leaf and nibbled at it from its edges. Then, when they had eaten everything, they crawled on the paper and looked for more food. Then I put on them new sheets of perforated paper with mulberry leaves upon them, and they crawled over to the new food.

They were lying on my shelf, and when there was no leaf, they climbed about the shelf, and came to its very edge, but they never fell down, though they are blind. The moment a worm comes to an edge, it lets out a web from its mouth before descending, and then it attaches itself to it and lets itself down; it hangs awhile in the air, and watches, and if it wants to get down farther, it does so, and if not, it pulls itself up by its web.

For days at a time the worms did nothing but eat. I had to give them more and more leaves. When a new leaf was brought, and they transferred themselves to it, they made a noise as though a rain were falling on leaves,—that was when they began to eat the new leaf.

Thus the older worms lived for five days. They had grown very large and began to eat ten times as much as ever. On the fifth day, I knew, they would fall asleep, and waited for that to happen. Toward evening, on the fifth day, one of the older worms stuck to the paper and stopped eating and stirring.

[Pg 167]

The whole next day I watched it for a long time. I knew that worms moulted several times, because they grew up and found it close in their old hide, and so put on a new one.

My friend and I watched it by turns. In the evening my friend called out:

"It has begun to undress itself,—come!"

I went up to him, and saw that the worm had stuck with its old hide to the paper, had torn a hole at the mouth, thrust forth its head, and was writhing and working to get out, but the old shirt held it fast. I watched it for a long time as it writhed and could not get out, and I wanted to help it. I barely touched it with my nail, but soon saw that I had done something foolish. Under my nail there was something liquid, and the worm died. At first I thought that it was blood, but later I learned that the worm has a liquid mass under its skin, so that the shirt may come off easier. With my nail I no doubt disturbed the new shirt, for, though the worm crawled out, it soon died.

The other worms I did not touch. All of them came out of their shirts in the same manner; only a few died, and nearly all came out safely, though they struggled hard for a long time.

After shedding their skins, the worms began to eat more voraciously, and more leaves were devoured. Four days later they again fell asleep, and again crawled out of their skins. A still larger quantity of leaves was now consumed by them, and they were now a quarter of an inch in length. Six days later they fell asleep once more, and once more came out in new skins, and now were very large and fat, and we had barely time to get leaves ready for them.

On the ninth day the oldest worms quit eating entirely and climbed up the shelves and rods. I gathered them in and gave them fresh leaves, but they turned their[Pg 168] heads away from them, and continued climbing. Then I remembered that when the worms get ready to roll up into larvæ, they stop eating and climb upward.

I left them alone, and began to watch what they would do.

The eldest worms climbed to the ceiling, scattered about, crawled in all directions, and began to draw out single threads in various directions. I watched one of them. It went into a corner, put forth about six threads each two inches long, hung down from them, bent over in a horseshoe, and began to turn its head and let out a silk web which began to cover it all over. Toward evening it was covered by it as though in a mist; the worm could scarcely be seen. On the following morning the worm could no longer be seen; it was all wrapped in silk, and still it spun out more.

Three days later it finished spinning, and quieted down. Later I learned how much web it had spun in those three days. If the whole web were to be unravelled, it would be more than half a mile in length, seldom less. And if we figure out how many times the worm has to toss its head in these three days in order to let out all the web, it will appear that in these three days the worm tosses its head 300,000 times. Consequently, it makes one turn a second, without stopping. But after the work, when we took down a few cocoons and broke them open, we found inside the worms all dried up and white, looking like pieces of wax.

I knew that from these larvæ with their white, waxen bodies would come butterflies; but as I looked at them, I could not believe it. None the less I went to look at them on the twentieth day, to see what had become of them.

On the twentieth day, I knew, there was to be a change. Nothing was to be seen, and I was beginning to think that something was wrong, when suddenly I noticed that[Pg 169] the end of one of the cocoons grew dark and moist. I thought that it had probably spoiled, and wanted to throw it away. But then I thought that perhaps it began that way, and so I watched to see what would happen. And, indeed, something began to move at the wet end. For a long time I could not make out what it was. Later there appeared something like a head with whiskers. The whiskers moved. Then I noticed a leg sticking out through the hole, then another, and the legs scrambled to get out of the cocoon. It came out more and more, and I saw a wet butterfly. When all six legs scrambled out, the back jumped out, too, and the butterfly crawled out and stopped. When it dried it was white; it straightened its wings, flew away, circled around, and alighted on the window.

Two days later the butterfly on the window-sill laid eggs in a row, and stuck them fast. The eggs were yellow. Twenty-five butterflies laid eggs. I collected five thousand eggs. The following year I raised more worms, and had more silk spun.

[Pg 170]

## STORIES FROM BOTANY
## THE APPLE-TREE

I set out two hundred young apple-trees, and for three years I dug around them in the spring and the fall, and in winter wrapped them with straw against the hares. On the fourth year, when the snow melted, I went to take a look at my apple-trees. They had grown stouter during the winter: the bark was glossy and filled with sap; all the branches were sound, and at all the tips and axils there were pea-shaped flower-buds. Here and there the buds were bursting, and the purple edges of the flower-leaves could be seen. I knew that all the buds would be blossoms and fruit, and I was delighted as I looked at the apple-trees. But when I took off the wrapping from the first tree, I saw that down at the ground the bark was nibbled away, like a white ring, to the very wood. The mice had done that. I unwrapped a second tree, and the same had happened there. Of the two hundred trees not one was unharmed. I smeared pitch and wax on the nibbled spots; but when the trees were all in bloom, the blossoms at once fell off; there came out small leaves, and they, too, dropped off. The bark became wrinkled and black. Out of the two hundred apple-trees only nine were left. On these nine trees the bark had not been gnawed through all around, but strips of bark were left on the white ring. On the strips, where the bark held[Pg 171] together, there grew out knots, and, although the trees suffered, they lived. All the rest were ruined; below the rings there came out shoots, but they were all wild.

The bark of the tree is like the arteries in man: through the arteries the blood goes to the whole body, and through the bark the sap goes along the tree and reaches the branches, leaves, and flowers. The whole inside of a tree may be taken out, as is often the case with old willows, and yet the tree will live so long as the bark is alive; but when the bark is ruined, the tree is gone. If a man's arteries are cut through, he will die, in the first place, because the blood will flow out, and in the second, because the blood will not be distributed through the body.

64

Even thus a birch dries up when the children bore a hole into it, in order to drink its sap, and all the sap flows out of it.

Just so the apple-trees were ruined because the mice gnawed the bark all around, and the sap could not rise from the roots to the branches, leaves, and flowers.

[Pg 172]
## THE OLD POPLAR

For five years our garden was neglected. I hired labourers with axes and shovels, and myself began to work with them in the garden. We cut out and chopped out all the dry branches and wild shoots, and the superfluous trees and bushes. The poplars and bird-cherries grew ranker than the rest and choked the other trees. A poplar grows out from the roots, and it cannot be dug out, but the roots have to be chopped out underground.

Beyond the pond there stood an enormous poplar, two men's embraces in circumference. About it there was a clearing, and this was all overgrown with poplar shoots. I ordered them to be cut out: I wanted the spot to look more cheerful, but, above all, I wanted to make it easier for the old poplar, because I thought that all those young trees came from its roots, and were draining it of its sap. When we cut out these young poplars, I felt sorry as I saw them chop out the sap-filled roots underground, and as all four of us pulled at the poplar that had been cut down, and could not pull it out. It held on with all its might, and did not wish to die. I thought that, no doubt, they had to live, since they clung so much to life. But it was necessary to cut them down, and so I did it. Only later, when nothing could be done, I learned that they ought not to have been cut down.

I thought that the shoots were taking the sap away from the old poplar, but it turned out quite differently. When I was cutting them down, the old poplar was already dying. When the leaves came out, I saw (it grew from two boughs) that one bough was bare; and[Pg 173] that same summer it dried up completely. The tree had been dying for quite awhile, and the tree knew it, so it tried to give its life to the shoots.

That was the reason why they grew so fast. I wanted to make it easier for the tree, and only killed all its children.

[Pg 174]
## THE BIRD-CHERRY

A bird-cherry grew out on a hazel bush path and choked the bushes. I deliberated for a long time whether I had better cut down the bird-cherry, or not. This bird-cherry grew not as a bush, but as a tree, about six inches in diameter and thirty feet high, full of branches and bushy, and all besprinkled with bright, white, fragrant blossoms. You could smell it from a distance. I should not have cut it down, but one of the labourers (to whom I had before given the order to cut down the bird-cherry) had begun to chop it without me. When I came, he had already cut in about three inches, and the sap splashed under the axe whenever it struck the same cut. "It cannot be helped,—apparently such is its fate," I thought, and I picked up an axe myself and began to chop it with the peasant.

It is a pleasure to do any work, and it is a pleasure to chop. It is a pleasure to let the axe enter deeply in a slanting line, and then to chop out the chip by a straight stroke, and to chop farther and farther into the tree.

I had entirely forgotten the bird-cherry, and was thinking only of felling it as quickly as possible. When I got tired, I put down my axe and with the peasant pressed against the tree and tried to make it fall. We bent it: the tree trembled with its leaves, and the dew showered down upon us, and the white, fragrant petals of the blossoms fell down.

At the same time something seemed to cry,—the middle of the tree creaked; we pressed against it, and it was as though something wept, there was a crash in the middle,[Pg 175] and the tree tottered. It broke at the notch and, swaying, fell with its branches and blossoms into the grass. The twigs and blossoms trembled for awhile after the fall, and stopped.

"It was a fine tree!" said the peasant. "I am mightily sorry for it!"

I myself felt so sorry for it that I hurried away to the other labourers.

[Pg 176]

## HOW TREES WALK

One day we were cleaning an overgrown path on a hillock near the pond. We cut down a lot of brier bushes, willows, and poplars,—then came the turn of a bird-cherry. It was growing on the path, and it was so old and stout that it could not be less than ten years old. And yet I knew that five years ago the garden had been cleaned. I could not understand how such an old bird-cherry could have grown out there. We cut it down and went farther. Farther away, in another thicket, there grew a similar bird-cherry, even stouter than the first. I looked at its root, and saw that it grew under an old linden. The linden with its branches choked it, and it had stretched out about twelve feet in a straight line, and only then came out to the light, raised its head, and began to blossom.

I cut it down at the root, and was surprised to find it so fresh, while the root was rotten. After we had cut it down, the peasants and I tried to pull it off; but no matter how much we jerked at it, we were unable to drag it away: it seemed to have stuck fast. I said:

"Look whether it has not caught somewhere."

A workman crawled under it, and called out:

"It has another root; it is out on the path!"

I walked over to him, and saw that it was so.

Not to be choked by the linden, the bird-cherry had gone away from underneath the linden out on the path, about eight feet from its former root. The root which I had cut down was rotten and dry, but the new one was fresh. The bird-cherry had evidently felt that it could[Pg 177] not exist under the linden, so it had stretched out, dropped a branch to the ground, made a root of that branch, and left the other root. Only then did I understand how the first bird-cherry had grown out on the road. It had evidently done the same,—only it had had time to give up the old root, and so I had not found it.

[Pg 178]
[Pg 179]

## THE DECEMBRISTS
### Fragments of a Novel
### 1863-1878

[Pg 180]
[Pg 181]

THE DECEMBRISTS
A Novel
## FIRST FRAGMENT
### I.

This happened not long ago, in the reign of Alexander II., in our days of civilization, progress, questions, regeneration of Russia, and so forth, and so forth; at a time when the victorious Russian army was returning from Sevastopol, surrendered to the enemy; when all of Russia celebrated the annihilation of the Black Sea fleet, and white-stoned Moscow received and congratulated with this happy event the remainders of the crews of that fleet, offering them a good Russian cup of vódka, and bread and salt, according to the good Russian custom, and bowing down to their feet. It was that time when Russia, in the person of far-sighted virgin politicians, lamented the shattered dream of a Te Deum in the Cathedral of St. Sophia, and the loss of two great men, so painful for the country, who had perished during the war (one, who had been carried away by the desire to celebrate the Te Deum in the above-mentioned cathedral at the earliest time possible, and who fell in the fields of Wallachia, but who, at least, left two squadrons of hussars in the same fields, and the other, an unappreciated man, who had distributed tea,[Pg 182] other people's money, and bed-sheets to the wounded, without stealing any of these things); that time, when on all sides, in all branches of human activities, great men—generals, administrators, economists, writers, orators, and simply great men, without any especial calling or purpose—sprang up in Russia like mushrooms; that time, when, at the jubilee of a Moscow actor, there appeared the public opinion, confirmed by a toast, which began to rebuke all the criminals,—when menacing commissions galloped south from St. Petersburg, to convict and punish the evil-doers of the commissariat,—when in all the cities dinners with speeches were given to the heroes of Sevastopol, and when to them, with arms and legs torn off, toasts were drunk, on meeting them on the bridges and on the highways; that time, when oratorical talents developed so rapidly in the nation that a certain dram-shopkeeper everywhere and upon all occasions wrote and printed and recited by rote at dinners such strong speeches, that the guardians of the peace had to take repressive measures against the dram-shopkeeper's eloquence,—when in the very English club a special room was set aside for the discussion of public matters,—when periodicals sprang up under the most diversified standards,—periodicals that evolved European principles on a European basis, but with a Russian world conception, and periodicals on an exclusively Russian basis, but with a European world conception,—when suddenly there appeared so many periodicals that all names seemed to be exhausted,—"The Messenger," and "The Word," and "The Speaker," and "The Observer," and "The Star," and "The Eagle," and many more, and, in spite of it, there appeared ever new names; that time, when the constellation of philosophic writers made its appearance to prove that science was national, and not national, and non-national, and so forth, and the constellation of artistic writers, who described a grove, and the sunrise, and a[Pg 183] storm, and the love of a Russian maiden, and the indolence of a certain official, and the bad conduct of many officials; that time, when on all sides appeared questions (as in the year '56 they called every concourse of circumstances, of which no one could make any sense), questions of cadet corps, universities, censorship, oral judicature, finance, banking, police, emancipation, and many more:—everybody tried to discover ever new questions, everybody tried to solve them, wrote, read, spoke, made projects, wanted to mend everything, destroy, change, and all Russians, like one man, were in indescribable ecstasy.

That is a state of affairs which has been twice repeated in the Russia of the nineteenth century,—the first time, when in the year '12 we repulsed Napoleon I., and the second time, when in the year '56 we were repulsed by Napoleon III. Great, unforgettable time of the regeneration of the Russian people! Like the Frenchman who said that he has not lived who has not lived through the great French Revolution, I venture to say that he who has not lived through the year '56 in Russia does not know what life is. The writer of these lines not only lived through that time, but was one of the actors of that period. Not only did he pass several weeks in one of the blindages of Sevastopol, but he also wrote a work on the Crimean War, which brought him great fame, and in which he described clearly and minutely how the soldiers fired their guns from the bastions, how the wounds were dressed at the ambulance, and how they buried people in the cemetery. Having achieved these deeds, the writer of these lines arrived in the centre of the empire,—a rocket establishment,—where he cut the laurels for his deeds. He saw the transports of the two capitals and of the whole nation, and experienced in his person to what extent Russia knew how to reward real deserts. The mighty of this world sought his friendship, pressed his hands, gave him dinners, urged him to come to their[Pg 184] houses, and, in order to learn the details of the war from him, informed him of their own sentimentalities. Consequently the writer of these lines can appreciate that great and memorable time. But that is another matter.

At that very time, two vehicles on wheels and a sleigh were standing at the entrance of the best Moscow hotel. A young man ran through the door, to find out about quarters. In one of the vehicles sat an old man with two ladies. He was talking about the condition of Blacksmith Bridge in the days of the French. It was the continuation of a conversation started as they entered Moscow, and now the old man with the white beard, in his unbuttoned fur coat, calmly continued his conversation in the vehicle, as though he intended to stay in it overnight. His wife and daughter listened to him, but kept looking at the door with some impatience. The young man emerged from the door with the porter and room servant.

"Well, Sergyéy," asked the mother, thrusting her emaciated face out into the glare of the lamplight.

Either because it was his habit, or because he did not wish the porter to take him for a lackey on account of the short fur coat which he wore, Sergyéy replied in French that there were rooms to be had, and opened the carriage door. The old man looked for a moment at his son, and again turned to the dark corner of the vehicle, as though nothing else concerned him:

"There was no theatre then."

"Pierre!" said his wife, lifting her cloak; but he continued:

"Madame Chalmé was in Tverskáya Street—"

Deep in the vehicle could be heard a youthful, sonorous laugh.

"Papa, step out! You are forgetting where we are."

The old man only then seemed to recall that they had arrived, and looked around him.

[Pg 185]

"Do step out!"

He pulled his cap down, and submissively passed through the door. The porter took him under his arm, but, seeing that the old man was walking well, he at once offered his services to the lady. Judging from the sable cloak, and from the time it took for her to emerge, and from the way she pressed down on his arm, and from the way she, leaning on her son's arm, walked straight toward the porch, without looking to either side, Natálya Nikoláevna, his wife, seemed to the porter to be an important personage. He did not even separate the young lady from the maids, who climbed out from the other vehicle; like them, she carried a bundle and a pipe, and walked behind. He recognized her only by her laughing and by her calling the old man father.

"Not that way, father,—to the right!" she said, taking hold of the sleeve of his sheepskin coat. "To the right."

On the staircase there resounded, through the noise of the steps, the doors, and the heavy breathing of the elderly lady, the same laughter which had been heard in the vehicle, and about which any one who heard it thought: "How excellently she laughs,—I just envy her."

Their son, Sergyéy, had attended to all the material conditions on the road, and, though he lacked knowledge of the matter, he had attended to it with the energy and self-satisfying activity which are characteristic of twenty-five years of age. Some twenty times, and apparently for no important reason, he ran down to the sleigh in his greatcoat, and ran up-stairs again, shivering in the cold and taking two or three steps at a time with his long, youthful legs. Natálya Nikoláevna asked him not to catch a cold, but he said that it was all right, and continued to give orders, slamming doors, and walking, and, when it seemed that only the servants and peasants had[Pg 186] to be attended to, he several times walked through all the rooms, leaving the drawing-room by one door, and coming in through another, as though he were looking for something else to do.

"Well, papa, will you be driven to the bath-house? Shall I find out?" he asked.

His papa was deep in thought and, it seemed, was not at all conscious of where he was. He did not answer at once. He heard the words, but did not comprehend them. Suddenly he comprehended.

"Yes, yes, yes. Find out, if you please, at Stone Bridge."

The head of the family walked through the rooms with hasty, agitated steps, and seated himself in a chair.

"Now we must decide what to do, how to arrange matters," he said. "Help along, children, lively! Like good fellows, drag things around, put them up, and to-morrow we shall send Serézha with a note to sister Márya Ivánovna, to the Nikítins, or we shall go there ourselves. Am I right, Natásha? But now, fix things!"

"To-morrow is Sunday. I hope, Pierre, that first of all you will go to mass," said his wife, kneeling in front of a trunk and opening it.

"That is so, it is Sunday! We shall by all means all of us go to the Cathedral of the Assumption. Thus will our return begin. O Lord! When I think of the day when I was for the last time in the Cathedral of the Assumption! Do you remember, Natásha? But that is another matter."

And the head of the family rose quickly from the chair, on which he had just seated himself.

"Now we must settle down!"

And without doing anything, he kept walking from one room to another.

"Well, shall we drink tea? Or are you tired, and do you want to rest?"

[Pg 187]

"Yes, yes," replied his wife, taking something out from the trunk. "You wanted to go to the bath-house, did you not?"

"Yes—in my day it was near Stone Bridge. Serézha, go and find out whether there is still a bath-house near Stone Bridge. This room here Serézha and I shall occupy. Serézha! Will you be comfortable here?"

But Serézha had gone to find out about the bath-house.

"No, that will not do," he continued. "You will not have a straight passage to the drawing-room. What do you think, Natásha?"

"Calm yourself, Pierre, everything will come out all right," Natásha said, from another room, where peasants were bringing in things.

But Pierre was still under the influence of that ecstatic mood which the arrival had evoked in him.

"Look there,—don't mix up Serézha's things! You have thrown his snow-shoes down in the drawing-room." And he himself picked them up and with great care, as though the whole future order of the quarters depended upon it, leaned them against the door-post and tried to make them stand there. But the snow-shoes did not stick to it, and, the moment Pierre walked away from them, fell with a racket across the door. Natálya Nikoláevna frowned and shuddered, but, seeing the cause of the fall, she said:

"Sónya, darling, pick them up!"

"Pick them up, darling," repeated the husband, "and I will go to the landlord, or else you will never get done. I must talk things over with him."

"You had better send for him, Pierre. Why should you trouble yourself?"

Pierre assented.

"Sónya, bring him here, what do you call him? M. Cavalier, if you please. Tell him that we want to speak about everything."

[Pg 188]

"Chevalier, papa," said Sónya, ready to go out.

Natálya Nikoláevna, who was giving her commands in a soft voice, and was softly stepping from room to room, now with a box, now with a pipe, now with a pillow, imperceptibly finding places for a mountain of baggage, in passing Sónya, had time to whisper to her:

"Do not go yourself, but send a man!"

While a man went to call the landlord, Pierre used his leisure, under the pretext of aiding his consort, in crushing a garment of hers and in stumbling against an empty box. Steadying himself with his hand against the wall, the Decembrist looked around with a smile; but Sónya was looking at him with such smiling eyes that she seemed to be waiting for permission to laugh. He readily granted her that permission, and himself burst out into such a good-natured laugh that all those who were in the room, his wife, the maids, and the peasants, laughed with him. This laughter animated the old man still more. He discovered that the divan in the room for his wife and daughter was not standing very conveniently for them, although they affirmed the opposite, and asked him to calm himself. Just as he was trying with his own hands to help a peasant to change the position of that piece of furniture, the landlord, a Frenchman, entered the room.

"You sent for me," the landlord asked sternly and, in proof of his indifference, if not contempt, slowly drew out his handkerchief, slowly unfolded it, and slowly cleared his nose.

"Yes, my dear sir," said Peter Ivánovich, stepping up toward him, "you see, we do not know ourselves how long we are going to stay here, I and my wife—" and Peter Ivánovich, who had the weakness of seeing a neighbour in every man, began to expound his plans and affairs to him.

M. Chevalier did not share that view of people and was not interested in the information communicated to[Pg 189] him by Peter Ivánovich, but the good French which Peter Ivánovich spoke (the French language, as is known, is something like rank in Russia) and his lordly manner somewhat raised the landlord's opinion about the newcomers.

69

"What can I do for you?" he asked.

This question did not embarrass Peter Ivánovich. He expressed his desire to have rooms, tea, a samovár, supper, dinner, food for the servants, in short, all those things for which hotels exist, and when M. Chevalier, marvelling at the innocence of the old man, who apparently imagined that he was in the Trukhmén steppe, or supposed that all these things would be given him without pay, informed him that he could have all those things, Peter Ivánovich was in ecstasy.

"Now that is nice! Very nice! And so we shall get things all fixed. Well, then please—" but he felt embarrassed to be speaking all the time about himself, and he began to ask M. Chevalier about his family and his business. When Sergyéy Petróvich returned to the room, he did not seem to approve of his father's address; he observed the landlord's dissatisfaction, and reminded his father of the bath. But Peter Ivánovich was interested in the question of how a French hotel could be run in Moscow in the year '56, and of how Madame Chevalier passed her time. Finally the landlord himself bowed and asked him whether he was not pleased to order anything.

"We will have tea, Natásha. Yes? Tea, then, if you please! We will have some other talks, my dear monsieur! What a charming man!"

"And the bath, papa?"

"Oh, yes, then we shall have no tea."

Thus the only result from the conversation with the newly arrived guests was taken from the landlord. But Peter Ivánovich was now proud and happy of his arrangements.[Pg 190] The drivers, who came to ask a *pourboire*, vexed him, because Serézha had no change, and Peter Ivánovich was on the point of sending once more for the landlord, but the happy thought that others, too, ought to be happy on that evening helped him out of that predicament. He took two three-rouble bills, and, sticking one bill into the hand of one of the drivers, he said, "This is for you" (Peter Ivánovich was in the habit of saying "you" to all without exception, unless to a member of his family); "and this is for you," he said, transferring the other bill from the palm of his hand to that of the driver, in some such manner as people do when paying a doctor for a visit. After attending to all these things, he was taken to the bath-house.

Sónya, who was sitting on the divan, put her hand under her head and burst out laughing.

"Oh, how nice it is, mamma! Oh, how nice!"

Then she placed her feet on the divan, stretched herself, adjusted herself, and fell into the sound, calm sleep of a healthy girl of eighteen years of age, after six weeks on the road. Natálya Nikoláevna, who was still busy taking out things in her sleeping-room, heard, no doubt with her maternal ear, that Sónya was not stirring, and went out to take a look at her. She took a pillow and, raising the girl's reddened, dishevelled head with her large white hand, placed her on the pillow. Sónya drew a deep, deep sigh, shrugged her shoulders, and put her head on the pillow, without saying "*Merci*," as though that had all been done of its own accord.

"Not on that bed, not on that, Gavrílovna, Kátya," Natálya Nikoláevna immediately turned to the maids who were making a bed, and with one hand, as though in passing, she adjusted the straying hair of her daughter. Without stopping and without hurrying, Natálya Nikoláevna dressed herself, and upon the arrival of her husband and her son everything was ready: the trunks were no[Pg 191] longer in the rooms; in Pierre's sleeping-room everything was arranged as it had been for several decades in Irkútsk: the morning-gown, the pipe, the tobacco-pouch, the sugared water, the Gospel, which he read at night, and even the image stuck to the rich wall-paper in the rooms of Chevalier, who never used such adornments, but on that evening they appeared in all the rooms of the third division of the hotel.

Having dressed herself, Natálya Nikoláevna adjusted her collar and cuffs, which, in spite of the journey, were still clean, combed herself, and seated herself opposite the table. Her beautiful black eyes gazed somewhere into the distance: she looked and rested herself. She seemed to be resting, not from the unpacking alone, nor from the road, nor from the oppressive years,—she seemed to be resting from her whole life, and the distance into which she was gazing, and in which she saw living and beloved faces, was that rest which she was wishing for. Whether it was an act of love, which she had done for her husband, or the love which she had experienced for her children when they were young, or whether it was a heavy loss, or a peculiarity of her character,—everyone who looked at that woman could not help seeing that nothing could be expected from her, that she had long ago given all of herself to life, and that nothing was left of her. All that there was left was something worthy of respect, something beautiful and sad, as a reminiscence, as the moonlight. She could not be imagined otherwise than surrounded by all the comforts of life. It was impossible for her ever to be hungry, or to eat eagerly, or to have on soiled clothes, or to stumble, or to forget to clear her nose. It was a physical impossibility. Why it was so, I do not know, but every motion of hers was dignity, grace, gentleness toward all those who could enjoy her sight.

"Sie pflegen und weben Himmlische Rosen ins irdische Leben."[Pg 192]

She knew those verses and loved them, but was not guided by them. All her nature was an expression of that thought; all her life was this one unconscious weaving of invisible roses in the lives of those with whom she came in contact. She had followed her husband to Siberia only because she loved him; she had not thought what she could do for him, and instinctively had done everything. She had made his bed, had put away his things, had prepared his dinner and his tea, and, above all, had always been where he was, and no woman could have given more happiness to her husband.

In the drawing-room the samovár was boiling on the round table. Natálya Nikoláevna sat near it. Sónya wrinkled her face and smiled under her mother's hand, which was tickling her, when father and son, with wrinkled finger-tips and glossy cheeks and foreheads (the father's bald spot was particularly glistening), with fluffy white and black hair, and with beaming countenances, entered the room.

"It has grown brighter since you have come in," said Natálya Nikoláevna. "O Lord, how white you are!"

She had been saying that each Saturday, for several decades, and each Saturday Pierre experienced bashfulness and delight, whenever he heard that. They seated themselves at the table; there was an odour of tea and of the pipe, and there were heard the voices of the parents, the children, and the servants, who received their cups in the same room. They recalled everything funny that had happened on the road, admired Sónya's hair-dressing, and laughed. Geographically they were all transferred a distance of five thousand versts, into an entirely different, strange milieu, but morally they were that evening still at home, just such as the peculiar, long, solitary family life had made them to be. It will not be so to-morrow. Peter Ivánovich seated himself near the samovár, and lighted his pipe. He was not in a cheerful mood.

[Pg 193]

"So here we are," he said, "and I am glad that we shall not see any one to-night; this is the last evening we shall pass with the family," and he washed these words down with a large mouthful of tea.

"Why the last, Pierre?"

"Why? Because the eaglets have learned to fly, and they have to make their own nests, and from here they will fly each in a different direction—"

"What nonsense!" said Sónya, taking his glass from him, and smiling at him, as she smiled at everything. "The old nest is good enough!"

"The old nest is a sad nest; the old man did not know how to make it,—he was caught in a cage, and in the cage he reared his young ones, and was let out only when his wings no longer would hold him up. No, the eaglets must make their nests higher up, more auspiciously, nearer to the sun; that is what they are his children for, that his example might serve them; but the old one will look on, so long as he is not blind, and will listen, when he becomes blind— Pour in some rum, more, more—enough!"

"We shall see who is going to leave," replied Sónya, casting a cursory glance at her mother, as though she felt uneasy speaking in her presence. "We shall see who is going to leave," she continued. "I am not afraid for myself, neither am I for Serézha." (Serézha was walking up and down in the room, thinking of how clothes would be ordered for him to-morrow, and wondering whether he had better go to the tailor, or send for him; he was not interested in Sónya's conversation with his father.) Sónya began to laugh.

"What is the matter? What?" asked her father.

"You are younger than we, papa. Much younger, indeed," she said, again bursting out into a laugh.

"Indeed!" said the old man, and his austere wrinkles formed themselves into a gentle, and yet contemptuous, smile.

[Pg 194]

Natálya Nikoláevna bent away from the samovár which prevented her seeing her husband.

"Sónya is right. You are still sixteen years old, Pierre. Serézha is younger in feelings, but you are younger in soul. I can foresee what he will do, but you will astound me yet."

Whether he recognized the justice of this remark, or was flattered by it, he did not know what reply to make, and only smoked in silence, drank his tea, and beamed with his eyes. But Serézha, with characteristic egoism of youth, interested in what was said about him, entered into the conversation and affirmed that he was really old, that his arrival in Moscow and the new life, which was opening before him, did not gladden him in the least, and that he calmly reflected on the future and looked forward toward it.

"Still, it is the last evening," repeated Peter Ivánovich. "It will not be again to-morrow."

And he poured a little more rum into his glass. He sat for a long time at the tea-table, with an expression as though he wished to say many things, but had no hearers. He moved up the rum toward him, but his daughter softly carried away the bottle.

## II.

When M. Chevalier, who had been up-stairs to look after his guests, returned to his room and gave the benefit of his observations on the newcomers to his life companion, in laces and a silk garment, who in Parisian fashion was sitting back of the counter, several habitual visitors of the establishment were sitting in the room. Serézha, who had been down-stairs, had taken notice of that room and of its visitors. If you have been in Moscow, you have, no doubt, noticed that room yourself.

If you, a modest man who do not know Moscow, have missed a dinner to which you are invited, or have made[Pg 195] a mistake in your calculations, imagining that the hospitable Muscovites would invite you to dinner, or simply wish to dine in the best restaurant, you enter the lackeys' room. Three or four lackeys jump up: one of them takes off your fur coat and congratulates you on the occasion of the New Year, or of the Butter-week, or of your arrival, or simply remarks that you have not called for a long while, though you have never been in that establishment before.

You enter, and the first thing that strikes your eyes is a table set, as you in the first moment imagine, with an endless quantity of palatable dishes. But that is only an optical illusion, for the greater part of that table is occupied by pheasants in feather, raw lobsters, boxes with perfume and pomatum, and bottles with cosmetics and candy. Only at the very edge, if you look well, will you find the vódka and a piece of bread with butter and sardines, under a wire globe, which is quite useless in Moscow in the month of December, even though it is precisely such as those which are used in Paris. Then, beyond the table, you see the room, where behind a counter sits a Frenchwoman, of extremely repulsive exterior, but wearing the cleanest of gloves and a most exquisite, fashionable gown. Near the Frenchwoman you will see an officer in unbuttoned uniform, taking a dram of vódka, a civilian reading a newspaper, and somebody's military or civilian legs lying on a velvet chair, and you will hear French conversation, and more or less sincere, loud laughter.

If you wish to know what is going on in that room, I should advise you not to enter within, but only to look in, as though merely passing by to take a sandwich. Otherwise you will feel ill at ease from the interrogative silence and glances, and you will certainly take your tail between your legs and skulk away to one of the tables in the large hall, or to the winter garden. Nobody will keep[Pg 196]you from doing so. These tables are for everybody, and there, in your solitude, you may call Dey a garçon and order as many truffles as you please.

72

The room with the Frenchwoman, however, exists for the select, golden Moscow youth, and it is not so easy to find your way among the select as you imagine.

On returning to this room, M. Chevalier told his wife that the gentleman from Siberia was dull, but that his son and daughter were fine people, such as could be raised only in Siberia.

"You ought just to see the daughter! She is a little rose-bush!"

"Oh, this old man is fond of fresh-looking women," said one of the guests, who was smoking a cigar. (The conversation, of course, was carried on in French, but I render it in Russian, as I shall continue to do in this story.)

"Oh, I am very fond of them!" replied M. Chevalier. "Women are my passion. Do you not believe me?"

"Do you hear, Madame Chevalier?" shouted a stout officer of Cossacks, who owed a big bill in the institution and was fond of chatting with the landlord.

"He shares my taste," said M. Chevalier, patting the stout man on his epaulet.

"And is this Siberian young lady really pretty?"

M. Chevalier folded his fingers and kissed them.

After that the conversation between the guests became confidential and very jolly. They were talking about the stout officer; he smiled as he listened to what they were saying about him.

"How can one have such perverted taste!" cried one, through the laughter. "Mlle. Clarisse! You know, Strúgov prefers such of the women as have chicken calves."

Though Mlle. Clarisse did not understand the salt of that remark, she behind her counter burst out into a[Pg 197] laughter as silvery as her bad teeth and advanced years permitted.

"Has the Siberian lady turned him to such thoughts?" and she laughed more heartily still. M. Chevalier himself roared with laughter, as he said:

"*Ce vieux coquin*," patting the officer of Cossacks on his head and shoulders.

"But who are they, those Siberians? Mining proprietors or merchants?" one of the gentlemen asked, during a pause in the laughter.

"Nikíta, ask ze passport from ze chentleman zat as come," said M. Chevalier.

"We, Alexander, ze Autocrat—" M. Chevalier began to read the passport, which had been brought in the meantime, but the officer of Cossacks tore it out of his hands, and his face expressed surprise.

"Guess who it is," he said, "for you all know him by reputation."

"How can we guess? Show it to us! Well, Abdel Kader, ha, ha, ha! Well, Cagliostro— Well, Peter III.—ha, ha, ha, ha!"

"Well, read it!"

The officer of Cossacks unfolded the paper and read the name of him who once had been Prince Peter Ivánovich, and the family name which everybody knows and pronounces with a certain respect and pleasure, when speaking of a person bearing that name, as of a near and familiar person. We shall call him Labázov. The officer of Cossacks had a dim recollection that this Peter Labázov had been something important in the year '25, and that he had been sent to hard labour,—but what he had been famous for, he did not exactly know. But of the others not one knew anything about him, and they replied:

"Oh, yes, the famous prince," just as they would have said, "Of course, he is famous!" about Shakespeare, who had written the "Æneid." But they recognized him from[Pg 198] the explanations of the stout officer, who told them that he was a brother of Prince Iván, an uncle of the Chíkins, of Countess Prut, in short, the well-known—

"He must be very rich, if he is a brother of Prince Iván," remarked one of the young men, "if the fortune has been returned to him. It has been returned to some."

"What a lot of exiles are returning nowadays!" remarked another. "Really, fewer seem to have been sent away, than are returning now. Zhikínski, tell us that story of the 18th!" he turned to an officer of sharp-shooters, who had the reputation of being a good story-teller.

"Do tell it!"

"In the first place, it is a true story, and happened here, at Chevalier's, in the large hall. Three Decembrists came to have their dinner. They were sitting at one table, eating, drinking, talking. Opposite them sat down a gentleman of respectable mien, of about the same age, and he listened to their talking about Siberia. He asked them something, they exchanged a few words, began to converse, and it turned out that he, too, was from Siberia.

"'And do you know Nerchínsk?'

"'Indeed I do, I lived there.'

"'And do you know Tatyána Ivánovna?'

"'Of course I do!'

"'Permit me to ask you,—were you, too, exiled?'

"'Yes, I had the misfortune to suffer, and you?'

"'We are all exiles of the 14th of December. It is strange that we should not know you, if you, too, were exiled for the 14th. Permit me to know your name!'

"'Fédorov.'

"'Also for the 14th?'

"'No, for the 18th.'

"'For the 18th?'

[Pg 199]

"'For the 18th of September, for a gold watch. I was falsely accused of having stolen it, and I suffered, though innocent.'"

All of them rolled in laughter, except the story-teller, who with a most serious face looked at the outstretched hearers and swore that it was a true story.

Soon after the story one of the young men got up and went to the club. He passed through the halls which were filled with tables at which old men were playing whist; turned into the "infernal region," where the famous "Puchin" had begun his game against the "company;" stood for awhile near one of the billiard-tables, where, holding on to the cushion, a distinguished old man was fumbling around and with difficulty striking a ball; looked into the library, where a general, holding a newspaper a distance away from him, was reading it slowly above his glasses, and a registered young man turned the leaves of one periodical after another, trying to make no noise; and finally seated himself on a divan in the billiard-room, near some young people who were playing pyramids, and who were as much gilded as he was.

It was a day of dinners, and there were there many gentlemen who always frequented the club. Among them was Iván Vavílovich Pákhtin. He was a man of about forty years of age, of medium stature, fair-complexioned, with broad shoulders and hips, with a bare head, and a glossy, happy, clean-shaven face. He was not playing at pyramids, but had just sat down beside Prince D——, with whom he was on "thou" terms, and had accepted a glass of champagne which had been offered to him. He had located himself so comfortably after the dinner, having quietly unbuckled his trousers at the back, that it looked as though he could sit there all his life, smoking a cigar, drinking champagne, and feeling the proximity of princes, counts, and the children of[Pg 200]ministers. The news of the arrival of the Labázovs interfered with his calm.

"Where are you going, Pákhtin," said a minister's son, having noticed during the game that Pákhtin had got up, pulled his waistcoat down, and emptied his champagne in a large gulp.

"Syévernikov has invited me," said Pákhtin, feeling a restlessness in his legs. "Well, will you go there?"

"Anastásya, Anastásya, please unlock the door for me." That was a well-known gipsy-song, which was in vogue at that time.

"Perhaps. And you?"

"Where shall I, an old married man, go?"

"Well!"

Pákhtin, smiling, went to the glass hall, to join Syévernikov. He was fond of having his last word appear to be a joke. And so it came out at that time, too.

"Well, how is the countess's health?" he asked, walking over to Syévernikov, who had not called him at all, but who, according to Pákhtin's surmise, should more than any one else learn of the arrival of the Labázovs. Syévernikov had somehow been mixed up with the affair of the 14th, and was a friend of the Decembrists. The countess's health was much better, and Pákhtin was very glad to hear it.

"Do you know, Labázov has arrived; he is staying at Chevaliers."

"You don't say so! We are old friends. How glad I am! How glad! The poor old fellow must have grown old. His wife wrote to my wife—"

But Syévernikov did not finish saying what it was she had written, because his partners, who were playing without trumps, had made some mistake. While speaking with Iván Pávlovich, he kept an eye on them, and now he leaned forward with his whole body against the table, and, thumping it with his hands, he tried to prove that[Pg 201] they ought to have played from the seven. Iván Pávlovich got up and, going up to another table, in the middle of a conversation informed another worthy gentleman of his bit of news, again got up, and repeated the same at a third table. The worthy gentlemen were all glad to hear of the arrival of the Labázovs, so that, upon returning to the billiard-room, Iván Pávlovich, who at first had had his misgivings about whether he had to rejoice in the return of the Labázovs, or not, no longer started with an introduction about the ball, about an article in the *Messenger*, about health, or weather, but approached everybody directly with the enthusiastic announcement of the safe return of the famous Decembrist.

The old man, who was still vainly endeavouring to hit the white ball with his cue, would, in Pákhtin's opinion, be very much delighted to hear the news. He went up to him.

"Are you playing well, your Excellency?" he said, just as the old man stuck his cue into the marker's red waistcoat, wishing to indicate that it had to be chalked.

"Your Excellency" was not said, as you might think, from a desire of being subservient (no, that was not the fashion in '56). Iván Pávlovich was in the habit of calling the old man by his name and patronymic, but this was said partly as a joke on men who spoke that way, partly in order to hint that he knew full well to whom he was talking, and yet was taking liberties, and partly in truth: altogether it was a very delicate jest.

"I have just learned that Peter Labázov has returned. Straight from Siberia, with his whole family."

These words Pákhtin pronounced just as the old man again missed his ball, for such was his bad luck.

"If he has returned as cracked as he went away, there is no cause for rejoicing," gruffly said the old man, who was irritated by his incomprehensible failure.

This statement vexed Iván Pávlovich, and again he[Pg 202] was at a loss whether there was any cause for rejoicing at Labázov's return, and, in order fully to settle his doubt, he directed his steps to a room, where generally assembled the clever people, who knew the meaning and value of each thing, and, in short, knew everything. Iván Pávlovich was on the same footing of friendship with the frequenters of the intellectual room as with the gilded youths and with the dignitaries. It is true, he had no special place of his own in the intellectual room, but nobody was surprised to see him enter and seat himself on a divan. They were just discussing in what year and upon what occasion there had taken place a quarrel between two Russian journalists. Waiting for a moment of silence, Iván Pávlovich communicated his bit of news, not as something joyous, nor as an unimportant event, but as though part of the conversation. But immediately, from the way the "intellectuals" (I use the word "intellectuals" as a name for the frequenters of the "intellectual" room) received the news and began to discuss it, Iván Pávlovich understood that it belonged there, and that only there would it receive such an elaboration as to enable him to carry it farther and *savoir à quoi s'en tenir*.

"Labázov was the only one who was wanting," said one of the intellectuals; "now all the living Decembrists have returned to Russia."

"He was one of the herd of the famous—" said Pákhtin, still with an inquisitive glance, prepared to make that quotation both jocular and serious.

"Indeed, Labázov was one of the most remarkable men of that time," began an intellectual. "In 1819 he was an ensign of the Seménovski regiment, and was sent abroad with messages to Duke Z——. Then he returned and in the year '24 was received in the First Masonic lodge. The Masons of that time used all to gather at the house of D—— and at his house. He was very[Pg 203] rich. Prince Zh——, Fédor D——, Iván P——, those were his nearest friends. Then his uncle, Prince Visarión, to remove the young man from that society, took him to Moscow."

"Pardon me, Nikoláy Stepánovich," another intellectual interrupted him, "it seems to me that that happened in the year '23, because Visarión Labázov was appointed a commander of the Third Corps in '24, and was then in Warsaw. He had offered him an adjutantship, and after his refusal, he was removed. However, pardon me for interrupting you."

"Not at all. Proceed!"

"Pardon me!"

"Proceed! You ought to know that better than I, and, besides, your memory and knowledge have been sufficiently attested here."

"In Moscow he against his uncle's will left the army," continued the one whose memory and knowledge had been attested, "and there he gathered around him a second society, of which he was the progenitor and the heart, if it be possible so to express it. He was rich, handsome, clever, educated; they say he was exceedingly amiable. My aunt used to tell me that she did not know a more bewitching man. Here he married Miss Krínski, a few months before the revolt broke out."

"The daughter of Nikoláy Krínski, the one of Borodinó fame, you know," somebody interrupted him.

"Well, yes. Her immense fortune he still possesses, but his own paternal estate passed over to his younger brother, Prince Iván, who is now Ober-Hof-Kaffermeister" (he gave him some such name) "and was a minister."

"The best thing is what he did for his brother," continued the narrator. "When he was arrested, there was one thing which he succeeded in destroying, and that was his brother's letters and documents."

"Was his brother mixed up in it, too?"

[Pg 204]

The narrator did not say "Yes," but compressed his lips and gave a significant wink.

"Then, during all the inquests Peter Labázov kept denying everything which concerned his brother, and so suffered more than the rest. But the best part of it is that Prince Iván got all the property, and never sent a penny to his brother."

"They say that Peter Labázov himself declined it," remarked one of the hearers.

"Yes; but he declined it only because Prince Iván wrote him before the coronation, excusing himself and saying that if he had not taken it, it would have been confiscated, and that he had children and debts, and that now he was unable to return it to him. Peter Labázov replied to him in two lines: 'Neither I nor my heirs have any right, nor can have any right, to the property legally appropriated by you.' That was all. How was that? And Prince Iván swallowed it, and in delight locked up that document with the notes in a safe, and showed it to no one."

One of the peculiarities of the intellectual room was that its visitors knew, whenever they wanted to know, everything that was taking place in the world, no matter how secret the event might have been.

"Still it is a question," said a new interlocutor, "whether it was just to deprive the children of Prince Iván of the property, with which they have grown up and have been educated, and to which they thought they had a right."

Thus the conversation was transferred to an abstract sphere, which did not interest Pákhtin.

He felt the necessity of communicating the news to fresh people, and so he rose and, speaking to the right and to the left, walked from one hall to another. One of his fellow officers stopped him to give him the news of Labázov's arrival.

"Who does not know that?" replied Iván Pávlovich,[Pg 205] with a calm smile, turning to the exit. The news had had time to complete its circle, and was again returning to him.

There was nothing else to do in the club, and he went to an evening party. It was not a special entertainment, but a salon where guests were received any evening. There were there eight ladies, and one old colonel, and all found it terribly dull. Pákhtin's firm gait alone and his smiling face cheered the ladies and maidens. And the news was the more appropriate, since the old Countess Fuks and her daughter were present in the salon. When Pákhtin told nearly word for word what he had heard in the intellectual room, Madame Fuks, shaking her head and marvelling at her old age, began to recall how she used to go out together with Natásha Krínski, the present Princess Labázov.

"Her marriage is a very romantic story, and all that happened under my eyes. Natásha was almost engaged to Myátlin, who was later killed in a duel with Debras. Just then Prince Peter arrived in Moscow, fell in love with her, and proposed to her. But her father, who wanted Myátlin very much,—they were, in general, afraid of Labázov because he was a Mason,—refused him. The young man continued to see her at balls, everywhere, and became friendly with Myátlin, whom he begged to decline. Myátlin agreed to do so, and he persuaded her to elope. She, too, agreed, but the last repentance——" (the conversation was taking place in French), "and she went to her father and said that everything was ready for the elopement, and she could leave him, but hoped for his magnanimity. And, indeed, her father forgave her,—everybody begged for her,—and gave his consent. Thus the wedding was celebrated, and it was a jolly wedding! Who of us thought that a year later she would follow him to Siberia! She, an only daughter, the most beautiful, the richest woman of that time. Emperor[Pg 206] Alexander always used to notice her at balls, and had danced with her so often. Countess G—— gave a *bal costumé*,—I remember it as though it were to-day,— and she was a Neapolitan maid, oh, so charming! Whenever he came to Moscow, he used to ask, '*que fait la belle Napolitaine?*' And suddenly this woman, in such a condition (she bore a child on the way), did not stop for a moment to think, without preparing anything, without collecting her things, just as she was, when they took him, followed him a distance of five thousand versts."

"Oh, what a remarkable woman!" said the hostess.

"Both he and she were remarkable people," said another lady. "I have been told,—I don't know whether it is true,—that wherever they worked in the mines in Siberia, or whatever it is called, the convicts, who were with them, improved in their presence."

"But she has never worked in the mines," Pákhtin corrected her.

How much that year '56 meant! Three years before no one had been thinking of the Labázovs, and if any one recalled them, it was with that unaccountable feeling of dread with which one speaks of one lately dead; but now they vividly recalled all the former relations, all the beautiful qualities, and each lady was making a plan for getting the monopoly of the Labázovs, in order to treat the other guests to them.

"Their son and their daughter have come with them," said Pákhtin.

"If they are only as handsome as their mother used to be," said Countess Fuks. "Still, their father, too, was very, very handsome."

"How could they educate their children there?" asked the hostess.

"They say, nicely. They say that the young man is as nice, as amiable, and as cultured as though he had been brought up in Paris."

[Pg 207]

"I predict great success to that young person," said a homely spinster. "All those Siberian ladies have something pleasantly trivial about them, which everybody, however, likes."

"Yes, yes," said another spinster.

"Here we have another rich prospective bride," said a third spinster.

The old colonel, of German origin, who had come to Moscow three years before, in order to marry a rich girl, decided as quickly as possible, before the young people knew anything about it, to present himself and propose. But the spinsters and ladies thought almost the same about the young Siberian.

"No doubt that is the one I am destined to marry," thought a spinster who had been going out for eight years.

"No doubt it was for the best that that stupid officer of the Chevalier Guards did not propose to me. I should certainly have been unhappy."

"Well, they will again grow yellow with envy, if this one, too, falls in love with me," thought a young and pretty lady.

77

We hear much about the provincialism of small towns,—but there is nothing worse than the provincialism of the upper classes. There are no new persons there, and society is prepared to receive all kinds of new persons, if they should make their appearance; but they are rarely, very rarely, recognized as belonging to their circle and accepted, as was the case with the Labázovs, and the sensation produced by them is stronger than in a provincial town.

### III.

"This is Moscow, white-stoned Mother Moscow," said Peter Ivánovich, rubbing his eyes in the morning, and listening to the tolling of the bells which was proceeding[Pg 208] from Gazette Lane. Nothing so vividly resurrects the past as sounds, and these sounds of the Moscow bells, combined with the sight of a white wall opposite the window, and with the rumbling of wheels, so vividly reminded him not only of the Moscow which he had known thirty-five years before, but also of the Moscow with the Kremlin, with the palaces, with Iván the bell, and so forth, which he had been carrying in his heart, that he experienced a childish joy at being a Russian, and in Moscow.

There appeared the Bukhara morning-gown, wide open over the broad chest with its chintz shirt, the pipe with its amber, the lackey with soft manners, tea, the odour of tobacco; a loud male voice was heard in Chevalier's apartments; there resounded the morning kisses, and the voices of daughter and son, and the Decembrist was as much at home as in Irkútsk, and as he would have been in New York or in Paris.

No matter how much I should like to present to my readers the Decembrist hero above all foibles, I must confess, for truth's sake, that Peter Ivánovich took great pains in shaving and combing himself, and in looking at himself in the mirror. He was dissatisfied with the garments, which had been made in Siberia with little elegance, and two or three times he buttoned and unbuttoned his coat.

But Natálya Nikoláevna entered the drawing-room, rustling with her black moire gown, with mittens and with ribbons in her cap, which, though not according to the latest fashion, were so arranged that, far from making her appear *ridicule*, they made her look *distinguée*. For this ladies have a special sixth sense and perspicacity, which cannot be compared to anything.

Sónya, too, was so dressed that, although she was two years behind in fashion, she could not be reproached in any way. On her mother everything was dark and simple, and on the daughter bright and cheerful.

[Pg 209]

Serézha had just awakened, and so they went by themselves to mass. Father and mother sat in the back seat, and their daughter was opposite them. Vasíli climbed on the box, and the hired carriage took them to the Kremlin. When they got out of the carriage, the ladies adjusted their robes, and Peter Ivánovich took the arm of his Natálya Nikoláevna, and, throwing back his head, walked up to the door of the church. Many people, merchants, officers, and everybody else, could not make out what kind of people they were.

Who was that old man with his old sunburnt, and still unblanched face, with the large, straight work wrinkles of a peculiar fold, different from the wrinkles acquired in the English club, with snow-white hair and beard, with a good, proud glance and energetic movements? Who was that tall lady with that determined gait, and those weary, dimmed, large, beautiful eyes? Who was that fresh, stately, strong young lady, neither fashionable, nor timid? Merchants? No, no merchants. Germans? No, no Germans. Gentlefolk? No, they are different,—they are distinguished people. Thus thought those who saw them in church, and for some reason more readily and cheerfully made way for them than for men in thick epaulets. Peter Ivánovich bore himself just as majestically as at the entrance, and prayed quietly, with reserve, and without forgetting himself. Natálya Nikoláevna glided down on her knees, took out a handkerchief, and wept much during the cherubical song. Sónya seemed to be making an effort over herself in order to pray. Devotion did not come to her, but she did not look around, and diligently made the signs of the cross.

Serézha stayed at home, partly because he had overslept himself, partly because he did not like to stand through a mass, which made his legs faint,—a matter he was unable to understand, since it was a mere trifle for[Pg 210] him to walk forty miles on snow-shoes, whereas standing through twelve pericopes was the greatest physical torture for him,—but chiefly because he felt that more than anything he needed a new suit of clothes. He dressed himself and went to Blacksmith Bridge. He had plenty of money. His father had made it a rule, ever since his son had passed his twenty-first year, to let him have as much money as he wished. It lay with him to leave his parents entirely without money.

How sorry I am for the 250 roubles which he threw away in Kuntz's shop of ready-made clothes! Any one of the gentlemen who met Serézha would have been only too happy to show him around, and would have regarded it as a piece of happiness to go with him to get his clothes made. But, as it was, he was a stranger in the crowd, and, making his way in his cap along Blacksmith Bridge, he went to the end, without looking into the shops, opened the door, and came out from it in a cinnamon-coloured half-dress coat, which was tight (though at that time they wore wide coats), and in loose black trousers (though they wore tight trousers), and in a flowery atlas waistcoat, which not one of the gentlemen, who were in Chevalier's special room, would have allowed their lackeys to wear, and bought a number of other a things; on the other hand, Kuntz marvelled at the young man's slender waist, the like of which, as he explained to everybody, he had never seen. Serézha knew that he had a beautiful waist, and he was very much flattered by the praise of a stranger, such as Kuntz was.

He came out with 250 roubles less, but was dressed badly, in fact so badly that his apparel two days later passed over into Vasíli's possession and always remained a disagreeable memory for Serézha.

At home he went down-stairs, seated himself in the large hall, looking now and then into the sanctum, and ordered a breakfast of such strange dishes that the servant[Pg 211] in the kitchen had to laugh. Then he asked for a periodical, and pretended to be reading. When the servant, encouraged by the inexperience of the young man, addressed some questions to him, Serézha said, "Go to your place!" and blushed. But he said this so proudly that the servant obeyed. Mother, father, and daughter, upon returning home, found his clothes excellent.

Do you remember that joyous sensation of childhood, when you were dressed up for your name-day and taken to mass, and when, upon returning with a holiday expression in your clothes, upon your countenance, and in your soul, you found toys and guests at home? You knew that on that day there would be no classes, that even the grown-ups celebrated on that day, and that that was a day of exceptions and pleasures for the whole house; you knew that you alone were the cause of that holiday, and that you would be forgiven, no matter what you might do, and you were surprised to see that the people in the streets did not celebrate along with your home folk, and the sounds were more audible, and the colours brighter,—in short, a name-day sensation. It was a sensation of that kind that Peter Ivánovich experienced on his return from church.

Pákhtin's solicitude of the evening before did not pass in vain: instead of toys Peter Ivánovich found at home several visiting-cards of distinguished Muscovites, who, in the year '56, regarded it as their peremptory duty to show every attention possible to a famous exile, whom they would under no consideration have wished to see three years before. In the eyes of Chevalier, the porter, and the servants of the hotel, the appearance of carriages asking for Peter Ivánovich, on that one morning increased their respect and subserviency tenfold.

All those were name-day toys for Peter Ivánovich. No matter how much tried in life, how clever a man may be, the expression of respect from people respected by a[Pg 212] large number of men is always agreeable. Peter Ivánovich felt light of heart when Chevalier, bowing, offered to change his apartments and asked him to order anything he might need, and assured him that he regarded Peter Ivánovich's visit as a piece of luck, and when, examining the visiting-cards and throwing them into a vase, he called out the names of Count S——, Prince D——, and so forth.

Natálya Nikoláevna said that she would not receive anybody and that she would go at once to the house of Márya Ivánovna, to which Peter Ivánovich consented, though he wished very much to talk to some of the visitors.

Only one visitor managed to get through before the refusal to meet him. That was Pákhtin. If this man had been asked why he went away from the Prechístenka to go to

Gazette Lane, he would have been unable to give any excuse, except that he was fond of everything new and remarkable, and so had come to see Peter Ivánovich, as something rare. One would think that, coming to see a stranger for no other reason than that, he would have been embarrassed. But the contrary was true. Peter Ivánovich and his son and Sónya Petróvna became embarrassed. Natálya Nikoláevna was too much of a *grande dame* to become embarrassed for any reason whatever. The weary glance of her beautiful black eyes was calmly lowered on Pákhtin. But Pákhtin was refreshing, self-contented, and gaily amiable, as always. He was a friend of Márya Ivánovna's.

"Ah!" said Natálya Nikoláevna.

"Not a friend,—the difference of our years,—but she has always been kind to me."

Pákhtin was an old admirer of Peter Ivánovich's,—he knew his companions. He hoped that he could be useful to the newcomers. He would have appeared the previous evening, but could not find the time, and[Pg 213] begged to be excused, and sat down and talked for a long time.

"Yes, I must tell you, I have found many changes in Russia since then," Peter Ivánovich said, in reply to a question.

The moment Peter Ivánovich began to speak, you ought to have seen with what respectful attention Pákhtin received every word that flew out of the mouth of the distinguished old man, and how after each sentence, at times after a word, Pákhtin with a nod, a smile, or a motion of his eyes gave him to understand that he had received and accepted the memorable sentence or word.

The weary glance approved of that manœuvre. Sergyéy Petróvich seemed to be afraid lest his father's conversation should not be weighty enough, corresponding to the attention of the hearer. Sónya Petróvna, on the contrary, smiled that imperceptible self-satisfied smile which people smile who have caught a man's ridiculous side. It seemed to her that nothing was to be got from him, that he was a "shyúshka," as she and her brother nicknamed a certain class of people.

Peter Ivánovich declared that during his journey he had seen enormous changes, which gave him pleasure.

"There is no comparison, the masses—the peasants—stand so much higher now, have so much greater consciousness of their dignity," he said, as though repeating some old phrases. "I must say that the masses have always interested me most. I am of the opinion that the strength of Russia does not lie in us, but in the masses," and so forth.

Peter Ivánovich with characteristic zeal evolved his more or less original ideas in regard to many important subjects. We shall hear more of them in fuller form. Pákhtin was melting for joy, and fully agreed with him in everything.

"You must by all means meet the Aksátovs. Will you[Pg 214] permit me to introduce them to you, prince? You know they have permitted him to publish his periodical. To-morrow, they say, the first number will appear. I have also read his remarkable article on the consistency of the theory of science in the abstract. Remarkably interesting. Another article, the history of Servia in the eleventh century, of that famous general Karbovánets, is also very interesting. Altogether an enormous step."

"Indeed," said Peter Ivánovich. But he was apparently not interested in all these bits of information; he did not even know the names and merits of all those men whom Pákhtin quoted as universally known.

But Natálya Nikoláevna, without denying the necessity of knowing all these men and conditions, remarked in justification of her husband that Pierre received his periodicals very late. He read entirely too much.

"Papa, shall we not go to aunty?" asked Sónya, upon coming in.

"We shall, but we must have our breakfast. Won't you have anything?"

Pákhtin naturally declined, but Peter Ivánovich, with the hospitality characteristic of every Russian and of him in particular, insisted that Pákhtin should eat and drink something. He himself emptied a wine-glass of vódka and a tumbler of Bordeaux. Pákhtin noticed that as he was filling his glass, Natálya accidentally turned away from it, and the son cast a peculiar glance on his father's hands.

After the wine, Peter Ivánovich, in response to Pákhtin's questions about what his opinion was in respect to the new literature, the new tendency, the war, the peace (Pákhtin had a knack of uniting the most diversified subjects into one senseless but smooth conversation), in response to these questions Peter Ivánovich at once replied with one general *profession de foi*, and either under the influence of the wine, or of the subject of the conversation,[Pg 215] he became so excited that tears appeared in his eyes, and Pákhtin, too, was in ecstasy, and himself became tearful, and without embarrassment expressed his conviction that Peter Ivánovich was now in advance of all the foremost men and should become the head of all the parties. Peter Ivánovich's eyes became inflamed,—he believed what Pákhtin was telling him,—and he would have continued talking for a long time, if Sónya Petróvna had not schemed to get Natálya Nikoláevna to put on her mantilla, and had not come herself to raise Peter Ivánovich from his seat. He poured out the rest of the wine into a glass, but Sónya Petróvna drank it.

"What is this?"

"I have not had any yet, papa, pardon."

He smiled.

"Well, let us go to Márya Ivánovna's. You will excuse us, Monsieur Pákhtin."

And Peter Ivánovich left the room, carrying his head high. In the vestibule he met a general, who had come to call on his old acquaintance. They had not seen each other for thirty-five years. The general was toothless and bald.

"How fresh you still are!" he said. "Evidently Siberia is better than St. Petersburg. These are your family,—introduce me to them! What a fine fellow your son is! So to dinner to-morrow?"

"Yes, yes, by all means."

On the porch they met the famous Chikháev, another old acquaintance.

"How did you find out that I had arrived?"

"It would be a shame for Moscow if it did not know it. It is a shame that you were not met at the barrier. Where do you dine? No doubt with your sister, Márya Ivánovna. Very well, I shall be there myself."

Peter Ivánovich always had the aspect of a proud man for one who could not through that exterior make out the[Pg 216] expression of unspeakable goodness and impressionableness; but just then even Márya Nikoláevna was delighted to see his unwonted dignity, and Sónya Petróvna smiled with her eyes, as she looked at him. They arrived at the house of Márya Ivánovna. Márya Ivánovna was Peter Ivánovich's godmother and ten years his senior. She was an old maid.

Her history, why she did not get married, and how she had passed her youth, I will tell some time later.

She had lived uninterruptedly for forty years in Moscow. She had neither much intelligence, nor great wealth, and she did not think much of connections,—on the contrary; and there was not a man who did not respect her. She was so convinced that everybody ought to respect her that everybody actually respected her. There were some young liberals from the university who did not recognize her power, but these gentlemen made a bold front only in her absence. She needed only to enter the drawing-room with her royal gait, to say something in her calm manner, to smile her kindly smile, and they were vanquished. Her society consisted of everybody. She looked upon all of Moscow as her home folk, and treated them as such. She had friends mostly among the young people and clever men, but women she did not like. She had also dependents, whom our literature has for some reason included with the Hungarian woman and with generals in one common class for contempt; but Márya Ivánovna considered it better for Skópin, who had been ruined in cards, and Madame Byéshev, whom her husband had driven away, to be living with her than in misery, and so she kept them.

But the two great passions in Márya Ivánovna's present life were her two brothers. Peter Ivánovich was her idol. Prince Iván was hateful to her. She had not known that Peter Ivánovich had arrived; she had attended mass, and was just finishing her coffee.

[Pg 217]

81

At the table sat the vicar of Moscow, Madame Byéshev, and Skópin. Márya Ivánovna was telling them about young Count V——, the son of P—— Z——, who had returned from Sevastopol, and with whom she was in love. (She had some passion all the time.) He was to dine with her on that day. The vicar got up and bowed himself out. Márya Ivánovna did not keep him,—she was a freethinker in this respect: she was pious, but had no use for monks and laughed at the ladies that ran after them, and boldly asserted that in her opinion monks were just such men as we sinful people, and that it was better to find salvation in the world than in a monastery.

"Give the order not to receive anybody, my dear," she said, "I will write to Pierre. I cannot understand why he is not coming. No doubt, Natálya Nikoláevna is ill."

Márya Ivánovna was of the opinion that Natálya Nikoláevna did not like her and was her enemy. She could not forgive her because it was not she, his sister, who had given up her property and had followed him to Siberia, but Natálya Nikoláevna, and because her brother had definitely declined her offer when she got ready to go with him. After thirty-five years she was beginning to believe that Natálya Nikoláevna was the best woman in the world and his guardian angel; but she was envious, and it seemed all the time to her that she was not a good woman.

She got up, took a few steps in the parlour, and was on the point of entering the cabinet when the door opened, and Madame Byéshev's wrinkled, grayish face, expressing joyous terror, was thrust through the door.

"Márya Ivánovna, prepare yourself," she said.

"A letter?"

"No, something better—"

But before she had a chance to finish, a man's loud voice was heard in the antechamber:

"Where is she? Go, Natásha."

[Pg 218]

"He!" muttered Márya Ivánovna, walking with long, firm steps toward her brother. She met them all as though she had last seen them the day before.

"When didst thou arrive? Where have you stopped? How have you come,—in a carriage?" Such were the questions which Márya Ivánovna put, walking with them to the drawing-room and not hearing the answers, and looking with large eyes, now upon one, and now upon another. Madame Byéshev was surprised at this calm, even indifference, and did not approve of it. They all smiled; the conversation died down, and Márya Ivánovna looked silently and seriously at her brother.

"How are you?" asked Peter Ivánovich, taking her hand, and smiling.

Peter Ivánovich said "you" to her, though she had said "thou." Márya Ivánovna once more looked at his gray beard, his bald head, his teeth, his wrinkles, his eyes, his sunburnt face, and recognized all that.

"Here is my Sónya."

But she did not look around.

"What a stup—" her voice faltered, and she took hold of his bald head with her large white hands. "What a stupid you are," she had intended to say, "not to have prepared me," but her shoulders and breast began to tremble, her old face twitched, and she burst out into sobs, pressing to her breast his bald head, and repeating: "What a stupid you are not to have prepared me!"

Peter Ivánovich no longer appeared as such a great man to himself, not so important as he had appeared on Chevalier's porch. His back was resting against a chair, but his head was in his sister's arms, his nose was pressed against her corset, his nose was tickled, his hair dishevelled, and there were tears in his eyes. But he felt happy.

When this outburst of joyous tears was over, Márya Ivánovna understood what had happened and believed it,[Pg 219] and began to examine them all. But several times during the course of the day, whenever she recalled what he had been then, and what she had been, and what they were now, and whenever the past misfortunes, and past joys and loves, vividly rose in her imagination, she was again seized by emotion, and got up and repeated: "What a stupid you are, Pierre, what a stupid not to have prepared me!"

"Why did you not come straight to me? I should have found room for you," said Márya Ivánovna. "At least, stay to dinner. You will not feel lonesome, Sergyéy,—a young, brave Sevastopol soldier is dining here to-day. Do you not know Nikoláy Mikháylovich's son? He is a writer,—has written something nice. I have not read it, but they praise it, and he is a dear fellow,—I shall send for him. Chikháev, too, wanted to come. He is a babbler,—I do not like him. Has he already called on you? Have you seen Nikíta? That is all nonsense. What do you intend to do? How are you, how is your health, Natálya? What are you going to do with this young fellow, and with this beauty?"

But the conversation somehow did not flow.

Before dinner Natálya Nikoláevna went with the children to an old aunt; brother and sister were left alone, and he began to tell her of his plans.

"Sónya is a young lady, she has to be taken out; consequently, we are going to live in Moscow," said Márya Ivánovna.

"Never."

"Serézha has to serve."

"Never."

"You are still as crazy as ever."

But she was just as fond of the crazy man.

"First we must stay here, then go to the country, and show everything to the children."

"It is my rule not to interfere in family matters," said[Pg 220] Márya Ivánovna, after calming down from her agitation, "and not to give advice. A young man has to serve, that I have always thought, and now more than ever. You do not know, Pierre, what these young men nowadays are. I know them all: there, Prince Dmítri's son is all ruined. Their own fault. I am not afraid of anybody, I am an old woman. It is not good." And she began to talk about the government. She was dissatisfied with it for the excessive liberty which was given to everything. "The one good thing they have done was to let you out. That is good."

Pierre began to defend it, but Márya Ivánovna was not Pákhtin: they could come to no terms. She grew excited.

"What business have you to defend it? You are just as senseless as ever, I see."

Peter Ivánovich grew silent, with a smile which showed that he did not surrender, but that he did not wish to quarrel with Márya Ivánovna.

"You are smiling. We know that. You do not wish to discuss with me, a woman," she, said, merrily and kindly, and casting a shrewd, intelligent glance at her brother, such as could not be expected from her old, large-featured face. "You could not convince me, my friend. I am ending my three score and ten. I have not been a fool all that time, and have seen a thing or two. I have read none of your books, and I never will. There is only nonsense in them!"

"Well, how do you like my children? Serézha?" Peter Ivánovich said, with the same smile.

"Wait, wait!" his sister replied, with a threatening gesture. "Don't switch me off on your children! We shall have time to talk about them. Here is what I wanted to tell you. You are a senseless man, as senseless as ever, I see it in your eye. Now they are going to carry you in their arms. Such is the fashion. You are all in vogue now. Yes, yes, I see by your eyes that you[Pg 221] are as senseless as ever," she added, in response to his smile. "Keep away, I implore you in the name of Jesus Christ our Lord, from those modern liberals. God knows what they are up to. I know it will not end well. Our government is silent just now, but when it comes later to showing up the nails, you will recall my words. I am afraid lest you should get mixed up in things again. Give it up! It is all nonsense. You have children."

"Evidently you do not know me, Márya Ivánovna," said her brother.

"All right, all right, we shall see. Either I do not know you, or you do not know yourself. I just told you what I had on my heart, and if you will listen to me, well and good. Now we can talk about Serézha. What kind of a lad is he?" She wanted to say, "I do not like him very much," but she only said: "He resembles his mother remarkably: they are like two drops of water. Sónya is you all over,—I like her very much, very much—so sweet and open. She is a dear. Where is she, Sónya? Yes, I forgot."

"How shall I tell you? Sónya will make a good wife and a good mother, but my Serézha is clever, very clever,—nobody will take that from him. He studied well,—a little lazy. He is very fond of the natural sciences. We have been fortunate: we had an excellent, excellent teacher. He wants to enter the university,—to attend lectures on the natural sciences, chemistry—"

Márya Ivánovna scarcely listened when her brother began to speak of the natural sciences. She seemed to feel sad, especially when he mentioned chemistry. She heaved a deep sigh and replied directly to that train of thoughts which the natural sciences evoked in her.

"If you knew how sorry I am for them, Pierre," she said, with sincere, calm, humble sadness. "So sorry, so sorry. A whole life before them. Oh, how much they will suffer yet!"

[Pg 222]

"Well, we must hope that they will be more fortunate than we."

"God grant it, God grant it! It is hard to live, Pierre! Take this one advice from me, my dear: don't philosophize! What a stupid you are, Pierre, oh, what a stupid! But I must attend to matters. I have invited a lot of people, but how am I going to feed them?" She flared up, turned away, and rang the bell.

"Call Tarás!"

"Is the old man still with you?"

"Yes; why, he is a boy in comparison with me."

Tarás was angry and clean, but he undertook to get everything done.

Soon Natálya Nikoláevna and Sónya, agleam with cold and happiness, and rustling in their dresses, entered the room; Serézha was still out, attending to some purchases.

"Let me get a good look at her!"

Márya Ivánovna took her face. Natálya Nikoláevna began to tell something.

[Pg 223]

THE DECEMBRISTS

SECOND FRAGMENT

(Variant of the First Chapter)

The litigation "about the seizure in the Government of Pénza, County of Krasnoslobódsk, by the landed proprietor and ex-lieutenant of the Guards, Iván Apýkhtin, of four thousand desyatínas of land from the neighbouring Crown peasants of the village of Izlegóshcha," was through the solicitude of the peasants' representative, Iván Mirónov, decided in the court of the first instance—the County Court—in favour of the peasants, and the enormous parcel of land, partly in forest, and partly in ploughings which had been broken by Apýkhtin's serfs, in the year 1815 returned into the possession of the peasants, and they in the year 1816 sowed in this land and harvested.

The winning of this irregular case by the peasants surprised all the neighbours and even the peasants themselves. This success of theirs could be explained only on the supposition that Iván Petróvich Apýkhtin, a very meek, peaceful man, who was opposed to litigations and was convinced of the righteousness of this matter, had taken no measures against the action of the peasants. On the other hand, Iván Mirónov, the peasants' representative, a dry, hook-nosed, literate peasant, who had been a township elder and had acted in the capacity of collector of taxes, had collected fifty kopeks from each peasant,[Pg 224] which money he cleverly applied in the distribution of presents, and had very shrewdly conducted the whole affair.

Immediately after the decision handed down by the County Court, Apýkhtin, seeing the danger, gave a power of attorney to the shrewd manumitted serf, Ilyá Mitrofánov, who appealed to the higher court against the decision of the County Court. Ilyá Mitrofánov managed the affair so shrewdly that, in spite of all the cunning of the peasants' representative, Iván Mirónov, in spite of the considerable presents distributed by him to the members of the higher court, the case was retried in the Government Court in favour of the proprietor, and the land was to go back to him from the peasants, of which fact their representative was duly informed.

The representative, Iván Mirónov, told the peasants at the meeting of the Commune that the gentleman in the Government capital had pulled the proprietor's leg and had "mixed up" the whole business, so that they wanted to take the land back again, but that the proprietor would not be successful, because he had a petition all written up to be sent to the Senate, and that then the land would be for ever confirmed to the peasants; all they had to do was to collect a rouble from each soul. The peasants decided to collect the money and again to entrust the whole matter to Iván Mirónov. When Mirónov had all the money in his hands, he went to St. Petersburg.

When, in the year 1817, during Passion-week,—it fell late that year,—the time came to plough the ground, the Izlegóshcha peasants began to discuss at a meeting whether they ought to plough the land under litigation during that year, or not; and, although Apýkhtin's clerk had come to see them during Lent with the order that they should not plough the land and should come to some agreement with him in regard to the rye already planted in what had been the doubtful, and now was Apýkhtin's[Pg 225] land, the peasants, for the very reason that the winter crop had been sowed on the debatable land, and because Apýkhtin, in his desire to avoid being unfair to them, wished to arbitrate the matter with them, decided to plough the land under litigation and to take possession of it before touching any other fields.

On the very day when the peasants went out to plough, which was Maundy Thursday, Iván Petróvich Apýkhtin, who had been preparing himself for communion during the Passion-week, went to communion, and early in the morning drove to the church in the village of Izlegóshcha, of which he was a parishioner, and there he, without knowing anything about the matter, amicably chatted with the church elder. Iván Petróvich had been to confession the night before, and had attended vigils at home; in the morning he had himself read the Rules, and at eight o'clock had left the house. They waited for him with the mass. As he stood at the altar, where he usually stood, Iván Petróvich rather reflected than prayed, which made him dissatisfied with himself.

Like many people of that time, and, so far as that goes, of all times, he was not quite clear in matters of religion. He was past fifty years of age; he never omitted carrying out any rite, attended church, and went to communion once a year; in talking to his only daughter, he instructed her in the articles of faith; but, if he had been asked whether he really believed, he would not have known what to reply.

On that day more than on any other, he felt meek of spirit, and, standing at the altar, he, instead of praying, thought of how strangely everything was constructed in the world: there he was, almost an old man, taking the communion for perhaps the fortieth time in his life, and he knew that everybody, all his home folk and all the people in the church, looked at him as a model and took him for an example, and he felt himself obliged to act as[Pg 226] an example in matters of religion, whereas he himself did not know anything, and soon, very soon, he would die, and even if he were killed he could not tell whether that in which he was showing an example to others was true. And it also seemed strange to him how every one considered—that he saw—old people to be firm and to know what was necessary and what not (thus he always thought about old men), and there he was old and positively failed to know, and was just as frivolous as he had been twenty years before; the only difference was that formerly he did not conceal it, while now he did. Just as in his childhood it had occurred to him during the service that he might crow like a cock, even so now all kinds of foolish things passed through his mind, and he, the old man, reverentially bent his head, touching the flagstones of the church with the old knuckles of his hands, and Father Vasíli was evidently timid in celebrating mass in his presence, and incited to zeal by his zeal.

"If they only knew what foolish things are running through my head! But that is a sin, a sin; I must pray," he said to himself, when the service commenced; and, trying to catch the meaning of the responses, he began to pray. Indeed, he soon transferred himself in feeling to the prayer and thought of his sins and of everything which he regretted.

A respectable-looking old man, bald-headed, with thick gray hair, dressed in a fur coat with a new white patch on one-half of his back, stepping evenly with his out-toeing bast shoes, went up to the altar, bowed low to him, tossed his hair, and went beyond the altar to place some tapers. This was the church elder, Iván Fedótov, one of the best peasants of the village of Izlegóshcha. Iván Petróvich knew him. The sight of this stern, firm face led Iván Petróvich to a new train of thoughts. He was one of those peasants who wanted to take the land away from him, and one of the best and richest married farmers,[Pg 227] who needed the land, who could manage it, and had the means to work it. His stern aspect, ceremonious bow, and measured gait, and the exactness of his wearing-apparel,—the leg-rags fitted his legs like stockings and the laces crossed each other symmetrically on either leg,—all his appearance seemed to express rebuke and enmity on account of the land.

"I have asked forgiveness of my wife, of Mánya" (his daughter), "of the nurse, of my valet, Volódya, but it is his forgiveness that I ought to ask for, and I ought to forgive him," thought Iván Petróvich, and he decided that after matins he would ask Iván Fedótov to forgive him.

And so he did.

There were but few people in church. The country people were in the habit of going to communion in the first and in the fourth week. Now there were only forty men and women present, who had not had time to go to communion before, a few old peasant women, the church servants, and the manorial people of the Apýkhtins and his rich neighbours, the Chernýshevs. There was also there an old woman, a relative of the Chernýshevs, who was living with them, and a deacon's widow, whose son the Chernýshevs, in the goodness of their hearts, had educated and made a man of, and who now was serving as an official in the Senate. Between the matins and the mass there were even fewer people left in the church. There were left two beggar women, who were sitting in the corner and conversing with each other and looking at Iván Petróvich with the evident desire to congratulate him and talk with him, and two lackeys,—one his own, in livery, and the other, Chernýshev's, who had come with the old woman. These two were also whispering in an animated manner to each other, just as Iván Petróvich came out from the altar-place; when they saw him,[Pg 228] they grew silent. There was also a woman in a tall head-gear with a pearl face-ornament and in a white fur coat, with which she covered up a sick child, who was crying, and whom she was attempting to quiet; and another, a stooping old woman, also in a head-gear, but with a woollen face-ornament and a white kerchief, which was tied in the fashion of old women, and in a gray gathered coat with an iris-design on the back, who, kneeling in the middle of the church, and turning to an old image between two latticed windows, over which hung a new scarf with red edges, was praying so fervently, solemnly, and impassionately that one could not fail directing one's attention to her.

Before reaching the elder, who, standing at the little safe, was kneading over the remnants of some tapers into one piece of wax, Iván Petróvich stopped to take a look at the praying woman. The old woman was praying well. She knelt as straight as it was possible to kneel in front of the image; all the members of her body were mathematically symmetrical; her feet behind her pressed with the tips of her bast shoes at the same angle against the stone floor; her body was bent back, to the extent to which her stooping shoulders permitted her to do so; her hands were quite regularly placed below her abdomen; her head was thrown back, and her face, with an expression of bashful commiseration, wrinkled, and with a dim glance, was turned straight toward the image with the scarf. Having remained in an immobile position for a minute or less,—evidently a definite space of time,—she heaved a deep sigh and, taking her right hand away, swung it above her head-gear, touched the crown of her head with folded fingers, and made ample crosses by carrying her hand down again to her abdomen and to her shoulders; then she swayed back and dropped her head on her hands, which were placed evenly on the floor, and again raised herself, and repeated the same.

[Pg 229]

"Now she is praying," Iván Petróvich thought, as he looked at her. "She does it differently from us sinners: this is faith, though I know that she is praying to her own image, or to her scarf, or to her adornment on the image, just like the rest of them. All right. What of it?" he said to himself, "every person has his own faith: she prays to her image, and I consider it necessary to beg the peasant's forgiveness."

And he walked over to the elder, instinctively scrutinizing the church in order to see who was going to see his deed, which both pleased and shamed him. It was disagreeable to him, because the old beggar women would see it, and more disagreeable still, because Míshka, his lackey, would see it. In the presence of Míshka,—he knew how wide-awake and shrewd he was,—he felt that he should not have the strength to walk up to Iván Fedótov. He beckoned to Míshka to come up to him.

"What is it you wish?"

"Go, my dear, and bring me the rug from the carriage, for it is too damp here for my feet."

"Yes, sir."

When Míshka went away, Iván Petróvich at once went up to Iván Fedótov. Iván Fedótov was disconcerted, like a guilty person, at the approach of the gentleman. Timidity and hasty motions formed a queer contradiction to his austere face and curly steel-gray hair and beard.

"Do you wish a dime taper?" he said, raising the desk, and now and then casting his large, beautiful eyes upon the master.

"No, I do not want a taper, Iván. I ask you to forgive me for Christ's sake, if I have in any way offended you. Forgive me, for Christ's sake," Iván Petróvich repeated, with a low bow.

Iván Fedótov completely lost his composure and began to move restlessly, but when he comprehended it all, he smiled a gentle smile:

[Pg 230]

"God forgives," he said. "It seems to me, I have received no offence from you. God will forgive you,—I have not been offended by you," he hastened to repeat.

"Still—"

"God will forgive you, Iván Petróvich. So you want two dime tapers?"

"Yes, two."

"He is an angel, truly, an angel. He begs even a base peasant to forgive him. O Lord, true angels," muttered the deacon's widow, in an old black capote and black kerchief. "Truly, we ought to understand that."

"Ah, Paramónovna!" Iván Petróvich turned to her. "Are you getting ready for communion, too? You, too, must forgive me, for Christ's sake."

"God will forgive you, sir, angel, merciful benefactor! Let me kiss your hand!"

"That will do, that will do, you know I do not like that," said Iván Petróvich, smiling, and going away from the altar.

The mass, as always, did not take long to celebrate in the parish of Izlegóshcha, the more so since there were few communicants. Just as, after the Lord's Prayer, the regal doors were closed, Iván Petróvich looked through the north door, to call Míshka to take off his fur coat. When the priest saw that motion, he angrily beckoned to the deacon, and the deacon almost ran out to call in the lackey. Iván Petróvich was in a pretty good humour, but this subserviency and expression of respect from the priest who was celebrating mass again soured him entirely; his thin, bent, shaven lips were bent still more and his kindly eyes were lighted up by sarcasm.

"He acts as though I were his general," he thought, and immediately he thought of the words of the German tutor, whom he had once taken to the altar to attend a[Pg 231] Russian divine service, and who had made him laugh and had angered his wife, when he said, "*Der Pop war ganz böse, dass ich ihm Alles nachgesehen hatte.*" He also recalled the answer of the young Turk that there was no God, because he had eaten up the last piece of him. "And here I am going to communion," he thought, and, frowning, he made a low obeisance.

He took off his bear-fur coat, and in his blue dress coat with bright buttons and in his tall white neckerchief and waistcoat, and tightly fitting trousers, and heelless, sharp-toed boots, went with his soft, modest, and light gait to make his obeisances to the large images. Here he again met that same obsequiousness from the other communicants, who gave up their places to him.

"They act as though they said, '*Après vous, s'il en reste,*'" he thought, awkwardly making side obeisances; this awkwardness was due to the fact that he was trying to find that mean in which there would be neither disrespect, nor hypocrisy. Finally the doors were opened. He said the prayer after the priest, repeating the words, "As a robber;" his neckerchief was covered with the chalice cloth, and he received his communion and the lukewarm water in the ancient dipper, having put new silver twenty-kopek pieces on ancient plates; after hearing the last prayers, he kissed the cross and, putting on his fur coat left the church, receiving congratulations and experiencing the pleasant sensation of having everything over. As he left the church, he again fell in with Iván Fedótov.

"Thank you, thank you!" he replied to his congratulations. "Well, are you going to plough soon?"

"The boys have gone out, the boys have," replied Iván Fedótov, more timidly even than before. He supposed that Iván Petróvich knew whither the Izlegóshcha peasants had gone out to plough. "It is damp, though. Damp it is. It is early yet, early it is."

Iván Petróvich went up to his parents' monument,[Pg 232] bowed to it, and went back to be helped into his six-in-hand with an outrider.

"Well, thank God," he said to himself, swaying on the soft, round springs and looking at the vernal sky with the scattering clouds, at the bared earth and the white spots of unmelted snow, and at the tightly braided tail of a side horse, and inhaling the fresh spring air, which was particularly pleasant after the air in the church.

"Thank God that I have been through the communion, and thank God that I now may take a pinch of snuff." And he took out his snuff-box and for a long time held the pinch between his fingers, smiling and, without letting the pinch out of the hand, raising his cap in response to the low bows of the people on the way, especially of the women, who were washing the tables and chairs in front of their houses, just as the carriage at a fast trot of the large horses of the six-in-hand plashed and clattered through the mud of the street of the village of Izlegóshcha.

Iván Petróvich held the pinch of snuff, anticipating the pleasure of snuffing, not only down the whole village, but even until they got out of a bad place at the foot of a hill, toward which the coachman descended not without anxiety: he held up the reins, seated himself more firmly, and shouted to the outrider to go over the ice. When they went around the bridge, over the bed of the river, and scrambled out of the breaking ice and mud, Iván Petróvich, looking at two plovers that rose from the hollow, took the snuff and, feeling chilly, put on his glove, wrapped himself in his fur coat, plunged his chin into the high neckerchief, and said to himself, almost aloud, "Glorious!" which he was in the habit of saying secretly to himself whenever he felt well.

In the night snow had fallen, and when Iván Petróvich had driven to church the snow had not yet disappeared, but was soft; now, though there was no sun, it was[Pg 233] all melted from the moisture, and on the highway, on which he had to travel for three versts before turning into Chirakóvo, the snow was white only in last year's grass, which grew in parallel lines along the ruts; but on the black road the horses splashed through the viscous mud. The good, well-fed, large horses of his own stud had no difficulty in pulling the carriage, and it just rolled over the grass, where it left black marks, and over the mud, without being at all detained. Iván Petróvich was having pleasant reveries; he was thinking of his home, his wife, and his daughter.

"Mánya will meet me at the porch, and with delight. She will see such holiness in me! She is a strange, sweet girl, but she takes everything too much to heart. The rôle of importance and of knowing everything that is going on in this world, which I must play before her, is getting to be too serious and ridiculous. If she knew that I am afraid of her!" he thought. "Well, Káto," (his wife) "will no doubt be in good humour to-day, she will purposely be in good humour, and we shall have a fine day. It will not be as it was last week on account of the Próshkin women. What a remarkable creature! How afraid of her I am! What is to be done? She does not like it herself." And he recalled a famous anecdote about a calf. A proprietor, having quarrelled with his wife, was sitting at a window, when he saw a frisky calf: "I should like to get you married!" he said. And Iván Petróvich smiled again, according to his custom solving every difficulty and every perplexity by a joke, which generally was directed against himself.

At the third verst, near a chapel, the outrider bore to the left, into a cross-road, and the coachman shouted to him for having turned in so abruptly that the centre horses were struck by the shaft; and the carriage almost glided all the way down-hill. Before reaching the house, the outrider looked back at the coachman and pointed to[Pg 234] something; the coachman looked back at the lackey, and indicated something to him. And all of them looked in the same direction.

"What are you looking at?" asked Iván Petróvich.

"Geese," said Míshka.

"Where?"

Though he strained his vision, he could not see them.

"There they are. There is the forest, and there is the cloud, so be pleased to look between the two."

Iván Petróvich could not see anything.

"It is time for them. Why, it is less than a week to Annunciation."

"That's so."

"Well, go on!"

Near a puddle, Míshka jumped down from the footboard and tested the road, again climbed up, and the carriage safely drove on the pond dam in the garden, ascended the avenue, drove past the cellar and the laundry, from which water was falling, and nimbly rolled up and stopped at the porch. The Chernýshev calash had just left the yard. From the house at once ran the servants: gloomy old Danílych with the side whiskers, Nikoláy, Míshka's brother, and the boy Pavlúshka; and after them came a girl with large black eyes and red arms, which were bared above the elbow, and with just such a bared neck.

"Márya Ivánovna, Márya Ivánovna! Where are you going? Your mother will be worried. You will have time," was heard the voice of fat Katerína behind her.

But the girl paid no attention to her; just as her father had expected her to do, she took hold of his arm and looked at him with a strange glance.

"Well, papa, have you been to communion?" she asked, as though in dread.

"Yes. You look as though you were afraid that I am such a sinner that I could not receive the communion."

[Pg 235]

The girl was apparently offended by her father's jest at such a solemn moment. She heaved a sigh and, following him, held his hand, which she kissed.

"Who is here?"

"Young Chernýshev. He is in the drawing-room."

"Is mamma up? How is she?"

"Mamma feels better to-day. She is sitting down-stairs."

In the passage room Iván Petróvich was met by nurse Evprakséya, clerk Andréy Ivánovich, and a surveyor, who was living at the house, in order to lay out some land. All of them congratulated Iván Petróvich. In the drawing-room sat Luíza Kárlovna Trugóni, for ten years a friend of the house, an emigrant governess, and a young man of sixteen years, Chernýshev, with his French tutor.

[Pg 236]

THE DECEMBRISTS

THIRD FRAGMENT

(Variant of the First Chapter)

On the 2d of August, 1817, the sixth department of the Directing Senate handed down a decision in the debatable land case between the economic peasants of the village of Izlegóshcha and Chernýshev, which was in favour of the peasants and against Chernýshev. This decision was an unexpected and important calamitous event for Chernýshev. The case had lasted five years. It had been begun by the attorney of the rich village of Izlegóshcha with its three thousand inhabitants, and was won by the peasants in the County Court; but when, with the advice of lawyer Ilyá Mitrofánov, a manorial servant bought of Prince Saltykóv, Prince Chernýshev carried the case to the Government, he won it and besides, the Izlegóshcha peasants were punished by having six of them, who had insulted the surveyor, put in jail.

After that, Prince Chernýshev, with his good-natured and merry carelessness, entirely acquiesced, the more so since he knew full well that he had not "appropriated" any land of the peasants, as was said in the petition of the peasants. If the land was "appropriated," his father had done it, and since then more than forty years had passed. He knew that the peasants of the village of[Pg 237]Izlegóshcha were getting along well without that land, had no need of it, and lived on terms of friendship with him, and was unable to understand why they had become so infuriated against him. He knew that he never offended and never wished to offend any one, that he lived in peace with everybody, and that he never wished to do otherwise, and so could not believe that any one should think of offending him. He hated litigations, and so did not defend his case in the Senate, in spite of the advice and earnest solicitations of his lawyer, Ilyá Mitrofánov; by allowing the time for the appeal to lapse, he lost the case in the Senate, and lost it in such a way that he was confronted with complete ruin. By the decree of the Senate he not only was to be deprived of five thousand desyatínas of land, but also, for the illegal tenure of that land, was to be mulcted to the amount of 107,000 roubles in favour of the peasants.

Prince Chernýshev had eight thousand souls, but all the estates were mortgaged and he had large debts, so that this decree of the Senate ruined him with his whole large family. He had a son and five daughters. He thought of his case when it was too late to attend to it in the Senate. According to Ilyá Mitrofánov's words there was but one salvation, and that was, to petition the sovereign and to transfer the case to the Imperial Council. To obtain this it was necessary in person to approach one of the ministers or a member of the Council, or, better still, the emperor himself. Taking all that into consideration, Prince Grigóri Ivánovich in the fall of the year 1817 with his whole family left his beloved estate of Studénets, where he had lived so long without leaving it, and went to Moscow. He started for Moscow, and not for St. Petersburg, because in the fall of that year the emperor with his whole court, with all the highest dignitaries, and with part of the Guards, in which the son of Grigóri Ivánovich was serving, was to arrive in Moscow to lay the corner-stone[Pg 238] of the Church of the Saviour in commemoration of the liberation of Russia from the French invasion.

In August, immediately after receiving the terrible news of the decree of the Senate, Prince Grigóri Ivánovich got ready to go to Moscow. At first the majordomo was sent away to fix the prince's own house on the Arbát; then was sent out a caravan with furniture, servants, horses, carriages, and provisions. In September the prince with his whole family travelled in seven carriages, drawn by his own horses, and, after arriving in Moscow, settled in his house. Relatives, friends, visitors from the province and from St. Petersburg began to assemble in Moscow in the month of September. The Moscow life, with its entertainments, the arrival of his son, the débuts of his daughters, and the success of his eldest daughter, Aleksándra, the only blonde among all the brunettes of the Chernýshevs, so much occupied and diverted the prince's attention that, in spite of the fact that here in Moscow he was spending everything which would be left to him after paying all he owed, he forgot his affair and was annoyed and tired whenever Ilyá Mitrofánov talked of it, and undertook nothing for the success of his case.

Iván Mirónovich Baúshkin, the chief attorney of the peasants, who had conducted the case against the prince with so much zeal in the Senate, who knew all the approaches to the secretaries and departmental chiefs, and who had so skilfully distributed the ten thousand roubles, collected from the peasants, in the shape of presents, now himself brought his activity to an end and returned to the village, where, with the money collected for him as a reward and with what was left of the presents, he bought himself a grove from a neighbouring proprietor and built there a hut and an office. The case was finished in the court of the highest instance, and everything would now proceed of its own accord.

The only ones of those concerned in the case who could[Pg 239] not forget it were the six peasants who were passing their seventh month in jail, and their families that were left without their heads. But nothing could be done in the matter. They were imprisoned in Krasnoslobódsk, and their families tried to get along as well as they could. Nobody could be invoked in the case. Iván Mirónovich himself said that he could not take it up, because it was not a communal, nor a civil, but a criminal case. The peasants were in prison, and nobody paid any attention to them; but one family, that of Mikhaíl Gerásimovich, particularly his wife Tíkhonovna, could not get used to the idea that the precious old man, Gerásimovich, was sitting in prison with a shaven head. Tíkhonovna could not rest quiet. She begged

Mirónovich to take the case, but he declined it. Then she decided to go herself to pray to God for the old man. She had made a vow the year before that she would go on a pilgrimage to a saint, and had delayed it for another year only because she had had no time and did not wish to leave the house to the young daughters-in-law. Now that the misfortune had happened and Gerásimovich was put into jail, she recalled her vow; she turned her back on her house and, together with the deacon's wife of the same village, got ready to go on the pilgrimage.

First they went to the county seat to see her old man in the prison and to take him some shirts; from there they went through the capital of the Government to Moscow. On her way Tíkhonovna told the deacon's wife of her sorrow, and the latter advised her to petition the emperor who, it was said, was to be in Pénza, telling her of various cases of pardon granted by him.

When the pilgrims arrived in Pénza, they heard that there was there, not the emperor, but his brother Grand Duke Nikoláy Pávlovich. When he came out of the cathedral, Tíkhonovna pushed herself forward, dropped down on her knees, and began to beg for her husband.[Pg 240] The grand duke was surprised, the governor was angry, and the old woman was taken to the lockup. The next day she was let out and she proceeded to Tróitsa. In Tróitsa she went to communion and confessed to Father Paísi. At the confession she told him of her sorrow, and repented having petitioned the brother of the Tsar. Father Paísi told her that there was no sin in that and that there was no sin in petitioning the Tsar even in a just case, and dismissed her. In Khótkov she called on the blessed abbess, and she ordered her to petition the Tsar himself.

On their way back, Tíkhonovna and the deacon's wife stopped in Moscow to see the saints. Here she heard that the Tsar was there, and she thought that it was evidently God's command that she should petition the Tsar. All that had to be done was to write the petition.

In Moscow the pilgrims stopped in a hostelry. They begged permission to stay there overnight; they were allowed to do so. After supper the deacon's wife lay down on the oven, and Tíkhonovna, placing her wallet under her head, lay down on a bench and fell asleep. In the morning, before daybreak, Tíkhonovna got up, woke the deacon's wife, and went out. The innkeeper spoke to her just as she walked into the yard.

"You are up early, granny," he said.

"Before we get there, it will be time for matins," Tíkhonovna replied.

"God be with you, granny!"

"Christ save you!" said Tíkhonovna, and the pilgrims went to the Kremlin.

After standing through the matins and the mass, and having kissed the relics, the old women, with difficulty making their way, arrived at the house of the Chernýshevs. The deacon's wife said that the old lady had[Pg 241] given her an urgent invitation to stop at her house, and had ordered that all pilgrims should be received.

"There we shall find a man who will write the petition," said the deacon's wife, and the pilgrims started to blunder through the streets and ask their way. The deacon's wife had been there before, but had forgotten where it was. Two or three times they were almost crushed, and people shouted at them and scolded them. Once a policeman took the deacon's wife by the shoulder and, giving her a push, forbade her to walk through the street on which they were, and directed them through a forest of lanes. Tíkhonovna did not know that they were driven off the Vozdvízhenka for the very reason that through that street was to drive the Tsar, of whom she was thinking all the time, and to whom she intended to give the petition.

The deacon's wife walked, as always, heavily and complainingly, while Tíkhonovna, as usual, walked lightly and briskly, with the gait of a young woman. At the gate the pilgrims stopped. The deacon's wife did not recognize the house: there was there a new hut which she had not seen before; but on scanning the well with the pumps in the corner of the yard, she recognized it all. The dogs began to bark and made for the women with the staffs.

"Don't mind them, aunties, they will not touch you. Away there, accursed ones!" the janitor shouted to the dogs, raising the broom on them. "They are themselves from the country, and just see them bark at country people! Come this way! You will stick in the mud,—God has not given any frost yet."

But the deacon's wife, frightened by the dogs, and muttering in a whining tone, sat down on a bench near the gate and asked the janitor to take her by. Tíkhonovna made her customary bow to the janitor and, leaning on her crutch and spreading her feet, which were tightly covered[Pg 242] with leg-rags, stopped near her, looking as always calmly in front of her and waiting for the janitor to come up to them.

"Whom do you want?" the janitor asked.

"Do you not recognize us, dear man? Is not your name Egór?" asked the deacon's wife. "We are coming back from the saints, and so are calling on her Serenity."

"You are from Izlegóshcha," said the janitor. "You are the wife of the old deacon,—of course. All right, all right. Go to the house! Everybody is received here,—nobody is refused. And who is this one?"

He pointed to Tíkhonovna.

"From Izlegóshcha, Gerásimovich's wife,—used to be Fadyéev's,—I suppose you know her?" said Tíkhonovna. "I myself am from Izlegóshcha."

"Of course! They say your husband has been put into jail."

Tíkhonovna made no reply; she only sighed and with a strong motion threw her wallet and fur coat over her shoulder.

The deacon's wife asked whether the old lady was at home and, hearing that she was, asked him to announce them to her. Then she asked about her son, who was an official and, thanks to the prince's influence, was serving in St. Petersburg. The janitor could not give her any information about him and directed them over a walk, which crossed the yard, to the servants' house. The old women went into the house, which was full of people,—women, children, both old and young,—all of them manorial servants, and prayed turning to the front corner. The deacon's wife was at once recognized by the laundress and the old lady's maid, and she was at once surrounded and overwhelmed with questions: they took off her wallet, placed her at the table, and offered her something to eat. In the meantime Tíkhonovna, having made the sign of the cross to the images and saluted[Pg 243] everybody, was standing at the door, waiting to be invited in. At the very door, in front of the first window, sat an old man, making boots.

"Sit down, granny! Don't stand up. Sit down here, and take off your wallet," he said.

"There is not enough room to turn around as it is. Take her to the 'black' room," said a woman.

"This comes straight from Madame Chalmé," said a young lackey, pointing to the iris design on Tíkhonovna's peasant coat, "and the pretty stockings and shoes."

He pointed to her leg-rags and bast shoes, which were new, as she had specially put them on for Moscow.

"Parásha, you ought to have such."

"If you are to go to the 'black' room, all right; I will take you there." And the old man stuck in his awl and got up; but, on seeing a little girl, he called her to take the old woman to the black room.

Tíkhonovna not only paid no attention to what was being said in her presence and of her, but did not even look or listen. From the time that she entered the house, she was permeated with the feeling of the necessity of working for God and with the other feeling, which had entered her soul, she did not know when, of the necessity of handing the petition. Leaving the clean servant room, she walked over to the deacon's wife and, bowing, said to her:

"Mother Paramónovna, for Christ's sake do not forget about my affair! See whether you can't find a man."

"What does that woman need?"

"She has suffered insult, and people have advised her to hand a petition to the Tsar."

"Take her straight to the Tsar!" said the jesting lackey.

"Oh, you fool, you rough fool," said the old shoemaker. "I will teach you a lesson with this last, then you will know how to grin at old people."

[Pg 244]

The lackey began to scold, but the old man, paying no attention to him, took Tíkhonovna to the black room.

Tíkhonovna was glad that she was sent out of the baking-room, and was taken to the black, the coachmen's room. In the baking-room everything looked clean, and the people were all clean, and Tíkhonovna did not feel at ease there. The black coachmen's room was more like the inside of a peasant house, and Tíkhonovna was more at home there. The black hut was a dark pine building, twenty by twenty feet, with a large oven, bed places, and hanging-beds, and a newly paved, dirt-covered floor. When Tíkhonovna entered the room, there were there the cook, a white, ruddy-faced, fat, manorial woman, with the sleeves of her chintz dress rolled up, who with difficulty was moving a pot in the oven with an oven-fork; then a young, small coachman, who was learning to play the balaláyka; an old man with an unshaven, soft white beard, who was sitting on a bed place with his bare feet and, holding a skein of silk between his lips, was sewing on some fine, good material, and a shaggy-haired, swarthy young man, in a shirt and blue trousers, with a coarse face, who, chewing bread, was sitting on a bench at the oven and leaning his head on both his arms, which were steadied against his knees.

Barefoot Nástka with sparkling eyes ran into the room with her lithe, bare feet, in front of the old woman, jerking open the door, which stuck fast from the steam within, and squeaking in her thin voice:

"Aunty Marína, Simónych sends this old woman, and says that she should be fed. She is from our parts: she has been with Paramónovna to worship the saints. Paramónovna is having tea.—Vlásevna has sent for her—"

The garrulous little girl would have gone on talking for quite awhile yet; the words just poured forth from her and, apparently, it gave her pleasure to hear her own voice. But Marína, who was in a perspiration, and who[Pg 245] had not yet succeeded in pushing away the pot with the beet soup, which had caught in the hearth, shouted angrily at her:

"Stop your babbling! What old woman am I to feed now? I have enough to do to feed our own people. Shoot you!" she shouted to the pot, which came very near falling down, as she removed it from the spot where it was caught.

But when she was satisfied in regard to the pot, she looked around and, seeing trim Tíkhonovna with her wallet and correct peasant attire, making the sign of the cross and bowing low toward the front corner, felt ashamed of her words and, as though regaining her consciousness after the cares which had worn her out, she put her hand to her breast, where beneath the collar-bone buttons clasped her dress, and examined it to see whether it was buttoned, and then put her hands to her head to fasten the knot of the kerchief, which covered her greasy hair, and took up an attitude, leaning against the oven-fork and waiting for the salute of the trim old woman. Tíkhonovna made her last low obeisance to God, and turned around and saluted in three directions.

"God aid you, good day!" she said.

"You are welcome, aunty!" said the tailor.

"Thank you, granny, take off your wallet! Sit down here," said the cook, pointing to a bench where sat the shaggy-haired man. "Move a little, can't you? Are you stuck fast?"

The shaggy man, scowling more angrily still, rose, moved away, and, continuing to chew, riveted his eyes on the old woman. The young coachman made a bow and, stopping his playing, began to tighten the strings of his balaláyka, looking now at the old woman, and now at the tailor, not knowing how to treat the old woman,—whether respectfully, as he thought she ought to be treated, because the old woman wore the same kind[Pg 246] of attire that his grandmother and mother wore at home (he had been taken from the village to be an outrider), or making fun of her, as he wished to do and as seemed to him to accord with his present condition, his blue coat and his boots. The tailor winked with one eye and seemed to smile, drawing the silk to one side of his mouth, and looked on. Marína started to put in another pot, but, even though she was busy working, she kept looking at the old woman, while she briskly and nimbly took off her wallet and, trying not to disturb any one, put it under the bench. Nástka ran up to her and helped her, by taking away the boots, which were lying in her way under the bench.

"Uncle Pankrát," she turned to the gloomy man, "I will put the boots here. Is it all right?"

"The devil take them! Throw them into the oven, if you wish," said the gloomy man, throwing them into another corner.

"Nástka, you are a clever girl," said the tailor. "A pilgrim has to be made comfortable."

"Christ save you, girl! That is nice," said Tíkhonovna. "I am afraid I have put you out, dear man," she said, turning to Pankrát.

"All right," said Pankrát.

Tíkhonovna sat down on the bench, having taken off her coat and carefully folded it, and began to take off her footgear. At first she untied the laces, which she had taken special care in twisting smooth for her pilgrimage; then she carefully unwrapped the white lambskin leg-rags and, carefully rubbing them soft, placed them on her wallet. Just as she was working on her other foot, another of awkward Marína's pots got caught and spilled over, and she again started to scold somebody, catching the pot with the fork.

"The hearth is evidently burned out, grandfather. It ought to be plastered," said Tíkhonovna.

[Pg 247]

"When are you going to plaster it? The chimney never cools off: twice a day you have to bake bread; one set is taken out, and the other is started."

In response to Marína's complaint about the bread-baking and the burnt-out hearth, the tailor defended the ways of the Chernýshev house and said that they had suddenly arrived in Moscow, that the hut was built and the oven put up in three weeks, and that there were nearly one hundred servants who had to be fed.

"Of course, lots of cares. A large establishment," Tíkhonovna confirmed him.

"Whence does God bring you?" the tailor turned to her.

And Tíkhonovna, continuing to take off her foot-gear, at once told him where she came from, whither she had gone, and how she was going home. She did not say anything about the petition. The conversation never broke off. The tailor found out everything about the old woman, and the old woman heard all about awkward, pretty Marína. She learned that Marína's husband was a soldier, and she was made a cook; that the tailor was making caftans for the driving coachmen; that the stewardess's errand girl was an orphan, and that shaggy-haired, gloomy Pankrát was a servant of the clerk, Iván Vasílevich.

Pankrát left the room, slamming the door. The tailor told her that he was a gruff peasant, but that on that day he was particularly rude because the day before he had smashed the clerk's knickknacks on the window, and that he was going to be flogged to-day in the stable. As soon as Iván Vasílevich should come, he would be flogged. The little coachman was a peasant lad, who had been made an outrider, and now that he was grown he had nothing to do but attend to the horses, and strum the balaláyka. But he was not much of a hand at it.

[Pg 248]
[Pg 249]

## ON POPULAR EDUCATION
### 1875

[Pg 250]
[Pg 251]

ON POPULAR EDUCATION

I suppose each of us has had more than one occasion to come in contact with monstrous, senseless phenomena, and to find back of these phenomena put forward some important principle, which overshadowed those phenomena, so that in our youthful and even maturer years we began to doubt whether it was true that those phenomena were monstrous, and whether we were not mistaken. And having been unable to convince ourselves that monstrous phenomena might be good, or that the protection of an important principle was illegitimate, or that the principle was only a word, we remained in regard to those phenomena in an ambiguous, undecided condition.

In such a state I was, and I assume many of us are, in respect to the principle of "development" which obfuscates pedagogy, in its connection with the rudiments. But popular education is too near to my heart, and I have busied myself too much with it, to remain too long in indecision. The monstrous phenomena of the imaginary development I could not call good, nor could I be persuaded that the development of the pupil was bad, and so I began to inquire what that development was. I do not consider it superfluous to communicate the deductions to which I have been led during the study of this matter.

To define what is understood by the word "development," I shall take the manuals of Messrs. Bunákov and|Pg 252| Evtushévski, as being new works, which combine all the latest deductions of German pedagogy, intended as guides for the teachers in the popular schools, and selected by the advocates of the sound method as manuals in their schools.

In discussing what is to form the foundation for a choice of this or that method for the teaching of reading, Mr. Bunákov says:

"No, an opinion about the method of construction based on such near-sighted and flimsy foundations (that is, on experience) will be too doubtful. Only the theoretical substratum, based on the study of human nature, can make the judgments in this sphere firm and independent of all casualties, and to a considerable degree guard them against gross errors. Consequently for the final choice of the best method of teaching the rudiments, it is necessary first of all to stand on theoretic soil, on the basis of previous considerations, the general conditions of which give to this or that method the actual right to be called satisfactory from the pedagogical standpoint. These conditions are: (1) It has to be a method which is capable of developing the child's mental powers, so that the acquisition of the rudiments may be obtained together with the development and the strengthening of the reasoning powers. (2) It must introduce into the instruction the child's personal interest, so that the matter be furthered by this interest, and not by dulling violence. (3) It must represent in itself the process of self-instruction, inciting, supporting, and directing the child's self-activity. (4) It must be based on the impressions of hearing, as of the sense which serves for the acquisition of language. (5) It has to combine analysis with synthesis, beginning with the dismemberment of the complex whole into simple principles, and passing over to the composition of a complex whole out of the simple principles."

So this is what the method of instruction is to be based|Pg 253| upon. I will remark, not for contradiction, but for the sake of simplicity and clearness, that the last two statements are quite superfluous, because without the union of analysis and synthesis there can be not only no instruction, but also no other activity of the mind, and every instruction, except that of the deaf and dumb, is based on the sense of hearing. These two conditions are put down only for beauty's sake and for the obscuration of the style, so common in pedagogical treatises, and so have no meaning whatever. The first three at first sight appear quite true as a programme. Everybody, of course, would like to know how the method is secured that will "develop," that will "introduce into the instruction the pupil's personal interest," and that will "represent the process of self-instruction."

But to the questions as to why this method combines all those qualities you will find an answer neither in the books of Messrs. Bunákov and Evtushévski, nor in any other pedagogical work of the founders of this school of pedagogy, unless they be those hazy discussions of this nature, such as that every instruction must be based on the union of analysis and synthesis, and by all means on the sense of hearing, and so forth; or you will find, as in Mr. Evtushévski's book, expositions about how in man are formed impressions, sensations, representations, and concepts, and you will find the rule that "it is necessary to start from the object and lead the pupil up to the idea, and not start with the idea, which has no point of contact in his consciousness," and so forth. After such discussions there always follows the conclusion that therefore the method advocated by the pedagogue gives that exclusive real development which it was necessary to find.

After the above-cited definition of what a good method ought to be, Mr. Bunákov explains how children ought to be educated, and, having given an exposition of all the methods, which in my opinion and experience lead to|Pg 254| results which are diametrically opposite to development, he says frankly and definitely:

"From the standpoint of the above-mentioned fundamental principles for estimating the value of the satisfactoriness of the methods of rudimentary instruction, the method which we have just elucidated in its general features presents the following plastic qualities and peculiarities: (1) As a sound method it wholly preserves the characteristic peculiarities of all sound method,—it starts from the impressions of hearing, at once establishing the regular relation to language, and only later adds to them the impressions of sight, thus clearly distinguishing sound, matter, and the letter, its representation. (2) As a method which unites reading with writing it begins with decomposition and passes over to composition, combining analysis with synthesis. (3) As a method which passes over to the study of words and sounds from the study of objects it proceeds along a natural path, coöperates with the regular formation of concepts and ideas, and acts in a developing way on all the sides of the child's nature: it incites the children to be observant, to group their observations, to render them orally; it develops the external senses, mind, imagination, memory, the gift of speech, concentration, self-activity, the habit of work, the respect for order. (4) As a method which provides ample work to all the mental powers of the child, it introduces into instruction the personal interest, rousing in children willingness and love of work, and transforming it into a process of self-instruction."

This is precisely what Mr. Evtushévski does; but why it is all so remains inexplicable to him who is looking for actual reasons and does not become entangled in such words as psychology, didactics, methodics, heuristics. I advise all those who have no inclination for philosophy and therefore have no desire to verify all those deductions of the pedagogues not to be embarrassed by these words[Pg 255] and to be assured that a thing which is not clear cannot be the basis of anything, least of all of such an important and simple thing as popular education.

All the pedagogues of this school, especially the Germans, the founders of the school, start with the false idea that those philosophical questions which have remained as questions for all the philosophers from Plato to Kant, have been definitely settled by them. They are settled so definitely that the process of the acquisition by man of impressions, sensations, concepts, ratiocinations, has been analyzed by them down to its minutest details, and the component parts of what we call the soul or the essence of man have been dissected and divided into parts by them, and that, too, in such a thorough manner that on this firm basis can go up the faultless structure of the science of pedagogy. This fancy is so strange that I do not regard it as necessary to contradict it, more especially as I have done so in my former pedagogical essays. All I will say is that those philosophical considerations which the pedagogues of this school put at the basis of their theory not only fail to be absolutely correct, not only have nothing in common with real philosophy, but even lack a clear, definite expression with which the majority of the pedagogues might agree.

But, perchance, the theory of the pedagogues of the new school, in spite of its unsuccessful references to philosophy, has some value in itself. And so we will examine it, to see what it consists in. Mr. Bunákov says:

"To these little savages (that is, the pupils) must be imparted the main order of school instruction, and into their consciousness must be introduced such initial concepts as they will have to come in contact with from the start, during the first lessons of drawing, reading, writing, and every elementary instruction, such as: the right side and the left, to the right—to the left, up—down, near by—around, in front—in back, close by—in[Pg 256] the distance, before—behind, above—below, fast—slow, softly—aloud, and so forth. No matter how simple these concepts may be, I know from practice that even city children, from well-to-do families, are frequently, when they come to the elementary schools, unable to distinguish the right side from the left. I assume that there is no need of expatiating on the necessity of explaining such concepts to village children, for any one who has had to deal with village schools knows this as well as I do."

And Mr. Evtushévski says:

"Without entering into the broad field of the debatable question about the innate ability of man, we only see that the child can have no innate concepts and ideas about real things,—they have to be formed, and on the skill with which they are formed by the educator and teacher depends both their regularity and their permanency. In watching the development of the child's soul one has to be much more cautious than in attending to his body. If the food for the body and the various bodily exercises are carefully chosen both as regards their quantity and their quality, in conformity with the man's growth, so much more cautious have we to be in the choice of food and exercises for the mind. A badly placed foundation will precariously support what is fastened to it."

Mr. Bunákov advises that ideas be imparted as follows:

"The teacher may begin a conversation such as he deems fit: one will ask every pupil for his name; another about what is going on outside; a third about where each comes from, where he lives, what is going on at home,—and then he may pass over to the main subject. 'Where are you sitting now? Why did you come here? What are we going to do in this room? Yes, we are going to study in this room,—so let us call it a class-room. See what there is under your feet, below you. Look, but do not say anything. The one I will tell to speak shall answer. Tell me, what do you see under your feet? Repeat[Pg 257] everything we have found out and have said about this room: in what room are we sitting? What are the parts of the room? What is there on the walls? What is standing on the floor?'

"The teacher from the start establishes the order which is necessary for the success of his work: each pupil is to answer only when asked to do so; all the others are to listen and should be able to repeat the words of the teacher and of their companions; the desire to answer, when the teacher directs a question to everybody, is to be expressed by raising the left hand; the words are to be pronounced neither in a hurry, nor by drawing them out, but loudly, distinctly, and correctly. To obtain this latter result the teacher gives them a living example by his loud, correct, distinct enunciation, showing them in practice the difference between soft and loud, distinct and correct, slow and fast. The teacher should see to it that all the children take part in the work, by having somebody's question answered or repeated, now by one, now by another, and now by the whole class at once, but especially by rousing the indifferent, inattentive, and playful children: the first he must enliven by frequent questions, the second he must cause to concentrate themselves on the subject of the common work, and the third he must curb. During the first period the children ought to answer in full, that is, by repeating the question: 'We are sitting in the class-room' (and not in brief, 'In the class-room'); 'Above, over my head, I see the ceiling;' 'On the left I see three windows,' and so forth."

Mr. Evtushévski advises that in this way be begun all the lessons on numbers from 1 to 10, of which there are to be 120, and which are to be continued through the year.

"One. The teacher shows the pupils a cube, and asks: 'How many cubes have I?' and taking several cubes into the other hand, he asks, 'And how many are there here?'—'Many, a few.'

[Pg 258]

"'Name here in the class-room an object of which there are several.'—'Bench, window, wall, copy-book, pencil, slate-pencil, pupil, and so forth.'—'Name an object of which there is only one in the class-room.'—'The blackboard, stove, door, ceiling, floor, picture, teacher, and so forth.'—'If I put this cube away in my pocket, how many cubes will there be left in my hand?'—'Not one.'—'And how many must I again put into my hand, to have as many as before?'—'One.'—'What is meant by saying that Pétya fell down once? How many times did Pétya fall? Did he fall another time? Why does it say once?'—'Because we are speaking only of one case and not of another case.'—'Take your slates (or copy-books). Make on them a line of this size.' (The teacher draws on the blackboard a line two or four inches in length, or shows on the ruler that length.) 'Rub it off. How many lines are left?'—'Not one.'—'Draw several such lines.' It would be unnatural to invent any other exercises in order to acquaint the children with number one. It suffices to rouse in them that conception of unity which they, no doubt, had previous to their school instruction."

Then Mr. Bunákov speaks of exercises on the board, and so on, and Mr. Evtushévski of the number four with its decomposition. Before examining the theory itself of the transmission of ideas, the question involuntarily arises whether that theory is not mistaken in its very problem. Has the condition of the pedagogical material with which it has to do been correctly defined? The first thing that startles us is the strange relation to some imaginary children, to such as I, at least, have never seen in the Russian Empire. The conversations, and the information which they impart, refer to children of less than two years of age, because two-year-old children know all that is contained in them, but as to the questions which have to be asked, they have reference to parrots. Any pupil of six, seven, eight, or nine years will not understand a thing in these[Pg 259] questions, because he knows all about that, and cannot make out what it all means. The demands for such conversations evince either complete ignorance, or a desire to ignore that degree of development on which the pupils stand.

Maybe the children of Hottentots and negroes, or some German children, do not know what is imparted to them in such conversations, but Russian children, except demented ones, all those who come to a school, not only know what is up and what down, what is a bench and what a table, what is two and what one, and so forth, but, in my experience, the peasant children who are sent to school by their parents can every one of them express their thoughts well and correctly, can understand another person's thought (if it is expressed in Russian), and can count to twenty and more; playing with knuckle-bones they count in pairs and sixes, and they know how many points and pairs there are in a six. Frequently the pupils who came to my school brought with them the problem with the geese, and explained it to me. But even if we admit that children possess no such conceptions as those the pedagogues want to impart to them by means of conversations, I do not find the method chosen by them to be correct.

Thus, for example, Mr. Bunákov has written a reader. This book is to be used in conjunction with the conversations to teach the children language. I have run through the book and have found it to be a series of bad language blunders, wherever extracts from other books are not quoted. The same complete ignorance of language I have found in Mr. Evtushévski's problems. Mr. Evtushévski wants to give ideas by means of problems. First of all he ought to have seen to it that the tool for the transmission of ideas, that is, the language, was correct.

What has been mentioned here refers to the form in which the development is imparted. Let us look at the[Pg 260] contents themselves. Mr. Bunákov proposes the following questions to be put to the children: "Where can you see cats? where a magpie? where sand? where a wasp and a suslik? what are a suslik and a magpie and a cat covered with, and what are the parts of their bodies?" (The suslik is a favourite animal of pedagogy, no doubt because not one peasant child in the centre of Russia knows that word.)

"Naturally the teacher does not always put these questions straight to the children, as forming the predetermined programme of the lesson; more frequently the small and undeveloped children have to be led up to the solution of the question of the programme by a series of suggestive questions, by directing their attention to the side of the subject which is more correct at the given moment, or by inciting them to recall something from their previous observations. Thus the teacher need not put the question directly: 'Where can a wasp be seen?' but, turning to this or that pupil, he may ask him whether he has seen a wasp, where he has seen it, and then only, combining the replies of several pupils, compose an answer to the first question of his programme. In answering the teacher's questions, the children will often connect several remarks that have no direct relation to the matter; for example, when the question is about what the parts of a magpie are, one may say irrelevantly that a magpie jumps, another that it chatters funnily, a third that it steals things,—let them add and give utterance to everything that arises in their memory or imagination,—it is the teacher's business to concentrate their attention in accordance with the programme, and these remarks and additions of the children he should take notice of for the purpose of elaborating the other parts of the programme. In viewing a new subject, the children at every convenient opportunity return to the subjects which have already been under consideration. Since they have observed that[Pg 261] a magpie is covered with feathers, the teacher asks: 'Is the suslik also covered with feathers? What is it covered with? And what is a chicken covered with? and a horse? and a lizard?' When they have observed that a magpie has two legs, the teacher asks: 'How many legs has a dog? and a fox? and a chicken? and a wasp? What other animals do you know with two legs? with four? with six?'"

Involuntarily the question arises: Do the children know, or do they not know, what is so well explained to them in these conversations? If the pupils know it all, then, upon

98

occasion, in the street or at home, where they do not need to raise their left hands, they will certainly be able to tell it in more beautiful and more correct Russian than they are ordered to do. They will certainly not say that a horse is "covered" with wool; if so, why are they compelled to repeat these questions just as the teacher has put them? But if they do not know them (which is not to be admitted except as regards the suslik), the question arises: by what will the teacher be guided in what is with so much unction called the programme of questions,—by the science of zoology, or by logic? or by the science of eloquence? But if by none of the sciences, and merely by the desire to talk about what is visible in the objects, there are so many visible things in objects, and they are so diversified, that a guiding thread is needed to show what to talk upon, whereas in objective instruction there is no such thread, and there can be none.

All human knowledge is subdivided for the purpose that it may more conveniently be gathered, united, and transmitted, and these subdivisions are called sciences. But outside their scientific classifications you may talk about objects anything you please, and you may say all the nonsense imaginable, as we actually see. In any case, the result of the conversation will be that the children[Pg 262] are either made to learn by heart the teacher's words about the suslik, or to change their own words, place them in a certain order (not always a correct order), and to memorize and repeat them. For this reason all the manuals of this kind, in general all the exercises of development, suffer on the one hand from absolute arbitrariness, and on the other from superfluity. For example, in Mr. Bunákov's book the only story which, it seems, is not copied from another author, is the following:

"A peasant complained to a hunter about his trouble: a fox had carried off several of his chickens and one duck; the fox was not in the least afraid of watch-dog Dandy, who was chained up and kept barking all night long; in the morning he had placed a trap with a piece of roast meat in the fresh tracks on the snow,—evidently the red-haired sneak was disporting near the house, but he did not go into the trap. The hunter listened to what the peasant had to say to him, and said: 'Very well; now we will see who will be shrewder!' The hunter walked all day with his gun and with his dog, over the tracks of the fox, to discover how he found his way into the yard. In the daytime the sneak sleeps in his lair, and knows nothing of what is going on, so that had to be considered: on its path the hunter dug a hole and covered it with boards, dirt, and snow; a few steps from it he put down a piece of horseflesh. In the evening he seated himself with a loaded gun in his ambush, fixed things in such a way that he could see everything and shoot comfortably, and there he waited. It grew dark. The moon swam out. Cautiously, looking around and listening, the fox crept out of his lair, raised his nose, and sniffed. He at once smelled the odour of horseflesh, and ran at a slow trot to the place, and suddenly stopped and pricked his ears: the shrewd one saw that there was a mound there which had not been in that spot the previous evening. This mound apparently vexed him, and made him think;[Pg 263] he took a large circle around it, and sniffed and listened, and sat down, and for a long time looked at the meat from a distance, so that the hunter could not shoot him,—it was too far. The fox thought and thought, and suddenly ran at full speed between the meat and the mound. Our hunter was careful, and did not shoot. He knew that the sneak was merely trying to find out whether anybody was sitting behind that mound; if he had shot at the running fox, he would certainly have missed him, and then he would not have seen the sneak, any more than he could see his own ears. Now the fox quieted down,—the mound no longer disturbed him: he walked briskly up to the meat, and ate it with great delight. Then the hunter aimed carefully, without haste, so that he might not miss him. Bang! The fox jumped up from pain and fell down dead."

Everything is arbitrary here: it is an arbitrary invention to say that a fox could carry off a peasant's duck in winter, that peasants trap foxes, that a fox sleeps in the daytime in his lair (for he sleeps only at night); arbitrary is that hole which is uselessly dug in winter and covered with boards without being made use of; arbitrary is the statement that the fox eats horseflesh, which he never does; arbitrary is the supposed cunning of the fox, who runs past the hunter; arbitrary are the mound and the hunter, who does not shoot for fear of missing, that is, everything, from beginning to end, is bosh, for which any peasant boy might arraign the author of the story, if he could talk without raising his hand.

Then a whole series of so-called exercises in Mr. Bunákov's lessons is composed of such questions as: "Who bakes? Who chops? Who shoots?" to which the pupil is supposed to answer: "The baker, the wood-chopper, and the marksmen," whereas he might just as correctly answer that the woman bakes, the axe chops, and the teacher shoots, if he has a gun. Another arbitrary statement|Pg 264|in that book is that the throat is a part of the mouth, and so on.

All the other exercises, such as "The ducks fly, and the dogs?" or "The linden and birch are trees, and the horse?" are quite superfluous. Besides, it must be observed that if such conversations are really carried on with the pupils (which never happens) that is, if the pupils are permitted to speak and ask questions, the teacher, choosing simple subjects (they are most difficult), is at each step perplexed, partly through ignorance, and partly because *ein Narr kann mehr fragen, als zehn Weise antworten.*

Exactly the same takes place in the instruction of arithmetic, which is based on the same pedagogical principle. Either the pupils are informed in the same way of what they already know, or they are quite arbitrarily informed of combinations of a certain character that are not based on anything. The lesson mentioned above and all the other lessons up to ten are merely information about what the children already know. If they frequently do not answer questions of that kind, this is due to the fact that the question is either wrongly expressed in itself, or wrongly expressed as regards the children. The difficulty which the children encounter in answering a question of that character is due to the same cause which makes it impossible for the average boy to answer the question: Three sons were to Noah,[1]—Shem, Ham, and Japheth,—who was their father? The difficulty is not mathematical, but syntactical, which is due to the fact that in the statement of the problem and in the question there is not one and the same subject; but when to the syntactical difficulty there is added the awkwardness of the proposer of the problems in expressing himself in Russian, the matter becomes of greater difficulty still to the pupil; but the trouble is no longer mathematical.

[Pg 265]

[1] The Russian way of saying "Noah had three sons."

Let anybody understand at once Mr. Evtushévski's problem: "A certain boy had four nuts, another had five. The second boy gave all his nuts to the first, and this one gave three nuts to a third, and the rest he distributed equally to three other friends. How many nuts did each of the last get?" Express the problem as follows: "A boy had four nuts. He was given five more. He gave away three nuts, and the rest he wants to give to three friends. How many can he give to each?" and a child of five years of age will solve it. There is no problem here at all, but the difficulty may arise only from a wrong statement of the problem, or from a weak memory. And it is this syntactical difficulty, which the children overcome by long and difficult exercises, that gives the teacher cause to think that, teaching the children what they know already, he is teaching them anything at all. Just as arbitrarily are the children taught combinations in arithmetic and the decomposition of numbers according to a certain method and order, which have their foundation only in the fancy of the teacher. Mr. Evtushévski says:

"Four. (1) The formation of the number. On the upper border of the board the teacher places three cubes together—I I I. How many cubes are there here? Then a fourth cube is added. And how many are there now? I I I I. How are four cubes formed from three and one? We have to add one cube to the three.

"(2) Decomposition into component parts. How can four cubes be formed? or, How can four cubes be broken up? Four cubes may be broken up into two and two: II + II. Four cubes may be formed from one, and one, and one, and one more, or by taking four times one cube: I + I + I + I. Four cubes may be broken up into three and one: III + I. It may be formed from one, and one, and two: I + I + II. Can four cubes be put together in any other way? The pupils convince themselves that there can be no other decomposition, distinct from those[Pg 266] already given. If the pupils begin to break the four cubes in this way: one, two, and one, or, two, one and one; or, one and three, the teacher will easily point out to them that these decompositions are only repetitions of what has been got before, only in a different order.

100

"Every time, whenever the pupils indicate a new method of decomposition, the teacher places the cubes on a ledge of the blackboard in the manner here indicated. Thus there will be four cubes on the upper ledge; two and two in a second place; in a third place the four cubes will be separated at some distance from each other; in a fourth place, three and one, and in a fifth one, one, and two.

"(3) Decomposition in order. It may easily happen that the children will at once point out the decomposition of the number into component parts in order; even then the third exercise cannot be regarded as superfluous: Here we have formed four cubes of twos, of separate cubes, and of threes,—in what order had we best place the cubes on the board? With what shall the decomposition of the four cubes begin? With the decomposition into separate cubes. How are four cubes to be formed from separate cubes? We must take four times one cube. How are four cubes to be formed from twos, from a pair? We must take two twos,—twice two cubes, two pairs of cubes. How shall we afterward break up the four cubes? They can be formed of threes: for this purpose we take three and one, or one and three. The teacher explains to the pupils that the last decomposition, that is, 1 1 2, does not come under the accepted order, and is a modification of one of the first three."

Why does Mr. Evtushévski not admit this last decomposition? Why must there be the order indicated by him? All that is a matter of mere arbitrariness and fancy. In reality, it is apparent to every thinking man that there is only one foundation for any composition and decomposition, and for the whole of mathematics. Here[Pg 267] is the foundation: $1 + 1 = 2$, $2 + 1 = 3$, $3 + 1 = 4$, and so forth,—precisely what the children learn at home, and what in common parlance is called counting to ten, to twenty, and so forth. This process is known to every pupil, and no matter what decomposition Mr. Evtushévski may make, it is to be explained from this one. A boy that can count to four, considers four as a whole, and so also three, and two, and one. Consequently, he knows that four was produced from the consecutive addition of one. Similarly he knows that four is produced by adding twice one to two, just as he knows twice one is two. What, then, are the children taught here? That which they know, or that process of counting which they must learn according to the teacher's fancy.

The other day I happened to witness a lesson in mathematics according to Grube's method. The pupil was asked: "How much is 8 and 7?" He hastened to answer and said 16. His neighbour, too, was in a hurry and, without raising his left hand, said: "8 and 8 is 16, and one less is 15." The teacher sternly stopped him, and compelled the first boy to add one after one to 8, until he came to 15, though the boy knew long ago that he had made a blunder. In that school they had reached the number 15, but 16 was supposed to be unknown yet.

I am afraid that many people, reading all these long refutals of the methods of object instruction and counting according to Grube, which I am making, will say: "What is there here to talk about? Is it not evident that it is all mere nonsense which it is not worth while to criticize? Why pick out the errors and blunders of a Bunákov and Evtushévski, and criticize what is beneath all criticism?"

That was the way I myself thought before I was led to see what was going on in the pedagogical world, when I convinced myself that Messrs. Bunákov and Evtushévski were not mere individuals, but authorities in our pedagogics,[Pg 268] and that what they prescribe is actually carried out in our schools. In the backwoods we may find teachers, especially women, who spread Evtushévski's and Bunákov's manuals out before them and ask according to their prescription how much one feather and one feather is, and what a hen is covered with. All that would be funny if it were only an invention of the theorist, and not a guide in practical work, a guide that some follow already, and if it did not concern one of the most important affairs of life,—the education of the children. I was amused at it when I read it as theoretical fancies; but when I learned and saw that that was being practised on children, I felt pity for them and ashamed.

From a theoretical standpoint, not to mention the fact that they faultily define the aim of education, the pedagogues of this school make this essential error, that they depart from the conditions of all instruction, whether this instruction be on the highest or lowest stage of the science, in a university or in a popular school. The essential conditions of all instruction consist in selecting the homogeneous phenomena from an endless number of heterogeneous

101

phenomena, and in imparting the laws of these phenomena to the students. Thus, in the study of language, the pupils are taught the laws of the word, and in mathematics, the laws of the numbers. The study of language consists in imparting the laws of the decomposition and of the reverse composition of sentences, words, syllables, sounds,—and these laws form the subject of instruction. The instruction of mathematics consists in imparting the laws of the composition and decomposition of the numbers (but I beg to observe,—not in the process of the composition and the decomposition of the numbers, but in imparting the laws of that composition and decomposition). Thus, the first law consists in the ability of regarding a collection of units as a unit of a higher order, precisely what a child does when he says: "2 and 1 = 3." He regards 2[Pg 269] as a kind of unit. On this law are based the consequent laws of numeration, then of addition, and of the whole of mathematics. But arbitrary conversations about the wasp, and so forth, or problems within the limit of 10,—its decomposition in every manner possible,—cannot form a subject of instruction, because, in the first place, they transcend the subject and, in the second place, because they do not treat of its laws.

That is the way the matter presents itself to me from its theoretical side; but theoretical criticism may frequently err, and so I will try to verify my deductions by means of practical data. G—— P—— has given us a sample of the practical results of both object instruction and of mathematics according to Grube's method. One of the older boys was told: "Put your hand under your book!" in order to prove that he had been taught the conceptions of "over" and "under," and the intelligent boy, who, I am sure, knew what "over" and "under" was, when he was three years old, put his hand on the book when he was told to put it under it. I have all the time observed such examples, and they prove more clearly than anything else how useless, strange, and disgraceful, I feel like saying, this object instruction is for Russian children. A Russian child cannot and will not believe (he has too much respect for the teacher and for himself) that the teacher is in earnest when he asks him whether the ceiling is above or below, or how many legs he has. In arithmetic, too, we have seen that pupils who did not even know how to write the numbers and during the whole time of the instruction were exercised only in mental calculations up to 10, for half an hour did not stop blundering in every imaginable way in response to questions which the teacher put to them within the limit of 10. Evidently the instruction of mental calculation brought no results, and the syntactical difficulty, which consists in unravelling a question that is improperly put, has remained[Pg 270] the same as ever. And thus, the practical results of the examination which took place did not confirm the usefulness of the development.

But I will be more exact and conscientious. Maybe the process of development, which at first is confined not so much to the study, as to the analysis of what the pupils know already, will produce results later on. Maybe the teacher, who at first takes possession of the pupils' minds by means of the analysis, later guides them firmly and with ease, and from the narrow sphere of the descriptions of a table and the count of 2 and 1 leads them into the real sphere of knowledge, in which the pupils are no longer confined to learning what they know already, but also learn something new, and learn that new information in a new, more convenient, more intelligent manner. This supposition is confirmed by the fact that all the German pedagogues and their followers, among them Mr. Bunákov, say distinctly that object instruction is to serve as an introduction to "home science" and "natural science." But we should be looking in vain in Mr. Bunákov's manual to find out how this "home science" is to be taught, if by this word any real information is to be understood, and not the descriptions of a hut and a vestibule,—which the children know already. Mr. Bunákov, on page 200, after having explained that it is necessary to teach where the ceiling is and where the stove, says briefly:

"Now it is necessary to pass over to the third stage of object instruction, the contents of which have been defined by me as follows: The study of the country, county, Government, the whole realm with its natural products and its inhabitants, in general outline, as a sketch of home science and the beginning of natural science, with the predominance of reading, which, resting on the immediate observations of the first two grades, broadens the mental horizon of the pupils,—the sphere of their concepts and ideas. We can see from the mere definition that here the[Pg 271] objectivity appears as a

102

complement to the explanatory reading and narrative of the teacher,—consequently, what is said in regard to the occupations of the third year has more reference to the discussion of the second occupation, which enters into the composition of the subject under instruction, which is called the native language,—the explanatory reading."

We turn to the third year,—the explanatory reading, but there we find absolutely nothing to indicate how the new information is to be imparted, except that it is good to read such and such books, and in reading to put such and such questions. The questions are extremely queer (to me, at least), as, for example, the comparison of the article on water by Ushínski and of the article on water by Aksákov, and the request made of the pupils that they should explain that Aksákov considers water as a phenomenon of Nature, while Ushínski considers it as a substance, and so forth. Consequently, we find here again the same foisting of views on the pupils, and of subdivisions (generally incorrect) of the teacher, and not one word, not one hint, as to how any new knowledge is to be imparted.

It is not known what shall be taught: natural history, or geography. There is nothing there but reading with questions of the character I have just mentioned. On the other side of the instruction about the word,—grammar and orthography,—we should just as much be looking in vain for any new method of instruction which is based on the preceding development. Again the old Perevlévski's grammar, which begins with philosophical definitions and then with syntactical analysis, serves as the basis of all new grammatical exercises and of Mr. Bunákov's manual.

In mathematics, too, we should be looking in vain, at that stage where the real instruction in mathematics begins, for anything new and more easy, based on the whole previous instruction of the exercises of the second[Pg 272] year up to 20. Where in arithmetic the real difficulties are met with, where it becomes necessary to explain the subject from all its sides to the pupil, as in numeration, in addition, subtraction, division, in the division and multiplication of fractions, you will not find even a shadow of anything easier, any new explanation, but only quotations from old arithmetics.

The character of this instruction is everywhere one and the same. The whole attention is directed toward teaching the pupil what he already knows. And since the pupil knows what he is being taught, and easily recites in any order desired what he is asked to recite by the teacher, the teacher thinks that he is really teaching something, and the pupil's progress is great, and the teacher, paying no attention to what forms the real difficulty of teaching, that is, to teaching something new, most comfortably stumps about in one spot.

This explains why our pedagogical literature is overwhelmed with manuals for object-lessons, with manuals about how to conduct kindergartens (one of the most monstrous excrescences of the new pedagogy), with pictures and books for reading, in which are eternally repeated the same articles about the fox and the blackcock, the same poems which for some reason are written out in prose in all kinds of permutations and with all kinds of explanations; but we have not a single new article for children's reading, not one Russian, nor Church-Slavic grammar, nor a Church-Slavic dictionary, nor an arithmetic, nor a geography, nor a history for the popular schools. All the forces are absorbed in writing text-books for the instruction of children in subjects they need not and ought not to be taught in school, because they are taught them in life. Of course, there is no end to the writing of such books; for there can be only one grammar and arithmetic, but of exercises and reflections, like those I have quoted from Bunákov, and of the orders of the decomposition of[Pg 273] numbers from Evtushévski, there may be an endless number.

Pedagogy is in the same condition in which a science would be that would teach how a man ought to walk; and people would try to discover rules about how to teach the children, how to enjoin them to contract this muscle, stretch that muscle, and so forth. This condition of the new pedagogy results directly from its two fundamental principles: (1) that the aim of the school is development and not science, and (2) that development and the means for attaining it may be theoretically defined. From this has consistently resulted that miserable and frequently ridiculous condition in which the whole matter of the schools now is. Forces are wasted in vain, and the masses, who at the present moment are thirsting for education, as the dried-up grass thirsts for rain, and are ready to receive it, and beg for it,—instead of a loaf receive a stone, and are perplexed to understand whether they were mistaken in regarding education as something good, or whether something is wrong in what is being offered to them. That matters are really so there cannot be the least doubt for any man who becomes acquainted with the present theory of teaching and knows the actual condition of the school among the masses. Involuntarily there arises the question: how could honest, cultured people, who sincerely love their work and wish to do good,—for such I regard the majority of my opponents to be,—have arrived at such a strange condition and be in such deep error?

This question has interested me, and I will try to communicate those answers which have occurred to me. Many causes have led to it. The most natural cause which has led pedagogy to the false path on which it now stands, is the criticism of the old order, the criticism for the sake of criticism, without positing new principles in the place of those criticized. Everybody knows that criticizing[Pg 274] is an easy business, and that it is quite fruitless and frequently harmful, if by the side of what is condemned one does not point out the principles on the basis of which this condemnation is uttered. If I say that such and such a thing is bad because I do not like it, or because everybody says that it is bad, or even because it is really bad, but do not know how it ought to be right, the criticism will always be useless and injurious. The views of the pedagogues of the new school are, above all, based on the criticism of previous methods. Even now, when it seems there would be no sense in striking a prostrate person, we read and hear in every manual, in every discussion, "that it is injurious to read without comprehension; that it is impossible to learn by heart the definitions of numbers and operations with numbers; that senseless memorizing is injurious; that it is injurious to operate with thousands without being able to count 2-3," and so forth. The chief point of departure is the criticism of the old methods and the concoction of new ones to be as diametrically opposed to the old as possible, but by no means the positing of new foundations of pedagogy, from which new methods might result.

It is very easy to criticize the old-fashioned method of studying reading by means of learning by heart whole pages of the psalter, and of studying arithmetic by memorizing what a number is, and so forth. I will remark, in the first place, that nowadays there is no need of attacking these methods, because there will hardly be found any teachers who would defend them, and, in the second place, that if, criticizing such phenomena, they want to let it be known that I am a defender of the antiquated method of instruction, it is no doubt due to the fact that my opponents, in their youth, do not know that nearly twenty years ago I with all my might and main fought against those antiquated methods of pedagogy and coöperated in their abolition.

[Pg 275]

And thus it was found that the old methods of instruction were not good for anything, and, without building any new foundation, they began to look for new methods. I say "without building any new foundation," because there are only two permanent foundations of pedagogy:

(1) The determination of the criterion of what ought to be taught, and (2) the criterion of how it has to be taught, that is, the determination that the chosen subjects are most necessary, and that the chosen method is the best.

Nobody has even paid any attention to these foundations, and each school has in its own justification invented quasi-philosophical justificatory reflections. But this "theoretical substratum," as Mr. Bunákov has accidentally expressed himself quite well, cannot be regarded as a foundation. For the old method of instruction possessed just such a theoretical substratum.

The real, peremptory question of pedagogy, which fifteen years ago I vainly tried to put in all its significance, "Why ought we to know this or that, and how shall we teach it?" has not even been touched. The result of this has been that as soon as it became apparent that the old method was not good, they did not try to find out what the best method would be, but immediately set out to discover a new method which would be the very opposite of the old one. They did as a man may do who finds his house to be cold in winter and does not trouble himself about learning why it is cold, or how to help matters, but at once tries to find another house which will as little as possible resemble the one he is living in. I was then

104

abroad, and I remember how I everywhere came across messengers roving all over Europe in search of a new faith, that is, officials of the ministry, studying German pedagogy.

We have adopted the methods of instruction current with our nearest neighbours, the Germans, in the first[Pg 276] place, because we are always prone to imitate the Germans; in the second, because it was the most complicated and cunning of methods, and if it comes to taking something from abroad, of course, it has to be the latest fashion and what is most cunning; in the third, because, in particular, these methods were more than any others opposed to the old way. And thus, the new methods were taken from the Germans, and not by themselves, but with a theoretical substratum, that is, with a quasi-philosophical justification of these methods.

This theoretical substratum has done great service. The moment parents or simply sensible people, who busy themselves with the question of education, express their doubt about the efficacy of these methods, they are told: "And what about Pestalozzi, and Diesterweg, and Denzel, and Wurst, and methodics, heuristics, didactics, concentrism?" and the bold people wave their hands, and say: "God be with them,—they know better." In these German methods there also lay this other advantage (the cause why they stick so eagerly to this method), that with it the teacher does not need to try too much, does not need to go on studying, does not need to work over himself and the methods of instruction. For the greater part of the time the teacher teaches by this method what the children know, and, besides, teaches it from a text-book, and that is convenient. And unconsciously, in accordance with an innate human weakness, the teacher is fond of this convenience. It is very pleasant for me, with my firm conviction that I am teaching and doing an important and very modern work, to tell the children from the book about the suslik, or about a horse's having four legs, or to transpose the cubes by twos and by threes, and ask the children how much two and two is; but if, instead of telling about the suslik, the teacher had to tell or read something interesting, to give the foundations of grammar, geography, sacred history, and of the four operations,[Pg 277] he would at once be led to working over himself, to reading much, and to refreshing his knowledge.

Thus, the old method was criticized, and a new one was taken from the Germans. This method is so foreign to our Russian un-pedantic mental attitude, its monstrosity is so glaring, that one would think that it could never have been grafted on Russia, and yet it is being applied, even though only in a small measure, and in some way gives at times better results than the old church method. This is due to the fact that, since it was taken in our country (just as it originated in Germany) from the criticism of the old method, the faults of the former method have really been rejected, though, in its extreme opposition to the old method, which, with the pedantry characteristic of the Germans, has been carried to the farthest extreme, there have appeared new faults, which are almost greater than the former ones.

Formerly reading was taught in Russia by attaching to the consonants useless endings (*buki—uki*, *tyedi—yedi*), and in Germany *es em de ce*, and so forth, by attaching a vowel to each consonant, now in front, and now behind, and that caused some difficulty. Now they have fallen into the other extreme, by trying to pronounce the consonants without the vowels, which is an apparent impossibility. In Ushínski's grammar (Ushínski is with us the father of the sound method), and in all the manuals on sound, a consonant is defined thus: "That sound which cannot be pronounced by itself." And it is this sound which the pupil is taught before any other. When I remarked that it is impossible to pronounce *b* alone, but that it always gives you *bu*, I was told that was due to the inability of some persons, and that it took great skill to pronounce a consonant. And I have myself seen a teacher correct a pupil more than ten times, though he seemed quite satisfactorily to pronounce short *b*, until at last the pupil began to talk nonsense. And it is with[Pg 278] these *b's*, that is, sounds that cannot be pronounced, as Ushínski defines them, or the pronunciation of which demands special skill, that the instruction of reading begins according to the pedantic German manuals.

Formerly syllables were senselessly learned by heart (that was bad); diametrically opposed to this, the new fashion enjoins us not to divide up into syllables at all, which is absolutely impossible in a long word, and which in reality is never done. Every teacher, according to the sound method, feels the necessity of letting a pupil rest after a part of a word, having him pronounce it separately. Formerly they used to read the psalter, which, on account of its high and deep style, is incomprehensible to the children (which was bad); in contrast to this the children are made to read sentences without any contents whatever, to explain intelligible words, or to learn by heart what they cannot understand. In the old school the teacher did not speak to the pupil at all; now the teacher is ordered to talk to them on anything and everything, on what they know already, or what they do not need to know. In mathematics they formerly learned by heart the definition of operations, but now they no longer have anything to do with operations, for, according to Evtushévski, they reach numeration only in the third year, and it is assumed that for a whole year they are to be taught nothing but numbers up to ten. Formerly the pupils were made to work with large abstract numbers, without paying any attention to the other side of mathematics, to the disentanglement of the problem (the formation of an equation). Now they are taught solving puzzles, forming equations with small numbers before they know numeration and how to operate with numbers, though experience teaches any teacher that the difficulty of forming equations or the solution of puzzles are overcome by a general development in life, and not in school.

It has been observed—quite correctly—that there[Pg 279] is no greater aid for a pupil, when he is puzzled by a problem with large numbers, than to give him the same problem with smaller numbers. The pupil, who in life learns to grope through problems with small numbers, is conscious of the process of solving, and transfers this process to the problem with large numbers. Having observed this, the new pedagogues try to teach only the solving of puzzles with small numbers, that is, what cannot form the subject of instruction and is only the work of life.

In the instruction of grammar the new school has again remained consistent with its point of departure,—with the criticism of the old and the adoption of the diametrically opposite method. Formerly they used to learn by heart the definition of the parts of speech, and from etymology passed over to syntax; now they not only begin with syntax, but even with logic, which the children are supposed to acquire. According to the grammar of Mr. Bunákov, which is an abbreviation of Perevlévski's grammar, even with the same choice of examples, the study of grammar begins with syntactical analysis, which is so difficult and, I will say, so uncertain for the Russian language, which does not fully comply with the classic forms of syntax. To sum up, the new school has removed certain disadvantages, of which the chief are the superfluous addition to the consonants and the memorizing of definitions, and in this it is superior to the old method, and in reading and writing sometimes gives better results; but, on the other hand, it has introduced new defects, which are that the contents of the reading are most senseless and that arithmetic is no longer taught as a study.

In practice (I can refer in this to all the inspectors of schools, to all the members of school councils, who have visited the schools, and to all the teachers), in practice, in the majority of schools, where the German method is prescribed, this is what takes place, with rare exceptions.[Pg 280] The children learn not by the sound system, but by the method of letter composition; instead of saying *b,r*, they say *bŭ, rŭ*, and break up the words into syllables. The object instruction is entirely lost sight of, arithmetic does not proceed at all, and the children have absolutely nothing to read. The teachers quite unconsciously depart from the theoretical demands and fall in with the needs of the masses. These practical results, which are repeated everywhere, should, it seems, prove the incorrectness of the method itself; but among the pedagogues, those that write manuals and prescribe rules, there exists such a complete ignorance of and aversion to the knowledge of the masses and their demands that the relation of reality to these methods does not in the least impair the progress of their business. It is hard to imagine the conception about the masses which exists in this world of the pedagogues, and from which result their method and all the consequent manner of instruction.

Mr. Bunákov, in proof of how necessary the object instruction and development is for the children of a Russian school, with extraordinary naïveté adduces Pestalozzi's words: "Let any one who has lived among the common people," he says, "contradict my words that there is nothing more difficult than to impart any idea to these creatures. Nobody, indeed, gainsays that. The Swiss pastors affirm that when the people come to them to receive instruction they do not understand what they are told, and the pastors do not understand what the people say to them. City dwellers who settle in the country are amazed at the inability of the country population to express themselves; years pass before the country servants learn to express themselves to their masters." This relation of the common people in Switzerland to the cultured class is assumed as the foundation for just such a relation in Russia.

I regard it as superfluous to expatiate on what is known to everybody, that in Germany the people speak a special[Pg 281] language, called Plattdeutsch, and that in the German part of Switzerland this Plattdeutsch is especially far removed from the German language, whereas in Russia we frequently speak a bad language, while the masses always speak a good Russian, and that in Russia it will be more correct to put these words of Pestalozzi in the mouth of peasants speaking of the teachers. A peasant and his boy will say quite correctly that it is very hard to understand what those creatures, meaning the teachers, say. The ignorance about the masses is so complete in this world of the pedagogues that they boldly say that to the peasant school come little savages, and therefore boldly teach them what is down and what up, that a blackboard is placed on a stand, and that underneath it there is a groove. They do not know that if the pupils asked the teacher, there would turn up very many things which the teacher would not know; that, for example, if you rub off the paint from the board, nearly any boy will tell you of what kind of wood the board is made, whether of pine, linden, or aspen, which the teacher cannot tell; that a boy will always tell better than the teacher about a cat or a chicken, because he has observed them better than the teacher; that instead of the problem about the wagons the boy knows the problems about the crows, about the cattle, and about the geese. (About the crows: There flies a flock of crows, and there stand some oak-trees: if two crows alight on each, a crow will be lacking; if one on each, an oak-tree will be lacking. How many crows and how many oak-trees are there? About the cattle: For one hundred roubles buy one hundred animals,—calves at half a rouble, cows at three roubles, and oxen at ten roubles. How many oxen, cows, and calves are there?) The pedagogues of the German school do not even suspect that quickness of perception, that real vital development, that contempt for everything false, that ready ridicule of everything false, which are inherent in every Russian peasant boy,—and[Pg 282] only on that account so boldly (as I myself have seen), under the fire of forty pairs of intelligent youthful eyes, perform their tricks at the risk of ridicule. For this reason, a real teacher, who knows the masses, no matter how sternly he is enjoined to teach the peasant children what is up and what down, and that two and three is five, not one real teacher, who knows the pupils with whom he has to deal, will be able to do that.

Thus, the chief causes which have led us into such error are: (1) the ignorance about the masses; (2) the involuntarily seductive ease of teaching the children what they already know; (3) our proneness to imitate the Germans, and (4) the criticism of the old, without putting down a new, foundation. This last cause has led the pedagogues of the new school to this, that, in spite of the extreme external difference of the new method from the old, it is identical with it in its foundation, and, consequently, in the methods of instruction and in the results. In either method the essential principle consists in the teacher's firm and absolute knowledge of what to teach and how to teach, and this knowledge of his he does not draw from the demands of the masses and from experience, but simply decides theoretically once for all that he must teach this or that and in such a way, and so he teaches. The pedagogue of the ancient school, which for briefness' sake I shall call the church school, knows firmly and absolutely that he must teach from the prayer-book and the psalter by making the children learn by rote, and he admits no alterations in his methods; in the same manner the teacher of the new, the German, school knows firmly and absolutely that he must teach according to Bunákov and Evtushévski, begin with the words "whisker" and "wasp," ask what is up and what down, and tell about the favourite suslik, and he admits no alterations in his method. Both of them base their opinion on the firm conviction that they know the best[Pg 283] methods. From the identity of the foundations arises also a further similarity. If you tell a teacher of the church reading that it takes the children a long time and causes them difficulty to acquire reading and writing, he will reply that the main interest is not in the reading and writing, but in the "divine instruction," by which he means the study of the church books. The same you will be told by a teacher of Russian reading according to the German method. He will tell you (all say and write it) that the main question is not the rapidity of the acquisition of the art of reading, writing, and arithmetic, but in the "development." Both place the aim of instruction in something independent of reading, writing, and arithmetic, that is, of science, in something else, which is absolutely necessary.

This similarity continues down to the minutest details. In either method all instruction previous to the school, all knowledge acquired outside the school, is not taken into account,—all entering pupils are regarded as equally ignorant, and all are made to learn from the beginning. If a boy who knows the letters and the syllables *a*, *be*, enters a church school, he is made to change them to *buki-az*—*ba*. The same is true of the German school.

Just so, in either school it happens that some children cannot learn the rudiments.

Just so, with either method, the mechanical side of instruction predominates over the mental. In either school the pupils excel in a good handwriting and good enunciation with absolutely exact reading, that is, not as it is spoken, but as it is written. Just so, with either method, there always reigns an external order in the school, and the children are in constant fear and can be guided only with the greatest severity. Mr. Korolév has incidentally remarked that in instruction according to the sound method blows are not neglected. I have seen the same in the schools of the German method, and[Pg 284] I assume that without blows it is impossible to get along even in the new German school, because, like the church school, it teaches without asking what the pupil finds interesting to know, but what, in the teacher's opinion, seems necessary, and so the school can be based only on compulsion. Compulsion is attained with children generally by means of blows. The church and the new German school, starting from the same principles and arriving at the same results, are absolutely identical. But, if it came to choosing one of the two, I should still prefer the church school. The defects are the same, but on the side of the church school is the custom of a thousand years and the authority of the church, which is so powerful with the masses.

Having finished the analysis and criticism of the German school, I consider it necessary,—in view of what I have said, namely, that criticism is fruitful only when, condemning, it points out how that which is bad ought to be,—I consider it necessary to speak of those foundations of instruction which I regard as legitimate, and on which I rear my method of instruction.

In order to elucidate in what I find these unquestionable foundations of every pedagogical activity, I shall be compelled to repeat myself, that is, to repeat what I said fifteen years ago in the pedagogical periodical, *Yásnaya Polyána*, which I then published. This repetition will not be tedious for the pedagogues of the new school, because what I then wrote is not exactly forgotten, but has never been considered by the pedagogues,—and yet I still think that just what was expressed by me at that time might have placed pedagogy, as a theory, on a firm foundation. Fifteen years ago, when I took up the matter of popular education without any preconceived theories or views on the subject, with the one desire to advance the matter in a direct and straightforward manner, I, as a teacher in my school, was at once confronted with two[Pg 285] questions: (1) What must I teach? and (2) How must I teach it?

At that time, even as at the present, there existed the greatest diversity of opinion in the answers to these questions.

I know that some pedagogues, who are locked up in their narrow theoretical world, think that there is no other light than what peeps through the windows, and that there is no longer any diversity of opinions.

I ask those who think so to observe that it only seems so to them, just as it seems so to the circles that are opposed to them. In the whole mass of people who are interested in education, there exists, as it has existed before, the greatest diversity of opinions. Formerly, just as now, some, in reply to the question of what ought to be taught, said that outside of the rudiments the most useful information for a primary school is obtained from the natural sciences; others, even as now, that that was not necessary, and was even injurious; even as now, some proposed history, or geography, while others denied their necessity; some

108

proposed the Church-Slavic language and grammar, and religion, while others found that, too, superfluous, and ascribed a prime importance to "development." On the question of how to teach there has always been a still greater diversity of answers. The most diversified methods of instructing in reading and arithmetic have been proposed.

In the bookstalls there were sold, side by side, the self-teachers according to the *buki-az—ba*, Bunákov's lessons, Zolotóv's charts, Madame Daragán's alphabets, and all had their advocates. When I encountered these questions and found no answer for them in Russian literature, I turned to the literature of Europe. After having read what had been written on the subject and having made the personal acquaintance of the so-called best representatives of the pedagogical science in Europe, I not only[Pg 286] failed to find anywhere an answer to the question I was interested in, but I convinced myself that this question does not even exist for pedagogy, as a science; that every pedagogue of any given school firmly believed that the methods which he used were the best, because they were based on absolute truth, and that it would be useless for him to look at them with a critical eye.

However, because, as I said, I took up the matter of popular education without any preconceived notions, or because I took up the matter without prescribing laws from a distance about how I ought to teach, but became a schoolmaster in a village popular school in the backwoods,—I could not reject the idea that there must of necessity exist a criterion by means of which the question could be solved: What to teach and how to teach it. Should I teach the psalter by heart, or the classification of the organisms? Should I teach according to the sound alphabet, translated from the German, or from the prayer-book? In the solution of this question I was aided by a certain pedagogical tact, with which I am gifted, and especially by that close and impassioned relation in which I stood to the matter.

When I entered at once into the closest direct relations with those forty tiny peasants that formed my school (I call them tiny peasants because I found in them the same characteristics of perspicacity, the same immense store of information from practical life, of jocularity, simplicity, and loathing for everything false, which distinguish the Russian peasant), when I saw that susceptibility, that readiness to acquire the information which they needed, I felt at once that the antiquated church method of instruction had outlived its usefulness and was not good for them. I began to experiment on other proposed methods of instruction; but, because compulsion in education, both by my conviction and by my character, are repulsive to me, I did not exercise any[Pg 287]pressure, and, the moment I noticed that something was not readily received, I did not compel them, and looked for something else. From these experiments it appeared to me and to those teachers who instructed with me at Yásnaya Polyána and in other schools on the same principle of freedom, that nearly everything which in the pedagogical world was written about schools was separated by an immeasurable abyss from reality, and that many of the proposed methods, such as object-lessons, the natural sciences, the sound method, and others, called forth contempt and ridicule, and were not accepted by the pupils. We began to look for those contents and those methods which were readily taken up by the pupils, and struck that which forms my method of instruction.

But this method stood in a line with all other methods, and the question of why it was better than the rest remained as unsolved as before. Consequently, the question of what the criterion was as to what to teach and how to teach received an even greater meaning for me; only by solving it could I be convinced that what I taught was neither injurious nor useless. This question both then and now has appeared to me as a corner-stone of the whole pedagogy, and to the solution of this question I devoted the publication of the pedagogical periodical *Yásnaya Polyána*. In several articles (I do not renounce anything I then said) I tried to put the question in all its significance and to solve it as much as I could. At that time I found no sympathy in all the pedagogical literature, not even any contradiction, but the most complete indifference to the question which I put. There were some attacks on certain details and trifles, but the question itself evidently did not interest any one. I was young then, and that indifference grieved me. I did not understand that with my question, "How do you know what to teach and how to teach?" I was like a man who, let us say, in a gathering of Turkish pashas discussing[Pg 288] the question in what manner they may collect the greatest revenue from the people, should propose to them the following: "Gentlemen, in order to

109

know how much revenue to collect from each, we must first analyze the question on what your right to exact that revenue is based." Obviously all the pashas would continue their discussion of the measures of extortion, and would reply only with silence to his irrelevant question. But the question cannot be circumvented. Fifteen years ago no attention was paid to it, and the pedagogues of every school, convinced that everybody else was talking to the wind and that they were right, most calmly prescribed their laws, basing their principles on philosophies of a very doubtful character, which they used as a substratum for their wee little theories.

And yet, this question is not quite so difficult if we only renounce completely all preconceived notions. I have tried to elucidate and solve this question, and, without repeating those proofs, which he who wishes may read in the article, I will enunciate the results to which I was led. "The only criterion of pedagogy is freedom, the only method— experience." After fifteen years I have not changed my opinion one hair's breadth; but I consider it necessary to define with greater precision what I understand by these words, not only in respect to education in general, but also in respect to the particular question of popular education in a primary school. One hundred years ago the question what to teach and how to teach could have had no place either in Europe or with us. Education was inseparably connected with religion. To learn reading meant to learn Holy Writ. In the Mohammedan countries this relation of the rudiments and religion still persists in its full force. To learn means to learn the Koran, and, therefore, Arabic. But the moment religion ceased to be the criterion of what ought to be taught, and the school became independent of[Pg 289] it, this question had to arise. But it did not arise because the school was not suddenly freed from its dependence on religion, but by imperceptible steps. Now it is accepted by everybody that religion cannot serve as the contents, nor as an indication of the method of education, and that education has different demands for its basis. In what do these demands consist? On what are they based? In order that these principles should be incontrovertible, it is necessary either that they be proved philosophically, incontrovertibly, or that, at least, all educated people should be agreed on them. But is it so? There can be no doubt whatsoever about this, that in philosophy have not been found those principles on which could be built up the decision of what ought to be taught, the more so since the matter itself is not an abstract, but a practical affair, which depends on an endless number of vital conditions. Still less can these principles be discovered in the common consent of all men who busy themselves with this matter, in the consent which we may take as a practical foundation, as an expression of the universal common sense. Not only in matters of popular, but even of higher education do we see a complete diversity of opinions among the best representatives of education, as, for example, in the question of classicism and realism. And yet, in spite of the absence of any foundations, we see education proceeding on its own path and on the whole being guided by only one principle, namely by freedom. There exist side by side the classical and the real school, each of which is prepared to regard itself as the only natural school, and both satisfy some want, for parents send their children to either.

In the popular school the right to determine what the children shall learn, no matter from what standpoint we may consider this question, belongs just as much to the masses, that is, either to the pupils themselves, or to the parents who send the children to school, and so the[Pg 290] answer to the question what the children are to be taught in a popular school can be got only from the masses. But, perhaps, we shall say that we, as highly cultured people, must not submit to the demands of the rude masses and that we must teach the masses what to wish. Thus many think, but to that I can give this one answer: give us a firm, incontrovertible foundation why this or that is chosen by you, show me a society in which the two diametrically opposed views on education do not exist among the highly cultured people; where it is not eternally repeated that if education falls into the hands of the clergy, the masses are educated in one sense, and if education falls into the hands of the progressists, the people are educated in another sense,—show me a state of society where that does not exist, and I will agree with you. So long as that does not exist, there is no criterion except the freedom of the learner, where, in matters of the popular school, the place of the learning children is taken by their parents, that is, by the needs of the masses.

These needs are not only definite, quite clear, and everywhere the same throughout Russia, but also so intelligent and broad that they include all the most diversified demands of the people who are debating what the masses ought to be taught. These needs are: the knowledge of Russian and Church-Slavic reading, and calculation. The masses everywhere and always regard the natural sciences as useless trifles. Their programme is remarkable not only by its unanimity and firm definiteness, but, in my opinion, also by the breadth of its demands and the correctness of its view. The masses admit two spheres of knowledge, the most exact and the least subject to vacillation from a diversity of views,—the languages and mathematics; everything else they regard as trifles. I think that the masses are quite correct,—in the first place, because in this knowledge there can be no half information, no falseness, which they[Pg 291] cannot bear, and, in the second, because the sphere of those two kinds of knowledge is immense. Russian and Church-Slavic grammar and calculation, that is, the knowledge of one dead and one living language, with their etymological and syntactical forms and their literatures, and arithmetic, that is, the foundation of all mathematics, form their programme of knowledge, which, unfortunately, but the rarest of the cultured class possess. In the third place, the masses are right, because by this programme they will be taught in the primary school only what will open to them the more advanced paths of knowledge, for it is evident that the thorough knowledge of two languages and their forms, and, in addition to them, of arithmetic, completely opens the paths to an independent acquisition of all other knowledge. The masses, as though feeling the false relation to them, when they are offered incoherent scraps of all kinds of information, repel that lie from themselves, and say: "I need know but this much,—the church language and my own and the laws of the numbers, but that other knowledge I will take myself if I want it."

Thus, if we admit freedom as the criterion of what is to be taught, the programme of the popular schools is clearly and firmly defined, until the time when the masses shall express some new demands. Church-Slavic and Russian and arithmetic to their highest possible stages, and nothing else but that. That is the determination of the limits of the programme of the popular school, which, however, does not presume that all three subjects be introduced systematically. With such a programme the attainment of symmetrical results in all three subjects would naturally be desirable; but it cannot be said that the predominance of one subject over another would be injurious. The problem consists only in keeping within the limits of the programme. It may happen that from the demands of the parents, and especially[Pg 292] from the knowledge of the teacher, this or that subject will be more prominent,—with a clerical person the Church-Slavic language, with a teacher from a county school—either Russian or arithmetic; in all these cases the demands of the masses will be satisfied, and the instruction will not depart from its fundamental criterion.

The second part of the question, how to teach, that is, how to discover which method is the best, has remained just as unsolved.

Just as in the first part of the question of what to teach, the assumption that on the basis of reflections it is possible to build a programme of instruction leads to contradictory schools, so it is also with the question as to how to teach. Let us take the very first stage of the teaching of reading. One asserts that it is easier to teach so from cards; another—according to the *b, v* system; a third—according to Korf; a fourth—according to the *be, ve, ge* system, and so forth. It is said that the nuns teach reading in six weeks by the *buki-az—ba* system. And every teacher, convinced of the superiority of his method, proves this superiority either by the fact that he teaches with it faster than others, or by reflections of the character which Mr. Bunákov and the German pedagogues adduce. At the present time, when there are thousands of examples, we ought to know precisely by what to be guided in our choice. Neither theory, nor reflections, nor even the results of instruction can show this completely.

Education and instruction are generally considered in the abstract, that is, the question is discussed how in the best and easiest manner to produce a certain act of instruction on a certain subject (whether it be one child or a mass of children). This view is quite faulty. All education and instruction can be viewed only as a certain relation of two persons or of two groups of persons having for their aim education or instruction. This

111

definition,[Pg 293] more general than all the other definitions, has special reference to popular education, where the question is the education of an immense number of persons, and where there can be no question about an ideal education. In general, with the popular education we cannot put the question, "How is the best education to be given?" just as with the question of the nutrition of the masses we cannot ask how the most nutritious and best loaf is to be baked. The question has to be put like this: "How is the best relation to be established between given people who want to learn and others who want to teach?" or, "How is the best bread to be made from given bolted flour?" Consequently the question of how to teach and what is the best method is a question of what will be the best relation between teacher and pupil.

Nobody, I suppose, will deny that the best relation between teacher and pupil is that of naturalness, and that the contrary relation is that of compulsion. If so, the measure of all methods is to be found in the greater or lesser naturalness of relations and, therefore, in the lesser or greater compulsion in instruction. The less the children are compelled to learn, the better is the method; the more—the worse. I am glad that I do not have to prove this evident truth. Everybody is agreed that just as in hygiene the use of any food, medicine, exercise, that provokes loathing or pain, cannot be useful, so also in instruction can there be no necessity of compelling children to learn anything that is tiresome and repulsive to them, and that, if necessity demands that children be compelled, it only proves the imperfection of the method. Any one who has taught children has no doubt observed that the less the teacher himself knows the subject which he teaches and the less he likes it, the more will he have to have recourse to severity and compulsion; on the contrary, the more the teacher knows and loves his subject, the more natural and easy will his instruction be. With[Pg 294] the idea that for successful instruction not compulsion is wanted, but the rousing of the pupil's interest, all the pedagogues of the school which is opposed to me agree. The only difference between us is that the conception that the teaching must rouse the child's interest is with them lost in a mass of other conflicting notions about "development," of the value of which they are convinced and in which they exercise compulsion; whereas I consider the rousing of the pupil's interest, the greatest possible ease, and, therefore, the non-compulsion and naturalness of instruction as the fundamental and only measure of good and bad instruction.

Every progress of pedagogy, if we attentively consider the history of this matter, consists in an ever increasing approximation toward naturalness of relations between teacher and pupil, in a lessened compulsion, and in a greater ease of instruction.

The objection was formerly made and, I know, is made even now that it is hard to find the limit of freedom which shall be permitted in school. To this I will reply that this limit is naturally determined by the teacher, his knowledge, his ability to manage the school; that this freedom cannot be prescribed; the measure of this freedom is only the result of the greater or lesser knowledge and talent of the teacher. This freedom is not a rule, but serves as a check in comparing schools between themselves, and as a check in comparing new methods which are introduced into the school curriculum. The school in which there is less compulsion is better than the one in which there is more. The method which at its introduction into the school does not demand an increase of discipline is good; but the one which demands greater severity is certainly bad. Take, for example, a more or less free school, such as mine was, and try to start a conversation in it about the table and the ceiling, or to transpose cubes,—you will see what it hubbub will arise in the school[Pg 295] and how you will feel the necessity of restoring order by means of severity; try to tell them an interesting story, or to give them problems, or make one write on the board and let the others correct his mistakes, and allow them to leave the benches, and you will find them all occupied and there will be no naughtiness, and you will not have to increase your severity,— and you may safely say that the method is good.

In my pedagogical articles I have given theoretical reasons why I find that only the freedom of choice on the side of the learners as to what they are to be taught and how can form a foundation of any instruction; in practice I have always applied these rules in the schools under my guidance, at first on a large scale, and later in narrower limits, and the results have always been very good, both for the teachers and the pupils, as also for the evolution of new methods,—and this I assert boldly, for hundreds of visitors have come to the Yásnaya Polyána school and know all about it.

The consequences of such a relation to the pupils has been for the teachers that they did not consider that method best which they knew, but tried to discover other methods, became acquainted with other teachers for the purpose of learning their methods, tested new methods, and, above all, were learning something all the time. A teacher never permitted himself to think that in cases of failure it was the pupils' fault,—their laziness, playfulness, dulness, deafness, stammering,—but was firmly convinced that he alone was to blame for it, and for every failure of a pupil or of all the pupils he tried to find a remedy. For the pupils the result was that they learned readily, always begged the teachers to give them evening classes in the winter, and were absolutely free in the school,—which, in my conviction and experience, is the chief condition for successful progress in instruction. Between teachers and pupils there were always established[Pg 296] friendly, natural relations, with which alone it is possible for the teacher to know his pupils well. If, from a first, external impression of the school, we were to determine the difference between the church, the German, and my own school, it would be this: in a church school you hear a peculiar, unnatural, monotonous shouting of all the pupils and now and then the stern cries of the teacher; in the German school you hear only the teacher's voice and now and then the timid voices of the pupils; in mine you hear the loud voices of the teachers and the pupils, almost simultaneously.

As for the methods of instruction the consequences were that not one method of instruction was adopted or rejected because it was liked or not, but only because it was accepted or not by the pupils without compulsion. But in addition to the good results which were always obtained without fail from the application of my method by myself and by everybody else (more than twenty teachers), who taught according to my method ("without fail" I say for the reason that not once did we have a pupil who did not learn the rudiments), besides these results, the application of the principles of which I have spoken had the effect that during these fifteen years all the various modifications, to which my method was subjected, not only did not remove it from the needs of the masses, but, on the contrary, brought it nearer and nearer to them. The masses, at least in our parts, know the method itself and discuss it, and prefer it to the church method, which I cannot say of the sound method. In the schools which are conducted according to my method the teacher cannot remain motionless in his knowledge, such as he is and must be with the method of sounds. If a teacher according to the new German fashion wants to go ahead and perfect himself, he has to follow the pedagogical literature, that is, to read all those new inventions about the conversations about the suslik and about[Pg 297] the transposition of the squares. I do not think that that can promote his personal education. On the contrary, in my school, where the subjects of instruction, language and mathematics, demand positive knowledge, every teacher, in advancing his pupils, feels the need of learning himself, which was constantly the case with all the teachers I had.

Besides, the methods of instruction themselves, which are not settled once for all, but always strive to be as easy and as simple as possible, are modified and improved from the indications which the teacher discovers in the relations of the learners to his instruction.

The very opposite to this I see in what, unfortunately, takes place in the schools of the German pattern, which of late have been introduced in our country in an artificial manner. The failure to recognize that before deciding what to teach and how to teach we must solve the question how we can find that out has led the pedagogues to a complete disagreement with reality, and the abyss which fifteen years ago was felt to exist between theory and practice has now reached the farthest limits. Now that the masses are on all sides begging for education, while pedagogy has more than ever passed to personal fancies, this discord has reached incredible proportions.

This discord between the demands of pedagogy and reality has of late found its peculiarly striking expression not only in the matter of instruction itself, but also in another very important side of the school, namely in its administration. In order to show in what condition this matter has been and might be, I shall speak of Krapívensk County of the Government of Túla, in which I live, which I know, and which, from its position, forms the type of the majority of counties of central Russia.

113

In 1862 fourteen schools were opened in a district of ten thousand souls, when I was rural judge; besides, there existed about ten schools in the district among the[Pg 298] clericals and in the manors among the servants. In the three remaining districts of the county there were fifteen large and thirty small schools among the clericals and manorial servants. Without saying anything about the number of the learners, of which, I assume, there were in general not less than now, nor about the instruction itself, which was partly bad and partly good, but on the whole not worse than at present, I will tell how and on what that business was based.

All schools were then, with few exceptions, based on a free agreement of the teacher with the parents of the pupils, or with the whole partnership of the peasants paying a lump sum for everybody. Such a relation between the parents or Communes and the teachers is even now met with in some exceedingly rare places of our county and of the Government in general. Everybody will agree that, leaving aside the question of the quality of instruction, such a relation of the teacher to the parents and peasants is most just, natural, and desirable. But, with the introduction of the law of 1864, this relation was abolished and is being abolished more and more. Everybody who knows the matter as it is will observe that with the abolition of this relation the people take less and less part in the matter of their education, which is only natural. In some County Councils the school tax of the peasants is even turned into the County Council, and the salary, appointment of teachers, location of schools,—all that is done quite independently of those for whom it is intended (in theory the peasants, no doubt, are members of the County Council, but in practice they have through this mediation no influence on their own schools). Nobody will, I suppose, assert that that is just, but some will say: "The illiterate peasants cannot judge what is good and what bad, and we must build for them as well as we can." But how do we know? Do we know firmly, are we all of one opinion, how to build schools? And[Pg 299] does it not frequently turn out bad, for we have built much worse than they have?

Thus, in relation to the administrative side of the schools I have again to put a third question, on the same basis of freedom: Why do we know how best to arrange a school? To this question German pedagogy gives an answer which is quite consistent with its whole system. It knows what the best school is, it has formed a clear, definite ideal, down to the minutest details, the benches, the hours of instruction, and so forth, and gives an answer: the school has to be such and such, according to this pattern,—this alone is good and every other school is injurious. I know that, although the desire of Henry IV. to give each Frenchman soup and a chicken was unrealizable, it was impossible to say that the desire was false. But the matter assumes an entirely different aspect when the soup is of a very questionable quality and is not a chicken soup, but a worthless broth. And yet the so-called science of pedagogy is in this matter indissolubly connected with power; both in Germany and with us there are prescribed certain ideal one-class, two-class schools, and so forth; and the pedagogical and the administrative powers do not wish to know the fact that the masses would like to attend to their own education. Let us see how such a view of popular education has been reflected in practice on the question of education.

Beginning with the year 1862 the idea that education was necessary has more and more spread among the masses: on all sides schools were established by church servants, hired teachers, and the Communes. Whether good or bad, these schools were spontaneous and grew out directly from the needs of the masses; with the introduction of the law of 1864 this tendency was increased, and in 1870 there were, according to the reports, about sixty schools in Krapívensk County. Since then officials of the ministry and members of the County Council have[Pg 300] begun to meddle more and more with school matters, and in Krapívensk County forty schools have been closed and schools of a lower order have been prohibited from being opened. I know that those who closed those schools affirm that these schools existed only nominally and were very bad; but I cannot believe it, because I know well-instructed pupils from three villages, Trósna, Lamíntsovo, and Yásnaya Polyána, where schools were closed. I also know—and this will seem incredible to many—what is meant by prohibiting the opening of schools. It means that, on the basis of a circular of the ministry of public instruction, which spoke of the prohibition of unreliable teachers (this, no doubt, had reference to the Nihilists), the school council transferred this prohibition to the

114

minor schools, taught by sextons, soldiers, and so forth, which the peasants themselves had opened, and which, no doubt, are not at all comprised in the circular. But, instead, there exist twenty schools with teachers, who are supposed to be good because they receive a salary of two hundred roubles in silver, and the County Council has distributed Ushínski's text-books, and these schools are called one-class schools, because they teach in them according to a programme, and the whole year around, that is, also in summer, with the exception of July and August.

Leaving aside the question of the quality of the former schools, we shall now take a glance at their administrative side, and we will compare, from this side, what was before, with what is now. In the administrative, external side of the school there are five main subjects, which are so closely connected with the school business itself that on their good or bad structure depend to a great extent the success and dissemination of popular education. These five subjects are: (1) the school building, (2) the schedule of instruction, (3) the distribution of the schools according to localities, (4) the choice of the[Pg 301] teacher, and—what is most important—(5) the material means, the remuneration of the teachers.

In regard to the school building the masses rarely have any difficulty, when they start a school for themselves, and if the Commune is rich and there are any communal buildings, such as a storehouse or a deserted inn, the Commune fixes it up; if there is none, it buys a building, at times even from a landed proprietor, or it builds one of its own. If the Commune is not well-to-do and is small, it hires quarters from a peasant, or establishes a rotation, and the teacher passes from hut to hut. If the Commune, as it most generally does, selects a teacher from its own midst, a manorial servant, a soldier, or a church servant, the school is located at the house of that person, and the Commune looks only after the heating. In any case, I have never heard that the question of the location of the school ever troubled a Commune, or that half the sum set aside for instruction should be lost, as is done by school councils, on the buildings, nay, not even one-sixth or one-tenth of the whole sum. The peasant Communes have arranged it one way or another, but the question of the school building has never been regarded as troublesome. Only under the influence of the higher authorities do there occur cases where the Communes build brick buildings with iron roofs. The peasants assume that the school is not in the structure, but in the teacher, and that the school is not a permanent institution, but that as soon as the parents have acquired knowledge, the next generation will get the rudiments without a teacher. But the County Council department of the ministry always assumes—since for it the whole problem consists in inspecting and classifying—that the chief foundation of the school is the structure and that the school is a permanent establishment, and so, as far as I know, now spends about one-half of its money on buildings, and inscribes empty school buildings in the list of the schools[Pg 302] of the third order. In the Krapívensk County Council seven hundred roubles out of two thousand roubles are spent on buildings. The ministerial department cannot admit that the teacher (that educated pedagogue who is assumed for the masses) would lower himself to such an extent as to be willing to go, like a tailor, from hut to hut, or to teach in a smoky house. But the masses assume nothing and only know that for their money they can hire whom they please, and that, if they, the hiring peasants, live in smoky huts, the hired teacher has no reason to turn up his nose at them.

In regard to the second question, about the division of the school time, the masses have always and everywhere invariably expressed one demand, and that is that the instruction shall be carried on in the winter only.

Everywhere the parents quit sending their children in the spring, and those children who are left in the school, from one-fourth to one-fifth of the whole number, are the little tots or the children of rich parents, and they attend school unwillingly. When the masses hire a teacher themselves, they always hire him by the month and only for the winter. The ministerial department assumes that, just as in the institutions of learning there are two months of vacation, so it ought also to be in a one-class country school. From the standpoint of the ministerial department that is quite reasonable: the children will not forget their instruction, the teacher is provided for during the whole year, and the inspectors find it more comfortable to travel in the summer; but the masses know nothing about all that, and their common sense tells them that in winter the children sleep for ten hours, consequently

115

their minds are fresh; that in winter there are no plays and no work for the children, and that if they study in winter as long as possible, taking in even the evenings, for which a lamp costing one rouble fifty kopeks is needed and kerosene costing as much, there will be enough instruction.[Pg 303] Besides, in the summer every boy is of use to the peasant, and in summer proceeds the life instruction, which is more important than school learning. The masses say that there is no reason why they should pay the teacher during the summer. "Rather will we increase his pay for the winter months, and that will please him better. We prefer to hire a teacher at twenty-five roubles a month for seven months, than at twelve roubles a month for the whole year. For the summer the teacher will hire himself out elsewhere."

As to the third question, the distribution of the schools according to localities, the arrangements of the masses most markedly differ from those of the school council. In the first place, the distribution of the schools, that is, whether there shall be more or less of them for a certain locality, always depends on the character of the whole population (when the masses themselves attend to it). Wherever the masses are more industrial and work out, where they are nearer to the cities, where they need the rudiments,—there there are more schools; where the locality is more removed and agricultural, there there are fewer of them. In the second place, when the masses themselves attend to the matter, they distribute the schools in such a way as to give all the parents a chance to make use of the schools in return for their money, that is, to send their children to school. The peasants of small, remote villages of from thirty to forty souls, where half the population will be found, prefer to have a cheap teacher in their own village, than an expensive one in the centre of the township, whither their children cannot walk or be driven. By this distribution of the schools, the schools themselves, as arranged by the peasants, depart, it is true, from the required pattern of the school, but, instead, acquire the most diversified forms, everywhere adapting themselves to local conditions. Here a clerical person from a neighbouring village teaches eight boys at his house, receiving fifty[Pg 304] kopeks a month from each. Here a small village hires a soldier for eight roubles for the winter, and he goes from house to house. Here a rich innkeeper hires a teacher for his children for five roubles and board, and the neighbouring peasants join him, by adding two roubles for each of their boys. There a large village or a compact township levies fifteen kopeks from each of the twelve hundred souls and hires a teacher for 180 roubles for the winter. There the priest teaches, receiving as a remuneration either money, or labour, or both. The chief difference in this respect between the view of the peasants and that of the County Council is this: the peasants, according to the more or less favourable local conditions, introduce schools of a better or worse quality, but always in such a way that there is not a single locality where some kind of instruction is not offered; while with the arrangement of the County Council a large half of the population is left outside every possibility of partaking of that education even in the distant future.

In matters of the petty villages, forming one-half of the population, the ministerial department acts most decisively. It says: "We provide schools where there is a building and where the peasants of the township have collected enough money to support a teacher at two hundred roubles. We will contribute from the County Council what is wanting, and the school is entered on the lists." The villages that are removed from the school may send their children there, if they so wish. Of course, the peasants do not take their children there, because it is too far, and yet they pay. Thus, in the Yásenets township all pay for three schools, but only 450 souls in three villages make use of the school, though there are in all three thousand souls; thus, only one-seventh of the population makes use of the school, though all pay for it. In the Chermóshen township there are nine hundred souls and there is a school there, but only thirty pupils attend[Pg 305] it, because all the villages of that township are scattered. To nine hundred souls there ought to be four hundred pupils. And yet, both in the Yásenets and the Chermóshen townships the question of the distribution of schools is regarded as satisfactorily solved.

In matters of the choice of a teacher, the masses are again guided by quite different views from the County Council. In choosing a teacher, the masses look upon him in their own way, and judge him accordingly. If the teacher has been in the neighbourhood, and the masses know what the results of his teaching are, they value him according to these results as

116

a good or as a bad teacher; but, in addition to the scholastic qualities, the masses demand that the teacher shall be a man who stands in close relations to the peasant, able to understand his life and to speak Russian, and so they will always prefer a country to a city teacher. In doing so, the masses have no bias and no antipathy toward any class in particular: he may be a gentleman, official, burgher, soldier, sexton, priest,—that makes no difference so long as he is a simple man and a Russian. For this reason the peasants have no cause for excluding clerical persons, as the County Councils do. The County Councils select their teachers from among strangers, getting them from the cities, while the masses look for them among themselves. But the chief difference in this respect between the view of the Communes and that of the County Council consists in this: the County Council has only one type,—the teacher who has attended pedagogical courses, who has finished a course in a seminary or school, at two hundred roubles; but with the masses, who do not exclude this teacher and appreciate him, if he is good, there are gradations of all kinds of teachers. Besides, with the majority of school councils there are definite favourite types of teachers, for the most part such as are foreign to the masses and antagonistic to them, and other types which[Pg 306] the school councils dislike. Thus, evidently, the favourite type of many counties of the Government of Túla are lady teachers; the disliked type are the clerical persons, and in the whole of the Túla and Krapívensk counties there is not one school with a teacher from the clergy, which is quite remarkable from an administrative point of view. In Krapívensk County there are fifty parishes. The clerical persons are the cheapest of teachers, because they are permanently settled and for the most part can teach in their own houses with the aid of their wives and daughters,—and these are, it seems, purposely avoided, as though they were very harmful people.

In matters of the remuneration of the teachers, the difference between the view of the masses and that of the County Council has almost all been expressed in the preceding pages. It consists in this: (1) the masses choose a teacher according to their means, and they admit and know from experience that there are teachers at all prices, from two puds of flour a month to thirty roubles a month; (2) teachers are to be remunerated for the winter months, for those during which there can be some instruction; (3) the masses, in the housing of the school as also in matters of the remuneration of the teachers, always know how to find a cheap way: they give flour, hay, the use of carts, eggs, and all kinds of trifles, which are imperceptible to the world at large, but which improve the teacher's condition; (4) above all, a teacher is paid, or is remunerated in addition to the payment, by the parents of the pupils, who pay by the month, or by the whole Commune which enjoys the advantages of the school, and not by the administration that has no direct interest in the matter.

The ministerial department cannot act differently in this respect. The norm of the salary for a model teacher is given, consequently these means have to be got together in some way. For example: a Commune intends to open[Pg 307] a school,—the township gives it a certain number of kopeks per soul. The County Council calculates how much to add. If there are no demands made by other schools, it gives more, sometimes twice as much as the Commune has given; at times, when all the money has been distributed, it gives less, or entirely refuses to give any. Thus, there is in Krapívensk County a Commune which gives ninety roubles, and the County Council adds to that three hundred roubles for a school with an assistant; and there is another Commune which gives 250 roubles, and the County Council adds another fifty roubles; and a third Commune which offers fifty-six roubles, and the County Council refuses to add anything or to open the school, because that money is insufficient for a normal school, and all the money has been distributed.

Thus, the chief distinctions between the administrative view of the masses and that of the County Council are the following: (1) the County Council pays great attention to the housing and spends large sums upon it, while the masses obviate this difficulty by domestic, economic means, and look upon the primary schools as temporary, passing institutions; (2) the ministerial department demands that instruction be carried on during the whole year, with the exception of July and August, and nowhere introduces evening classes, while the masses demand that instruction be carried on only in the winter and are fond of evening classes; (3) the ministerial department has a definite type of teachers, without which it does not recognize the school, and has a loathing for clerical persons and, in general, for local instructors; the masses recognize no norm and choose their teachers preferably from local inhabitants; (4) the ministerial department distributes the schools by accident, that is, it is guided only by the desire of forming a normal school, and has no care for that greater half of the population which under such a distribution is left outside the school education; the[Pg 308] masses not only recognize no definite external form of the school, but in the greatest variety of ways get teachers with all kinds of means, arranging worse and cheaper schools with small means and good and expensive schools with greater means, and turn their attention to furnishing all localities with instruction in return for their money; (5) the ministerial department determines one measure of remuneration, which is sufficiently high, and arbitrarily increases the amount from the County Council; the masses demand the greatest possible economy and distribute the remuneration in such a way that those whose children are taught pay directly.

It seems as though it would be superfluous to expatiate on how clearly the common sense of the masses is expressed in these demands, in contradistinction to that artificial structure, in which, at its very birth, they are trying to imprison the business of popular education. Even besides this, the feeling of justice is involuntarily provoked against such an order of things. See what is taking place. The masses have felt the necessity of education, and have begun to work in the direction of attaining their end. In addition to all the taxes which they pay, they have voluntarily imposed upon themselves the tax for education, that is, they have begun to hire teachers. What have we done? "Oh, you are able to pay," we said, "wait, then, for you are stupid and rude. Let us have the money, and we will arrange it for you in the best manner possible."

The masses have given up their money (as I have said, in many County Councils the levy for the schools has been turned directly into a tax). The money was taken, and the education was arranged for them.

I am not going to repeat about the artificiality of the education, but how the whole matter has been arranged. In Krapívensk County there are forty thousand souls, including girls, according to the last census. According[Pg 309] to Bunyakóvski's table of the distribution of ten thousand of the Orthodox population for the year 1862, there ought to be, of the male sex between six and fourteen years, 1,834, and of the female sex, 1,989,—in all 3,823 to each ten thousand. According to my own observations, there ought to be more, no doubt on account of the increase of the population, so that the average school population may boldly be put at four thousand. In a school there are, on an average, in the large centres, about sixty pupils, and in the smaller, from ten to twenty-five. In order that all may receive instruction, the smaller centres, forming the greater half of the population, need schools for ten, fifteen, and twenty pupils, so that the average of a school, in my opinion, would be not more than thirty pupils. How many schools are, then, needed for sixteen thousand pupils? Divide sixteen thousand by thirty, and we get 530 schools. Let us assume that, although at the opening of the schools all pupils from seven to fifteen years of age will enter, not all will attend regularly for the period of eight years; let us reject one-fourth, that is 130 schools and, consequently, 4,200 pupils. Let us say that there are four hundred schools. Only twenty have been opened. The County Council gives two thousand roubles and has added one thousand roubles, making in all three thousand roubles. From some of the peasants, not from all, fifteen kopeks are levied from each soul, in all about four thousand roubles. On the building of schools seven hundred roubles are spent, and on the pedagogical courses twelve hundred roubles have been used in one year. But let us suppose that the County Council will act quite simply and sensibly, and will not waste money on pedagogical courses and other trifles; let us suppose that all peasants will pay the new school tax of fifteen kopeks, what will the future of this matter be? From the peasants six thousand, from the County Council three thousand, in all nine thousand. Let us assume that[Pg 310] ten more schools will be added. Nine thousand roubles will barely suffice for the support of these schools, and that only in case the school council will act most prudently and economically. Consequently, with the County Council administration, thirty schools to forty thousand of the population are the highest limit of what the dissemination of the schools in the county may reach. And this limit of the school business can be attained only if the peasants will levy fifteen kopeks on each soul, which is extremely doubtful, and if the disbursement of this money will be in the hands of the peasants, and not of the County Council. I do not speak of the possible increase of three thousand roubles, because this increase of three thousand roubles partly falls back on those same peasants, and on the other hand is not secured by anything, forming only an accidental means. Thus, in order to bring the business of popular education to the state in which it ought to be, that is, in order that there shall be four hundred schools to the forty thousand of the population, and in order that the schools shall not be a toy, but may answer a real want of the masses, there is no other issue than that the peasants be taxed, not fifteen kopeks, but three roubles a soul, in order that the necessary three hundred roubles to each school be obtained. Even then I do not see any reason for thinking that as many schools as are needed would be built.

Do we not see that now, when the simplest arithmetical calculation shows that the only means for the success of the schools is the simplification of methods, the simplicity and cheapness of the arrangement of the school,—the pedagogues are busy, as though having made a wager to concoct a most difficult, most complicated, and expensive (and, I must add, most bad) instruction? In the manuals of Messrs. Bunákov and Evtushévski I have figured up three hundred roubles' worth of aids to instruction which, in their opinion, are absolutely necessary for[Pg 311] the establishment of a primary school. All they talk about in pedagogical circles is how to prepare improved teachers in the seminaries, so that a village might not be able to get them even for four hundred roubles. On that road of perfection, on which pedagogy stands, it is quite apparent to me that if 120,000 roubles were collected in a county, the pedagogues would find use for them all in twenty schools, with adjustable tables, seminaries for teachers, and so forth. Have we not seen that forty schools were closed in Krapívensk County, and that those who closed them were fully convinced that they thus advanced the cause of education, for now they have twenty "good" schools? But what is most remarkable is that those who express these demands are not in the least interested in knowing whether the masses for whom they are preparing all these things want them, and still less, who is going to pay for it all. But the County Councils are so befogged by these demands that they do not see the simple calculation and the simple justice. It is as though a man asked me to buy him two puds of flour for a month, and I bought him for that rouble a box of perfumed confectionery and reproached him for his ignorance, because he was dissatisfied.

As I wish to remain true to my rule that criticism should point out how that which is not good ought to be, I shall try to show how the whole school business ought to be arranged, if it is not to be a plaything, and is to have a future. The answer is the same as to the first two questions,—freedom. The masses must be given the freedom to arrange their schools as they wish, and as little as possible should any one interfere in their arrangement. Only with such a view of the matter will all the obstacles to the dissemination of the schools be obviated, though they have seemed insuperable. The chief obstacles are the insufficiency of the means and the impossibility of increasing them. To the first the masses reply[Pg 312] that they are using all the measures at their command to make the schools cost little; to the second they reply that the means will always be found so long as they themselves are the masters, and that they are not willing to increase the means for the support of that which they do not need.

The essential difference between the view of the people and of the ministerial department consists in the following: (1) In the opinion of the masses there is no one definite norm and form of the school, outside and below which the school is not recognized, as is assumed by the ministerial department; a school may be of any kind, either a very good and expensive one, or a very poor and cheap one, but even in a very poor one reading and writing may be learned, and, as in a richer parish a better pope is appointed and a better church built, so also may a better school be built in a wealthy village, and a poorer school in a less well-to-do village; but just as one can pray equally well in a poor or in a rich parish, even so it is with learning. (2) The masses regard as the first condition of their education an even, equal distribution of this education, though it be in its lowest stage, and then only they propose a further, again an even, raising of the level of education, while the ministerial department considers it necessary to give to a certain chosen few, to one-twentieth of the whole number, a specimen of education, to show them how nice it is. (3) The ministerial

119

department, either unable or purposely unwilling to calculate, has raised the educational business to such a high, expensive level, and one which is so foreign to the masses, that considering the high price at which the education is acquired, no issue from that situation can be foreseen, and the number of learners can never be increased; but the masses, who know how to calculate, and who are interested in that calculation, have no doubt long ago figured out what I have pointed out above, and see as clear as[Pg 313] daylight that those expensive schools, which cost as much as four hundred roubles each, may be good indeed, but are not what they need, and try in every way possible to diminish the expenses for their schools.

What, then, is to be done? How are the County Councils to act in order that this business may not be a plaything and a pastime, but shall have a future? Let them conform with the needs of the masses, and, so far as possible, cheapen and free the forms of the school, and afford the Communes the greatest possible power in the establishment of the schools.

For this it is necessary that the County Councils shall entirely abandon the distribution of the taxes to the schools and the distribution of the schools according to localities, but shall leave this distribution to the peasants themselves. The determination of the pay to the teacher, the hiring, purchase, or building of the house, the choice of place and of the teacher himself,—all that ought to be left to the peasants. The County Council, that is, the school council, should only demand that the Communes inform it where and on what foundations schools have been established, not in order that, upon learning the facts, it shall prohibit them, as is done now, but in order that, learning about the conditions under which the school exists, it may add (if the conditions are in conformity with the demands of the council) from its County Council's sums, for the support of the school newly founded, a certain, definite part of what the school costs the Commune: a half, a third, a fourth, according to the quality of the school and the means and wishes of the County Council. Thus, for example, a village of twenty souls hires a transient man at two roubles a month to teach the children. The school council, that is, a person authorized by it, of whom I shall speak later, upon receiving that information, invites the transient to come to him, asks him what he knows and how he teaches, and, if the[Pg 314] transient is the least bit educated and does not represent anything harmful, apportions to him the amount determined upon by the County Council, one-half, one-third, or one-fourth, in precisely the same way the school council proceeds in reference to a clerical person hired by the Commune at five roubles per month, or in reference to a teacher hired at fifteen roubles per month. Of course, that is the way the school council acts in reference to the teachers hired by the Communes themselves; but if the Communes turn to the school council, the latter recommends to them teachers under the same conditions. But in doing so the County Council must not forget that there should not be merely teachers at two hundred roubles; the school council should be an employment agency for teachers of every description and of every price, from one rouble to thirty roubles a month. On buildings the school council ought not to spend or add anything, because they are one of the most unproductive items of expense. But the County Council ought not to disdain, as it now does, teachers at two, three, four, five roubles per month and locations in smoky huts or by rotation from farm to farm.

The County Council ought to remember that the prototype of the school, that ideal toward which it ought to tend, is not a stone building with an iron roof, with blackboards and desks, such as we see in model schools, but the very hut in which the peasant lives, with those benches and tables on which he eats, and not a teacher in a Prince Albert or a lady teacher in a chignon, but a male teacher in a caftan and shirt, or a female teacher in a peasant skirt and with a kerchief on her head, and not with one hundred pupils, but with five, six, or ten.

The County Council must have no bias or antipathy for certain types of teachers, as is the case at present. Thus, for example, the Túla County Council just now has a special bias for the type of school-teachers from the gymnasia and clerical schools, and the greater part of[Pg 315] the schools in Túla County are in their charge. In Krapívensk County there exists a strange antipathy for teachers from the clerical profession, so that in this county, where there are as many as fifty parishes, there is not one clerical person employed as a teacher.

The County Council, in proposing a teacher, ought to be guided by two chief considerations: in the first place, that the teacher should be as cheap as possible; in the second, that by his education he should stand as near to the masses as possible. Only thanks to the opposite view on the matter can be explained such an inexplicable phenomenon as that in Krapívensk County (almost the same is true of the whole Government and of the majority of Governments) there are fifty parishes and twenty schools, and that for these twenty schools there is not a single clerical teacher, although there is not a parish where a priest, or a deacon, or a sexton, or their daughters and wives could not be found, who would not be glad to do the teaching for one-fourth the pay that the teachers coming from the city would be willing to take.

But I shall be told: What kind of schools will those be with bigots, drunken soldiers, expelled scribes, and sextons? And what control can there be over those formless schools? To this I will reply that, in the first place, these teachers, bigots, soldiers, and sextons are not so bad as they are imagined to be. In my school practice I often had to do with pupils from these schools, and some of them could read fluently and write beautifully, and soon abandoned the bad habits which they brought with them from those schools. All of us know peasants who have learned the rudiments in such schools, and it cannot be said that this learning was useless or injurious. In the second place, I will say that teachers of that calibre are especially bad because they are quite abandoned in the backwoods and teach without any aid or instruction, and that now there is not to be found a single one of the old[Pg 316] teachers who would not tell you with regret that he does not know the new methods and has himself learned for copper pence, and that many of them, especially the younger church servants, are quite willing to learn the new methods. These teachers ought not to be rejected without further ado as absolutely worthless. There are among them better and worse teachers (and I have seen some very capable ones). They ought to be compared; the better of them ought to be selected, encouraged, brought together with other better teachers, and instructed,—which is quite feasible and precisely the thing in which the duty of the school council is to consist.

But how are they to be controlled, watched, and taught, if they breed by the hundred in each county? In my opinion the work of the County Council and school council ought to consist in nothing but watching the pedagogical side of the business, and that is feasible, if these means will be taken: in every County Council, which has taken upon itself the duty of the dissemination of popular education, or the coöperation with it, there ought to be one person—whether it be an unpaid member of the school council, or a man at a salary of not less than one thousand roubles, hired by the County Council—who is to attend to the pedagogical side of the business in the county. That person ought to have a general, fresh education within the limits of a gymnasium course, that is, he must know Russian thoroughly and Church-Slavic partly, arithmetic and algebra thoroughly, and be a teacher, that is, know the practice of pedagogy. This person must be freshly educated, because I have observed that frequently the information of a man who has long ago finished his course even in a university, and who has not refreshed his education, is insufficient, not only for the guidance of teachers, but even for the examination of a village school. This person must by all means be a teacher himself in the same locality, in order[Pg 317] that in his demands and instructions he may always have in view that pedagogical material with which the other teachers have to deal, and that he may sustain in himself that live relation to reality which is the chief preservative against error and delusion. If a County Council does not possess such a man and does not wish to employ one, it has, in my opinion, absolutely nothing to do with the popular education, except to give money, because every interference with the administrative side of the matter, in the way it is done now, can only be injurious.

This member of the County Council, or the educated person hired by it, must have the best model school, with an assistant, in the county. In addition to conducting this school and applying to it all the newest methods of instruction, this head teacher ought to keep an eye on all the other schools. This school is not to be a model in the sense of introducing into it all kinds of cubes and pictures and all kinds of nonsense invented by the Germans, but the teacher in this school should experiment on just such peasant children as the other schools consist of, in order to determine the simplest methods which may be adopted by the majority of the teachers, sextons, and soldiers, who form the bulk of all the schools. Since with the arrangement which I propose there will certainly be formed large complete schools in the larger centres (as I think, in the proportion of one to twenty of all the other schools), and in these large schools the teachers will be of a grade of education equal to that of the seminarists who have finished a course in a theological school, the head teacher will visit all these larger schools, bring together these teachers on Sundays, point out to them the defects, propose new methods, give counsel and books for their own education, and invite them to his school on Sundays. The library of the head teacher ought to consist of several copies of the Bible, of Church-Slavic and Russian grammars, arithmetic, and algebra. The head[Pg 318] teacher, whenever he has time, will visit also the small schools and invite their teachers to come to see him; but the duty of watching the minor teachers is imposed on the older teachers, who just in the same way visit their district and invite those teachers to come to see them on Sundays and on week-days. The County Council either pays the teachers for travelling, or, in adding its portion to what the Communes levy, makes it a condition that the Communes furnish transportation. The meetings of the teachers and the visits in similar or better schools are one of the chief conditions for the successful conduct of the business of education, and so the County Council ought to direct its main attention to the organization of these meetings, and not spare any money for them.

Besides, in the large schools, where there will be more than fifty pupils, there ought to be chosen, instead of the assistants which they now have, such of the pupils, of either sex, as show marked ability for a teacher's calling, and they should be made assistants, two or three in each school. These assistants should receive a salary of fifty kopeks to one rouble per month, and the teacher should work with them separately in the evenings, so that they may not fall behind the others. These assistants, chosen from among the best, are to form the future teachers, to take the place of the lowest in the minor schools.

Naturally the organization of these teachers' meetings, both for the smaller and the larger schools, and the head teacher's visits of inspection, and the formation of teachers from pupils acting as assistants may take place in a large variety of ways; the main point is that the surveillance of any number of schools (even though it may reach the norm of one school to every one hundred souls) is possible in this manner. With such an arrangement the teachers of both the large and the small schools will feel that their labours are appreciated, that they have not buried themselves in the backwoods without hope of salvation,[Pg 319] that they have companions and guides, and that in the matter of instruction, both for their own further education and for the improvement of their situation, they have means for advancement. With such an arrangement, the devotee and the sexton who are able to learn will learn; while those who are unable or unwilling to do so will be replaced by some one else.

The time of instruction ought to be, as is the wish of all peasants, during the seven winter months, and so the salary is to be determined by the month. With such an arrangement, leaving out the rapidity and the equal distribution of education, the advantage will be this, that the schools will be established in those centres where the necessity for them is felt by the masses, where they are established spontaneously and, therefore, firmly. Where the character of the population demands education it will be permanent. Just look: in the towns, the children of the innkeepers and well-to-do peasants learn to read in one way or another and never forget what they have learned; but in the backwoods, where a landed proprietor founds a school, the children learn well, but in ten years all is forgotten, and the population is as illiterate as ever. For this reason the centres, large or small, where the schools are established spontaneously, are particularly precious. Where such a school has germinated, no matter how poor it be, it will throw out roots, and sooner or later the population will be able to read and write. Consequently, these sprouts ought to be deemed precious, and not be treated, as they are everywhere,—they ought not to be forbidden, because the schools are not according to our taste, that is, the sprouts ought not to be killed, and branches stuck in the ground where they will not take root.

With merely such an arrangement, without the establishment of costly and artificial seminaries, the chosen ones—those selected from the best of the pupils themselves,[Pg 320] and those who are educated in the schools—will form that contingent of cheap popular teachers who will take the place of the soldiers and sextons and will fully satisfy all the demands of the masses and of the educated classes. The chief advantage of such an arrangement is that it alone gives the development of popular education a future, that is, takes us out from that blind alley into which the County Councils have gone, thanks to the expensive schools and to the absence of new sources for the increase of their numbers. Only when the masses themselves choose the centres for the schools, themselves choose teachers, determine the amount of the remuneration, and directly enjoy the advantages of the schools, will they be ready to add means for the schools if such should become necessary. I know Communes that paid fifty kopeks a soul for a school in each of their villages; but it is difficult to compel the peasants to pay fifteen kopeks for a school in the township, if not all of them can make use of it. For the whole county, for the County Council, the peasants will not add a single kopek, because they feel that they will not enjoy the advantages of their money. Only with such an arrangement will be found soon the means for the proper maintenance of all schools, of one to each one hundred souls, which seems so impossible in the present state of affairs.

In addition to this, with the arrangement which I propose, the interests of the peasant Communes and of the County Council, as the representative of the intelligence of the locality, will indissolubly be connected. Let us say that the County Council gives one-third of what the peasants give. In furnishing this amount, it will evidently, in one way or another, see to it that the money is not wasted, and, consequently, will also keep an eye on the two-thirds given by the peasant Communes. The peasant Commune sees that the County Council gives its part, and so admits the right of the Council to follow the[Pg 321] progress of the instruction. At the same time, it has an object-lesson in the difference which exists between a school maintained at a smaller and that maintained at a greater expense, and chooses the one which it needs or which is more accessible to it in accordance with its means.

I will again take Krapívensk County, with which I am familiar, to show what difference the proposed arrangement would make. I cannot have the slightest doubt that the moment permission is granted to open schools, wherever wanted and of any description desired, there will at once appear very many schools. I am convinced that in Krapívensk County, in which there are fifty parishes, there will always be a school in each parish, because the parishes are always centres of population, and because among the church servants there will always be found one who is capable of teaching, likes to teach, and will find his advantage in it. In addition to the schools maintained by the church servants there will be opened those forty schools that have been closed (more correctly thirty, because ten of them were church schools), and there will be opened very many new schools, so that in a very short time there will be not far from four hundred instead of the twenty at present.

I may be believed or not, but I will assume that in Krapívensk County 380 additional schools will be opened, the moment they are given over to the masses, so that there will be four hundred in all, and I will try to determine whether the existence of these four hundred schools, that is, of twenty times as many as at present, is possible under the conditions which I have assumed in discussing the existing order.

Assuming that all peasants pay fifteen kopeks per soul, and the County Council gives three thousand roubles, there will be nine thousand roubles, which will suffice only for thirty schools with the former arrangement. But with the new arrangement:

[Pg 322]

I assume that ten of the old schools are left intact; in these schools the teachers get twenty roubles per month, which, for the seven winter months, amounts to fourteen hundred roubles.

I assume that in every parish there will be established a school with the teacher's salary at five roubles per month, which, for fifty schools, amounts to 1,750 roubles.

I assume the remaining 340 schools are of the cheap character, at two roubles per month; fifteen roubles for each of the 340 schools makes 5,100 roubles.

Thus the four hundred schools will demand an expenditure in salaries amounting to 8,250 roubles. There are still left 750 roubles for school appliances and transportation.

The figures for the teachers' wages are not chosen arbitrarily by me: on the other hand, the expensive teachers are given a larger salary than they now get by the month for the whole year. Even so, the amount apportioned to the church servants is what they now receive in the majority of cases. But the cheap schools at two roubles per month are assumed by me at a higher rate than what the peasants in reality pay, so that the calculation may boldly be accepted. In this calculation is included the kernel of ten chief teachers and ten or more church servant teachers. It is evident that only with such a calculation will the school business be placed on a serious and possible basis and have a clear and definite future.

If what I have pointed out does not convince anybody that will mean that I did not express clearly what I wanted to say, and do not wish to enter into any disputes with anybody. I know that no deaf people are so hopeless as those who do not want to hear. I know how it is with farmers. A new threshing-machine has been bought at a great expense, and it is put up and started threshing. It threshes miserably, no matter how you set the[Pg 323] screw; it threshes badly, and the grain falls into the straw. There is a loss, and it is as clear as can be that the machine ought to be abandoned and another means be employed for threshing, but the money has been spent and the threshing-machine is put up. "Let her thresh," says the master. Precisely the same thing will happen with this matter. I know that for a long time to come there will flourish the object instruction, and cubes, and buttons instead of arithmetic, and hissing and sputtering, in teaching the letters, and twenty expensive schools of the German pattern, instead of the needed four hundred popular, cheap schools. But I know just as surely that the common sense of the Russian nation will not permit this false, artificial system of instruction to be foisted upon it.

The masses are the chief interested person and the judge, and now do not pay a particle of attention to our more or less ingenious discussions about the manner in which the spiritual food of education is best to be prepared for them. They do not care, because they are firmly convinced that in the great business of their mental development they will not make a false step and will not accept what is bad,—and it would be like making pease stick to the wall to attempt to educate, direct, and teach them in the German fashion.

[Pg 324]
[Pg 325]

## WHAT MEN LIVE BY
### 1881

[Pg 326]
[Pg 327]

### WHAT MEN LIVE BY

We know that we have passed from death unto life, because we love the brethren. He that loveth not his brother abideth in death. (First Ep. of John, iii. 14.)

But whoso hath this world's good, and seeth his brother have need, and shutteth, up his heart from him, how dwelleth the love of God in him? (*Ib*. iii. 17.)

My children, let us not love in word, neither in tongue; but in deed and in truth. (*Ib*. iii. 18.)

Love is of God; and every one that loveth is born of God, and knoweth God. (*Ib*. iv. 7.)

He that loveth not knoweth not God; for God is love. (*Ib*. iv. 8.)

No man hath seen God at any time. If we love one another, God dwelleth in us. (*Ib*. iv. 12.)

God is love; and he that dwelleth in love dwelleth in God, and God in him. (*Ib*. iv. 16.)

If a man say, I love God, and hateth his brother, he is a liar: for he that loveth not his brother whom he hath seen, how can he love God whom he hath not seen. (*Ib*.iv. 20.)

### I.

A shoemaker was lodging with his wife and children at the house of a peasant. He had no house, no land of his own, and supported his family by his shoemaker's trade. Bread was dear, but work was cheap, and he spent everything he made. The shoemaker and his wife had one fur coat between them, and even that was all worn to tatters; this was the second year that the shoemaker had been meaning to buy a sheepskin for a new fur coat.

[Pg 328]

Toward fall the shoemaker had saved some money: three roubles in paper lay in his wife's coffer, and five roubles and twenty kopeks were outstanding in the village.

In the morning the shoemaker went to the village to get him that fur coat. He put on his wife's wadded nankeen jacket over his shirt, and over it his cloth caftan; he put the three-rouble bill into his pocket, broke off a stick, and started after breakfast. He thought:

"I shall get the five roubles from the peasant, will add my own three, and with that will buy me a sheepskin for the fur coat."

The shoemaker came to the village, and called on the peasant: he was not at home, and his wife promised to send her husband with the money, but gave him none herself. He went to another peasant, but the peasant swore that he had no money, and gave him only twenty kopeks for mending a pair of boots. The shoemaker made up his mind to take the sheepskin on credit, but the furrier would not give it to him.

"Bring me the money," he said, "and then you can choose any you please; we know what it means to collect debts."

Thus the shoemaker accomplished nothing. All he got was the twenty kopeks for the boots he had mended, and a peasant gave him a pair of felt boots to patch with leather.

The shoemaker was grieved, spent all the twenty kopeks on vódka, and started home without the fur coat. In the morning it had seemed frosty to him, but now that he had drunk a little he felt warm even without the fur coat. The shoemaker walked along, with one hand striking the stick against the frozen mud clumps, and swinging the felt boots in the other, and talking to himself.

"I am warm even without a fur coat," he said. "I have drunk a cup, and the vódka is coursing through all[Pg 329] my veins. I do not need a sheepskin. I have forgotten my woe. That's the kind of a man I am! What do I care! I can get along without a fur coat: I do not need it all the time. The only trouble is the old woman will be sorry. It is a shame indeed: I work for him, and he leads me by the nose. Just wait! If you do not bring the money, I'll take away your cap, upon my word, I will! How is this? He pays me back two dimes at a time! What can you do with two dimes? Take a drink, that is all. He says he suffers want. You suffer want, and am I not suffering? You have a house, and cattle, and everything, and here is all I possess; you have your own grain, and I have to buy it. I may do as I please, but I have to spend three roubles a week on bread. I come home, and the bread is gone: again lay out a rouble and a half! So give me what is mine!"

Thus the shoemaker came up to a chapel at the turn of the road, and there he saw something that looked white, right near the chapel. It was growing dusk, and the shoemaker strained his eyes, but could not make out what it was.

"There was no stone here," he thought. "A cow? It does not look like a cow. It looks like the head of a man, and there is something white besides. And what should a man be doing there?"

He came nearer, and he could see plainly. What marvel was that? It was really a man, either alive or dead, sitting there all naked, leaning against the chapel, and not stirring in the least. The shoemaker was frightened, and thought to himself:

"Somebody must have killed a man, and stripped him of his clothes, and thrown him away there. If I go up to him, I shall never clear myself."

And the shoemaker went past. He walked around the chapel, and the man was no longer to be seen. He went past the chapel, and looked back, and saw the man leaning[Pg 330] away from the building and moving, as though watching him. The shoemaker was frightened even more than before, and he thought to himself:

"Shall I go up to him, or not? If I go up, something bad may happen. Who knows what kind of a man he is? He did not get there for anything good. If I go up, he will spring at me and choke me, and I shall not get away from him; and if he does not choke me, I may have trouble with him all the same. What can I do with him, since he is naked? Certainly I cannot take off the last from me and give it to him! May God save me!"

And the shoemaker increased his steps. He was already a distance away from the chapel, when his conscience began to smite him.

And the shoemaker stopped on the road.

"What are you doing, Semén?" he said to himself. "A man is dying in misery, and you go past him and lose your courage. Have you suddenly grown so rich? Are you afraid that they will rob you of your wealth? Oh, Semén, it is not right!"

Semén turned back, and went up to the man.

[Pg 331]

## II.

Semén walked over to the man, and looked at him; and saw that it was a young man, in the prime of his strength, with no bruises on his body, but evidently frozen and frightened: he was leaning back and did not look at Semén, as though he were weakened and could not raise his eyes. Semén went up close to him, and the man suddenly seemed to wake up. He turned his head, opened his eyes, and looked at Semén. And this one glance made Semén think well of the man. He threw down the felt boots, ungirt himself, put his belt on the boots, and took off his caftan.

"What is the use of talking?" he said. "Put it on! Come now!"

Semén took the man by his elbows and began to raise him. The man got up. And Semén saw that his body was soft and clean, his hands and feet not calloused, and his face gentle. Semén threw his caftan over the man's shoulders. He could not find his way into the sleeves. So Semén put them in, pulled the caftan on him, wrapped him in it, and girded it with the belt.

Semén took off his torn cap, intending to put it on the naked man, but his head grew cold, and so he thought: "My whole head is bald, while he has long, curly hair." He put it on again. "I had better put the boots on him."

He seated himself and put the felt boots on him.

The shoemaker addressed him and said:

"That's the way, my friend! Now move about and get warmed up. This business will be looked into without us. Can you walk?"

[Pg 332]

The man stood, looking meekly at Semén, but could not say a word.

"Why don't you speak? You can't stay here through the winter. We must make for a living place. Here, take my stick, lean on it, if you are weak. Tramp along!"

And the man went. And he walked lightly, and did not fall behind.

As they were walking along, Semén said to him:

"Who are you, please?"

"I am a stranger."

"I know all the people here about. How did you get near that chapel?"

"I cannot tell."

"Have people insulted you?"

"No one has. God has punished me."

"Of course, God does everything, but still you must be making for some place. Whither are you bound?"

"It makes no difference to me."

Semén was surprised. He did not resemble an evil-doer, and was gentle of speech, and yet did not say anything about himself. And Semén thought that all kinds of things happen, and so he said to the man:

"Well, come to my house and warm yourself a little."

Semén walked up to the farm, and the stranger did not fall behind, but walked beside him. A wind rose and blew into Semén's shirt, and his intoxication went away, and he began to feel cold. He walked along, sniffling, and wrapping himself in his wife's jacket, and he thought:

"There is your fur coat: I went to get myself a fur coat, and I am coming back without a caftan, and am even bringing a naked man with me. Matréna will not praise me for it!"

And as Semén thought of Matréna, he felt sorry; and as he looked at the stranger and recalled how he had looked at him at the chapel, his blood began to play in his heart.

"'Whither are you bound?'"

*Photogravure from Painting by A. Kivshénko*

126

## III.

Semén's wife got things done early. She chopped the wood, brought the water, fed the children, herself took a bite of something, and fell to musing. She was thinking about when to set the bread, whether to-day or to-morrow. There was a big slice of it left.

"If Semén has his dinner there," she thought, "and does not eat much for supper, the bread will last until to-morrow."

Matréna turned the slice around and a second time, and thought:

"I will not set any bread to-day. I have enough meal for just one setting. We shall somehow hold out until Friday."

Matréna put the bread away, and seated herself at the table to put a patch in her husband's shirt. She was sewing and thinking of how he would buy a sheepskin for a fur coat.

"If only the furrier does not cheat him, for my man is too simple for anything. He himself will not cheat a soul, but a little child can deceive him. Eight roubles is no small sum. One can pickup a good fur coat for it. It will not be tanned, still it will be a fur coat. How we suffered last winter without a fur coat! We could not get down to the river, or anywhere. And there he has gone out, putting everything on him, and I have nothing to dress in. He went away early; it is time for him to be back. If only my dear one has not gone on a spree!"

Just as Matréna was thinking this, the steps creaked[Pg 334] on the porch, and somebody entered. Matréna stuck the needle in the cloth, and went out into the vestibule. She saw two coming in: Semén, and with him a man without a cap and in felt boots.

Matréna at once smelt the liquor in her husband's breath. "Well," she thought, "so it is: he has been on a spree." And when she saw that he was without his caftan, in nothing but the jacket, and that he was not bringing anything, but only keeping silent and crouching, something broke in Matréna's heart. "He has spent all the money in drinks," she thought, "and has been on a spree with some tramp, and has even brought him along."

Matréna let them pass into the hut, and then stepped in herself. She saw the lean young man, and he had on him their caftan. No shirt was to be seen under the caftan, and he had no hat on his head. When he entered, he stood still, and did not stir, and did not raise his eyes. And Matréna thought: "He is not a good man,—he is afraid."

Matréna scowled and went to the oven, waiting to see what would happen.

Semén took off his cap and sat down on the bench like a good man.

"Well, Matréna, will you let us have something for supper, will you?" he said.

Matréna growled something under her breath. She stood at the oven, and did not stir: she looked now at the one, and now at the other, and shook her head. Semén saw that his wife was not in a good humour, but there was nothing to be done, and he acted as though he did not see it. He took the stranger by the arm:

"Sit down, my friend," he said, "we shall have our supper."

The stranger sat down on the bench.

"Well, have you not cooked anything?"

That simply roiled Matréna.

[Pg 335]

"I have cooked, but not for you. You seem to have drunk away your senses, I see. You went to get a fur coat, and come back without your caftan, and have even brought some kind of a naked tramp with you. I have no supper for you drunkards."

"Stop, Matréna! What is the use of wagging your tongue without any sense? First ask what kind of a man it is—"

"Tell me what you did with the money."

Semén stuck his hand into the caftan, took out the bill, and opened it before her.

"Here is the money. Trifónov has not paid me,—he promised to give it to me to-morrow."

That enraged Matréna even more: he had bought no fur coat, and the only caftan they had he had put on a naked fellow, and had even brought him along.

She grabbed the bill from the table, and ran to put it away, and said:

"I have no supper. One cannot feed all the drunkards."

127

"Oh, Matréna, hold your tongue. First hear what I have to say—"

"Much sense shall I hear from a drunken fool. With good reason did I object to marrying you, a drunkard. My mother gave me some linen, and you spent it on drinks; you went to buy a fur coat, and spent that, too."

Semén wanted to explain to his wife that he had spent twenty kopeks only, and wanted to tell her that he had found the man; but Matréna began to break in with anything she could think of, and to speak two words at once. Even what had happened ten years before, she brought up to him now.

Matréna talked and talked, and jumped at Semén, and grabbed him by the sleeve.

"Give me my jacket. That is all I have left, and you have taken it from me and put it on yourself. Give it to me, you freckled dog,—may the apoplexy strike you!"

[Pg 336]

Semén began to take off the bodice; as he turned back his arm, his wife gave the bodice a jerk, and it ripped at the seam. Matréna grabbed the jacket, threw it over her head, and made for the door. She wanted to go out, but stopped: her heart was doubled, for she wanted to have her revenge, and also to find out what kind of a man he was.

[Pg 337]

## IV.

Matréna stopped and said:

"If he were a good man, he would not be naked; but, as it is, he has not even a shirt on him. If he meant anything good, you would tell me where you found that dandy."

"I am telling you: as I was walking along, I saw him sitting at the chapel, without any clothes, and almost frozen. It is not summer, and he was all naked. God sent me to him, or he would have perished. Well, what had I to do? All kinds of things happen! I picked him up and dressed him, and brought him here. Calm yourself! It is a sin, Matréna. We shall all die."

Matréna wanted to go on scolding, but she looked at the stranger and kept silence. The stranger sat without moving, just as he had seated himself on the edge of the bench. His hands were folded on his knees, his head drooped on his breast, his eyes were not opened, and he frowned as though something were choking him. Matréna grew silent. And Semén said:

"Matréna, have you no God?"

When Matréna heard these words, she glanced at the stranger, and suddenly her heart became softened. She went away from the door, walked over to the oven corner, and got the supper ready. She placed a bowl on the table, filled it with kvas, and put down the last slice of bread. She handed them a knife and spoons.

"Eat, if you please," she said.

Semén touched the stranger.

"Creep through here, good fellow!" he said.

[Pg 338]

Semén cut up the bread and crumbled it into the kvas, and they began to eat. And Matréna sat down at the corner of the table, and leaned on her arm, and kept looking at the stranger.

And Matréna pitied the stranger, and took a liking for him. And suddenly the stranger grew merry, stopped frowning, raised his eyes on Matréna, and smiled.

They got through with their supper. The woman cleared the table, and began to ask the stranger:

"Who are you?"

"I am a stranger."

"How did you get on the road?"

"I cannot tell."

"Has somebody robbed you?"

"God has punished me."

"And you were lying there naked?"

"Yes, I was lying naked, and freezing. Semén saw me, took pity on me, pulled off his caftan, put it on me, and told me to come here. And you have given me to eat and to drink, and have pitied me. The Lord will save you!"

128

Matréna got up, took from the window Semén's old shirt, the same that she had been patching, and gave it to the stranger; and she found a pair of trousers, and gave them to him.

"Here, take it! I see that you have no shirt. Put it on, and lie down wherever it pleases you,—on the hanging bed or on the oven."

The stranger took off the caftan, put on the shirt, and lay down on the hanging bed. Matréna put out the light, took the caftan, and climbed to where her husband was.

Matréna covered herself with the corner of the caftan, and she lay and could not sleep: the stranger would not leave her mind.

As she thought how he had eaten the last slice of bread[Pg 339] and how there would be no bread for the morrow; as she thought how she had given him a shirt and a pair of trousers, she felt pretty bad; but when she thought of how he smiled, her heart was gladdened.

Matréna could not sleep for a long time, and she heard that Semén, too, was not sleeping; he kept pulling the caftan on himself.

"Semén!"

"What is it?"

"We have eaten up the last bread, and I have not set any. I do not know what to do for to-morrow. Maybe I had better ask Gossip Malánya for some."

"If we are alive we shall find something to eat."

The woman lay awhile and kept silence.

"He must be a good man. But why does he not tell about himself?"

"I suppose he cannot."

"Semén!"

"What?"

"We give, but why does nobody give to us?"

Semén did not know what to say. He only said, "Stop talking!" and turned over, and fell asleep.

[Pg 340]

## V.

In the morning Semén awoke. The children were asleep; his wife had gone to the neighbours to borrow some bread. The stranger of last night, in the old trousers and shirt, was alone, sitting on the bench and looking upward. And his face was brighter than on the day before.

And Semén said:

"Well, dear man, the belly begs for bread, and the naked body for clothes. We must earn our living. Can you work?"

"I do not know anything."

Semén wondered at him, and said:

"If only you are willing: people can learn anything."

"People work, and I, too, will work."

"What is your name?"

"Michael."

"Well, Mikháyla, you do not want to talk about yourself,—that is your business; but a man has to live. If you work as I order you, I will feed you."

"God save you, and I will learn. Show me what to do!"

Semén took the flax, put it on his fingers and began to make an end.

"It is not a hard thing to do, you see."

Mikháyla watched him, himself put the flax on his fingers, and made a thread end, as Semén had taught him.

Semén showed him how to wax it. Mikháyla again learned the way at once. The master showed him how to weld the bristle, and how to whet, and Mikháyla learned it all at once.

[Pg 341]

No matter what work Semén showed to him, he grasped it at once, and on the third day he began to sew as though he had done nothing else in all his life. He worked without unbending himself, ate little, between the periods of work kept silence, and all the time looked toward the sky. He did not go into the street, spoke no superfluous word, and did not jest or laugh.

Only once was he seen to smile, and that was the first evening, when the woman gave him a supper.

[Pg 342]

## VI.

Day was added to day, week to week, and the circle of a year went by. Mikháyla was living as before with Semén, and working. And the report spread about Semén's workman that nobody sewed a boot so neatly and so strongly as he. And people from all the surrounding country began to come to Semén for boots, and Semén's income began to grow.

One time, in the winter, Semén was sitting with Mikháyla and working, when a tróyka with bells stopped at the door. They looked through the window: the carriage had stopped opposite the hut, and a fine lad jumped down from the box and opened the carriage door. Out of the carriage stepped a gentleman in a fur coat. He came out of the carriage, walked toward Semén's house, and went on the porch. Up jumped Matréna and opened the door wide. The gentleman bent his head and entered the hut; he straightened himself up, almost struck the ceiling with his head, and took up a whole corner.

Semén got up, bowed to the gentleman, and wondered what he wanted. He had not seen such men. Semén himself was spare-ribbed, and Mikháyla was lean, and Matréna was as dry as a chip, while this one was like a man from another world: his face was red and blood-filled, his neck like a bull's, and altogether he looked as though cast in iron.

The gentleman puffed, took off his fur coat, seated himself on a bench, and said:

"Who is the master shoemaker?"

Semén stepped forward, and said:

[Pg 343]

"I, your Excellency."

The gentleman shouted to his lad:

"Oh, Fédka, let me have the material!"

The lad came running in and brought a bundle. The gentleman took it and put it on the table.

"Open it!" he said.

The lad opened it. The gentleman pointed to the material, and said to Semén:

"Listen now, shoemaker! Do you see the material?"

"I do," he said, "your Honour."

"Do you understand what kind of material this is?"

Semén felt of it, and said:

"It is good material."

"I should say it is! You, fool, have never seen such before. It is German material: it costs twenty roubles."

Semén was frightened, and he said:

"How could we have seen such?"

"That's it. Can you make me boots to fit my feet from this material?"

"I can, your Honour."

The gentleman shouted at him:

"That's it: you can. You must understand for whom you are working, and what material you have to work on. Make me a pair of boots that will wear a year without running down or ripping. If you can, undertake it and cut the material; if you cannot, do not undertake it and do not cut the material. I tell you in advance: if the boots wear off or rip before the year is over, I will put you into jail; if they do not wear off or rip for a year, I will give you ten roubles for the work."

Semén was frightened and did not know what to say. He looked at Mikháyla. He nudged him with his elbow, and said:

"Friend, what do you say?"

Mikháyla nodded to him: "Take the work!"

[Pg 344]

130

Semén took Mikháyla's advice and undertook to make a pair of boots that would not wear down or rip.

The gentleman shouted at his lad, told him to pull off the boot from his left foot, and stretched out his leg.

"Take the measure!"

Semén sewed together a piece of paper, ten inches in length, smoothed it out, knelt down, carefully wiped his hand on his apron so as not to soil the gentleman's stocking, and began to measure. He measured the sole, then the instep, and then the calf, but there the paper was not long enough. His leg at the calf was as thick as a log.

"Be sure and do not make them too tight in the boot-leg!"

Semén sewed up another piece to the strip. The gentleman sat and moved his toes in his stocking, and watched the people in the room. He caught sight of Mikháyla.

"Who is that man there?" he asked.

"That is my master workman,—he will make those boots."

"Remember," said the gentleman to Mikháyla, "remember! Make them so that they will wear a year."

Semén, too, looked at Mikháyla, and he saw that Mikháyla was not looking at the gentleman, but gazed at the corner, as though he saw some one there. Mikháyla looked and looked, suddenly smiled and shone bright.

"What makes you show your teeth, fool? You had better be sure and get the boots in time."

And Mikháyla said:

"They will be done in time."

"Exactly."

The gentleman put on his boot and his fur coat, and wrapped himself up, and went to the door. He forgot to bow down, and hit his head against the lintel.

The gentleman cursed awhile, and rubbed his head, and seated himself in the carriage, and drove away.

[Pg 345]

When the gentleman was gone, Semén said:

"He is mighty flinty! You can't kill him with a club. He has knocked out the lintel, but he himself took little harm."

And Matréna said:

"How can he help being smooth, with the life he leads? Even death will not touch such a sledge-hammer!"

[Pg 346]

### VII.

And Semén said to Mikháyla:

"To be sure, we have undertaken to do the work, if only we do not get into trouble! The material is costly, and the gentleman is cross. I hope we shall not make a blunder. Your eyes are sharper, and your hands are nimbler than mine, so take this measure! Cut the material, and I will put on the last stitches."

Mikháyla did not disobey him, but took the gentleman's material, spread it out on the table, doubled it, took the scissors, and began to cut.

Matréna came up and saw Mikháyla cutting, and was wondering at what he was doing. Matréna had become used to the shoemaker's trade, and she looked, and saw that Mikháyla was not cutting the material in shoemaker fashion, but in a round shape.

Matréna wanted to say something, but thought: "Perhaps I do not understand how boots have to be made for a gentleman; no doubt Mikháyla knows better, and I will not interfere."

Mikháyla cut the pair, and picked up the end, and began to sew, not in shoemaker fashion, with the two ends meeting, but with one end, like soft shoes.

Again Matréna marvelled, but did not interfere. And Mikháyla kept sewing and sewing. They began to eat their dinner, and Semén saw that Mikháyla had made a pair of soft shoes from the gentleman's material.

131

Semén heaved a sigh. "How is this?" he thought. "Mikháyla has lived with me a whole year, and has never made a mistake, and now he has made such trouble for me. The gentleman ordered boots with long boot-legs,[Pg 347] and he has made soft shoes, without soles, and has spoiled the material. How shall I now straighten it out with the master? No such material can be found."

And he said to Mikháyla:

"What is this, dear man, that you have done? You have ruined me. The master has ordered boots, and see what you have made!"

He had just begun to scold Mikháyla, when there was a rattle at the door ring,—some one was knocking. They looked through the window: there was there a man on horseback, and he was tying up his horse. They opened the door: in came the same lad of that gentleman.

"Good day!"

"Good day, what do you wish?"

"The lady has sent me about the boots."

"What about the boots?"

"What about the boots? Our master does not need them. Our master has bid us live long."

"You don't say!"

"He had not yet reached home, when he died in his carriage. The carriage drove up to the house, and the servants came to help him out, but he lay as heavy as a bag, and was stiff and dead, and they had a hard time taking him out from the carriage. So the lady has sent me, saying: 'Tell the shoemaker that a gentleman came to see him, and ordered a pair of boots, and left the material for them; well, tell him that the boots are not wanted, but that he should use the leather at once for a pair of soft shoes. Wait until they make them, and bring them with you.' And so that is why I have come."

Mikháyla took the remnants of the material from the table, rolled them up, and took the soft shoes which he had made, and clapped them against each other, and wiped them off with his apron, and gave them to the lad. The lad took the soft shoes.

"Good-bye, masters, good luck to you!"

[Pg 348]

## VIII.

There passed another year, and a third, and Mikháyla was now living the sixth year with Semén. He was living as before. He went nowhere, did not speak an unnecessary word, and all that time had smiled but twice: once, when they gave him the supper, and the second time when the gentleman came. Semén did not get tired admiring his workman. He no longer asked him where he came from; he was only afraid that Mikháyla might leave him.

One day they were sitting at home. The housewife was putting the iron pots into the oven, and the children were running on the benches, and looking out of the window. Semén was sharpening his knives at one window, and Mikháyla was heeling a shoe at the other.

One of the little boys ran up to Mikháyla on the bench, leaned against his shoulder, and looked out of the window.

"Uncle Mikháyla, look there: a merchant woman is coming to us with some little girls. One of the girls is lame."

When the boy said that, Mikháyla threw down his work, turned to the window, and looked out into the street.

And Semén marvelled. Mikháyla had never before looked into the street, and now he had rushed to the window, and was gazing at something. Semén, too, looked out of the window: he saw, indeed, a woman who was walking over to his yard. She was well dressed, and led two little girls in fur coats and shawls. The girls looked one like the other, so that it was hard to tell them apart,[Pg 349] only one had a maimed left leg,—she walked with a limp.

The woman walked up the porch to the vestibule, felt for the entrance, pulled at the latch, and opened the door. First she let the two girls in, and then entered herself.

"Good day, people!"

"You are welcome! What do you wish?"

The woman seated herself at the table. The girls pressed close to her knees: they were timid before the people.

"I want you to make some leather boots for the girls for the spring."

"Well, that can be done. We have not made such small shoes, but we can do it. We can make sharp-edged shoes, or turnover shoes on linen. Mikháyla is my master."

Semén looked around at Mikháyla, and he saw that Mikháyla had put away his work and was sitting and gazing at the girls.

And Semén marvelled at Mikháyla. Indeed, the girls were pretty: black-eyed, chubby, ruddy-faced, and the fur coats and shawls which they had on were fine; but still Semén could not make out why he was gazing at them as though they were friends of his.

Semén marvelled, and began to talk with the woman and to bargain. They came to an agreement, and he took the measures. The woman took the lame girl on her knees, and said:

"For this girl take two measures: make one shoe for the lame foot, and three for the sound foot. They have the same size of feet, exactly alike. They are twins."

Semén took the measure, and he said about the lame girl:

"What has made her lame? She is such a pretty girl. Was she born this way?"

"No, her mother crushed her."

[Pg 350]

Matréna broke in,—she wanted to know who the woman was, and whose the children were, and so she said:

"Are you not their mother?"

"I am not their mother, nor their kin, housewife! I am a stranger to them: I have adopted them."

"Not your children! How you care for them!"

"Why should I not care for them? I nursed them with my own breast. I had a child of my own, but God took him away. I did not care for him so much as I have cared for them."

"Whose are they, then?"

[Pg 351]

## IX.

The woman began to talk, and said:

"It was six years ago that these orphans lost their parents in one week: their father was buried on a Tuesday, and their mother died on Friday. These orphans were born three days after their father's death, and their mother did not live a day. At that time I was living with my husband in the village. We were their neighbours, our yard joining theirs. Their father was a lonely man; he worked in the forest. They dropped a tree on him, and it fell across his body and squeezed out his entrails. They had barely brought him home, when he gave up his soul to God, and that same week his wife bore twins,—these girls. The woman was poor and alone; she had neither old woman nor girl with her.

"Alone she bore them, and alone she died.

"I went in the morning to see my neighbour, but she, the dear woman, was already cold. As she died she fell on the girl, and wrenched her leg. The people came, and they washed and dressed her, and made a coffin, and buried her. All of them were good people. The girls were left alone. What was to be done with them? Of all the women I alone had a baby. I had been nursing my first-born boy for eight weeks. I took them for the time being to my house. The peasants gathered and thought and thought what to do with them, and they said to me: 'Márya, keep the girls awhile, and we will try and think what to do with them.' And I nursed the straight girl once, but the lame girl I would not nurse. I did not want her to live. But, I thought, why should[Pg 352] the angelic soul go out, and so I pitied her, too. I began to nurse her, and so I raised my own and the two girls, all three of them with my own breasts. I was young and strong, and I had good food. And God gave me so much milk in my breasts that at times they overflowed. I would feed two of them, while the third would be waiting. When one rolled away, I took the third. And God granted that I should raise the three, but my own child I lost in the second year. And God has given me no other children. We began to earn more and more, and now we are living here with the merchant at the mill. The wages are big, and our living is good. I have no children, and how should I live

133

if it were not for these girls? How can I help loving them? They are all the wax of my tapers that I have."

With one hand the woman pressed the lame girl to her side, and with the other she began to wipe off her tears.

And Matréna sighed, and said:

"Not in vain is the proverb: 'You can live without parents, but not without God.'"

And so they were talking among themselves, when suddenly the room was lighted as though by sheet lightning from the corner where sat Mikháyla. All looked at him, and they saw Mikháyla sitting with folded hands on his knees, and looking up, and smiling.

[Pg 353]

## X.

The woman went away with the girls, and Mikháyla got up from his bench. He lay down his work, took off his apron, bowed to the master and to the housewife, and said:

"Forgive me, people! God has forgiven me. You, too, should forgive me."

And the master and his wife saw a light coming from Mikháyla. And Semén got up, and bowed to Mikháyla, and said:

"I see, Mikháyla, you are not a simple man, and I cannot keep you, and must not beg you to remain. But tell me this: Why, when I found you and brought you home, were you gloomy, and when my wife gave you a supper, why did you smile at her and after that grow brighter? Later, when the gentleman ordered the boots, you smiled for the second time, and after that grew brighter, and now, when the woman brought her girls, you smiled for the third time, and grew entirely bright. Tell me, Mikháyla, why does such light come from you, and why did you smile three times?"

And Mikháyla said:

"The light comes from me, because I had been punished, and now God has forgiven me. And I smiled three times because I had to learn three words of God. And I have learned the three words: one word I learned when your wife took pity on me, and so I smiled for the first time. The second word I learned when the rich man ordered the boots, and then I smiled for the second time. And now, when I saw the girls, I learned the last, the third word, and I smiled for the third time."

[Pg 354]

And Semén said:

"Tell me, Mikháyla, for what did God punish you, and what are those words of God, that I may know them."

And Mikháyla said:

"God punished me for having disobeyed him. I was an angel in heaven, and I disobeyed God. I was an angel in heaven, and God sent me down to take the soul out of a woman. I flew down to the earth, and I saw the woman lying sick, and she had borne twins,—two girls. The girls were squirming near their mother, and she could not take them to her breasts. The woman saw me, and she knew that God had sent me for her soul. She wept, and said: 'Angel of God! My husband has just been buried,—he was killed by a tree in the forest. I have neither sister, nor aunt, nor granny,—there is no one to bring up my orphans, so do not take my soul! Let me raise my own children, and put them on their feet. Children cannot live without a father, without a mother.' And I listened to the mother, and placed one girl to her breast, and gave the other one into her hands, and rose up to the Lord in heaven. And I came before the Lord, and said: 'I cannot take the soul out of the mother in childbirth. The father was killed by a tree, the mother bore twins, and she begged me not to take the soul out of her, saying, Let me rear and bring up my children, and put them on their feet. Children cannot live without a father or mother. I did not take the soul out of the woman in childbirth.' And the Lord said: 'Go and take the soul out of the woman in childbirth! And you will learn three words: you will learn what there is in men, and what is not given to men, and what men live by. When you learn them, you will return to heaven.' I flew back to earth and took the soul out of the woman.

"The little ones fell away from the breasts. The dead body rolled over on the bed and crushed one of the girls, and wrenched her leg. I rose above the village and[Pg 355] wanted

134

to take the soul to God; but the wind caught me, and my wings fell flat; and dropped off, and the soul went by itself before God, and I fell near the road on the earth."

[Pg 356]

## XI.

And Semén and Matréna understood whom they had clothed and fed, and who had lived with them, and they wept for terror and for joy, and said the angel:

"I was left all alone in the field, and naked. I had not known before of human wants, neither of cold, nor of hunger, and I became a man. I was starved and chilled and did not know what to do. I saw in the field a chapel made for the Lord, and I went to God's chapel and wanted to hide myself in it. The chapel was locked, and I could not get in. And I seated myself behind the chapel, to protect myself against the wind. The evening came, I was hungry and chilled, and I ached all over. Suddenly I heard a man walking on the road; he was carrying a pair of boots and talking to himself. And I saw a mortal face, for the first time since I had become a man, and that face was terrible to me, and I turned away from it. And I heard the man talking to himself about how he might cover his body in the winter from the cold, and how he might feed his wife and children. And I thought: 'I am dying from hunger and cold, and here comes a man, who is thinking only of how to cover himself and his wife with a fur coat, and of how to feed his family. He cannot help me.' The man saw me; he frowned, and looked gloomier still, and passed by me. And I was in despair. Suddenly I heard the man coming back. I looked at him and did not recognize him: before that death had been in his face, and now he was revived, and in his face I saw God. He came up to me, and clothed me, and took me with him, and led me to his house. I came to[Pg 357] his house, and a woman came out of the house and began to talk. The woman was more terrible yet than the man; the dead spirit was coming out of her mouth, and I could not breathe from the stench of death. She wanted to send me out into the cold, and I knew that she would die if she drove me out. And suddenly her husband reminded her of God. And the woman suddenly changed. And when she gave us to eat, and looked at us, I glanced at her: there was no longer death in her,—she was alive, and I recognized God in her.

"And I recalled God's first word: 'You will know what there is in men.' And I learned that there was love in men. And I rejoiced at it, because God had begun to reveal to me what He had promised, and I smiled for the first time. But I could not yet learn everything. I could not understand what was not given to men, and what men lived by.

"I began to live with you, and lived a year, and there came a man, to order a pair of boots, such as would wear a year, without ripping or turning. I looked at him, and suddenly I saw behind his shoulder my companion, the angel of death. None but me saw that angel; but I knew him, and I knew that the sun would not go down before the rich man's soul would be taken away. And I thought: 'The man is providing for a year, and does not know that he will not live until evening.' And I thought of God's second word: 'You will learn what is not given to men.'

"I knew already what there was in men. Now I learned what was not given to men. It is not given men to know what they need for their bodies. And I smiled for the second time. I was glad because I had seen my comrade the angel, and because God had revealed the second word to me.

"But I could not understand everything. I could not understand what men lived by. And I lived and waited[Pg 358] for God to reveal to me the last word. And in the sixth year came the twin girls with the woman, and I recognized the girls and knew how they were kept alive. I recognized them, and I thought: 'The mother begged me for the sake of the children, and I believed the mother and thought that the children could not live without father and mother, and yet a strange woman has fed them and reared them.' And when the woman was touched as she looked at the children and wept, I saw in her the living God, and I understood what men lived by. And I learned that God had revealed the third word to me and forgave me. And I smiled for the third time."

[Pg 359]

## XII.

135

And the angel's body was bared and clothed in light, so that the eye could not behold him, and he spoke louder, as though the voice were coming not from him but from heaven. And the angel said:

"I have learned that every man lives not by the care for himself, but by love.

"It was not given to the mother to know what her children needed for life. It was not given to the rich man to know what he needed for himself. And it is not given to any man to know whether before evening he will need boots for his life, or soft shoes for his death.

"I was kept alive when I was a man not by what I did for myself, but because there was love in a passer-by and in his wife, and because they pitied and loved me. The orphans were left alive not by what was done for them, but because there was love in the heart of a strange woman, and she pitied and loved them. And all men live not by what they do for themselves, but because there is love in men.

"I knew before that God gave life to men and that He wanted them to live; now I understand even something else.

"I understand that God does not want men to live apart, and so He has not revealed to them what each needs for himself, but wants them to live together, and so He has revealed to them what they all need for themselves and for all.

"I understand now that it only seems to men that they live by the care for themselves, and that they live[Pg 360] only by love. He who has love, is in God, and God is in him, because God is love."

And the angel began to sing the praise of God, and from his voice the whole hut shook. And the ceiling expanded, and a fiery column rose from earth to heaven. And Semén and his wife and children fell to the ground. And the wings were unfolded on the angel's shoulders, and he rose to heaven.

And when Semén awoke, the hut was as before, and in the room were only his family.

[Pg 361]

# THE THREE HERMITS
## 1884

[Pg 362]
[Pg 363]

## THE THREE HERMITS

But when ye pray, use not vain repetitions, as the heathen do: for they think that they shall be heard for their much speaking. Be not ye therefore like unto them: for your Father knoweth what things ye have need of, before ye ask him. (Matt. vi. 7-8.)

A bishop was sailing in a ship from Arkhángelsk to Solóvki. On this ship there were pilgrims on their way to visit the saints. The wind was favourable, the weather clear, and the vessel did not roll. Of the pilgrims some were lying down, some eating, some sitting in groups, and some talking with each other. The bishop, too, came out on deck, and began to walk up and down on the bridge. He walked up to the prow and saw there several men sitting together. A peasant was pointing to something in the sea and talking, while the people listened to him. The bishop stopped to see what the peasant was pointing at: he could see nothing except that the sun was glistening on the water. The bishop came nearer and began to listen. When the peasant saw the bishop, he took off his cap and grew silent. And the people, too, when they saw the bishop, took off their caps and saluted him.

"Do not trouble yourselves, friends," said the bishop. "I have just come to hear what you, good man, are telling about."

"The fisherman is telling us about the hermits," said a merchant, who was a little bolder than the rest.

"What about those hermits?" asked the bishop. He[Pg 364] walked over to the gunwale and sat down on a box. "Tell me, too, and I will listen. What were you pointing at?"

"There is an island glinting there," said the peasant, pointing forward and to the right. "On that island the hermits are living and saving their souls."

"Where is that island?" asked the bishop.

136

"Please to follow my hand! There is a small cloud; below it and a little to the left of it the island appears like a streak."

The bishop looked and looked, but only the water was rippling in the sun, and he could not make out anything with his unaccustomed eye.

"I do not see it," he said. "What kind of hermits are living on that island?"

"God's people," replied the peasant. "I had heard about them for a long time, and never had any chance to see them; but two summers ago I saw them myself."

The fisherman went on to tell how he went out to catch fish and was driven to that island, and did not know where he was. In the morning he walked out and came to an earth hut, and there he saw one hermit, and then two more came out. They fed him and dried him and helped him to mend his boat.

"What kind of people are they?" asked the bishop.

"One is small and stooping, a very old man, in an old cassock; he must be more than a hundred years old, the gray of his beard is turning green, and he smiles all the time, and is as bright as an angel of heaven. The second is taller; he, too, is old, and wears a ragged caftan; his broad gray beard is streaked yellow, and he is a powerful man: he turned my boat around as though it were a vat, before I had a chance to help him; he also is a cheerful man. The third man is tall; his beard falls down to his knees and is as white as snow; he is a[Pg 365] gloomy man, and his brows hang over his eyes; he is all naked, and girded only with a piece of matting."

"What did they tell you?" asked the bishop.

"They did everything mostly in silence, and spoke little to one another. When one looked up, the others understood him. I asked the tall man how long they had been living there. He frowned and muttered something, as though he were angry, but the little hermit took his arm and smiled, and the tall one grew silent. All the little hermit said was: 'Have mercy on us,' and smiled."

While the peasant spoke, the ship came nearer to the island.

"Now you can see it plainly," said the merchant. "Please to look there, your Reverence!" he said, pointing to the island.

The bishop looked up and really saw a black strip, which was the island. The bishop looked at it for quite awhile, then he went away from the prow to the stern, and walked over to the helmsman.

"What island is this that we see there?"

"That is a nameless island. There are so many of them here."

"Is it true what they say, that some hermits are saving their souls there?"

"They say so, your Reverence, but I do not know whether it is so. Fishermen say that they have seen them. But they frequently speak to no purpose."

"I should like to land on that island and see the hermits," said the bishop. "How can I do it?"

"The ship cannot land there," said the helmsman. "You can get there by a boat, but you must ask the captain."

The captain was called out.

"I should like to see those hermits," said the bishop. "Can I not be taken there?"

[Pg 366]

The captain began to dissuade him.

"It can be done, but it will take much time, and, I take the liberty of informing your Reverence, it is not worth while to look at them. I have heard people say that they were foolish old men: they understand nothing and cannot speak, just like the fishes of the sea."

"I wish it," said the bishop. "I will pay you for the trouble, so take me there."

It could not be helped. The sailors shifted the sails and the helmsman turned the ship, and they sailed toward the island. A chair was brought out for the bishop and put at the prow. He sat down and looked. All the people gathered at the prow, and all kept looking at the island. Those who had sharper eyes saw the rocks on the island, and they pointed to the earth hut. And one man could make out the three hermits. The captain brought out his spy-glass and looked through it and gave it to the bishop.

137

"That's so," he said, "there, on the shore, a little to the right from that big rock, stand three men."

The bishop looked through the glass and turned it to the right spot. There were three men there: one tall, a second smaller, and a third a very small man. They were standing on the shore and holding each other's hands.

The captain walked over to the bishop, and said:

"Here, your Reverence, the ship has to stop. If you wish to go there by all means, you will please go from here in a boat, and we will wait here at anchor."

The hawsers were let out, the anchor dropped, the sails furled, and the vessel jerked and shook. A boat was lowered, the oarsmen jumped into it, and the bishop went down a ladder. He sat down on a bench in the boat, and the oarsmen pulled at the oars and rowed toward the island. They came near to the shore and could see clearly three men standing there: a tall man, all naked,[Pg 367]with a mat about his loins; the next in size, in a tattered caftan; and the stooping old man, in an old cassock. There they stood holding each other's hands.

The oarsmen rowed up to the shore and caught their hook in it. The bishop stepped ashore.

The old men bowed to him. He blessed them, and they bowed lower still. Then the bishop began to talk to them:

"I have heard," he said, "that you are here, hermits of God, saving your souls and praying to Christ our God for men. I, an unworthy servant of Christ, have been called here by the mercy of God to tend His flock, and so I wanted to see you, the servants of God, and to give you some instruction, if I can do so."

The hermits kept silence, and smiled, and looked at one another.

"Tell me, how do you save yourselves and serve God?" asked the bishop.

The middle-sized hermit heaved a sigh and looked at the older, the stooping hermit. And the stooping hermit smiled, and said:

"We do not know, O servant of God, how to serve God. We only support ourselves."

"How, then, do you pray to God?"

And the stooping hermit said:

"We pray as follows: There are three of you and three of us,—have mercy on us!"

And the moment the stooping hermit had said that, all three of them raised their eyes to heaven, and all three said:

"There are three of you and three of us,—have mercy on us!"

The bishop smiled, and said:

"You have heard that about the Holy Trinity, but you do not pray the proper way. I like you, hermits of God, and I see that you want to please God, but do not know[Pg 368] how to serve Him. I will teach you, not according to my way, but from the Gospel will I teach you as God has commanded all men to pray to Him."

And the bishop began to explain to the hermits how God had revealed Himself to men: he explained to them about God the Father, and God the Son, and God the Holy Ghost, and said:

"God the Son came down upon earth to save men and taught them to pray as follows. Listen, and repeat after me."

And the bishop began to say, "Our Father." And one of the hermits repeated, "Our Father," and the second repeated, "Our Father," and the third repeated, "Our Father."

"Which art in heaven." The hermit repeated, "Which art in heaven." But the middle hermit got mixed in his words, and did not say it right; and the tall, naked hermit did not say it right: his moustache was all over his mouth, and he could not speak clearly; and the stooping, toothless hermit, too, lisped it indistinctly.

The bishop repeated it a second time, and the hermits repeated it after him. And the bishop sat down on a stone, and the hermits stood around him and looked into his mouth and repeated after him so long as he spoke. And the bishop worked with them all day; he repeated one word ten, and twenty, and a hundred times, and the hermits repeated after him. They blundered, and he corrected them, and made them repeat from the beginning.

The bishop did not leave the hermits until he taught them the whole Lord's prayer. They said it with him and by themselves. The middle-sized hermit was the first to learn it, and he repeated it all by himself. The bishop made him say it over and over again, and both the others said the prayer, too.

It was beginning to grow dark, and the moon rose from the sea, when the bishop got up to go back to the ship.[Pg 369] The bishop bade the hermits good-bye, and they bowed to the ground before him. He raised each of them, and kissed them, and told them to pray as he had taught them, and entered the boat, and was rowed back to the ship.

And as the boat was rowed toward the ship, the bishop heard the hermits loudly repeating the Lord's prayer in three voices. The boat came nearer to the ship, and the voices of the hermits could no longer be heard, but in the moonlight they could be seen standing on the shore, in the spot where they had been left: the smallest of them was in the middle, the tallest on the right, and the middle-sized man on the left. The bishop reached the ship and climbed up to the deck. The anchors were weighed, the sails unfurled, and the wind blew and drove the ship, and on they sailed. The bishop went to the prow and sat down there and looked at the island. At first the hermits could be seen, then they disappeared from view, and only the island could be seen; then the island, too, disappeared, and only the sea glittered in the moonlight.

The pilgrims lay down to sleep, and everything grew quiet on the deck. But the bishop did not feel like sleeping. He sat by himself at the prow and looked out to sea to where the island had disappeared, and thought of the good hermits. He thought of how glad they had been to learn the prayer, and thanked God for having taken him there to help the God's people,—to teach them the word of God.

The bishop was sitting and thinking and looking out to sea to where the island had disappeared. There was something unsteady in his eyes: now a light quivered in one place on the waves, and now in another. Suddenly he saw something white and shining in the moonlight,—either a bird, a gull, or a white sail on a boat. The bishop watched it closely.

"A sailboat is following after us," he thought. "It[Pg 370] will soon overtake us. It was far, far away, but now it is very near. It is evidently not a boat, for there seems to be no sail. Still it is flying behind us and coming up close to us."

The bishop could not make out what it was: a boat, no, it was not a boat; a bird, no, not a bird; a fish, no, not a fish! It was like a man, but too large for that, and then, how was a man to be in the middle of the ocean? The bishop got up and walked over to the helmsman.

"See there, what is it?"

"What is it, my friend? What is it?" asked the bishop, but he saw himself that those were the hermits running over the sea. Their beards shone white, and, as though the ship were standing still, they came up to it.

The helmsman looked around and was frightened. He dropped the helm, and called out in a loud voice:

"O Lord! The hermits are running after us on the sea as though it were dry land!"

The people heard him, and rushed to the helm. All saw the hermits running and holding each other's hands. Those at the ends waved their hands, asking the ship to be stopped. All three were running over the water as though it were dry land, without moving their feet.

Before the ship could be stopped, the hermits came abreast with the ship. They came up to the gunwale, raised their heads, and spoke in one voice:

"O servant of God, we have forgotten your lesson. So long as we repeated it, we remembered it; but when we stopped for an hour, one word leaped out, and then the rest scattered. We do not remember a thing, so teach us again."

The bishop made the sign of the cross, bent down to the hermits, and said:

"Even your prayer, hermits of God, reaches the Lord. It is not for me to teach you. Pray for us sinful men!"

[Pg 371]

And the bishop made a low obeisance to the hermits. And the hermits stopped, turned around, and walked back over the sea. And up to morning a light could be seen on the side where the hermits had departed.

139

|Pg 372|
|Pg 373|

# NEGLECT THE FIRE
## And You Cannot Put It Out
### 1885

|Pg 374|
|Pg 375|

## NEGLECT THE FIRE
### And You Cannot Put It Out

Then came Peter to him, and said, Lord, how oft shall my brother sin against me, and I forgive him? till seven times?

Jesus saith unto him, I say not unto thee, Until seven times: but, Until seventy times seven.

Therefore is the kingdom of heaven likened unto a certain king, which would take account of his servants.

And when he had begun to reckon, one was brought unto him, which owed him ten thousand talents.

But forasmuch as he had not to pay, his lord commanded him to be sold, and his wife, and children, and all that he had, and payment to be made.

The servant therefore fell down, and worshipped him, saying, Lord, have patience with me, and I will pay thee all.

Then the lord of that servant was moved with compassion, and loosed him, and forgave him the debt.

But the same servant went out, and found one of his fellowservants, which owed him an hundred pence: and he laid hands on him, and took him by the throat, saying, Pay me that thou owest.

And his fellowservant fell down at his feet, and besought him, saying, Have patience with me, and I will pay thee all.

And he would not: but went and cast him into prison, till he should pay the debt.

So when his fellowservants saw what was done, they were very sorry, and came and told unto their lord all that was done.

Then his lord, after that he had called him, said unto him, O thou wicked servant, I forgave thee all that debt, because thou desiredst me:

Shouldest not thou also have had compassion on thy fellowservant, even as I had pity on thee?

|Pg 376|

And his lord was wroth, and delivered him to the tormentors, till he should pay all that was due unto him.

So likewise shall my heavenly Father do also unto you, if ye from your hearts forgive not every one his brother their trespasses. (Matt. xviii. 21-35.)

There lived in a village a peasant, by the name of Iván Shcherbakóv. He lived well; he was himself in full strength, the first worker in the village, and he had three sons,—all of them on their legs: one was married, the second about to marry, and the third a grown-up lad who drove horses and was beginning to plough. Iván's wife was a clever woman and a good housekeeper, and his daughter-in-law turned out to be a quiet person and a good worker. There was no reason why Iván should not have led a good life with his family. The only idle mouth on the farm was his old, ailing father (he had been lying on the oven for seven years, sick with the asthma).

Iván had plenty of everything, three horses and a colt, a cow and a yearling calf, and fifteen sheep. The women made the shoes and the clothes for the men and worked in the field; the men worked on their farms.

They had enough grain until the next crop. From the oats they paid their taxes and met all their obligations. An easy life, indeed, might Iván have led with his children. But next door to him he had a neighbour, Gavrílo the Lame, Gordyéy Ivánov's son. And there was an enmity between him and Iván.

140

So long as old man Gordyéy was alive, and Iván's father ran the farm, the peasants lived in neighbourly fashion. If the women needed a sieve or a vat, or the men had to get another axle or wheel for a time, they sent from one farm to another, and helped each other out in a neighbourly way. If a calf ran into the yard of the threshing-floor, they drove it out and only said: "Don't let it out, for the heap has not yet been put away." And it was not their custom to put it away and lock it[Pg 377] up in the threshing-floor or in a shed, or to revile each other.

Thus they lived so long as the old men were alive. But when the young people began to farm, things went quite differently.

The whole thing began from a mere nothing. A hen of Iván's daughter-in-law started laying early. The young woman gathered the eggs for Passion week. Every day she went to the shed to pick up an egg from the wagon-box. But, it seems, the boys scared away the hen, and she flew across the wicker fence to the neighbour's yard, and laid an egg there. The young woman heard the hen cackle, so she thought:

"I have no time now, I must get the hut in order for the holiday; I will go there later to get it."

In the evening she went to the wagon-box under the shed, to fetch the egg, but it was not there. The young woman asked her mother-in-law and her brother-in-law if they had taken it; but Taráska, her youngest brother-in-law, said:

"Your hen laid an egg in the neighbour's yard, for she cackled there and flew out from that yard."

The young woman went to look at her hen, and found her sitting with the cock on the perch; she had closed her eyes and was getting ready to sleep. The woman would have liked to ask her where she laid the egg, but she would not have given her any answer. Then the young woman went to her neighbour. The old woman met her.

"What do you want, young woman?"

"Granny, my hen has been in your yard to-day,—did she not lay an egg there?"

"I have not set eyes on her. We have hens of our own, thank God, and they have been laying for quite awhile. We have gathered our own eggs, and we do not need other people's eggs. Young woman, we do not go to other people's yards to gather eggs."

[Pg 378]

The young woman was offended. She said a word too much, the neighbour answered with two, and the women began to scold. Iván's wife was carrying water, and she, too, took a hand in it. Gavrílo's wife jumped out, and began to rebuke her neighbour. She reminded her of things that had happened, and mentioned things that had not happened at all. And the tongue-lashing began. All yelled together, trying to say two words at the same time. And they used bad words.

"You are such and such a one; you are a thief, a sneak; you are simply starving your father-in-law; you are a tramp."

"And you are a beggar: you have torn my sieve; and you have our shoulder-yoke. Give me back the yoke!"

They grabbed the yoke, spilled the water, tore off their kerchiefs, and began to fight. Gavrílo drove up from the field, and he took his wife's part. Iván jumped out with his son, and they all fell in a heap. Iván was a sturdy peasant, and he scattered them all. He yanked out a piece of Gavrílo's beard. People ran up to them, and they were with difficulty pulled apart.

That's the way it began.

Gavrílo wrapped the piece of his beard in a petition and went to the township court to enter a complaint.

"I did not raise a beard for freckled Iván to pull it out."

In the meantime his wife bragged to the neighbours that they would now get Iván sentenced and would have him sent to Siberia, and the feud began.

The old man on the oven tried to persuade them to stop the first day they started to quarrel, but the young people paid no attention to him. He said to them:

"Children, you are doing a foolish thing, and for a foolish thing have you started a feud. Think of it,—the whole affair began from an egg. The children picked up the egg,—

141

well, God be with them! There is no[Pg 379] profit in one egg. With God's aid there will be enough for everybody. Well, you have said a bad word, so correct it, show her how to use better words! Well, you have had a fight,—you are sinful people. That, too, happens. Well, go and make peace, and let there be an end to it! If you keep it up, it will only be worse."

The young people did not obey the old man; they thought that he was not using sense, but just babbling in old man's fashion.

Iván did not give in to his neighbour.

"I did not pull his beard," he said. "He jerked it out himself; but his son has yanked off my shirt-button and has torn my whole shirt. Here it is."

And Iván, too, took the matter to court. The case was heard before a justice of the peace, and in the township court. While they were suing each other, Gavrílo lost a coupling-pin out of his cart. The women in Gavrílo's house accused Iván's son of having taken it.

"We saw him in the night," they said, "making his way under the window to the cart, and the gossip says that he went to the dram-shop and asked the dram-shopkeeper to take the pin from him."

Again they started a suit. But at home not a day passed but that they quarrelled, nay, even fought. The children cursed one another,—they learned this from their elders,—and when the women met at the brook, they did not so much strike the beetles as let loose their tongues, and to no good.

At first the men just accused each other, but later they began to snatch up things that lay about loose. And they taught the women and children to do the same. Their life grew worse and worse. Iván Shcherbakóv and Gavrílo the Lame kept suing one another at the meetings of the Commune, and in the township court, and before the justices of the peace, and all the judges were tired of them. Now Gavrílo got Iván to pay a fine, or he sent[Pg 380] him to the lockup, and now Iván did the same to Gavrílo. And the more they did each other harm, the more furious they grew. When dogs make for each other, they get more enraged the more they fight. You strike a dog from behind, and he thinks that the other dog is biting him, and gets only madder than ever. Just so it was with these peasants: when they went to court, one or the other was punished, either by being made to pay a fine, or by being thrown into prison, and that only made their rage flame up more and more toward one another.

"Just wait, I will pay you back for it!"

And thus it went on for six years. The old man on the oven kept repeating the same advice. He would say to them:

"What are you doing, my children? Drop all your accounts, stick to your work, don't show such malice toward others, and it will be better. The more you rage, the worse will it be."

They paid no attention to the old man.

In the seventh year the matter went so far that Iván's daughter-in-law at a wedding accused Gavrílo before people of having been caught with horses. Gavrílo was drunk, and he did not hold back his anger, but struck the woman and hurt her so that she lay sick for a week, for she was heavy with child. Iván rejoiced, and went with a petition to the prosecuting magistrate.

"Now," he thought, "I will get even with my neighbour: he shall not escape the penitentiary or Siberia."

Again Iván was not successful. The magistrate did not accept the petition: they examined the woman, but she was up and there were no marks upon her. Iván went to the justice of the peace; but the justice sent the case to the township court. Iván bestirred himself in the township office, filled the elder and the scribe with half a bucket of sweet liquor, and got them to sentence[Pg 381] Gavrílo to having his back flogged. The sentence was read to Gavrílo in the court.

The scribe read:

"The court has decreed that the peasant Gavrílo Gordyéy receive twenty blows with rods in the township office."

Iván listened to the decree and looked at Gavrílo, wondering what he would do. Gavrílo, too, heard the decree, and he became as pale as a sheet, and turned away and

142

walked out into the vestibule. Iván followed him out and wanted to go to his horse, when he heard Gavrílo say:

"Very well, he will beat my back, and it will burn, but something of his may burn worse than that."

When Iván heard these words, he returned to the judges.

"Righteous judges! He threatens to set fire to my house. Listen, he said it in the presence of witnesses."

Gavrílo was called in.

"Is it true that you said so?"

"I said nothing. Flog me, if you please. Evidently I must suffer for my truth, while he may do anything he wishes."

Gavrílo wanted to say something more, but his lips and cheeks trembled. He turned away toward the wall. Even the judges were frightened as they looked at him.

"It would not be surprising," they thought, "if he actually did some harm to his neighbour or to himself."

And an old judge said to them:

"Listen, friends! You had better make peace with each other. Did you do right, brother Gavrílo, to strike a pregnant woman? Luckily God was merciful to you, but think what crime you might have committed! Is that good? Confess your guilt and beg his pardon! And he will pardon you. Then we shall change the decree."

[Pg 382]

The scribe heard that, and said:

"That is impossible, because on the basis of Article 117 there has taken place no reconciliation, but the decree of the court has been handed down, and the decree has to be executed."

But the judge paid no attention to the scribe.

"Stop currycombing your tongue. The first article, my friend, is to remember God, and God has commanded me to make peace."

And the judge began once more to talk to the peasants, but he could not persuade them. Gavrílo would not listen to him.

"I am fifty years old less one," he said, "and I have a married son. I have not been beaten in all my life, and now freckled Iván has brought me to being beaten with rods, and am I to beg his forgiveness? Well, he will—Iván will remember me!"

Gavrílo's voice trembled again. He could not talk. He turned around and went out.

From the township office to the village was a distance of ten versts, and Iván returned home late. The women had already gone out to meet the cattle. He unhitched his horse, put it away, and entered the hut. The room was empty. The children had not yet returned from the field, and the women were out to meet the cattle. Iván went in, sat down on a bench, and began to think. He recalled how the decision was announced to Gavrílo, and how he grew pale, and turned to the wall. And his heart was pinched. He thought of how he should feel if he were condemned to be flogged. He felt sorry for Gavrílo. He heard the old man coughing on the oven. The old man turned around, let down his legs, and sat up. He pulled himself with difficulty up to the bench, and coughed and coughed, until he cleared his throat, and leaned against the table, and said:

"Well, have they condemned him?"

[Pg 383]

Iván said:

"He has been sentenced to twenty strokes with the rods."

The old man shook his head.

"Iván, you are not doing right. It's wrong, not wrong to him, but to yourself. Well, will it make you feel easier, if they flog him?"

"He will never do it again," said Iván.

"Why not? In what way is he doing worse than you?"

"What, he has not harmed me?" exclaimed Iván. "He might have killed the woman; and he even now threatens to set fire to my house. Well, shall I bow to him for it?"

The old man heaved a sigh, and said:

143

"You, Iván, walk and drive wherever you please in the free world, and I have passed many years on the oven, and so you think that you see everything, while I see nothing. No, my son, you see nothing,—malice has dimmed your eyes. Another man's sins are in front of you, but your own are behind your back. You say that he has done wrong. If he alone had done wrong, there would be no harm. Does evil between people arise from one man only? Evil arises between two. You see his badness, but you do not see your own. If he himself were bad, and you good, there would be no evil. Who pulled out his beard? Who blasted the rick which was at halves? Who is dragging him to the courts? And yet you put it always on him. You yourself live badly, that's why it is bad. Not thus did I live, and no such thing, my dear, did I teach you. Did I and the old man, his father, live this way? How did we live? In neighbourly fashion. If his flour gave out, and the woman came: 'Uncle Frol, I need some flour.'—'Go, young woman, into the granary, and take as much as you need.' If he had nobody to send out with the horses,—'Go, Iván, and look after his horses!' And if I was short of anything, I[Pg 384] used to go to him. 'Uncle Gordyéy, I need this and that.' And how is it now? The other day a soldier was talking about Plévna. Why, your war is worse than what they did at Plévna. Do you call this living? It is a sin! You are a peasant, a head of a house. You will be responsible. What are you teaching your women and your children? To curse. The other day Taráska, that dirty nose, cursed Aunt Arína, and his mother only laughed at him. Is that good? You will be responsible for it. Think of your soul. Is that right? You say a word to me, and I answer with two; you box my ears, and I box you twice. No, my son, Christ walked over the earth and taught us fools something quite different. If a word is said to you,—keep quiet, and let conscience smite him. That's what he, my son, has taught us. If they box your ears, you turn the other cheek to them: 'Here, strike it if I deserve it.' His own conscience will prick him. He will be pacified and will do as you wish. That's what he has commanded us to do, and not to crow. Why are you silent? Do I tell you right?"

Iván was silent, and he listened.

The old man coughed again, and with difficulty coughed up the phlegm, and began to speak again:

"Do you think Christ has taught us anything bad? He has taught us for our own good. Think of your earthly life: are you better off, or worse, since that Plévna of yours was started? Figure out how much you have spent on these courts, how much you have spent in travelling and in feeding yourself on the way? See what eagles of sons you have! You ought to live, and live well, and go up, but your property is growing less. Why? For the same reason. From your pride. You ought to be ploughing with the boys in the field and attend to your sowing, but the fiend carries you to court or to some pettifogger. You do not plough in time and do not sow in time, and mother earth does not bring forth[Pg 385] anything. Why did the oats not do well this year? When did you sow them? When you came back from the city. And what did you gain from the court? Only trouble for yourself. Oh, son, stick to your business, and attend to your field and your house, and if any one has offended you, forgive him in godly fashion, and things will go better with you, and you will feel easier at heart."

Iván kept silence.

"Listen, Iván! Pay attention to me, an old man. Go and hitch the gray horse, and drive straight back to the office: squash there the whole business, and in the morning go to Gavrílo, make peace with him in godly fashion, and invite him to the holiday" (it was before Lady-day), "have the samovár prepared, get a half bottle, and make an end to all sins, so that may never happen again, and command the women and children to live in peace."

Iván heaved a sigh, and thought: "The old man is speaking the truth," and his heart melted. The only thing he did not know was how to manage things so as to make peace with his neighbour.

And the old man, as though guessing what he had in mind, began once more:

"Go, Iván, do not put it off! Put out the fire at the start, for when it burns up, you can't control it."

The old man wanted to say something else, but did not finish, for the women entered the room and began to prattle like magpies. The news had already reached them about how Gavrílo had been sentenced to be flogged, and how he had threatened to set fire to the house. They had found out everything, and had had time in the pasture to exchange words with the women of Gavrílo's house. They said that Gavrílo's daughter-in-law had threatened them with the examining magistrate. The magistrate, they said, was receiving gifts from Gavrílo. He would now upset the whole case, and the teacher had already written another[Pg 386] petition to the Tsar about Iván, and that petition mentioned all the affairs, about the coupling-pin, and about the garden,—and half of the estate would go back to him. Iván listened to their talk, and his heart was chilled again, and he changed his mind about making peace with Gavrílo.

In a farmer's yard there is always much to do. Iván did not stop to talk with the women, but got up and went out of the house, and walked over to the threshing-floor and the shed. Before he fixed everything and started back again, the sun went down, and the boys returned from the field. They had been ploughing up the field for the winter crop. Iván met them, and asked them about their work and helped them to put up the horses. He laid aside the torn collar and was about to put some poles under the shed, when it grew quite dark. Iván left the poles until the morrow; instead he threw some fodder down to the cattle, opened the gate, let Taráska out with the horses into the street, to go to the night pasture, and again closed the gate and put down the gate board.

"Now to supper and to bed," thought Iván. He took the torn collar and went into the house. He had entirely forgotten about Gavrílo, and about what his father had told him. As he took hold of the ring and was about to enter the vestibule, he heard his neighbour on the other side of the wicker fence scolding some one in a hoarse voice.

"The devil take him!" Gavrílo was crying to some one. "He ought to be killed."

These words made all the old anger toward his neighbour burst forth in Iván. He stood awhile and listened to Gavrílo's scolding. Then Gavrílo grew quiet, and Iván went into the house.

He entered the room. Fire was burning within. The young woman was sitting in the corner behind the spinning-wheel; the old woman was getting supper ready;[Pg 387] the eldest son was making laces for the bast shoes, the second was at the table with a book, and Taráska was getting ready to go to the night pasture.

In the house everything was good and merry, if it were not for that curse,—a bad neighbour.

Iván was angry when he entered the room. He knocked the cat down from the bench and scolded the women because the vat was not in the right place. Iván felt out of humour. He sat down, frowning, and began to mend the collar. He could not forget Gavrílo's words, with which he had threatened him in court, and how he had said about somebody, speaking in a hoarse voice: "He ought to be killed."

The old woman got Taráska something to eat. When he was through with his supper, he put on a fur coat and a caftan, girded himself, took a piece of bread, and went out to the horses. The eldest brother wanted to see him off, but Iván himself got up and went out on the porch. It was pitch-dark outside, the sky was clouded, and a wind had risen. Iván stepped down from the porch, helped his little son to get on a horse, frightened a colt behind him, and stood looking and listening while Taráska rode down the village, where he met other children, and until they all rode out of hearing. Iván stood and stood at the gate, and could not get Gavrílo's words out of his head, "Something of yours may burn worse."

"He will not consider himself," thought Iván. "It is dry, and a wind is blowing. He will enter somewhere from behind, the scoundrel, and will set the house on fire, and he will go free. If I could catch him, he would not get away from me."

This thought troubled Iván so much that he did not go back to the porch, but walked straight into the street and through the gate, around the corner of the house.

"I will examine the yard,—who knows?"

And Iván walked softly down along the gate. He had[Pg 388] just turned around the corner and looked up the fence, when it seemed to him that something stirred at the other end, as though it got up and sat down again. Iván stopped and stood still,—he listened and looked: everything was quiet, only the wind rustled the leaves in the willow-tree and crackled through the straw. It was pitch-dark, but his eyes got used to the darkness: Iván could see the whole corner and the plough and the penthouse. He stood and looked, but there was no one there.

"It must have only seemed so to me," thought Iván, "but I will, nevertheless, go and see," and he stole up along the shed. Iván stepped softly in his bast shoes, so that he did not hear his own steps. He came to the corner, when, behold, something flashed by near the plough, and disappeared again. Iván felt as though something hit him in the heart, and he stopped. As he stopped he could see something flashing up, and he could see clearly some one in a cap squatting down with his back toward him, and setting fire to a bunch of straw in his hands. He stood stock-still. "Now," he thought, "he will not get away from me. I will catch him on the spot."

Before Iván had walked two lengths of the fence it grew quite bright, and no longer in the former place, nor was it a small fire, but the flame licked up in the straw of the penthouse and was going toward the roof, and there stood Gavrílo so that the whole of him could be seen.

As a hawk swoops down on a lark, so Iván rushed up against Gavrílo the Lame.

"I will twist him up," he thought, "and he will not get away from me."

But Gavrílo the Lame evidently heard his steps and ran along the shed with as much speed as a hare.

"You will not get away," shouted Iván, swooping down on him.

[Pg 389]

He wanted to grab him by the collar, but Gavrílo got away from him, and Iván caught him by the skirt of his coat. The skirt tore off, and Iván fell down.

Iván jumped up.

"Help! Hold him!" and again he ran.

As he was getting up, Gavrílo was already near his yard, but Iván caught up with him. He was just going to take hold of him, when something stunned him, as though a stone had come down on his head. Gavrílo had picked up an oak post near his house and hit Iván with all his might on the head, when he ran up to him.

Iván staggered, sparks flew from his eyes, then all grew dark, and he fell down. When he came to his senses, Gavrílo was gone. It was as light as day, and from his yard came a sound as though an engine were working, and it roared and crackled there. Iván turned around and saw that his back shed was all on fire and the side shed was beginning to burn; the fire, and the smoke, and the burning straw were being carried toward the house.

"What is this? Friend!" cried Iván. He raised his hands and brought them down on his calves. "If I could only pull it out from the penthouse, and put it out! What is this? Friends!" he repeated. He wanted to shout, but he nearly strangled,—he had no voice. He wanted to run, but his feet would not move,—they tripped each other up. He tried to walk slowly, but he staggered, and he nearly strangled. He stood still again and drew breath, and started to walk. Before he came to the shed and reached the fire, the side shed was all on fire, and he could not get into the yard. People came running up, but nothing could be done. The neighbours dragged their own things out of their houses, and drove the cattle out. After Iván's house, Gavrílo's caught fire; a wind rose and carried the fire across the street. Half the village burned down.

[Pg 390]

All they saved from Iván's house was the old man, who was pulled out, and everybody jumped out in just what they had on. Everything else was burned, except the horses in the pasture: the cattle were burned, the chickens on their roosts, the carts, the ploughs, the harrows, the women's chests, the grain in the granary,—everything was burned.

Gavrílo's cattle were saved, and they dragged a few things out of his house.

It burned for a long time, all night long. Iván stood near his yard, and kept looking at it, and saying:

"What is this? Friends! If I could just pull it out and put it out!"

But when the ceiling in the hut fell down, he jumped into the hottest place, took hold of a brand, and wanted to pull it out. The women saw him and began to call him back, but he pulled out one log and started for another: he staggered and fell on the fire. Then his son rushed after him and dragged him out. Iván had his hair and beard singed and his garments burnt and his hands blistered, but he did not feel anything.

"His sorrow has bereft him of his senses," people said.

146

The fire died down, but Iván was still standing there, and saying:

"Friends, what is this? If I could only pull it out."

In the morning the elder sent his son to Iván.

"Uncle Iván, your father is dying: he has sent for you, to bid you good-bye."

Iván had forgotten about his father, and did not understand what they were saying to him.

"What father?" he said. "Send for whom?"

"He has sent for you, to bid you good-bye. He is dying in our house. Come, Uncle Iván!" said the elder's son, pulling him by his arm.

Iván followed the elder's son.

When the old man, was carried out, burning straw fell on[Pg 391] him and scorched him. He was taken to the elder's house in a distant part of the village. This part did not burn.

When Iván came to his father, only the elder's wife was there, and the children on the oven. The rest were all at the fire. The old man was lying on a bench, with a taper in his hand, and looking toward the door. When his son entered, he stirred a little. The old woman went up to him and said that his son had come. He told her to have him come closer to him. Iván went up, and then the old man said:

"What have I told you, Iván? Who has burned the village?"

"He, father," said Iván, "he,—I caught him at it. He put the fire to the roof while I was standing near. If I could only have caught the burning bunch of straw and put it out, there would not have been anything."

"Iván," said the old man, "my death has come, and you, too, will die. Whose sin is it?"

Iván stared at his father and kept silence; he could not say a word.

"Speak before God: whose sin is it? What have I told you?"

It was only then that Iván came to his senses, and understood everything. And he snuffled, and said:

"Mine, father." And he knelt before his father, and wept, and said: "Forgive me, father! I am guilty toward you and toward God."

The old man moved his hands, took the taper in his left hand, and was moving his right hand toward his brow, to make the sign of the cross, but he did not get it so far, and he stopped.

"Glory be to thee, O Lord! Glory be to thee, O Lord!" he said, and his eyes were again turned toward his son.

"Iván! Oh, Iván!"

"What is it, father?"

"What is to be done now?"

[Pg 392]

Iván was weeping.

"I do not know, father," he said. "How am I to live now, father?"

The old man closed his eyes and lisped something, as though gathering all his strength, and he once more opened his eyes and said:

"You will get along. With God's aid will you get along." The old man was silent awhile, and he smiled and said:

"Remember, Iván, you must not tell who started the fire. Cover up another man's sin! God will forgive two sins."

And the old man took the taper into both hands, folded them over his heart, heaved a sigh, stretched himself, and died.

Iván did not tell on Gavrílo, and nobody found out how the fire had been started.

And Iván's heart was softened toward Gavrílo, and Gavrílo marvelled at Iván, because he did not tell anybody. At first Gavrílo was afraid of him, but later he got used to him. The peasants stopped quarrelling, and so did their families. While they rebuilt their homes, the two families lived in one house, and when the village was built again, and the farmhouses were built farther apart, Iván and Gavrílo again were neighbours, living in the same block.

And Iván and Gavrílo lived neighbourly together, just as their fathers had lived. Iván Shcherbakóv remembered his father's injunction and God's command to put out the fire in the beginning. And if a person did him some harm, he did not try to have his revenge on the man, but to mend matters; and if a person called him a bad name, he did not try to answer with worse words still, but to teach him not to speak badly. And thus he taught, also the women folk and the children. And Iván Shcherbakóv improved and began to live better than ever.

[Pg 393]

# THE CANDLE
## 1885

[Pg 394]
[Pg 395]

### THE CANDLE

Ye have heard that it hath been said, An eye for an eye, and a tooth for a tooth: but I say unto you, That ye resist not evil. (Matt. v. 38, 39.)

This happened in the days of slavery. There were then all kinds of masters. There were such as remembered their hour of death and God, and took pity on their people, and there were dogs,—not by that may their memory live! But there were no meaner masters than those who from serfdom rose, as though out of the mud, to be lords! With them life was hardest of all.

There happened to be such a clerk in a manorial estate. The peasants were doing manorial labour. There was much land, and the land was good, and there was water, and meadows, and forests. There would have been enough for everybody, both for the master and for the peasants, but the master had placed over them a clerk, a manorial servant of his from another estate.

The clerk took the power into his own hand, and sat down on the peasants' necks. He was a married man,—he had a wife and two married daughters,—and had saved some money: he might have lived gloriously without sin, but he was envious, and stuck fast in sin. He began by driving the peasants to manorial labour more than the usual number of days. He started a brick-kiln, and he drove all the men and women to work in it above[Pg 396] their strength, and sold the brick. The peasants went to the proprietor in Moscow to complain against him, but they were not successful. When the clerk learned that the peasants had entered a complaint against him, he took his revenge out of them. The peasants led a harder life still. There were found faithless people among the peasants: they began to denounce their own brothers to the clerk, and to slander one another. And all the people became involved, and the clerk was furious.

The further it went, the worse it got, and the clerk carried on so terribly that the people became afraid of him as of a wolf. When he drove through the village, everybody ran away from him as from a wolf, so as not to be seen by him. The clerk saw that and raved more than ever because people were afraid of him. He tortured the peasants with beating and with work, and they suffered very much from him.

It used to happen that such evil-doers were put out of the way, and the peasants began to talk that way about him. They would meet somewhere secretly, and such as were bolder would say:

"How long are we going to endure this evil-doer? We are perishing anyway,—and it is no sin to kill a man like him."

One day the peasants met in the forest, before Easter week: the clerk had sent them to clean up the manorial woods. They came together at dinner-time, and began to talk:

"How can we live now?" they said. "He will root us up. He has worn us out with work: neither in the daytime nor at night does he give any rest to us or to the women. And the moment a thing does not go the way he wants it to, he nags at us and has us flogged. Semén died from that flogging; Anísim he wore out in the stocks. What are we waiting for? He will come here in the evening and will again start to torment us.[Pg 397] We ought just to pull him down from his horse, whack him with an axe, and that will be the end of it. We will

148

bury him somewhere like a dog, and mum is the word. Let us agree to stand by each other and not give ourselves away."

Thus spoke Vasíli Mináev. He was more furious at the clerk than anybody else. The clerk had him flogged every week, and had taken his wife from him and made her a cook at his house.

Thus the peasants talked, and in the evening the clerk came. He came on horseback, and immediately began to nag them because they were not cutting right. He found a linden-tree in the heap.

"I have commanded you not to cut any lindens down," he said. "Who cut it down? Tell me, or I will have every one of you flogged!"

He tried to find out in whose row the linden was. They pointed to Sídor. The clerk beat Sídor's face until the blood came, and struck Vasíli with a whip because his pile was small. He rode home.

In the evening the peasants met again, and Vasíli began to speak.

"Oh, people, you are not men, but sparrows! 'We will stand up, we will stand up!' but when the time for action came, they all flew under the roof. Even thus the sparrows made a stand against the hawk: 'We will not give away, we will not give away! We will make a stand, we will make a stand!' But when he swooped down on them, they made for the nettles. And the hawk seized one of the sparrows, the one he wanted, and flew away with him. Out leaped the sparrows: 'Chivik, chivik!' one of them was lacking. 'Who is gone? Vánka. Well, served him right!' Just so you did. 'We will not give each other away, we will not give each other away!' When he took hold of Sídor, you ought to have come together and made an end of him. But there you say,[Pg 398] We will not give away, we will not give away! We will make a stand, we will make a stand!' and when he swooped down on you, you made for the bushes."

The peasants began to talk that way oftener and oftener, and they decided fully to make away with the clerk. During Passion week the clerk told the peasants to get ready to plough the manorial land for oats during Easter week. That seemed offensive to the peasants, and they gathered during Passion week in Vasíli's back yard, and began to talk.

"If he has forgotten God," they said, "and wants to do such things, we must certainly kill him. We shall be ruined anyway."

Peter Mikhyéev came to them. He was a peaceable man, and did not take counsel with the peasants. He came, and listened to their speeches, and said:

"Brothers, you are planning a great crime. It is a serious matter to ruin a soul. It is easy to ruin somebody else's soul, but how about our own souls? He is doing wrong, and the wrong is at his door. We must suffer, brothers."

Vasíli grew angry at these words.

"He has got it into his head that it is a sin to kill a man. Of course it is, but what kind of a man is he? It is a sin to kill a good man, but such a dog even God has commanded us to kill. A mad dog has to be killed, if we are to pity men. If we do not kill him, there will be a greater sin. What a lot of people he will ruin! Though we shall suffer, it will at least be for other people. Men will thank us for it. If we stand gaping he will ruin us all. You are speaking nonsense, Mikhyéev. Will it be a lesser sin if we go to work on Christ's holiday? You yourself will not go."

And Mikhyéev said:

"Why should I not go? If they send me, I will go to plough. It is not for me. God will find out whose sin[Pg 399] it is, so long as we do not forget him. Brothers, I am not speaking for myself. If we were enjoined to repay evil with evil, there would be a commandment of that kind, but we are taught just the opposite. You start to do away with evil, and it will only pass into you. It is not a hard thing to kill a man. But the blood sticks to your soul. To kill a man means to soil your soul with blood. You imagine that when you kill a bad man you have got rid of the evil, but, behold, you have reared a worse evil within you. Submit to misfortune, and misfortune will be vanquished."

The peasants could not come to any agreement: their thoughts were scattered. Some of them believed with Vasíli, and others agreed with Peter's speech that they ought not commit a crime, but endure.

The peasants celebrated the first day, the Sunday. In the evening the elder came with the deputies from the manor, and said:

"Mikhaíl Seménovich, the clerk, has commanded me to get all the peasants ready for the morrow, to plough the field for the oats." The elder made the round of the village with the deputies and ordered all to go out on the morrow to plough, some beyond the river, and some from the highway. The peasants wept, but did not dare to disobey, and on the morrow went out with their ploughs and began to plough.

Mikhaíl Seménovich, the clerk, awoke late, and went out to look after the farm. His home folk—his wife and his widowed daughter (she had come for the holidays)—were all dressed up. A labourer hitched a cart for them, and they went to mass, and returned home again. A servant made the samovár, and when Mikhaíl Seménovich came, they sat down to drink tea. Mikhaíl Seménovich drank his tea, lighted a pipe, and sent for the elder.

"Well," he said, "have you sent out the peasants to plough?"

[Pg 400]

"Yes, Mikhaíl Seménovich."

"Well, did all of them go?"

"All. I placed them myself."

"Of course, you have placed them,—but are they ploughing? Go and see, and tell them that I will be there in the afternoon, and by that time they are to plough a desyatína to each two ploughs, and plough it well. If I find any unploughed strips, I will pay no attention to the holiday."

"Yes, sir."

The elder started to go out, but Mikhaíl Seménovich called him back. He called him back, but he hesitated, for he wanted to say something and did not know how to say it. He hesitated awhile, and then he said:

"Listen to what those robbers are saying about me. Tell me everything,—who is scolding me, or whatever they may be saying. I know those robbers: they do not like to work; all they want to do is to lie on their sides and loaf. To eat and be idle, that is what they like; they do not consider that if the time of ploughing is missed it will be too late. So listen to what they have to say, and let me know everything you may hear! Go, but be sure you tell me everything and keep nothing from me!"

The elder turned around and left the room. He mounted his horse and rode into the field to the peasants.

The clerk's wife had heard her husband's talk with the elder, and she came in and began to implore him. The wife of the clerk was a peaceable woman, and she had a good heart. Whenever she could, she calmed her husband and took the peasants' part.

She came to her husband, and began to beg him: "My dear Míshenka, do not sin, for the Lord's holiday! For Christ's sake, send the peasants home!"

Mikhaíl Seménovich did not accept his wife's words, but only laughed at her:

[Pg 401]

"Is it too long a time since the whip danced over you that you have become so bold, and meddle in what is not your concern?"

"Míshenka, my dear, I have had a bad dream about you. Listen to my words and send the peasants home!"

"Precisely, that's what I say. Evidently you have gathered so much fat that you think the whip will not hurt you. Look out!"

Seménovich grew angry, knocked the burning pipe into her teeth, sent her away, and told her to get the dinner ready.

Mikhaíl Seménovich ate cold gelatine, dumplings, beet soup with pork, roast pig, and milk noodles, and drank cherry cordial, and ate pastry for dessert; he called in the cook and made her sit down and sing songs to him, while he himself took the guitar and accompanied her.

Mikhaíl Seménovich was sitting in a happy mood and belching, and strumming the guitar, and laughing with the cook. The elder came in, made a bow, and began to report what he had seen in the field.

"Well, are they ploughing? Will they finish the task?"

"They have already ploughed more than half."

"No strips left?"

"I have not seen any. They are afraid, and are working well."

"And are they breaking up the dirt well?"

"The earth is soft and falls to pieces like a poppy."

The clerk was silent for awhile.

"What do they say about me? Are they cursing me?"

The elder hesitated, but Mikhaíl Seménovich commanded him to tell the whole truth.

"Tell everything! You are not going to tell me your words, but theirs. If you tell me the truth, I will reward you; and if you shield them, look out, I will have you flogged. O Kátyusha, give him a glass of vódka to brace him up!"

[Pg 402]

The cook went and brought the elder the vódka. The elder saluted, drank the vódka, wiped his mouth, and began to speak. "I cannot help it," he thought, "it is not my fault if they do not praise him; I will tell him the truth, if he wants it." And the elder took courage and said:

"They murmur, Mikhaíl Seménovich, they murmur."

"What do they say? Speak!"

"They keep saying that you do not believe in God."

The clerk laughed.

"Who said that?"

"All say so. They say that you are submitting to the devil."

The clerk laughed.

"That is all very well," he said, "but tell me in particular what each says. What does Vasíli say?"

The elder did not wish to tell on his people, but with Vasíli he had long been in a feud.

"Vasíli," he said, "curses more than the rest."

"What does he say? Tell me!"

"It is too terrible to tell. He says that you will die an unrepenting death."

"What a brave fellow!" he said. "Why, then, is he gaping? Why does he not kill me? Evidently his arms are too short. All right," he said, "Vasíli, we will square up accounts. And Tíshka, that dog, I suppose he says so, too?"

"All speak ill of you."

"But what do they say?"

"I loathe to tell."

"Never mind! Take courage and speak!"

"They say: 'May his belly burst, and his guts run out!'"

Mikhaíl Seménovich was delighted, and he even laughed.

"We will see whose will run out first. Who said that? Tíshka?"

**"But the candle was still burning"**

*Photogravure from Painting by A. Kivshénko*

[Pg 403]

"Nobody said a good word. All of them curse you and threaten you."

"Well, and Peter Mikhyéev? What does he say? He, too, I suppose, is cursing me?"

"No, Mikhaíl Seménovich, Peter is not cursing."

"What does he say?"

"He is the only one of all the peasants who is not saying anything. He is a wise peasant. I wondered at him, Mikhaíl Seménovich."

"How so?"

"All the peasants were wondering at what he was doing."

"What was he doing?"

"It is wonderful. I rode up to him. He is ploughing the slanting desyatína at Túrkin Height. As I rode up to him, I heard some one singing such nice, high tones, and on the plough-staff something was shining."

151

"Well?"

"It was shining like a light. I rode up to him, and there I saw a five-kopek wax candle was stuck on the cross-bar and burning, and the wind did not blow it out. He had on a clean shirt, and was ploughing and singing Sunday hymns. And he would turn over and shake off the dirt, but the candle did not go out. He shook the plough in my presence, changed the peg, and started the plough, but the candle was still burning and did not go out."

"And what did he say?"

"He said nothing. When he saw me, he greeted me and at once began to sing again."

"What did you say to him?"

"I did not say anything to him, but the peasants came up and laughed at him: 'Mikhyéev will not get rid of his sin of ploughing during Easter week even if he should pray all his life.'"

"What did he say to that?"

[Pg 404]

"All he said was: 'Peace on earth and good-will to men.' He took his plough, started his horses, and sang out in a thin voice, but the candle kept burning and did not go out."

The clerk stopped laughing. He put down the guitar, lowered his head, and fell to musing.

He sat awhile; then he sent away the cook and the elder, went behind the curtain, lay down on the bed, and began to sigh and to sob, just as though a cart were driving past with sheaves. His wife came and began to speak to him; he gave her no answer. All he said was:

"He has vanquished me. My turn has come."

His wife tried to calm him.

"Go and send them home! Maybe it will be all right. See what deeds you have done, and now you lose your courage."

"I am lost," he said. "He has vanquished me."

His wife cried to him:

"You just have it on your brain, 'He has vanquished me, he has vanquished me.' Go and send the peasants home, and all will be well. Go, and I will have your horse saddled."

The horse was brought up, and the clerk's wife persuaded him to ride into the field to send the peasants home.

Mikhaíl Seménovich mounted his horse and rode into the field. He drove through the yard, and a woman opened the gate for him, and he passed into the village. The moment the people saw the clerk, they hid themselves from him, one in the yard, another around a corner, a third in the garden.

The clerk rode through the whole village and reached the outer gate. The gate was shut, and he could not open it while sitting on his horse. He called and called for somebody to open the gate, but no one would come. He got down from his horse, opened the gate, and in the gateway[Pg 405] started to mount again. He put his foot into the stirrup, rose in it, and was on the point of vaulting over the saddle, when his horse shied at a pig and backed up toward the picket fence; he was a heavy man and did not get into his saddle, but fell over, with his belly on picket. There was but one sharp post in the picket fence, and it was higher than the rest. It was this post that he struck with his belly. He was ripped open and fell to the ground.

When the peasants drove home from their work, the horses snorted and would not go through the gate. The peasants went to look, and saw Mikhaíl lying on his back. His arms were stretched out, his eyes stood open, and all his inside had run out and the blood stood in a pool,—the earth had not sucked it in.

The peasants were frightened. They took their horses in by back roads, but Mikhyéev alone got down and walked over to the clerk. He saw that he was dead, so he closed his eyes, hitched his cart, with the aid of his son put the dead man in the bed of the cart, and took him to the manor.

The master heard about all these things, and to save himself from sin substituted tenant pay for the manorial labour.

And the peasants saw that the power of God was not in sin, but in goodness.

[Pg 406]

[Pg 407]

# THE TWO OLD MEN
## 1885

[Pg 408]
[Pg 409]

### THE TWO OLD MEN

Therefore, being wearied with his journey, sat thus on the well: and it was about the sixth hour. There cometh a woman of Samaria to draw water: Jesus saith unto her, Give me to drink. (For his disciples were gone away unto the city to buy meat.) Then saith the woman of Samaria unto him, How is it that thou, being a Jew, askest drink of me, which am a woman of Samaria? for the Jews have no dealings with the Samaritans. Jesus answered and said unto her, If thou knewest the gift of God, and who it is that saith to thee, Give me to drink; thou wouldest have asked of him, for the Father seeketh such to worship him. (John iv. 19-23.)

### I.

Two old men got ready to go to old Jerusalem to pray to God. One of them was a rich peasant; his name was Efím Tarásych Shevelév. The other was not a well-to-do man, and his name was Eliséy Bodróv.

Efím was a steady man: he did not drink liquor, nor smoke tobacco, nor take snuff, had never cursed in his life, and was a stern, firm old man. He had served two terms as an elder, and had gone out of his office without a deficit. He had a large family,—two sons and a married grandson,—and all lived together. As to looks he was a sound, bearded, erect man, and only in his seventh decade did a gray streak appear in his beard.

Eliséy was neither wealthy nor poor; in former days he used to work out as a carpenter, but in his old age he[Pg 410] stayed at home and kept bees. One son was away earning money, and another was living at home. Eliséy was a good-natured and merry man. He liked to drink liquor and take snuff, and sing songs; but he was a peaceable man, and lived in friendship with his home folk and with the neighbours. In appearance he was an undersized, swarthy man, with a curly beard and, like his saint, Prophet Elisha, his whole head was bald.

The old men had long ago made the vow and agreed to go together, but Tarásych had had no time before: he had so much business on hand. The moment one thing came to an end, another began; now he had to get his grandson married, now he was expecting his younger son back from the army, and now he had to build him a new hut.

On a holiday the two old men once met, and they sat down on logs.

"Well," said Eliséy, "when are we going to carry out our vow?"

Efím frowned.

"We shall have to wait," he said, "for this is a hard year for me. I have started to build a house,—I thought I could do it with one hundred, but it is going on now in the third. And still it is not done. We shall have to let it go till summer. In the summer, God willing, we shall go by all means."

"According to my understanding," said Eliséy, "there is no sense in delaying. We ought to go at once. Spring is the best time."

"The time is all right, but the work is begun, so how can I drop it?"

"Have you nobody to attend to it? Your son will do it."

"Do it? My eldest is not reliable,—he drinks."

"When we die, friend, they will get along without us. Let your son learn it!"

"That is so, but still I want to see things done under my eyes."

[Pg 411]

"Oh, dear man! You can never attend to everything. The other day the women in my house were washing and cleaning up for the holidays. This and that had to be done, and everything could not be looked after. My eldest daughter-in-law, a clever woman, said: 'It is a lucky thing the holidays come without waiting for us, for else, no matter how much we might work, we should never get done.'"

Tarásych fell to musing.

"I have spent a great deal of money on this building," he said, "and I can't start out on the pilgrimage with empty hands. One hundred roubles are not a trifling matter."

Eliséy laughed.

"Don't sin, friend!" he said. "You have ten times as much as I, and yet you talk about money. Only say when we shall start. I have no money, but that will be all right."

Tarásych smiled.

"What a rich man you are!" he said. "Where shall you get the money from?"

"I will scratch around in the house and will get together some there; and if that is not enough, I will let my neighbour have ten hives. He has been asking me for them."

"You will have a fine swarm! You will be worrying about it."

"Worrying? No, my friend! I have never worried about anything in life but sins. There is nothing more precious than the soul."

"That is so; but still, it is not good if things do not run right at home."

"If things do not run right in our soul, it is worse. We have made a vow, so let us go! Truly, let us go!"

[Pg 412]

## II.

Eliséy persuaded his friend to go. Efím thought and thought about it, and on the following morning he came to Eliséy.

"Well, let us go," he said, "you have spoken rightly. God controls life and death. We must go while we are alive and have strength."

A week later the old men started.

Tarásych had money at home. He took one hundred roubles with him and left two hundred with his wife.

Eliséy, too, got ready. He sold his neighbour ten hives and the increase of ten other hives. For the whole he received seventy roubles. The remaining thirty roubles he swept up from everybody in the house. His wife gave him the last she had,—she had put it away for her funeral; his daughter-in-law gave him what she had.

Efím Tarásych left all his affairs in the hands of his eldest son: he told him where to mow, and how many fields to mow, and where to haul the manure, and how to finish the hut and thatch it. He considered everything, and gave his orders. But all the order that Eliséy gave was that his wife should set out the young brood separately from the hives sold and give the neighbour what belonged to him without cheating him, but about domestic affairs he did not even speak: "The needs themselves," he thought, "will show you what to do and how to do it. You have been farming yourselves, so you will do as seems best to you."

The old men got ready. The home folk baked a lot of flat cakes for them, and they made wallets for themselves,[Pg 413] cut out new leg-rags, put on new short boots, took reserve bast shoes, and started. The home folk saw them off beyond the enclosure and bade them good-bye, and the old men were off for their pilgrimage.

Eliséy left in a happy mood, and as soon as he left his village he forgot all his affairs. All the care he had was how to please his companion, how to keep from saying an unseemly word to anybody, how to reach the goal in peace and love, and how to get home again. As Eliséy walked along the road he either muttered some prayer or repeated such of the lives of the saints as he knew. Whenever he met a person on the road, or when he came to a hostelry, he tried to be as kind to everybody as he could, and to say to them God-fearing words. He walked along and was happy. There was only one thing Eliséy could not do: he wanted to stop taking snuff and had left his snuff-box at home, but he hankered for it. On the road a man offered him some. He wrangled with himself and stepped away from his companion so as not to lead him into sin, and took a pinch.

Efím Tarásych walked firmly and well; he did no wrong and spoke no vain words, but there was no lightness in his heart. The cares about his home did not leave his mind. He was thinking all the time about what was going on at home,—whether he had not forgotten to give his son some order, and whether his son was doing things in the right way. When he saw along the road that they were setting out potatoes or hauling manure, he wondered whether his son was doing as he had been ordered. He just felt like returning, and showing him what to do, and doing it himself.

154

## III.

The old men walked for live weeks. They wore out their home-made bast shoes and began to buy new ones. They reached the country of the Little-Russians. Heretofore they had been paying for their night's lodging and for their dinner, but when they came to the Little-Russians, people vied with each other in inviting them to their houses. They let them come in, and fed them, and took no money from them, but even filled their wallets with bread, and now and then with flat cakes. Thus the old men walked without expense some seven hundred versts. They crossed another Government and came to a place where there had been a failure of crops. There they let them into the houses and did not take any money for their night's lodging, but would not feed them. And they did not give them bread everywhere,—not even for money could the old men get any in some places. The previous year, so the people said, nothing had grown. Those who had been rich were ruined,—they sold everything; those who had lived in comfort came down to nothing; and the poor people either entirely left the country, or turned beggars, or just managed to exist at home. In the winter they lived on chaff and orach.

One night the two old men stayed in a borough. There they bought about fifteen pounds of bread. In the morning they left before daybreak, so that they might walk a good distance before the heat. They marched some ten versts and reached a brook. They sat down, filled their cups with water, softened the bread with it and ate it, and changed their leg-rags. They sat awhile and rested[Pg 415]themselves. Eliséy took out his snuff-horn. Efím Tarásych shook his head at him.

"Why don't you throw away that nasty thing?" he asked.

Eliséy waved his hand.

"Sin has overpowered me," he said. "What shall I do?"

They got up and marched on. They walked another ten versts. They came to a large village, and passed through it. It was quite warm then. Eliséy was tired, and wanted to stop and get a drink, but Tarásych would not stop. Tarásych was a better walker, and Eliséy had a hard time keeping up with him.

"I should like to get a drink," he said.

"Well, drink! I do not want any."

Eliséy stopped.

"Do not wait for me," he said. "I will just run into a hut and get a drink of water. I will catch up with you at once."

"All right," he said. And Efím Tarásych proceeded by himself along the road, while Eliséy turned to go into a hut.

Eliséy came up to the hut. It was a small clay cabin; the lower part was black, the upper white, and the clay had long ago crumbled off,—evidently it had not been plastered for a long time,—and the roof was open at one end. The entrance was from the yard. Eliséy stepped into the yard, and there saw that a lean, beardless man with his shirt stuck in his trousers in Little-Russian fashion was lying near the earth mound. The man had evidently lain down in a cool spot, but now the sun was burning down upon him. He was lying there awake. Eliséy called out to him, asking him to give him a drink, but the man made no reply. "He is either sick, or an unkind man," thought Eliséy, going up to the door. Inside he heard a child crying. He knocked with the door-ring.[Pg 416] "Good people!" No answer. He struck with his staff against the door. "Christian people!" No stir. "Servants of the Lord!" No reply. Eliséy was on the point of going away, when he heard somebody groaning within. "I wonder whether some misfortune has happened there to the people. I must see." And Eliséy went into the hut.

## IV.

Eliséy turned the ring,—the door was not locked. He pushed the door open and walked through the vestibule. The door into the living-room was open. On the left there was an oven; straight ahead was the front corner; in the corner stood a shrine and a table; beyond the table was a bench, and on it sat a bareheaded old woman, in nothing but a shirt; her head was leaning on the table, and near her stood a lean little boy, his face as yellow as wax and his belly swollen, and he was pulling the old woman's sleeve, and crying at the top of his voice and begging for something.

Eliséy entered the room. There was a stifling air in the house. He saw a woman lying behind the oven, on the floor. She was lying on her face without looking at anything, and snoring, and now stretching out a leg and again drawing it up. And she tossed from side to side,—and from her came that oppressive smell: evidently she was very sick, and there was nobody to take her away. The old woman raised her head, when she saw the man.

"What do you want?" she said, in Little-Russian. "What do you want? We have nothing, my dear man."

Eliséy understood what she was saying: he walked over to her.

"Servant of the Lord," he said, "I have come in to get a drink of water."

"There is none, I say, there is none. There is nothing here for you to take. Go!"

Eliséy asked her:

[Pg 418]

"Is there no well man here to take this woman away?"

"There is nobody here: the man is dying in the yard, and we here."

The boy grew quiet when he saw the stranger, but when the old woman began to speak, he again took hold of her sleeve.

"Bread, granny, bread!" and he burst out weeping.

Just as Eliséy was going to ask the old woman another question, the man tumbled into the hut; he walked along the wall and wanted to sit down on the bench, but before reaching it he fell down in the corner, near the threshold. He did not try to get up, but began to speak. He would say one word at a time, then draw his breath, then say something again.

"We are sick," he said, "and—hungry. The boy is starving." He indicated the boy with his head and began to weep.

Eliséy shifted his wallet on his back, freed his arms, let the wallet down on the ground, lifted it on the bench, and untied it. When it was open, he took out the bread and the knife, out off a slice, and gave it to the man. The man did not take it, but pointed to the boy and the girl, to have it given to them. Eliséy gave it to the boy. When the boy saw the bread, he made for it, grabbed the slice with both his hands, and stuck his nose into the bread. A girl crawled out from behind the oven and gazed at the bread. Eliséy gave her, too, a piece. He cut off another slice and gave it to the old woman. She took it and began to chew at it.

"If you would just bring us some water," she said. "Their lips are parched. I wanted to bring some yesterday or to-day,—I do not remember when,—but I fell down and left the pail there, if nobody took it away."

Eliséy asked where their well was. The old woman told him where. Eliséy went out. He found the pail, brought some water, and gave the people to drink. The[Pg 419] children ate some more bread with water, and the old woman ate some, but the man would not eat.

"My stomach will not hold it," he said.

The woman did not get up or come to: she was just tossing on the bed place. Eliséy went to the shop, and bought millet, salt, flour, and butter. He found an axe, chopped some wood, and made a fire in the oven. The girl helped him. Eliséy cooked a soup and porridge, and fed the people.

[Pg 420]

## V.

The man ate a little, and so did the old woman, and the girl and the little boy licked the bowl clean and embraced each other and fell asleep.

The man and the old woman told Eliséy how it had all happened.

"We lived heretofore poorly," they said, "but when the crop failed us, we ate up in the fall everything we had. When we had nothing left, we began to beg from our neighbours and from good people. At first they gave us some, but later they refused. Some of them would have been willing to give us to eat, but they had nothing themselves. Besides we felt ashamed to beg: we owed everybody money and flour and bread. I looked for work," said the man, "but could find none. People were everywhere looking for work to get something to eat. One day I would work, and two I would go around looking for more work. The old woman and the girl went a distance away to beg, but the alms were poor,—nobody had any bread. Still, we managed to get something to eat: we thought we might squeeze through until the new crop; but in the spring they quit giving us alms altogether, and sickness fell upon us. It grew pretty bad: one day we would have something to eat, and two we went without it. We began to eat grass. And from the grass, or from some other reason, the woman grew sick. She lay down, and I had no strength, and we had nothing with which to improve matters."

"I was the only one," the old woman said, "who worked: but I gave out and grew weak, as I had nothing[Pg 421] to eat. The girl, too, grew weak and lost her courage. I sent her to the neighbours, but she did not go. She hid herself in a corner and would not go. A neighbour came in two days ago, but when she saw that we were hungry and sick, she turned around and went out. Her husband has left, and she has nothing with which to feed her young children. So we were lying here and waiting for death."

When Eliséy heard what they said, he changed his mind about catching up with his companion, and remained there overnight. In the morning Eliséy got up and began to work about the house as though he were the master. He set bread with the old woman and made a fire in the oven. He went with the girl to the neighbours to fetch what was necessary. Everything he wanted to pick up was gone: there was nothing left for farming, and the clothes were used up. Eliséy got everything which was needed: some things he made himself, and some he bought. Eliséy stayed with them one day, and a second, and a third. The little boy regained his strength, and he began to walk on the bench and to make friends with Eliséy. The girl, too, became quite cheerful and helped him in everything. She kept running after Eliséy: "Grandfather, grandfather!"

The old woman got up and went to her neighbour. The man began to walk by holding on to the wall. Only the woman was lying down. On the third day she came to and asked for something to eat.

"Well," thought Eliséy, "I had not expected to lose so much time. Now I must go."

[Pg 422]

## VI.

The fourth day was the last of a fast, and Eliséy said to himself:

"I will break fast with them. I will buy something for them for the holidays, and in the evening I must leave."

Eliséy went once more to the village and bought milk, white flour, and lard. He and the old woman cooked and baked a lot of things, and in the morning Eliséy went to mass and came back and broke fast with the people. On that day the woman got up and began to move about. The man shaved himself, put on a clean shirt,—the old woman had washed it for him,—and went to a rich peasant to ask a favour of him. His mowing and field were mortgaged to the rich man, so he went to ask him to let him have the mowing and the field until the new crop. He came back gloomy in the evening, and burst out weeping. The rich man would not show him the favour; he had asked him to bring the money.

Eliséy fell to musing.

"How are they going to live now? People will be going out to mow, but they cannot go, for it is all mortgaged. The rye will ripen and people will begin to harvest it (and there is such a fine stand of it!), but they have nothing to look forward to,—their desyatína is sold to the rich peasant. If I go away, they will fall back into poverty."

And Eliséy was in doubt, and did not go away in the evening, but put it off until morning. He went into the yard to sleep. He said his prayers and lay down, but could not fall asleep.

[Pg 423]

"I ought to go,—as it is I have spent much time and money; but I am sorry for the people. You can't help everybody. I meant to bring them some water and give each a slice of bread, but see how far I have gone. Now I shall have to buy out his mowing and field. And if I buy out the field, I might as well buy a cow for the children, and a horse for the man to haul his sheaves with. Brother Eliséy Kuzmích, you are in for it! You have let yourself loose, and now you will not straighten out things."

Eliséy got up, took the caftan from under his head, and unrolled it; he drew out his snuff-horn and took a pinch, thinking that he would clear his thoughts, but no,—he thought and thought and could not come to any conclusion. He ought to get up and go, but he was sorry for the people. He did not know what to do. He rolled the caftan up under his head and lay down to sleep. He lay there for a long time, and the cocks crowed, and then only did he fall asleep. Suddenly he felt as though some one had wakened him. He saw himself all dressed, with his wallet and staff, and he had to pass through a gate, but it was just open enough to let a man squeeze through. He went to the gate and his wallet caught on one side, and as he was about to free it, one of his leg-rags got caught on the other side and came open. He tried to free the leg-rag, but it was not caught in the wicker fence: it was the girl who was holding on to it, and crying, "Grandfather, grandfather, bread!" He looked at his foot, and there was the little boy holding on to it, and the old woman and the man were looking out of the window. Eliséy awoke, and he began to speak to himself in an audible voice:

"I will buy out the field and the mowing to-morrow, and will buy a horse, and flour to last until harvest-time, and a cow for the children. For how would it be to go beyond the sea to seek Christ and lose him within me? I must get the people started."

[Pg 424]

And Eliséy fell asleep until morning. He awoke early. He went to the rich merchant, bought out the rye and gave him money for the mowing. He bought a scythe,—for that had been sold, too,—and brought it home. He sent the man out to mow, and himself went to see the peasants: he found a horse and a cart for sale at the innkeeper's. He bargained with him for it, and bought it; then he bought a bag of flour, which he put in the cart, and went out to buy a cow. As he was walking, he came across two Little-Russian women, and they were talking to one another. Though they were talking in their dialect, he could make out what they were saying about him:

"You see, at first they did not recognize him; they thought that he was just a simple kind of a man. They say, he went in to get a drink, and he has just stopped there. What a lot of things he has bought them! I myself saw him buy a horse and cart to-day of the innkeeper. Evidently there are such people in the world. I must go and take a look at him."

When Eliséy heard that, he understood that they were praising him, and so he did not go to buy the cow. He returned to the innkeeper and gave him the money for the horse. He hitched it up and drove with the flour to the house. When he drove up to the gate, he stopped and climbed down from the cart. When the people of the house saw the horse, they were surprised. They thought that he had bought the horse for them, but did not dare say so. The master came out to open the gates.

"Grandfather, where did you get that horse?"

"I bought it," he said. "I got it cheap. Mow some grass and put it in the cart, so that the horse may have some for the night. And take off the bag!"

The master unhitched the horse, carried the bag to the granary, mowed a lot of grass, and put it into the cart. They lay down to sleep. Eliséy slept in the street, and[Pg 425] thither he had carried his wallet in the evening. All the people fell asleep. Eliséy got up, tied his wallet, put on his shoes and his caftan, and started down the road to catch up with Efím.

[Pg 426]

## VII.

Eliséy had walked about five versts, when day began to break. He sat down under a tree, untied his wallet, and began to count his money. He found that he had seventeen roubles twenty kopeks left.

"Well," he thought, "with this sum I cannot travel beyond the sea, but if I beg in Christ's name, I shall only increase my sin. Friend Efím will reach the place by himself, and will put up a candle for me. But I shall evidently never fulfil my vow. The master is merciful, and he will forgive me."

Eliséy got up, slung his wallet over his shoulders, and turned back. He made a circle around the village so that people might not see him. And soon he reached home. On his way out he had found it hard: it was hard keeping up with Efím; but on his way home God made it easy for him, for he did not know what weariness was. Walking was just play to him, and he swayed his staff, and made as much as seventy versts a day.

Eliséy came back home. The harvest was all in. The home folk were glad to see the old man. They asked all about him, why he had left his companion and why he had not gone to Jerusalem, but had returned home. Eliséy did not tell them anything.

"God did not grant me that I should," he said. "I spent my money on the way, and got separated from my companion. And so I did not go. Forgive me for Christ's sake."

He gave the old woman what money he had left. He asked all about the home matters: everything was right;[Pg 427] everything had been attended to and nothing missed, and all were living in peace and agreement.

Efím's people heard that very day that Eliséy had come back, and so they came to inquire about their old man. And Eliséy told them the same story.

"You see," he said, "the old man started to walk briskly, and three days before St. Peter's day we lost each other. I wanted to catch up with him, but it happened that I spent all my money and could not go on, so I returned home."

The people marvelled how it was that such a clever man had acted so foolishly as to start and not reach the place and merely spend his money. They wondered awhile, and forgot about it. Eliséy, too, forgot about it. He began to work about the house: he got the wood ready for the winter with his son, threshed the grain with the women, thatched the sheds, gathered in the bees, and gave ten hives with the young brood to his neighbour. When he got all the work done, he sent his son out to earn money, and himself sat down in the winter to plait bast shoes and hollow out blocks for the hives.

[Pg 428]

## VIII.

All that day that Eliséy passed with the sick people, Efím waited for his companion. He walked but a short distance and sat down. He waited and waited, and fell asleep; when he awoke, he sat awhile,—but his companion did not turn up. He kept a sharp lookout for him, but the sun was going down behind a tree, and still Eliséy was not there.

"I wonder whether he has not passed by me," he thought. "Maybe somebody drove him past, and he did not see me while I was asleep. But how could he help seeing me? In the steppe you can see a long distance off. If I go back, he may be marching on, and we shall only get farther separated from each other. I will walk on,—we shall meet at the resting-place for the night."

When he came to a village, he asked the village officer to look out for an old man and bring him to the house where he stayed. Eliséy did not come there for the night. Efím marched on, and asked everybody whether they had seen a bald-headed old man. No one had seen him. Efím was surprised and walked on.

"We shall meet somewhere in Odessa," he thought, "or on the boat," and then he stopped thinking about it.

On the road he fell in with a pilgrim. The pilgrim, in calotte, cassock, and long hair, had been to Mount Athos, and was now going for the second time to Jerusalem. They met at a hostelry, and they had a chat and started off together.

They reached Odessa without any accident. They waited for three days for a ship. There were many pilgrims[Pg 429] there, and they had come together from all directions. Again Efím asked about Eliséy, but nobody had seen him.

Efím provided himself with a passport,—that cost five roubles. He had forty roubles left for his round trip, and he bought bread and herring for the voyage. The ship was loaded, then the pilgrims were admitted, and Tarásych sat down beside the pilgrim he had met. The anchors were weighed, they pushed off from the shore, and the ship sailed across the sea.

During the day they had good sailing; in the evening a wind arose, rain fell, and the ship began to rock and to be washed by the waves. The people grew excited; the women began to shriek, and such men as were weak ran up and down the ship, trying to find a safe place. Efím, too, was frightened, but he did not show it: where he had sat down on the floor on boarding the ship by the side of Tambóv peasants, he sat through the night and the following day; all of them held on to their wallets and did not speak. On the third day it grew calmer. On the fifth day they landed at Constantinople.

Some of the pilgrims went ashore there, to visit the Cathedral of St. Sophia, which now the Turks hold; Tarásych did not go, but remained on board the ship. All he did was to

159

buy some white bread. They remained there a day, and then again sailed through the sea. They stopped at Smyrna town, and at another city by the name of Alexandria, and safely reached the city of Jaffa. In Jaffa all pilgrims go ashore: from there it is seventy versts on foot to Jerusalem. At the landing the people had quite a scare: the ship was high, and the people were let down into boats below; but the boats were rocking all the time, and two people were let down past the boat and got a ducking, but otherwise all went safely.

When all were ashore, they went on afoot; on the third day they reached Jerusalem at dinner-time. They[Pg 430] stopped in a suburb, in a Russian hostelry; there they had their passports stamped and ate their dinner, and then they followed a pilgrim to the holy places. It was too early yet to be admitted to the Sepulchre of the Lord, so they went to the Monastery of the Patriarch. There all the worshippers were gathered, and the female sex was put apart from the male. They were all ordered to take off their shoes and sit in a circle. A monk came out with a towel, and began to wash everybody's feet. He would wash, and rub them clean, and kiss them, and thus he went around the whole circle. He washed Efím's feet and kissed them. They celebrated vigils and matins, and placed a candle, and served a mass for the parents. There they were fed, and received wine to drink.

On the following morning they went to the cell of Mary of Egypt, where she took refuge. There they placed candles, and a mass was celebrated. From there they went to Abraham's Monastery. They saw the Sebak garden, the place where Abraham wanted to sacrifice his son to God. Then they went to the place where Christ appeared to Mary Magdalene, and to the Church of Jacob, the brother of the Lord. The pilgrim showed them all the places, and in every place he told how much money they ought to give. At dinner they returned to the hostelry. They ate, and were just getting ready to lie down to sleep, when the pilgrim, who was rummaging through his clothes, began to sigh.

"They have pulled out my pocketbook with money in it," he said. "I had twenty-three roubles,—two ten-rouble bills, and three in change."

The pilgrim felt badly about it, but nothing could be done, and all went to sleep. [Pg 431]

## IX.

As Efím went to sleep, a temptation came over him.

"They have not taken the pilgrim's money," he thought, "he did not have any. Nowhere did he offer anything. He told me to give, but he himself did not offer any. He took a rouble from me."

As Efím was thinking so, he began to rebuke himself:

"How dare I judge the man, and commit a sin. I will not sin." The moment he forgot himself, he again thought that the pilgrim had a sharp eye on money, and that it was unlikely that they had taken the money from him. "He never had any money," he thought. "It's only an excuse."

They got up before evening and went to an early mass at the Church of the Resurrection,—to the Sepulchre of the Lord. The pilgrim did not leave Efím's side, but walked with him all the time.

They came to the church. There was there collected a large crowd of worshippers, Greeks, and Armenians, and Turks, and Syrians. Efím came with the people to the Holy Gate. A monk led them. He took them past the Turkish guard to the place where the Saviour was taken from the cross and anointed, and where candles were burning in nine large candlesticks. He showed and explained everything to them. Efím placed a candle there. Then the monks led Efím to the right over steps to Golgotha, where the cross stood; there Efím prayed; then Efím was shown the cleft where the earth was rent to the lowermost regions; then he was shown the place where Christ's hands and feet had been nailed to the[Pg 432] cross, and then he was shown Adam's grave, where Christ's blood dropped on his bones. Then they came to the rock on which Christ sat when they put the wreath of thorns on his head; then to the post to which Christ was tied when he was beaten. Then Efím saw the stone with the two holes, for Christ's feet. They wanted to show him other things, but the people hastened away: all hurried to the grotto of the Lord's Sepulchre. Some foreign mass was just ended, and the Russian began. Efím followed the people to the grotto.

160

He wanted to get away from the pilgrim, for in thought he still sinned against him, but the pilgrim stuck to him, and went with him to mass at the Sepulchre of the Lord. They wanted to stand close to it, but were too late. There was such a crowd there that it was not possible to move forward or back. Efím stood there and looked straight ahead and prayed, but every once in awhile he felt his purse, to see whether it was in his pocket. His thoughts were divided; now he thought that the pilgrim had deceived him; and then he thought, if he had not deceived him, and the pocketbook had really been stolen, the same might happen to him.

[Pg 433]

## X.

Efím stood there and prayed and looked ahead into the chapel where the Sepulchre itself was, and where over the Sepulchre thirty-six lamps were burning. Efím looked over the heads to see the marvellous thing: under the very lamps, where the blessed fire was burning, in front of all, he saw an old man in a coarse caftan, with a bald spot shining on his whole head, and he looked very much like Eliséy Bodróv.

"He resembles Eliséy," he thought. "But how can it be he? He could not have got here before me. The previous ship started a week ahead of us. He could not have been on that ship. On our ship he was not, for I saw all the pilgrims."

Just as Efím was thinking this, the old man began to pray, and made three bows: once in front of him, to God, and twice to either side, to all the Orthodox people. And as the old man turned his head to the right, Efím recognized him. Sure enough, it was Bodróv: it was his blackish, curly beard, and the gray streak on his cheeks, and his brows, his eyes, his nose, and full face,—all his. Certainly it was he, Eliséy Bodróv.

Efím was glad that he had found his companion, and he marvelled how Eliséy could have got there ahead of him.

"How in the world did Bodróv get to that place in front?" he thought. "No doubt he met a man who knew how to get him there. When all go out, I will hunt him up, and I will drop the pilgrim in the colette, and will walk with him. Maybe he will take me to the front place."

[Pg 434]

Efím kept an eye on Eliséy, so as not to lose him. When the masses were over, the people began to stir. As they went up to kiss the Sepulchre, they crowded and pushed Efím to one side. He was frightened lest his purse should be stolen. He put his hand to his purse and tried to make his way out into the open. When he got out, he walked and walked, trying to find Eliséy, both on the outside and in the church. In the church he saw many people in the cells: some ate, and drank wine, and slept there, and read their prayers. But Eliséy was not to be found. Efím returned to the hostelry, but he did not find his companion there either. On that evening the pilgrim, too, did not come back. He was gone, and had not returned the rouble to Efím. So Efím was left alone.

On the following day Efím went again to the Sepulchre of the Lord with a Tambóv peasant, with whom he had journeyed on the ship. He wanted to make his way to the front, but he was again pushed back, and so he stood at a column and prayed. He looked ahead of him, and there in front, under the lamps, at the very Sepulchre of the Lord, stood Eliséy. He had extended his hands, like a priest at the altar, and his bald spot shone over his whole head.

"Now," thought Efím, "I will not miss him."

He made his way to the front, but Eliséy was not there. Evidently he had left. On the third day he again went to the Sepulchre of the Lord, and there he saw Eliséy standing in the holiest place, in sight of everybody, and his hands were stretched out, and he looked up, as though he saw something above him. And his bald spot shone over his whole head.

"Now," thought Efím, "I will certainly not miss him; I will go and stand at the entrance, and then he cannot escape me."

Efím went out and stood there for a long time. He[Pg 435] stood until after noon: all the people had passed out, but Eliséy was not among them.

Efím passed six weeks in Jerusalem, and visited all the places, Bethlehem, and Bethany, and the Jordan, and had a stamp put on a new shirt at the Lord's Sepulchre, to be

161

buried in it, and filled a bottle of Jordan water, and got some earth, and candles with blessed fire, and in eight places inscribed names for the mass of the dead. He spent all his money and had just enough left to get home on, and so he started for home. He reached Jaffa, boarded a ship, landed at Odessa, and walked toward his home.

[Pg 436]

## XI.

Efím walked by himself the same way he had come out. As he was getting close to his village, he began to worry again about how things were going at his house without him. In a year, he thought, much water runs by. It takes a lifetime to get together a home, but it does not take long to ruin it. He wondered how his son had done without him, how the spring had opened, how the cattle had wintered, and whether the hut was well built. Efím reached the spot where the year before he had parted from Eliséy. It was not possible to recognize the people. Where the year before they had suffered want, now there was plenty. Everything grew well in the field. The people picked up again and forgot their former misery. In the evening Efím reached the very village where the year before Eliséy had fallen behind. He had just entered the village, when a little girl in a white shirt came running out of a hut.

"Grandfather, grandfather! Come to our house!"

Efím wanted to go on, but the girl would not let him. She took hold of his coat and laughed and pulled him to the hut. A woman with a boy came out on the porch, and she, too, beckoned to him:

"Come in, grandfather, and eat supper with us and stay overnight!"

Efím stepped in.

"I can, at least, ask about Eliséy," he thought. "This is the very hut into which he went to get a drink."

Efím went inside. The woman took off his wallet, gave him water to wash himself, and seated him at the table.[Pg 437] She fetched milk, cheese, cakes, and porridge, and placed it all on the table. Tarásych thanked her and praised the people for being hospitable to pilgrims. The woman shook her head.

"We cannot help receiving pilgrims," she said. "We received life from a pilgrim. We lived forgetting God, and God punished us in such a way that all of us were waiting for death. Last summer we came to such a point that we were all lying down sick and starved. We should certainly have died, but God sent us an old man like you. He stepped in during the daytime to get a drink; when he saw us, he took pity on us and remained at our house. He gave us to eat and to drink, and put us on our feet again. He cleared our land from debt, and bought a horse and cart and left it with us."

The old woman entered the room, and interrupted her speech:

"We do not know," she said, "whether he was a man or an angel of the Lord. He was good to us all, and pitied us, and then went away without giving his name, so that we do not know for whom to pray to God. I see it as though it happened just now: I was lying down and waiting for death to come; I looked up and saw a man come in,—just a simple, bald-headed man,—and ask for a drink. I, sinful woman, thought that he was a tramp, but see what he did! When he saw us he put down his wallet, right in this spot, and opened it."

The girl broke in.

"No, granny," she said, "first he put his wallet in the middle of the room, and only later did he put it on the bench."

And they began to dispute and to recall his words and deeds: where he had sat down, and where he had slept, and what he had done, and what he had said to each.

Toward evening the master of the house came home on[Pg 438] a horse, and he, too, began to tell about Eliséy, and how he had stayed at their house.

"If he had not come to us," he said, "we should all of us have died in sin. We were dying in despair, and we murmured against God and men. But he put us on our feet, and through him we found out God, and began to believe in good people. May Christ save him! Before that we lived like beasts, and he has made men of us."

They gave Efím to eat and to drink, and gave him a place to sleep, and themselves went to bed.

162

As Efím lay down, he could not sleep, and Eliséy did not leave his mind, but he thought of how he had seen him three times in Jerusalem in the foremost place.

"So this is the way he got ahead of me," he thought. "My work may be accepted or not, but his the Lord has accepted."

In the morning Efím bade the people good-bye: they filled his wallet with cakes and went to work, while Efím started out on the road.

[Pg 439]

## XII.

Efím was away precisely a year. In the spring he returned home.

He reached his house in the evening. His son was not at home,—he was in the dram-shop. He returned intoxicated, and Efím began to ask him about the house. He saw by everything that the lad had got into bad ways without him. He had spent all the money, and the business he had neglected. His father scolded him, and he answered his father with rude words.

"You ought to have come back yourself," he said. "Instead, you went away and took all the money with you, and now you make me responsible."

The old man became angry and beat his son.

The next morning Efím Tarásych went to the elder to talk to him about his son. As he passed Eliséy's farm, Eliséy's wife was standing on the porch and greeting him:

"Welcome, friend!" she said. "Did you, dear man, have a successful journey?"

Efím Tarásych stopped.

"Thank God," he said, "I have been at Jerusalem, but I lost your husband on the way. I hear that he is back."

And the old woman started to talk to him, for she was fond of babbling.

"He is back, my dear; he has been back for quite awhile. He returned soon after Assumption day. We were so glad to see him back. It was lonely without him. Not that we mean his work,—for he is getting old. But he is the head, and it is jollier for us. How happy our lad was! Without him, he said, it was as without light[Pg 440] for the eyes. It was lonely without him, my dear. We love him so much!"

"Well, is he at home now?"

"At home he is, neighbour, in the apiary, brushing in the swarms. He says it was a fine swarming season. The old man does not remember when there has been such a lot of bees. God gives us not according to our sins, he says. Come in, dear one! He will be so glad to see you."

Efím walked through the vestibule and through the yard to the apiary, to see Eliséy. When he came inside the apiary, he saw Eliséy standing without a net, without gloves, in a gray caftan, under a birch-tree, extending his arms and looking up, and his bald spot shone over his whole head, just as he had stood in Jerusalem at the Lord's Sepulchre, and above him, through the birch-tree, the sun glowed, and above his head the golden bees circled in the form of a wreath, and did not sting him. Efím stopped.

Eliséy's wife called out to her husband:

"Your friend is here."

Eliséy looked around. He was happy, and walked over toward his friend, softly brushing the bees out of his beard.

"Welcome, friend, welcome, dear man! Did you have a successful journey?"

"My feet took me there, and I have brought you some water from the river Jordan. Come and get it! But whether the Lord has received my work—"

"Thank God! Christ save you!"

Efím was silent.

"I was there with my feet, but in spirit you were there, or somebody else—"

"It is God's work, my friend, God's work."

"On my way home I stopped at the hut where I lost you."

[Pg 441]

Eliséy was frightened, and he hastened to say:

"It is God's work, my friend, God's work. Well, won't you step in? I will bring some honey."

And Eliséy changed the subject, and began to speak of home matters.

Efím heaved a sigh. He did not mention the people of the hut to Eliséy, nor what he had seen in Jerusalem. And he understood that God has enjoined that each man shall before his death carry out his vow—with love and good deeds.

[Pg 442]
[Pg 443]

## WHERE LOVE IS, THERE GOD IS ALSO
### 1885

[Pg 444]
[Pg 445]

### WHERE LOVE IS, THERE GOD IS ALSO

Shoemaker Martýn Avdyéich lived in the city. He lived in a basement, in a room with one window. The window looked out on the street. Through it the people could be seen as they passed by: though only the feet were visible, Martýn Avdyéich could tell the men by their boots. He had lived for a long time in one place and had many acquaintances. It was a rare pair of boots in the neighbourhood that had not gone once or twice through his hands. Some he had resoled; on others he had put patches, or fixed the seams, or even put on new uppers. Frequently he saw his own work through the window. He had much to do, for he did honest work, put in strong material, took no more than was fair, and kept his word. If he could get a piece of work done by a certain time he undertook to do it, and if not, he would not cheat, but said so in advance. Everybody knew Avdyéich, and his work never stopped.

Avdyéich had always been a good man, but in his old age he thought more of his soul and came near unto God. Even while Martýn had been living with a master, his wife had died, and he had been left with a boy three years of age. Their children did not live long. All the elder children had died before. At first Martýn had intended sending his son to his sister in a village, but[Pg 446] then he felt sorry for the little lad, and thought: "It will be hard for my Kapitóshka to grow up in somebody else's family, and so I will keep him."

Avdyéich left his master, and took up quarters with his son. But God did not grant Avdyéich any luck with his children. No sooner had the boy grown up so as to be a help to his father and a joy to him, than a disease fell upon him and he lay down and had a fever for a week and died. Martýn buried his son, and was in despair. He despaired so much that he began to murmur against God. He was so downhearted that more than once he asked God to let him die, and rebuked God for having taken his beloved only son, and not him. He even stopped going to church.

One day an old man, a countryman of Avdyéich's, returning from Tróitsa,—he had been a pilgrim for eight years,—came to see him. Avdyéich talked with him and began to complain of his sorrow:

"I have even no desire to live any longer, godly man. If I could only die. That is all I am praying God for. I am a man without any hope."

And the old man said to him:

"You do not say well, Martýn. We cannot judge God's works. Not by our reason, but by God's judgment do we live. God has determined that your son should die, and you live. Evidently it is better so. The reason you are in despair is that you want to live for your own enjoyment."

"What else shall we live for?" asked Martýn.

And the old man said:

"We must live for God, Martýn. He gives us life, and for Him must we live. When you shall live for Him and shall not worry about anything, life will be lighter for you."

Martýn was silent, and he said:

"How shall we live for God?"

[Pg 447]

And the old man said:

"Christ has shown us how to live for God. Do you know how to read? If so, buy yourself a Gospel and read it, and you will learn from it how to live for God. It tells all about it."

164

These words fell deep into Avdyéich's heart. And he went that very day and bought himself a New Testament in large letters, and began to read.

Avdyéich had meant to read it on holidays only, but when he began to read it, his heart was so rejoiced that he read it every day. Many a time he buried himself so much in reading that all the kerosene would be spent in the lamp, but he could not tear himself away from the book. And Avdyéich read in it every evening, and the more he read, the clearer it became to him what God wanted of him, and how he should live for God; and his heart grew lighter and lighter. Formerly, when he lay down to sleep, he used to groan and sob and think of his Kapitóshka, but now he only muttered:

"Glory be to Thee, glory to Thee, O Lord! Thy will be done!"

Since then Avdyéich's life had been changed. Formerly, he used on a holiday to frequent the tavern, to drink tea, and would not decline a drink of vódka. He would drink a glass with an acquaintance and, though he would not be drunk, he would come out of the tavern in a happier mood, and then he would speak foolish things, and would scold, or slander a man. Now all that passed away from him. His life came to be calm and happy. In the morning he sat down to work, and when he got through, he took the lamp from the hook, put it down on the table, fetched the book from the shelf, opened it, and began to read it. And the more he read, the better he understood it, and his mind was clearer and his heart lighter.

One evening Martýn read late into the night. He had[Pg 448] before him the Gospel of St. Luke. He read the sixth chapter and the verses: "And unto him that smiteth thee on the one cheek offer also the other; and him that taketh away thy cloke forbid not to take thy coat also. Give to every man that asketh of thee; and of him that taketh away thy goods ask them not again. And as ye would that men should do to you, do ye also to them likewise."

And he read also the other verses, where the Lord says: "And why call ye me, Lord, Lord, and do not the things which I say? Whosoever cometh to me, and heareth my sayings, and doeth them, I will shew you to whom he is like: he is like a man which built an house, and digged deep, and laid the foundation on a rock: and when the flood arose, the stream beat vehemently upon that house, and could not shake it: for it was founded upon a rock. But he that heareth, and doeth not, is like a man that without a foundation built an house upon the earth; against which the stream did beat vehemently, and immediately it fell; and the ruin of that house was great."

When Avdyéich read these words, there was joy in his heart. He took off his glasses, put them on the book, leaned his arms on the table, and fell to musing. And he began to apply these words to his life, and he thought:

"Is my house on a rock, or on the sand? It is well if it is founded on a rock: it is so easy to sit alone,—it seems to me that I am doing everything which God has commanded; but if I dissipate, I shall sin again. I will just proceed as at present. It is so nice! Help me, God!"

This he thought, and he wanted to go to sleep, but he was loath to tear himself away from the book. And he began to read the seventh chapter. He read about the centurion, about the widow's son, about the answer to[Pg 449] John's disciples, and he reached the passage where the rich Pharisee invited the Lord to be his guest, and where the sinning woman anointed His feet and washed them with her tears, and he justified her. And he reached the 44th verse, and read: "And he turned to the woman, and said unto Simon, Seest thou this woman? I entered into thine house, thou gavest me no water for my feet: but she hath washed my feet with tears, and wiped them with the hairs of her head. Thou gavest me no kiss: but this woman since the time I came in hath not ceased to kiss my feet. My head with oil thou didst not anoint: but this woman hath anointed my feet with ointment."

When he had read these verses, he thought:

"He gave no water for His feet; he gave no kiss; he did not anoint His head with oil."

And again Avdyéich took off his glasses and placed them on the book, and fell to musing.

"Evidently he was just such a Pharisee as I am. He, no doubt, thought only of himself: how to drink tea, and be warm, and in comfort, but he did not think of the guest.

About himself he thought, but no care did he have for the guest. And who was the guest?—The Lord Himself. Would I have done so, if He had come to me?"

And Avdyéich leaned his head on both his arms and did not notice how he fell asleep.

"Martýn!" suddenly something seemed to breathe over his very ear.

Martýn shuddered in his sleep: "Who is that?"

He turned around and looked at the door, but there was nobody there. He bent down again, to go to sleep. Suddenly he heard distinctly:

"Martýn, oh, Martýn, remember, to-morrow I will come to the street."

Martýn awoke, rose from his chair, and began to rub[Pg 450] his eyes. He did not know himself whether he had heard these words in his dream or in waking. He put out the light and went to sleep.

Avdyéich got up in the morning before daybreak, said his prayers, made a fire, put the beet soup and porridge on the stove, started the samovár, tied on his apron, and sat down at the window to work. And, as he sat there at work, he kept thinking of what had happened the night before. His thoughts were divided: now he thought that it had only seemed so to him, and now again he thought he had actually heard the voice.

"Well," he thought, "such things happen."

Martýn was sitting at the window and not so much working as looking out into the street, and if somebody passed in unfamiliar boots, he bent over to look out of the window, in order to see not merely the boots, but also the face. A janitor passed by in new felt boots; then a water-carrier went past; then an old soldier of the days of Nicholas, in patched old felt boots, holding a shovel in his hands, came in a line with the window. Avdyéich recognized him by his felt boots. The old man's name was Stepánych, and he was living with a neighbouring merchant for charity's sake. It was his duty to help the janitor. Stepánych began to clear away the snow opposite Avdyéich's window. Avdyéich cast a glance at him and went back to his work.

"Evidently I am losing my senses in my old age," Avdyéich laughed to himself. "Stepánych is clearing away the snow, and I thought that Christ was coming to see me. I, old fool, am losing my senses." But before he had made a dozen stitches, something drew him again toward the window. He looked out, and there he saw Stepánych leaning his shovel against the wall and either warming or resting himself.

He was an old, broken-down man, and evidently shovelling snow was above his strength. Avdyéich thought:[Pg 451] "I ought to give him some tea; fortunately the samovár is just boiling." He stuck the awl into the wood, got up, placed the samovár on the table, put some tea in the teapot, and tapped with his finger at the window. Stepánych turned around and walked over to the window. Avdyéich beckoned to him and went to open the door.

"Come in and get warmed up!" he said. "I suppose you are feeling cold."

"Christ save you! I have a breaking in my bones," said Stepánych.

He came in, shook off the snow and wiped his boots so as not to track the floor, but he was tottering all the time.

"Don't take the trouble to rub your boots. I will clean up,—that is my business. Come and sit down!" said Avdyéich. "Here, drink a glass of tea!"

Avdyéich filled two glasses and moved one of them up to his guest, and himself poured his glass into the saucer and began to blow at it.

Stepánych drank his glass; then he turned it upside down, put the lump of sugar on top of it, and began to express his thanks; but it was evident that he wanted another glass.

"Have some more," said Avdyéich; and he poured out a glass for his guest and one for himself. Avdyéich drank his tea, but something kept drawing his attention to the window.

"Are you waiting for anybody?" asked the guest.

"Am I waiting for anybody? It is really a shame to say for whom I am waiting: no, I am not exactly waiting, but a certain word has fallen deep into my heart: I do not know myself whether it is a vision, or what. You see, my friend, I read the Gospel yesterday about Father Christ and how He suffered and walked the earth. I suppose you have heard of it?"

"Yes, I have," replied Stepánych, "but we are ignorant people,—we do not know how to read."

"Well, so I read about how He walked the earth. I read, you know, about how He came to the Pharisee, and the Pharisee did not give Him a good reception. Well, my friend, as I was reading last night about that very thing, I wondered how he could have failed to honour Father Christ. If He should have happened to come to me, for example, I should have done everything to receive Him. But he did not receive Him well. As I was thinking of it, I fell asleep. And as I dozed off I heard some one calling me by name: I got up and it was as though somebody were whispering to me: 'Wait,' he said: 'I will come to-morrow.' This he repeated twice. Would you believe it,—it has been running through my head,—I blame myself for it,—and I am, as it were, waiting for Father Christ."

Stepánych shook his head and said nothing. He finished his glass and put it sidewise, but Avdyéich took it again and filled it with tea.

"Drink, and may it do you good! I suppose when He, the Father, walked the earth, He did not neglect anybody, and kept the company mostly of simple folk. He visited mostly simple folk, and chose His disciples mostly from people of our class, labouring men, like ourselves the sinners. He who raises himself up, He said, shall be humbled,—and he who humbles himself shall be raised. You call me Lord, He said, but I will wash your feet. He who wants to be the first, He said, let him be everybody's servant; because, He said, blessed are the poor, the meek the humble, and the merciful."

Stepánych forgot his tea. He was an old man and easily moved to tears. He sat there and listened, and tears flowed down his cheeks.

"Take another glass!" said Avdyéich.

But Stepánych made the sign of the cross, thanked him for the tea, pushed the glass away from him, and got up.

"Thank you, Martýn Avdyéich," he said. "You were hospitable to me, and have given food to my body and my soul."

"You are welcome. Come in again,—I shall be glad to see you," said Avdyéich.

Stepánych went away. Martýn poured out the last tea, finished another glass, put away the dishes, and again sat down at the window to work,—to tap a boot. And as he worked, he kept looking out of the window,—waiting for Christ and thinking of Him and His works. And all kinds of Christ's speeches ran through his head.

There passed by two soldiers, one in Crown boots, the other in boots of his own; then the proprietor of a neighbouring house came by in clean galoshes, and then a baker with a basket. All of these went past the window, and then a woman in woollen stockings and peasant shoes came in line with the window. She went by the window and stopped near a wall. Avdyéich looked at her through the window, and saw that she was a strange, poorly dressed woman, with a child: she had stopped with her back to the wind and was trying to wrap the child, though she did not have anything to wrap it in. The woman's clothes were for the summer, and scanty at that. Avdyéich could hear the child cry in the street, and her vain attempt to quiet it. Avdyéich got up and went out of his room and up to the staircase, and called out:

"Clever Woman! Clever woman!"

The woman heard him and turned around.

"Why are you standing there in the cold with the child? Come in here! It will be easier for you to wrap the child in a warm room. Here, this way!"

The woman was surprised. She saw an old man in an apron, with glasses over his nose, calling to her. She followed him in.

They went down the stairs and entered the room, and Martýn took the woman up to the bed.

"Sit down here, clever woman, nearer to the stove, and get warm and feed the child."

"There is no milk in my breasts,—I have not had anything to eat since morning," said the woman, but still she took the child to her breast.

Avdyéich shook his head, went to the table, fetched some bread and a bowl, opened a door in the stove, filled the bowl with beet soup, and took out the pot of porridge, but it was not done yet. He put the soup on the table, put down the bread, and took off a rag from a hook and put it down on the table.

"Sit down, clever woman, and eat, and I will sit with the babe,—I used to have children of my own, and so I know how to take care of them."

The woman made the sign of the cross, sat down at the table, and began to eat, while Avdyéich seated himself on the bed with the child. He smacked his lips at it, but could not smack well, for he had no teeth. The babe kept crying all the time. Avdyéich tried to frighten it with his finger: he quickly carried his finger down toward the babe's mouth and pulled it away again. He did not put his finger into the child's mouth, because it was black,—all smeared with pitch. But the child took a fancy for his finger and grew quiet, and then began even to smile. Avdyéich, too, was happy. The woman was eating in the meantime and telling him who she was and whither she was going.

"I am a soldier's wife," she said. "My husband was driven somewhere far away eight months ago, and I do not know where he is. I had been working as a cook when the baby was born; they would not keep me with the child. This is the third month that I have been without a place. I have spent all I had saved. I wanted to hire out as a wet-nurse, but they will not take me: they say that I am too thin. I went to a merchant woman, where our granny lives, and she promised she would take[Pg 455] me. I thought she wanted me to come at once, but she told me she wanted me next week. She lives a distance away. I am all worn out and have worn out the dear child, too. Luckily our landlady pities us for the sake of Christ, or else I do not know how we should have lived until now."

Avdyéich heaved a sigh, and said:

"And have you no warm clothes?"

"Indeed, it is time now to have warm clothing, dear man! But yesterday I pawned my last kerchief for twenty kopeks."

The woman went up to the bed and took her child, but Avdyéich got up, went to the wall, rummaged there awhile, and brought her an old sleeveless cloak.

"Take this!" he said. "It is an old piece, but you may use it to wrap yourself in."

The woman looked at the cloak and at the old man, and took the cloak, and burst out weeping. Avdyéich turned his face away; he crawled under the bed, pulled out a box, rummaged through it, and again sat down opposite the woman.

And the woman said:

"May Christ save you, grandfather! Evidently He sent me to your window. My child would have frozen to death. When I went out it was warm, but now it has turned dreadfully cold. It was He, our Father, who taught you to look through the window and have pity on me, sorrowful woman."

Avdyéich smiled, and said:

"It is He who has instructed me: clever woman, there was good reason why I looked through the window."

Martýn told the soldier woman about his dream, and how he had heard a voice promising him that the Lord would come to see him on that day.

"Everything is possible," said the woman. She got[Pg 456] up, threw the cloak over her, wrapped the child in it, and began to bow to Avdyéich and to thank him.

"Accept this, for the sake of Christ," said Avdyéich, giving her twenty kopeks, with which to redeem her kerchief.

The woman made the sign of the cross, and so did Avdyéich, and he saw the woman out.

She went away. Avdyéich ate some soup, put the things away, and sat down once more to work. He was working, but at the same time thinking of the window: whenever it grew dark there, he looked up to see who was passing. There went by acquaintances and strangers, and there was nothing peculiar.

Suddenly Avdyéich saw an old woman, a huckstress, stop opposite the very window. She was carrying a basket with apples. There were but few of them left,—evidently she had sold all, and over her shoulder she carried a bag with chips. No doubt, she had picked them up at some new building, and was on her way home. The bag was evidently pulling hard on her shoulder; she wanted to shift it to her other shoulder, so she let the bag down on the flagstones, set the apple-basket on a post, and began to shake down the chips. While she was doing that, a boy in a torn cap leaped out from somewhere, grasped any apple from the basket, and wanted to skip out, but the old woman saw him in time and turned around and grabbed the boy by the sleeve. The boy yanked and tried to get away, but the old woman held on to him with both her hands, knocked down his cap, and took hold of his hair. The boy cried, and the old woman scolded. Avdyéich did not have time to put away the awl. He threw it on the floor, jumped out of the room, stumbled on the staircase, and dropped his glasses. He ran out into the street. The old woman was pulling the boy's hair and scolding him. She wanted to take him to a policeman; the little fellow struggled and tried to deny what he had done:

[Pg 457]

"I did not take any, so why do you beat me? Let me go!"

Avdyéich tried to separate them. He took the boy's arm, and said:

"Let him go, granny, forgive him for Christ's sake!"

"I will forgive him in such a way that he will not forget until the new bath brooms are ripe. I will take the rascal to the police station!"

Avdyéich began to beg the old woman:

"Let him go, granny, he will not do it again. Let him go, for Christ's sake!"

The woman let go of him. The boy wanted to run, but Avdyéich held on to him.

"Beg the grandmother's forgiveness," he said. "Don't do that again,—I saw you take the apple."

The boy began to cry, and he asked her forgiveness.

"That's right. And now, take this apple!" Avdyéich took an apple from the basket and gave it to the boy. "I will pay for it, granny," he said to the old woman.

"You are spoiling these ragamuffins," said the old woman. "He ought to be rewarded in such a way that he should remember it for a week."

"Oh, granny, granny!" said Avdyéich. "That is according to our ways, but how is that according to God's ways? If he is to be whipped for an apple, what ought to be done with us for our sins?"

The old woman grew silent.

And Avdyéich told the old woman the parable of the lord who forgave his servant his whole large debt, after which the servant went and took his fellow servant who was his debtor by the throat. The old woman listened to him, and the boy stood and listened, too.

"God has commanded that we should forgive," said Avdyéich, "or else we, too, shall not be forgiven. All are to be forgiven, but most of all an unthinking person."

The old woman shook her head and sighed.

[Pg 458]

"That is so," said the old woman, "but they are very much spoiled nowadays."

"Then we old people ought to teach them," said Avdyéich.

"That is what I say," said the old woman. "I myself had seven of them,—but only one daughter is left now." And the old woman began to tell where and how she was living with her daughter, and how many grandchildren she had. "My strength is waning," she said, "but still I work. I am sorry for my grandchildren, and they are such nice children,—nobody else meets me the way they do. Aksyútka will not go to anybody from me. 'Granny, granny dear, darling!'" And the old woman melted with tenderness.

"Of course, he is but a child,—God be with him!" the old woman said about the boy.

She wanted to lift the bag on her shoulders, when the boy jumped up to her, and said:

"Let me carry it, granny! I am going that way."

The old woman shook her head and threw the bag on the boy's shoulders. They walked together down the street. The old woman had forgotten to ask Avdyéich to pay her for the apple. Avdyéich stood awhile, looking at them and hearing them talk as they walked along.

When they disappeared from sight, he returned to his room. He found his glasses on the staircase,—they were not broken,—and he picked up his awl and again sat down to work. He worked for awhile; he could not find the holes with the bristle, when he looked up and saw the lampman lighting the lamps.

169

"It is evidently time to strike a light," he thought, and he got up and fixed the lamp and hung it on the hook, and sat down again to work. He finished a boot: he turned it around and looked at it, and he saw that it was well done. He put down his tool, swept up the clippings, put away the bristles and the remnants and the awls, took[Pg 459] the lamp and put it on the table, and fetched the Gospel from the shelf. He wanted to open the book where he had marked it the day before with a morocco clipping, but he opened it in another place. And just as he went to open the Gospel, he thought of his dream of the night before. And just as he thought of it, it appeared to him as though something were moving and stepping behind him. He looked around, and, indeed, it looked as though people were standing in the dark corner, but he could not make out who they were. And a voice whispered to him:

"Martýn, oh, Martýn, have you not recognized me?"

"Whom?" asked Avdyéich.

"Me," said the voice. "It is I."

And out of the dark corner came Stepánych, and he smiled and vanished like a cloud and was no more.

"And it is I," said a voice.

And out of the dark corner came the woman with the babe, and the woman smiled and the child laughed, and they, too, disappeared.

"And it is I," said a voice.

And out came the old woman and the boy with the apple, and both smiled and vanished.

And joy fell on Avdyéich's heart, and he made the sign of the cross, put on his glasses, and began to read the Gospel, there where he had opened it. And at the top of the page he read:

"I was an hungered, and ye gave me meat: I was thirsty, and ye gave me drink: I was a stranger, and ye took me in."

And at the bottom of the page he read:

"Inasmuch as ye have done it unto one of the least of these my brethren, ye have done it unto me." (Matt. xxv.)

And Avdyéich understood that his dream had not deceived him, that the Saviour had really come to him on that day, and that he had received Him.

[Pg 460]
[Pg 461]

## TEXTS FOR CHAPBOOK
## ILLUSTRATIONS
### 1885

[Pg 462]
[Pg 463]

TEXTS FOR CHAPBOOK
ILLUSTRATIONS

### THE FIEND PERSISTS, BUT GOD RESISTS

In ancient times there lived a good master. He had plenty of everything, and many slaves served him. And the slaves prided themselves on their master. They said:

"There is not a better master under heaven. He feeds us and dresses us well, and gives us work to do according to our strength, and never offends us with a word, and bears no grudge against any one; he is not like other masters who torture their slaves worse than cattle, and punish them with cause and without cause, and never say a good word to them. Our master wishes us good, and does us good, and speaks good words to us. We do not want any better life."

Thus the slaves boasted of their master. And the devil was annoyed to see the slaves living well and in love with their master. And the devil took possession of one of the master's slaves, Aleb. He took possession of him and commanded him to seduce other slaves. And when all the slaves were resting and praising their master, Aleb raised his voice and said:

170

"Brothers, in vain do you pride yourselves on the goodness of your master. Try to do the devil's bidding, and he, too, will be kind to you. We serve our master well,[Pg 464] and please him in everything. He needs only to have a thing in mind, and we do it.—we guess his thoughts. Why, then, should he not be good to us? Stop doing his bidding and do him some wrong, and he will be like everybody else, and will repay evil with evil, much worse than the worst of masters."

And the other slaves began to dispute with Aleb. They disputed and made a wager. Aleb undertook to anger the good master. He undertook to do so on condition that if he did not succeed in making him angry, he should lose his holiday garment, but if he did, each should give him his own holiday garment, and, besides, they promised to defend him against the master and to free him if the master should put him in irons or throw him into prison. They made this wager, and Aleb promised to anger the master on the following morning.

Aleb was serving in the master's sheepfold and tended on costly thoroughbred rams. And so, when the good master came the next morning with his guests to the sheepfold to show them his favourite expensive rams, the devil's labourer winked to his companions: "Watch me now! I am going to anger the master." All the slaves gathered and looked through the door and over the enclosure, and the devil climbed a tree and looked from there into the yard, to see how his labourer was going to serve him. The master walked through the yard, showing his guests the sheep and lambs, and he wanted to show them his best ram.

"The other rams are nice, too, but the one with the twisted horns is priceless, and I think more of him than of the pupil of my eye."

The sheep and the lambs were shying from the people in the yard, and the guests could not get a good look at the expensive ram. The moment the ram stopped, the labourer of the devil, as though by accident, frightened the sheep, and they got all mixed. The guests could not[Pg 465] make out which was the expensive ram. The master got tired of it, so he said:

"Aleb, my dear friend, take the trouble carefully to catch the best ram with the twisted horns and to hold him awhile."

The moment the master had said that, Aleb rushed forward, like a lion, into the midst of the rams and caught the priceless ram by his fleece. He got hold of the wool, and with one hand he seized the left hind leg and raised it and in the eyes of the master jerked it in such a way that it snapped like a linden post. Aleb had broken the ram's leg beneath the knee. The ram began to bleat and fell down on his fore legs. Aleb grasped the right leg while the left hung loose like a whip-cord. The guests and all the slaves groaned, and the devil rejoiced, when he saw how cleverly Aleb had done his work. The master looked blacker than night. He frowned, lowered his head, and did not say a word. The guests and the slaves were silent. They waited to see what would happen.

The master was silent, then shook himself, as though he wanted to throw something off, and raised his head and lifted it to the sky. He looked at it for a short time, and the wrinkles on his face disappeared, and he smiled and lowered his eyes on Aleb. He looked at Aleb, and smiled, and said:

"O Aleb, Aleb! Your master has commanded you to anger me. But my master is stronger than yours: you have not angered me, but I will anger your master. You were afraid that I would punish you, and you wanted to be free, Aleb. Know, then, that you will receive no punishment from me, and, since you wanted to be free, I free you in the presence of these my guests. Go in all four directions and take your holiday garment with you!"

And the good master went with his guests to the house. But the devil ground his teeth and fell down from the tree and sank through the earth.

[Pg 466]

## LITTLE GIRLS WISER THAN OLD PEOPLE

It was an early Easter. They had just quit using sleighs. In the yards lay snow, and rills ran down the village. A large puddle had run down from a manure pile into a lane between two farms. And at this puddle two girls, one older than the other, had met. Both of them had been dressed by their mothers in new bodices. The little girl had a blue bodice, and the elder a yellow one with a design. Both had their heads wrapped in red kerchiefs. After mass the two girls went to the puddle, where they showed their new garments to each other, and began to play. They wanted to plash in the water. The little girl started to go into the puddle with her shoes on, but the older girl said to her:

"Don't go, Malásha, your mother will scold you. I will take off my shoes, and you do the same."

The girls took off their shoes, raised their skirts, and walked through the puddle toward each other. Malásha stepped in up to her ankles, and said:

"It is deep, Akúlka, I am afraid."

"Never mind," she replied, "it will not be any deeper. Come straight toward me!" They came closer to each other. Akúlka said:

"Malásha, look out, and do not splash it up, but walk softly."

She had barely said that when Malásha plumped her foot into the water and bespattered Akúlka's bodice, and not only her bodice, but also her nose and eyes. When Akúlka saw the spots on her bodice, she grew angry at Malásha, and scolded her, and ran after her, and wanted[Pg 467] to strike her. Malásha was frightened and, seeing what trouble she had caused, jumped out of the puddle and ran home.

Akúlka's mother passed by; she saw her daughter's bodice bespattered and her shirt soiled.

"Where, accursed one, did you get yourself so dirty?"

"Malásha has purposely splashed it on me."

Akúlka's mother grasped Malásha and gave her a knock on the nape of her neck. Malásha began to howl, and her mother ran out of the house.

"Why do you strike my daughter?" she began to scold her neighbour.

One word brought back another, and the women began to quarrel. The men, too, ran out, and a big crowd gathered in the street. All were crying, and nobody could hear his neighbour. They scolded and cursed each other; one man gave another man a push, and a fight had begun, when Akúlka's grandmother came out. She stepped in the midst of the peasants, and began to talk to them:

"What are you doing, dear ones? Consider the holiday. This is a time for rejoicing. And see what sin you are doing!"

They paid no attention to the old woman, and almost knocked her off her feet. She would never have stopped them, if it had not been for Akúlka and Malásha. While the women exchanged words, Akúlka wiped off her bodice, and went back to the puddle in the lane. She picked up a pebble and began to scratch the ground so as to let the water off into the street. While she was scratching, Malásha came up and began to help her: she picked up a chip and widened the rill. The peasants had begun to fight, just as the water went down the rill toward the place where the old woman was trying to separate the men. The girls ran, one from one side of the rill, the other from the other side.

"Look out, Malásha, look out!" shouted Akúlka.

[Pg 468]

Malásha wanted to say something herself, but could not speak for laughter.

The girls were running and laughing at a chip which was bobbing up and down the rill. They ran straight into the crowd of the peasants. The old woman saw them and said to the peasants:

"Shame on you before God, men! You have started fighting on account of these two girls, and they have long ago forgotten it: the dear children have been playing nicely together. They are wiser than you."

The men looked at the girls, and they felt ashamed. Then they laughed at themselves, and scattered to their farms.

"Except ye become as little children, ye shall not enter into the kingdom of heaven."

[Pg 469]

## THE TWO BROTHERS AND THE GOLD

In ancient times there lived not far from Jerusalem two brothers, the elder named Athanasius, and the younger John. They lived in a mountain, not far from the city, and supported themselves on what people offered them. The brothers passed all their days at work. They worked not for themselves, but for the poor. Wherever were those who were oppressed by labour, or sick people, or orphans, or widows, thither the brothers went, and there they worked, and received no pay. Thus the two brothers passed the whole week away from each other, and met only on Saturday evening in their abode. On Sunday alone did they stay at home, and then they prayed and talked with each other. And an angel of the Lord came down to them and blessed them. On Monday they separated each in his own direction. Thus they lived for many years, and each week the angel of the Lord came down to them and blessed them.

One Monday, when the brothers had already gone out to work and had gone each in his direction, the elder brother, Athanasius, was loath to part from his brother, and he stopped and looked back. John was walking with lowered head, in his direction, without looking back. But suddenly John, too, stopped and, as though he had suddenly noticed something, gazed at something, while shielding his eyes. Then he approached what he was gazing at, suddenly jumped to one side, and, without looking back, ran down-hill and up-hill again, away from the place, as though a wolf were after him. Athanasius was surprised. He went back to that spot, to see what it was[Pg 470] that had so frightened his brother. He went up to it and saw something shining in the sun. He came nearer, and there lay a heap of gold on the ground, as though poured out from a measure. And Athanasius was still more surprised, both at the gold and at his brother's leap.

"Why was he frightened, and why did he run away?" thought Athanasius. "There is no sin in gold. The sin is in man. With gold one may do wrong, but also some good. How many orphans and widows may be fed, how many naked people dressed, and the poor and sick aided with this gold! We now serve people, but our service is small, though it is to the best of our strength. With this gold, however, we can serve people better."

Thus Athanasius thought, and he wanted to tell it all to his brother; but John was out of the range of hearing, and could be seen only as a speck the size of a beetle on another mountain.

Athanasius took off his cloak, scooped up as much gold as he was able to carry away, threw it on his shoulder, and carried it into the city. He came to a hostelry and left the gold with the keeper, and went back for the rest. When he had brought all the gold, he went to the merchants, bought some land in the city, and stones and timber, and hired labourers, and began to build three houses.

Athanasius lived for three months in the city, and built three houses there: one—an asylum for widows and orphans, another—a hospital for the sick and the lame, and a third—for pilgrims and for the needy. And Athanasius found three God-fearing old men, and one of them he placed in charge of the asylum, the second—of the hospital, and the third—of the hostelry. And Athanasius had still three thousand gold coins left. He gave each old man one thousand coins to distribute them to the poor.

The three houses began to fill up with people, and the[Pg 471] people began to praise Athanasius for everything he had done. And Athanasius was glad of that and did not feel like leaving the city. But he loved his brother and so he bade the people farewell and, without keeping a single coin, went back to his abode, wearing the same old garment in which he had come.

As Athanasius was approaching his mountain, he thought:

"My brother did not judge rightly when he jumped from the gold and ran away from it. Have I not done better?"

And no sooner had Athanasius thought so than he saw the angel who used to bless him standing in the road and looking threateningly at him. And Athanasius was frightened and only said:

"For what, O Lord?"

And the angel opened his lips, and said:

"Go hence! You are not worthy of living with your brother. One leap of your brother is worth all the deeds which you have done with your gold."

And Athanasius began to speak of how many poor people and pilgrims he had fed, and how many orphans he had housed. And the angel said:

"The devil who placed the gold there has also taught you these words."

Then only did his conscience trouble him, and he saw that he had done his deeds not for God, and he wept and began to repent.

The angel stepped out of the road and opened the path on which his brother, John, was already standing and waiting for him. After that Athanasius no longer submitted to the temptation of the devil who had scattered the gold, and he understood that not with gold, but only with words can we serve God and men.

And the brothers began to live as before.

[Pg 472]

# ILYÁS

In the Government of Ufá there lived a Bashkir, Ilyás. His father had left him no wealth. His father had died a year after he had got his son married. At that time Ilyás had seven mares, two cows, and a score of sheep; but Ilyás was a good master and began to increase his possessions; he worked with his wife from morning until night, got up earlier than anybody, and went to bed later, and grew richer from year to year. Thus Ilyás passed thirty-five years at work, and came to have a vast fortune.

Ilyás finally had two hundred head of horses, 150 head of cattle, and twelve hundred sheep. Men herded Ilyás's herds and flocks, and women milked the mares and cows, and made kumys, butter, and cheese. Ilyás had plenty of everything, and in the district everybody envied him his life. People said:

"Ilyás is a lucky fellow. He has plenty of everything,—he does not need to die."

Good people made Ilyás's friendship and became his friends. And guests came to him from a distance. He received them all, and fed them, and gave them to drink. No matter who came, he received kumys, and tea, and sherbet, and mutton. If guests came to see him, a sheep or two were killed, and if many guests arrived, he had them kill a mare.

Ilyás had two sons and a daughter. He had got all of them married. When Ilyás had been poor, his sons had worked with him and had herded the horses and the cattle and the sheep; but when they grew rich, the sons[Pg 473] became spoiled, and one of them even began to drink. One of them, the eldest, was killed in a fight, and the other, the younger, had a proud wife, and did not obey his father, and his father had to give him a separate maintenance.

Ilyás gave him a house and cattle, and his own wealth was diminished. Soon after a plague fell on Ilyás's sheep, and many of them died. Then there was a famine year, the hay crop was a failure, and in the winter many head of cattle died. Then the Kirgizes drove off the best herd of horses. And thus Ilyás's estate grew less, and he fell lower and lower, and his strength began to wane.

When he was seventy years old, he began to sell off his furs, rugs, saddles, and tents, and soon had to sell his last head of cattle, so that he was left without anything. Before he knew it, all was gone, and in his old age he had to go with his wife to live among strangers. All that Ilyás had left of his fortune was what garments he had on his body, a fur coat, a cap, and his morocco slippers and shoes, and his wife, Sham-shemagi, who was now an old woman. The son to whom he had given the property had left for a distant country, and his daughter had died. And so there was nobody to help the old people.

Their neighbour, Muhamedshah, took pity on them. Muhamedshah was neither rich nor poor, and he lived an even life, and was a good man. He remembered Ilyás's hospitality, and so pitied him, and said to Ilyás:

"Come to live with me, Ilyás, and bring your wife with you! In the summer work according to your strength in my truck-garden, and in the winter feed the cattle, and let Sham-shemagi milk the mares and make kumys. I will feed and clothe you and will let you have whatever you may need."

Ilyás thanked his neighbour, and went to live with his wife as Muhamedshah's labourers. At first it was hard[Pg 474] for them, but soon they got used to the work, and the old people worked according to their strength.

It was profitable for the master to keep these people, for they had been masters themselves and knew all the order and were not lazy, but worked according to their strength; but it pained Muhamedshah to see the well-to-do people brought down so low.

One day distant guests, match-makers, happened to call on Muhamedshah; and the mulla, too, came. Muhamedshah ordered his men to catch a sheep and kill it. Ilyás flayed the sheep and cooked it and sent it in to the guests. They ate the mutton, drank tea, and then started to drink kumys. The guests and the master were sitting on down cushions on the rugs, drinking kumys out of bowls, and talking; but Ilyás got through with his work and walked past the door. When Muhamedshah saw him, he said to a guest:

"Did you see the old man who just went past the door?"

"I did," said the guest; "but what is there remarkable about him?"

"What is remarkable is that he used to be our richest man. Ilyás is his name; maybe you have heard of him?"

"Of course I have," said the guest. "I have never seen him, but his fame has gone far abroad."

"Now he has nothing left, and he lives with me as a labourer, and his wife is with him,—she milks the cows."

The guest was surprised. He clicked with his tongue, shook his head, and said:

"Evidently fortune flies around like a wheel: one it lifts up, another it takes down. Well, does the old man pine?"

"Who knows? He lives quietly and peaceably, and works well."

Then the guest said:

[Pg 475]

"May I speak with him? I should like to ask him about his life."

"Of course you may," said the master, and he called out of the tent: "Babay!" (This means "grandfather" in the Bashkia language.) "Come in and drink some kumys, and bring your wife with you!"

Ilyás came in with his wife. He exchanged greetings with the guests and with the master, said a prayer, and knelt down at the door; but his wife went back of a curtain and sat down with the mistress.

A bowl of kumys was handed to Ilyás. Ilyás saluted the guests and the master, made a bow, drank a little, and put down the bowl.

"Grandfather," the guest said to him, "I suppose it makes you feel bad to look at us and think of your former life, considering what fortune you had and how hard your life is now."

But Ilyás smiled and said:

"If I should tell you about my happiness and unhappiness, you would not believe me,—you had better ask my wife. She is a woman, and what is in her heart is on her tongue: she will tell you all the truth about this matter."

And the guest spoke to her behind the curtain:

"Well, granny, tell us how you judge about your former happiness and present sorrow."

And Sham-shemagi spoke from behind the curtain:

"I judge like this: My husband and I lived for fifty years trying to find happiness, and we did not find it; but now it is the second year that we have nothing left and that we live as labourers, and we have found that happiness and need no other."

The guests were surprised and the master marvelled, and he even got up to throw aside the curtain and to look at the old woman. But the old woman was standing with folded hands, smiling and looking at her husband,[Pg 476] and the old man was smiling, too. The old woman said once more:

"I am telling you the truth, without any jest: for half a century we tried to find happiness, and so long as we were rich, we did not find it; now nothing is left, and we are working out,—and we have come to have such happiness that we wish for no other.".

175

"Wherein does your happiness lie?"

"In this: when we were rich, my husband and I did not have an hour's rest: we had no time to talk together, to think of our souls, or to pray. We had so many cares! Now guests called on us,—and there were the cares about what to treat them to and what presents to make so that they should not misjudge us. When the guests left, we had to look after the labourers: they thought only of resting and having something good to eat, but we cared only about having our property attended to,—and so sinned. Now we were afraid that a wolf would kill a colt or a calf, and now that thieves might drive off a herd. When we lay down to sleep, we could not fall asleep, fearing lest the sheep might crush the lambs. We would get up in the night and walk around; no sooner would we be quieted than we would have a new care,—how to get fodder for the winter. And, worse than that, there was not much agreement between my husband and me. He would say that this had to be done so and so, and I would say differently, and so we began to quarrel, and sin. Thus we lived from one care to another, from one sin to another, and saw no happy life."

"Well, and now?"

"Now my husband and I get up, speak together peaceably, in agreement, for we have nothing to quarrel about, nothing to worry about,—all the care we have is to serve our master. We work according to our strength, and we work willingly so that our master shall have no loss, but profit. When we come back, dinner is ready, and supper,[Pg 477] and kumys. If it is cold, there are dung chips to make a fire with and a fur coat to warm ourselves. For fifty years we looked for happiness, but only now have we found it."

The guests laughed.

And Ilyás said:

"Do not laugh, brothers! This is not a joke, but a matter of human life. My wife and I were foolish and wept because we had lost our fortune, but now God has revealed the truth to us, and we reveal this to you, not for our amusement but for your good."

And the mulla said:

"That was a wise speech, and Ilyás has told the precise truth,—it says so, too, in Holy Writ."

And the guests stopped laughing and fell to musing.

[Pg 478]
[Pg 479]

## A FAIRY-TALE

About Iván the Fool and His Two Brothers, Semén the Warrior and Tarás the Paunch, and His Dumb Sister Malánya, and About the Old Devil and the Three Young Devils

1885

[Pg 480]
[Pg 481]

### A FAIRY-TALE

About Iván the Fool and His Two Brothers, Semén the Warrior and Tarás the Paunch, and His Dumb Sister Malánya, and About the Old Devil and the Three Young Devils

### I.

In a certain kingdom, in a certain realm, there lived a rich peasant. He had three sons, Semén the Warrior, Tarás the Paunch, and Iván the Fool, and a daughter Malánya, the dumb old maid.

Semén the Warrior went to war, to serve the king; Tarás the Paunch went to a merchant in the city, to sell wares; but Iván the Fool and the girl remained at home, to work and hump their backs.

Semén the Warrior earned a high rank and an estate, and married a lord's daughter. His salary was big, and his estate was large, but still he could not make both ends meet: whatever he collected, his wife scattered as though from a sleeve, and they had no money.

Semén the Warrior came to his estate, to collect the revenue. His clerk said to him:

176

"Where shall it come from? We have neither cattle, nor tools: neither horses, nor cows, nor plough, nor harrow.[Pg 482] Everything has to be provided, then there will be an income."

And Semén the Warrior went to his father:

"You are rich, father," he said, "and you have not given me anything. Cut off a third and I will transfer it to my estate."

And the old man said:

"You have brought nothing to my house, why should I give you a third? It will be unfair to Iván and to the girl."

But Semén said:

"But he is a fool, and she is a dumb old maid. What do they need?"

And the old man said:

"As Iván says so it shall be!"

But Iván said:

"All right, let him have it!"

So Semén the Warrior took his third from the house, transferred it to his estate, and again went away to serve the king.

Tarás the Paunch, too, earned much money,—and married a merchant woman. Still he did not have enough, and he came to his father, and said:

"Give me my part!"

The old man did not want to give Tarás his part:

"You," he said, "have brought nothing to the house, and everything in the house has been earned by Iván. I cannot be unfair to him and to the girl."

But Tarás said:

"What does he want it for? He is a fool. He cannot marry, for no one will have him; and the dumb girl does not need anything, either. Give me," he said, "half of the grain, Iván! I will not take your tools, and of your animals I want only the gray stallion,—you cannot plough with him."

Iván laughed.

[Pg 483]

"All right," he said, "I will earn it again."

So Tarás, too, received his part. Tarás took the grain to town, and drove off the gray stallion, and Iván was left with one old mare, and he went on farming and supporting his father and his mother.

[Pg 484]

## II.

The old devil was vexed because the brothers had not quarrelled in dividing up, but had parted in love. And so he called up three young devils.

"You see," he said, "there are three brothers, Semén the Warrior, Tarás the Paunch, and Iván the Fool. They ought to be quarrelling, but, instead, they live peacefully; they exchange with each other bread and salt. The fool has spoiled all my business. Go all three of you.—get hold of them, and mix them up in such a way that they shall tear out one another's eyes. Can you do it?"

"We can," they said.

"How are you going to do it?"

"We will do it like this," they said: "First we will ruin them, so that they will have nothing to eat; then we will throw them all in a heap, so that they will quarrel together."

"Very well," he said. "I see that you know your business. Go, and do not return to me before you have muddled all three, or else I will flay all three of you."

The three devils all went to a swamp, and considered how to take hold of the matter: they quarrelled and quarrelled, for they wanted each of them to get the easiest job, and finally they decided to cast lots for each man. If one of them got through first, he was to come and help the others. The devils cast lots, and set a time when they were to meet again in the swamp, in order to find out who was through, and who needed help.

When the time came, the devils gathered in the swamp.[Pg 485] They began to talk about their affairs. The first devil, Semén the Warrior's, began to speak.

"My affair," he said, "is progressing. To-morrow my Semén will go to his father."
His comrades asked him how he did it.

"In the first place," he said, "I brought such bravery over Semén that he promised his king to conquer the whole world, and the king made him a commander and sent him out to fight the King of India. They came together for a fight. But that very night I wet all his powder, and I went over to the King of India and made an endless number of soldiers for him out of straw. When Semén's soldiers saw the straw soldiers walking upon them on all sides, they lost their courage. Semén commanded them to fire their cannon and their guns, but they could not fire them. Semén's soldiers were frightened and ran away like sheep. And the King of India vanquished them. Semén is disgraced,—they have taken his estate from him, and to-morrow he is to be beheaded. I have only one day's work left to do: to let him out of the prison, so that he can run home. To-morrow I shall be through with him, so tell me which of you I am to aid!"

Then the other devil, Tarás's, began to speak:

"I do not need any help," he said, "for my affair is also progressing nicely,—Tarás will not live another week. In the first place, I have raised a belly on him, and made him envious. He is so envious of other people's property that, no matter what he sees, he wants to buy it. He has bought up an endless lot of things and spent all his money on them and is still buying. He now buys on other people's money. He has quite a lot on his shoulders, and is so entangled that he will never free himself. In a week the time will come for him to pay, and I will change all his wares into manure,—and he will not be able to pay his debts, and will go to his father's."

[Pg 486]

They began to ask the third devil, Iván's.

"How is your business?"

"I must say, my business is not progressing at all. The first thing I did was to spit into his kvas jug, so as to give him a belly-ache, and I went to his field and made the soil so hard that he should not be able to overcome it. I thought that he would never plough it up, but he, the fool, came with his plough and began to tear up the soil. His belly-ache made him groan, but he stuck to his ploughing. I broke one plough of his, but he went home, fixed another plough, wrapped new leg-rags on him, and started once more to plough. I crept under the earth, and tried to hold the ploughshare, but I could not do it,—he pressed so hard on the plough; the ploughshares are sharp, and he has cut up my hands. He has ploughed up nearly the whole of it,—only a small strip is left. Come and help me, brothers, or else, if we do not overpower him, all our labours will be lost. If the fool is left and continues to farm, they will have no want, for he will feed them all."

Semén's devil promised to come on the morrow to help him, and thereupon the devils departed.

[Pg 487]

### III.

Iván ploughed up all the fallow field, and only one strip was left. His belly ached, and yet he had to plough. He straightened out the lines, turned over the plough, and went to the field. He had just made one furrow, and was coming back, when something pulled at the plough as though it had caught in a root. It was the devil that had twined his legs about the plough-head and was holding it fast.

"What in the world is that?" thought Iván. "There were no roots here before, but now there are."

Iván stuck his hand down in the furrow, and felt something soft. He grabbed it and pulled it out. It was as black as a root, but something was moving on it. He took a glance at it, and, behold, it was a live devil.

"I declare," he said, "it is a nasty thing!" And Iván swung him and was about to strike him against the plough-handle; but the devil began to scream.

"Do not beat me," he said, "and I will do for you anything you wish."

"What will you do for me?"

"Say what you want!"

Iván scratched himself.

178

"My belly aches,—can you cure me?"

"I can," he said.

"Very well, cure me!"

The devil bent down to the furrow, scratched awhile in it, pulled out a few roots,—three of them in a bunch,—and gave them to Iván.

[Pg 488]

"Here," he said, "is a root, which, if you swallow, will make your ache go away at once."

Iván took the roots, tore them up, and swallowed one. His belly-ache stopped at once.

Then the devil began to beg again:

"Let me go, now, and I will slip through the earth, and will not come up again."

"All right," he said, "God be with you!"

And the moment Iván mentioned God's name, the devil bolted through the earth, as a stone plumps into the water, and only a hole was left. Iván put the remaining two roots in his cap, and started to finish his work. He ploughed up the strip, turned over the plough, and went home. He unhitched the horse, came to the house, and there found his eldest brother, Semén the Warrior, with his wife, eating supper. His estate had been taken from him, and he had with difficulty escaped from prison and come to his father's to live.

Semén saw Iván, and, "I have come to live with you," he said. "Feed me and my wife until I find a new place!"

"All right," he said, "stay here!"

Iván wanted to sit down on a bench, but the lady did not like the smell of Iván. So she said to her husband:

"I cannot eat supper with a stinking peasant."

"All right," he said, "I have to go anyway to pasture the mare for the night."

Iván took some bread and his caftan, and went out to herd his mare.

[Pg 489]

## IV.

That night Semén's devil got through with his work and by agreement went to find Iván's devil, to help to make an end of the fool. He came to the field and looked for him everywhere, but found only the hole.

"Something has evidently gone wrong with my comrade," he thought,—"I must take his place. The ploughing is done,—I shall have to catch him in the mowing time."

The devil went to the meadows and sent a flood on the mowing so that it was all covered with mud. Iván returned in the morning from the night watch, whetted his scythe, and went out to mow the meadows. He came, and began to mow: he swung the scythe once, and a second time, and it grew dull and would not cut,—it was necessary to grind it. Iván worked hard and in vain.

"No," he said, "I will go home, and will bring the grindstone with me, and a round loaf. If I have to stay here for a week, I will not give up until I mow it all."

When the devil heard it he thought:

"This fool is stiff-necked,—I cannot get at him. I must try something else."

Iván came back, ground his scythe, and began to mow. The devil crept into the grass and began to catch the scythe by the snath-end and to stick the point into the ground. It went hard with Iván, but he finished the mowing, and there was left only one scrubby place in the swamp. The devil crawled into the swamp and thought:

"If I get both my paws cut, I will not let him mow it."

[Pg 490]

Iván went into the swamp; the grass was not dense, but he found it hard to move the scythe. Iván grew angry and began to swing the scythe with all his might. The devil gave in; he had hardly time to get away,—he saw that matters were in bad shape, so he hid in a bush. Iván swung the scythe with all his might and struck the bush, and cut off half of the devil's tail. Iván finished the mowing, told the girl to rake it up, and himself went to cut the rye.

179

He went out with a round knife, but the bobtailed devil had been there before him and had so mixed up the rye that he could not cut it with the round knife. Iván went back, took the sickle, and began to cut it; he cut all the rye.

"Now I must go to the oats," he said.

The bobtailed devil heard it, and thought:

"I could not cope with him on the rye, but I will get the better of him in the oats,— just let the morning come."

The devil ran in the morning to the oats-field, but the oats were all cut down. Iván had cut them in the night, to keep them from dropping the seed.

The devil grew angry:

"The fool has cut me all up, and has worn me out. I have not seen such trouble even in war-time. The accursed one does not sleep,—I cannot keep up with him. I will go now to the ricks, and will rot them all."

And the devil went to the rye-rick, climbed between the sheaves, and began to rot them: he warmed them up, and himself grew warm and fell asleep.

Iván hitched his mare, and went with the girl to haul away the ricks. He drove up to one and began to throw the sheaves into the cart. He had just put two sheaves in when he stuck his fork straight into the devil's back; he raised it, and, behold, on the prongs was a live devil, and a bobtailed one at that, and he was writhing and twisting, and trying to get off.

[Pg 491]

"I declare," he said, "it is a nasty thing! Are you here again?"

"I am a different devil," he said. "My brother was here before. I was with your brother Semén."

"I do not care who you are," he replied, "you will catch it, too."

He wanted to strike him against the ground, but the devil began to beg him:

"Let me go, and I will not do it again, and I will do for you anything you please."

"What can you do?"

"I can make soldiers for you from anything."

"What good are they?"

"You can turn them to any use you please: they will do anything."

"Can they play music?"

"They can."

"All right, make them for me!"

And the devil said:

"Take a sheaf of rye, strike the lower end against the ground, and say: 'By my master's command not a sheaf shall you stand, but as many straws as there are so many soldiers there be.'"

Iván took the sheaf, shook it against the ground, and spoke as the devil told him to. And the sheaf fell to pieces, and the straws were changed into soldiers, and in front a drummer was drumming, and a trumpeter blowing the trumpet. Iván laughed.

"I declare," he said, "it is clever. This is nice to amuse the girls with."

"Let me go now," said the devil.

"No," he said, "I will do that with threshed straw, and I will not let full ears waste for nothing. I will thresh them first."

So the devil said:

"Say, 'As many soldiers, so many straws there be![Pg 492] With my master's command again a sheaf it shall stand.'"

Iván said this, and the sheaf was as before. And the devil begged him again:

"Let me go now!"

"All right!" Iván caught him on the cart-hurdle, held him down with his hand, and pulled him off the fork. "God be with you!" he said.

The moment he said, "God be with you," the devil bolted through the earth, as a stone plumps into the water, and only a hole was left.

Iván went home, and there he found his second brother. Tarás and his wife were sitting and eating supper. Tarás the Paunch had not calculated right, and so he ran away from his debts and came to his father's. When he saw Iván, he said:

180

"Iván, feed me and my wife until I go back to trading!"

"All right," he said, "stay with us!"

Iván took off his caftan, and seated himself at the table.

But the merchant's wife said:

"I cannot eat with a fool. He stinks of sweat."

So Tarás the Paunch said:

"Iván, you do not smell right, so go and eat in the vestibule!"

"All right," he said, and, taking bread, he went out. "It is just right," he said, "for it is time for me to go and pasture the mare for the night."

[Pg 493]

## V.

That night Tarás's devil got through with his job, and he went by agreement to help out his comrades,—to get the best of Iván the Fool. He came to the field and tried to find his comrades, but all he saw was a hole in the ground; he went to the meadows, and found a tail in the swamp, and in the rye stubbles he found another hole.

"Well," he thought, "evidently some misfortune has befallen my comrades; I must take their place, and go for the fool."

The devil went forth to find Iván. But Iván was through with the field, and was chopping wood in the forest.

The brothers were not comfortable living together, and they had ordered the fool to cut timber with which to build them new huts.

The devil ran to the woods, climbed into the branches, and did not let Iván fell the trees. Iván chopped the tree in the right way, so that it might fall in a clear place; he tried to make it fall, but it came down the wrong way, and fell where it had no business to fall, and got caught in the branches. Iván made himself a lever with his axe, began to turn the tree, and barely brought it down. Iván went to chop a second tree, and the same thing happened. He worked and worked at it, and brought it down. He started on a third tree, and again the same happened.

Iván had expected to cut half a hundred trunks, and before he had chopped ten it was getting dark. Iván[Pg 494] was worn out. Vapours rose from him as though a mist were going through the woods, but he would not give up. He chopped down another tree, and his back began to ache so much that he could not work: he stuck the axe in the wood, and sat down to rest himself.

The devil saw that Iván had stopped, and was glad:

"Well," he thought, "he has worn himself out, and he will stop soon. I will myself take a rest," and he sat astride a bough, and was happy.

But Iván got up, pulled out his axe, swung with all his might, and hit the tree so hard from the other side that it cracked and came down with a crash. The devil had not expected it and had no time to straighten out his legs. The bough broke and caught the devil's hand. Iván began to trim, and behold, there was a live devil. Iván was surprised.

"I declare," he said, "you are a nasty thing! Are you here again?"

"I am not the same," he said. "I was with your brother Tarás."

"I do not care who you are,—you will fare the same way." Iván swung his axe, and wanted to crush him with the back of the axe.

The devil began to beg him:

"Do not kill me,—I will do anything you please for you."

"What can you do?"

"I can make as much money for you as you wish."

"All right, make it for me!"

And the devil taught him how to do it.

"Take some oak leaves from this tree," he said, "and rub them in your hands. The gold will fall to the ground."

Iván took some leaves and rubbed them,—and the gold began to fall.

"This is nice to have," he said, "when you are out celebrating with the boys."

[Pg 495]

"Let me go now!" said the devil.

"All right!" Iván took his lever, and freed the devil. "God be with you," he said, and the moment he mentioned God's name, the devil bolted through the earth, as a stone plumps into the water, and only a hole was left.

[Pg 496]

## VI.

The brothers built themselves houses, and began to live each by himself. But Iván got through with his field work, and brewed some beer and invited his brothers to celebrate with him. They would not be Iván's guests:

"We have never seen a peasant celebration," they said.

Iván treated the peasants and their wives, and himself drank until he was drunk, and he went out into the street to the khorovód. He went up to the women, and told them to praise him.

"I will give you what you have not seen in all your lives."

The women laughed, and praised him. When they got through, they said:

"Well, let us have it!"

"I will bring it to you at once," he said.

He picked up the seed-basket and ran into the woods. The women laughed: "What a fool he is!" And they forgot about him, when, behold, he was running toward them, and carrying the basket full of something.

"Shall I let you have it?"

"Yes."

Iván picked up a handful of gold and threw it to the women. O Lord, how they darted for the money! The peasants rushed out and began to tear it out of the hands of the women. They almost crushed an old woman to death. Iván laughed.

"Oh, you fools," he said, "why did you crush that old woman? Be more gentle, and I will give you some[Pg 497] more." He began to scatter more gold. People ran up, and Iván scattered the whole basketful. They began to ask for more. But Iván said:

"That is all. I will give you more some other time. Now let us have music! Sing songs!"

The women started a song.

"I do not like your kind of songs," he said.

"What kind is better?"

"I will show you in a minute," he said. He went to the threshing-floor, pulled out a sheaf, straightened it up, placed it on end, and struck it against the ground.

"At your master's command not a sheaf shall you stand, each straw a soldier shall be."

The sheaf flew to pieces, and out came the soldiers, and the drums began to beat and the trumpets to sound. Iván told the soldiers to play songs, and went into the street with them. The people were surprised. The soldiers played songs, and then Iván took them back to the threshing-floor, and told nobody to follow him. He changed the soldiers back into a sheaf, and threw it on the loft. He went home and went to sleep behind the partition.

[Pg 498]

## VII.

On the next morning his eldest brother, Semén the Warrior, heard of it, and he went to see Iván.

"Reveal to me," he said, "where did you find those soldiers, and where did you take them to?"

"What is that to you?" he said.

"What a question! With soldiers anything may be done. You can get a kingdom for yourself."

Iván was surprised.

"Indeed? Why did you not tell me so long ago?" he said. "I will make as many for you as you please. Luckily the girl and I have threshed a lot of straw."

Iván took his brother to the threshing-floor, and said:

"Look here! I will make them for you, but you take them away, or else, if we have to feed them, they will ruin the village in one day."

182

Semén the Warrior promised that he would take the soldiers away, and Iván began to make them. He struck a sheaf against the floor, there was a company; he struck another, there was a second, and he made such a lot of them that they took up the whole field.

"Well, will that do?"

Semén was happy, and said:

"It will do. Thank you, Iván."

"All right," he said. "If you need more, come to me, and I will make you more. There is plenty of straw to-day."

Semén the Warrior at once attended to the army, collected it as was proper, and went forth to fight.

No sooner had Semén the Warrior left, than Tarás the[Pg 499] Paunch came. He, too, had heard of the evening's affair, and he began to beg his brother:

"Reveal to me, where do you get the gold money from? If I had such free money, I would with it gather in all the money of the whole world."

Iván was surprised.

"Indeed? You ought to have told me so long ago," he said. "I will rub up for you as much as you want."

His brother was glad:

"Give me at least three seed-baskets full!"

"All right," he said, "let us go to the woods! But hitch up the horse, or you will not be able to carry it away."

They went to the woods, and Iván began to rub the oak leaves. He rubbed up a large heap.

"Will that do, eh?"

Tarás was happy.

"It will do for awhile," he said. "Thank you, Iván."

"You are welcome. If you need more, come to me, and I will rub up some more,— there are plenty of leaves left."

Tarás the Paunch gathered a whole wagon-load of money, and went away to trade with it.

Both brothers left the home. And Semén went out to fight, and Tarás to trade. And Semén the Warrior conquered a whole kingdom for himself, while Tarás the Paunch made a big heap of money by trading.

The brothers met, and they revealed to one another where Semén got the soldiers, and Tarás the money.

Semén the Warrior said to his brother:

"I have conquered a kingdom for myself, and I lead a good life, only I have not enough money to feed my soldiers with."

And Tarás the Paunch said:

"And I have earned a whole mound of money, but here is the trouble: I have nobody to guard the money."

[Pg 500]

So Semén the Warrior said:

"Let us go to our brother! I will tell him to make me more soldiers, and I will give them to you to guard your money; and you tell him to rub me more money with which to feed the soldiers."

And they went to Iván. When they came to him, Semén said:

"I have not enough soldiers, brother. Make me some more soldiers,—if you have to work over two stacks."

Iván shook his head.

"I will not make you any soldiers, for nothing in the world."

"But you promised you would."

"So I did, but I will not make them for you."

"Why, you fool, won't you make them?"

"Because your soldiers have killed a man. The other day I was ploughing in the field, when I saw a woman driving with a coffin in the road, and weeping all the time. I asked her

183

who had died, and she said, 'Semén's soldiers have killed my husband in a war.' I thought that the soldiers would make music, and there they have killed a man. I will give you no more."

And he stuck to it, and made no soldiers for him.

Then Tarás the Paunch began to beg Iván to make him more gold money. But Iván shook his head.

"I will not rub any, for nothing in the world."

"But you promised you would."

"So I did, but I will not do it."

"Why, you fool, will you not do it?"

"Because your gold coins have taken away Mikháylovna's cow."

"How so?"

"They just did. Mikháylovna had a cow, whose milk the children sipped, but the other day the children came to me to ask for some milk. I said to them: 'Where is your cow?' And they answered: 'Tarás the Paunch's[Pg 501] clerk came, and he gave mother three gold pieces, and she gave him the cow, and now we have no milk to sip.' I thought you wanted to play with the gold pieces, and you take the cow away from the children. I will not give you any more."

And the fool stuck to it, and did not give him any. So the brothers went away.

They went away, and they wondered how they might mend matters. Then Semén said:

"This is what we shall do. You give me money to feed the soldiers with, and I will give you half my kingdom with the soldiers to guard your money." Tarás agreed to it. The brothers divided up, and both became kings, and rich men.

[Pg 502]

## VIII.

But Iván remained at home, supporting father and mother, and working the field with the dumb girl.

One day Iván's watch-dog grew sick: he had the mange and was dying. Iván was sorry for him, and he took some bread from the dumb girl, put it in his hat, and took it out and threw it to the dog. But the cap was torn, and with the bread one of the roots fell out. The old dog swallowed it with the bread. And no sooner had he swallowed it than he jumped up, began to play and to bark, and wagged his tail,—he was well again.

When his father and his mother saw that, they were surprised.

"With what did you cure the dog?"

And Iván said to them:

"I had two roots with which to cure all diseases, and he swallowed one."

It happened that at that time the king's daughter grew ill, and the king proclaimed in all the towns and villages that he would reward him who should cure her, and that if it should be an unmarried man, he should have his daughter for a wife. The same was also proclaimed in Iván's village.

Father and mother called Iván, and said to him:

"Have you heard what the king has proclaimed? You said that you had a root, so go and cure the king's daughter. You will get a fortune for the rest of your life."

"All right," he said. And he got ready to go. He was dressed up, and went out on the porch, and saw a beggar woman with a twisted arm.

[Pg 503]

"I have heard that you can cure," she said. "Cure my arm, for I cannot dress myself."

And Iván said:

"All right!" He took the root, gave it to the beggar woman, and told her to swallow it. She swallowed it, and was cured at once and could wave her arm. Iván's parents came out to see him off on his way to the king, and when they heard that he had given away the last root and had nothing left with which to cure the king's daughter, they began to upbraid him.

"You have taken pity on the beggar woman, but you have no pity on the king's daughter."

But he hitched his horse, threw a little straw into the hamper, and was getting ready to drive away.

"Where are you going, fool?"

"To cure the king's daughter."

"But you have nothing to cure her with!"

"All right," he said, and drove away.

He came to the king's palace, and the moment he stepped on the porch, the king's daughter was cured.

The king rejoiced, and sent for Iván. He had him all dressed up:

"Be my son-in-law!" he said.

"All right," he said.

And Iván married the king's daughter. The king died soon after, and Iván became king. Thus all three brothers were kings.

[Pg 504]

## IX.

The three brothers were reigning.

The elder brother, Semén the Warrior, lived well. With his straw soldiers he got him real soldiers. He commanded his people to furnish a soldier to each ten homes, and every such soldier had to be tall of stature, and white of body, and clean of face. And he gathered a great many such soldiers and taught them all what to do. And if any one acted contrary to his will, he at once sent his soldiers against that person, and did as he pleased. And all began to be afraid of him.

He had an easy life. Whatever he wished for, or his eyes fell upon, was his. He would send out his soldiers, and they would take away and bring to him whatever he needed.

Tarás the Paunch, too, lived well. The money which he had received from Iván he had not spent, but he had increased it greatly. He, too, had good order in his kingdom. The money he kept in coffers, and exacted more money from the people. He exacted money from each soul for walking past, and driving past, and for bast shoes, and leg-rags, and shoe-laces. And no matter what he wished, he had; for money they brought him everything, and they went to work for him, because everybody needs money.

Nor did Iván the Fool live badly. As soon as he had buried his father-in-law, he took off his royal garments and gave them to his wife to put away in the coffer. He put on his old hempen shirt and trousers, and his bast shoes, and began to work.

[Pg 505]

"I do not feel well," he said. "My belly is growing larger, and I cannot eat, nor sleep."

He brought his parents and the dumb girl, and began to work again.

People said to him:

"But you are a king!"

"All right," he said, "but a king, too, has to eat."

The minister came to him, and said:

"We have no money with which to pay salaries."

"All right," he said, "if you have none, pay no salaries!"

"But they will stop serving you."

"All right," he said, "Let them stop serving! They will have more time for work. Let them haul manure. They have not hauled any for a long time."

People came to Iván to have a case tried. One said:

"He stole money from me."

But Iván replied:

"All right, evidently he needed it."

All saw that Iván was a fool. His wife said to him:

"They say about you that you are a fool."

"All right," he said.

Iván's wife, too, was a fool, and she thought and thought.

"Why should I go against my husband?" she said. "The thread belongs where the needle is."

185

She took off her regal garments, put them in a coffer, and went to the dumb girl to learn to work. She learned, and began to help her husband.

All the wise men left Iván's kingdom, and only the fools were left. Nobody had any money. They lived and worked and fed themselves and all good people.

[Pg 506]

## X.

The old devil waited and waited for some news from the young devils about how they had destroyed the three brothers, but none came. He went to find out for himself: he looked everywhere for the three, but found only three holes.

"Well," he thought, "evidently they did not get the best of them. I shall have to try it myself."

He went to find the brothers, but they were no longer in their old places. He found them in different kingdoms. All three were living and reigning there. That vexed the old devil.

"I shall have to do the work myself," he said.

First of all he went to King Semén. He did not go to him in his own form, but in the shape of a general. He went to him, and said:

"I have heard that you, King Semén, are a great warrior. I have had good instruction in this business, and I want to serve you."

King Semén began to ask him questions, and he saw that he was a clever man, and so received him into his service.

The old general began to teach King Semén how to gather a great army.

"In the first place," he said, "you must collect more soldiers, for too many people in your kingdom are walking about idly. You must shave the heads of all the young men without exception, and then you will have an army which will be five times as large as it is now. In the second place, you must introduce new guns and cannon.[Pg 507] I will get you the kind of guns that fire one hundred bullets at once, as though pouring out pease. And I will get you cannon that burn with their fire: whether a man, or a horse, or a wall,—they burn everything."

King Semén listened to his new general, and ordered all the young men without exception to be drafted as soldiers, and started new factories. He had a lot of new guns and cannon made, and at once started a war against a neighbouring king. The moment the enemy's army came out against him, he ordered his soldiers to fire at them with bullets and to burn them with the cannon fire. He at once maimed and burnt one-half the army. The neighbouring king became frightened, and he surrendered and gave up his kingdom to him. King Semén was happy.

"Now I will vanquish the King of India," he said.

But the King of India heard of King Semén, and adopted all his inventions and added a few of his own. The King of India drafted not only all the young men, but he also made all the unmarried women serve as soldiers, and so he had even more soldiers than King Semén. He adopted all of King Semén's guns and cannon, and introduced flying in the air and throwing explosive bombs from above.

King Semén went out to make war on the King of India. He thought that he would conquer him as he had conquered before; but the scythe was cutting too fine,—the King of India did not give Semén's army a chance to fire a single shot, for he sent his women into the air, to throw explosive bombs on Semén's army. The women began to pour the bombs on Semén's army, like borax on cockroaches, and the whole army ran away, and King Semén was left alone. The King of India took possession of the whole of Semén's kingdom, and Semén the Warrior ran whither his eyes took him.

[Pg 508]

The old devil had done up this brother, and he made for King Tarás. He took the shape of a merchant and settled in Tarás's kingdom. He started an establishment, and began to issue money. The merchant paid high prices for everything, and the whole nation rushed to the merchant to get his money. And the people had so much money that they paid all their back taxes and paid on time all the taxes as they fell due. King Tarás was happy.

186

"Thanks to the merchant," he thought, "I shall now have more money than ever, and my life will improve."

And King Tarás fell on new plans. He began to build himself a new palace: he commanded the people to haul lumber and stone, and to come to work, and offered high prices for everything. King Tarás thought that as before the people would rush to work for him. But, behold, all the lumber and stone was being hauled to the merchant, and only the labourers were rushing to the king.

King Tarás offered higher prices, but the merchant went higher still. King Tarás had much money, but the merchant had more still, and the merchant could offer better pay than the king. The royal palace came to a standstill,—it could not be built.

King Tarás wanted to get a garden laid out. When the fall came, King Tarás proclaimed that he wanted people to come and set out trees for him; but nobody came, as they were all digging a pond for the merchant.

Winter came. King Tarás wanted to buy sable furs for a new coat, and he sent out men to buy them. The messenger came back, and said that there were no sables,—that all the furs were in the merchant's possession, as he had offered a higher price, and that he had made himself a sable rug.

King Tarás wanted to have some stallions. He sent messengers to buy them for him; but they came back, and said that the merchant had all the good stallions, and they were hauling water and filling up the pond.

[Pg 509]

All the business of the king came to a stop. Men would not do anything for him, but worked only for the merchant; all he received was the merchant's money, for taxes.

And the king collected such a mass of money that he did not know what to do with it, and his life grew bad. The king stopped planning things, and only thought of how he might pass his life peacefully, but he could not do so. He was oppressed in everything. His cooks, and his coachmen, and his servants began to leave him for the merchant. And he began to suffer for lack of food. He would send the women to market to buy provisions, but there was nothing there, for the merchant bought up everything, and all he received was money for taxes.

King Tarás grew angry and sent the merchant abroad; but the merchant settled at the border and continued to do his work: as before, people dragged for the merchant's money all the things from the king to him. The king was in a bad plight: he did not eat for days at a time, and the rumour was spread that the merchant was boasting that he was going to buy the king himself with his money. King Tarás lost his courage, and did not know what to do.

Semén the Warrior came to him, and said:

"Support me, for the King of India has vanquished me."

But Tarás himself was pinched.

"I have not eaten myself for two days," he said.

[Pg 510]

## XI.

The old devil had done up the two brothers, and now went to Iván. The old devil took the shape of a general, and he came to Iván and tried to persuade him to provide himself with an army.

"It will not do for a king to live without an army," he said. "Just command me, and I will gather soldiers from among your people, and will get you up an army."

Iván took his advice.

"All right," he said, "get me up an army: teach them to play good music,—I like that."

The old devil started to go over the kingdom, to gather volunteers. He said that they should go and get their crowns shaved, for which they would get a bottle of vódka each, and a red cap.

The fools laughed at him.

"We have all the liquor we want," they said, "for we distil it ourselves, and as for caps, our women will make us any we want, even motley ones, with tassels at that."

Not one of them would go. The old devil went to Iván and said:

"Your fools will not go of their own will; you will have to force them."

187

"All right," he said, "drive them by force!"

And so the old devil announced that all the fools were to inscribe themselves as soldiers, and that Iván would execute those who would not go.

The fools came to the general and said:

"You say that the king will have us killed if we do not become soldiers, but you do not tell us what we shall[Pg 511] have to do as soldiers. They say that soldiers, too, are killed."

"Yes, that cannot be helped."

When the fools heard that, they became stubborn.

"We will not go," they said. "If so, let us be killed at home! Death cannot be escaped anyway."

"Fools that you are!" said the old devil. "A soldier may be killed or not, but if you do not go, King Iván will certainly have you killed."

The fools considered the matter, and went to see Iván the Fool.

"Your general has come," they said, "and tells us all to turn soldiers. 'If you become soldiers,' he says, 'you may be killed, or not, but if you do not become soldiers King Iván will certainly put you to death.' Is that true?"

Iván began to laugh.

"How can I, one man, have you all put to death? If I were not a fool, I should explain that to you, but as it is, I do not understand it myself."

"If so," they said, "we shall not become soldiers."

"All right," he said, "don't."

The fools went to the general and refused to become soldiers.

The old devil saw that his business did not work, so he went to the King of Cockroachland, and got into his favour.

"Let us go," he said, "and wage war on King Iván, and vanquish him. He has no money, but he has plenty of grain, and cattle, and all kinds of things."

The King of Cockroachland went out to make war: he had gathered a large army, and collected guns and cannon, and left his borders, to enter Iván's kingdom.

People came to Iván and said:

"The King of Cockroachland is coming against us."

"All right," he said, "let him come."

The King of Cockroachland crossed the border, and[Pg 512] sent the advance-guard to find Iván's army. They looked and looked for it, and could not find it. They thought that they might wait for it to show up. But they heard nothing about it,—there was no army to fight.

The King of Cockroachland sent out his men to take possession of the villages. The soldiers came to one village,—and there the fools jumped out to look at the soldiers and to marvel at them. The soldiers began to take away the grain and the cattle: the fools gave it all up, and did not resist. The soldiers went to the next village, and the same happened. The soldiers walked for a day or two, and everywhere the same happened. They gave up all they had, and nobody resisted, and they invited the soldiers to come and live with them:

"If you, dear people," they said, "have not enough to live on in your country, come and settle among us."

The soldiers walked and walked, but no army was to be found; everywhere people were living, and feeding themselves and other people, and they did not resist, but invited them to come and live with them.

The soldiers felt bad, and they came back to the King of Cockroachland.

"We cannot fight here," they said, "so take us to some other place: war would be a good thing, but this is as though we were to cut soup. We cannot fight here."

The King of Cockroachland grew wroth, and commanded his soldiers to march through the whole kingdom, and destroy villages and houses, and burn the grain and kill the cattle.

"If you do not obey my command," he said, "I shall have you all executed."

The soldiers became frightened, and began to carry out the king's command. They started to burn the houses and the grain, and to kill the cattle. And still the fools did not resist, but only wept. The old men wept, and the old women wept, and the children wept.

[Pg 513]

"Why do you offend us? Why do you destroy the property? If you need it, take it along!"

The soldiers felt ashamed. They did not go any farther, and the whole army ran away.

[Pg 514]

## XII.

The old devil went away,—he could not get at Iván by means of the soldiers. The old devil changed into a clean-looking gentleman, and went to live in Iván's kingdom: he wished to get at him by means of money, as he had done with Tarás the Paunch.

"I want to do you good," he said, "and to teach you what is good and proper. I will build a house in your country, and will start an establishment."

"All right," he said, "stay here!"

The clean-looking gentleman stayed overnight, and the following morning he took a large bag of gold to the market-square, and a sheet of paper, and said:

"You are all of you living like pigs. I will teach you how to live. Build me a house according to this plan! You work, and I will show you how, and will pay gold money to you."

And he showed them the gold. The fools were astounded: they had no such a thing as money, and only exchanged things among themselves, or paid with work. They marvelled at the gold and said:

"They are nice things."

And for these gold things they began to give him what they had and to work for him. The old devil rejoiced and thought:

"My affair is proceeding favourably. I will now ruin Iván completely, as I have ruined Tarás, and will buy him up, guts and all."

As soon as the fools had any gold, they gave it all away to their women for necklaces, and their girls wove it into[Pg 515] their braids, and the children began to play in the streets with those pretty things. When all had enough of it, they refused to get any more. The clean-looking gentleman's palace was not half done, and the grain and the cattle were not yet attended to for the year. And the gentleman demanded that they should go and work for him, and haul his grain, and drive his cattle; he promised them much gold for everything and for all work.

But no one came to work, and they brought nothing to him. Only now and then a boy or girl would run in to exchange an egg for a gold coin; otherwise nobody came, and he had nothing to eat. The clean-looking gentleman was starved, and he went to the village to buy something to eat: he went into one yard, and offered a gold coin for a chicken, but the woman would not take it.

"I have too many of them as it is," she said.

He went to a homeless woman, to buy a herring of her, and offered her a gold coin.

"I do not want it, dear man," she said. "I have no children, and so there is nobody to play with it; I myself have three of these for show."

He went to a peasant to buy bread of him, but the peasant, too, would not take the money.

"I do not want it," he said. "If you want bread, for Christ's sake, wait, and I will have my wife cut you off a piece."

The devil just spit out and ran away from the peasant. Not only would he not take anything for Christ's sake, but it was worse than cutting him even to hear that word.

And so he did not get any bread. Everywhere it was the same; no matter where the devil went, they gave him nothing for money, but said:

"Bring us something else, or come and work for it, or take it for Christ's sake!"

[Pg 516]

But the devil had nothing but money. He did not like to work, and for Christ's sake he could not take anything. The old devil grew angry.

189

"What else do you want, if I give you money? You can buy anything for money, or hire a labourer."

The fools paid no attention to him.

"No," they said, "we do not want it. We have no taxes and no wages to pay, so what do we want with the money?"

The old devil went to bed without eating supper.

This affair reached the ears of Iván the Fool. They went to ask him:

"What shall we do? A clean-looking gentleman has appeared among us: he is fond of eating and drinking, and does not like to work, and does not beg for Christ's sake, but only offers us gold pieces. So long as we did not have enough of them, we gave him everything, but now we do not give him any more. What shall we do with him? We are afraid that he will starve."

Iván listened to what they had to say.

"All right," he said, "we shall have to feed him. Let him go from farm to farm as a shepherd!"

The old devil could not help himself, and he began to go from farm to farm. The turn came to Iván's farm. The old devil came to dinner, and the dumb girl was just fixing it. Those who were lazy used to deceive her. Without having worked they came to dinner earlier and ate up all the porridge. And so the dumb girl contrived to tell the good-for-nothing by their hands: if one had calluses, she seated him at the table, but if not, she gave him what was left of the dinner. The old devil climbed behind the table; but the dumb girl took hold of his hands, and there were no calluses; the hands were clean and smooth, and the nails long.

The dumb girl bawled, and pulled the devil out from behind the table.

[Pg 517]

Iván's wife said to him:

"Don't take it amiss, clean gentleman! My sister-in-law will not let a man without calluses sit down at the table. Wait awhile! Let the people eat first, and then you will get what is left."

The old devil was insulted, because at the king's house they would feed him with the swine. He said to Iván:

"What a fool's law you have in your country to let all men work with their hands! You have invented that in your stupidity. Do men work with their hands only? How do you suppose clever people work?"

But Iván said:

"How can we fools know? We labour mostly with our hands and with our backs."

"That is so, because you are fools. I will teach you," he said, "how to work with your heads. You will see that with your heads you can work faster than with your hands."

Iván marvelled.

"Indeed," he said, "we are called fools for good reason."

And the old devil said:

"But it is not easy to work with the head. You do not give me anything to eat because I have no calluses on my hands, and you do not know that it is a hundred times harder to work with the head. At times it just makes the head burst."

Iván fell to musing.

"But why do you torture yourself so much, my dear? It is no small matter to have your head burst. You had better do some easy work,—with your hands and back."

And the devil said:

"The reason I torture myself is because I pity you fools. If I did not torture myself, you would remain[Pg 518] fools to the end of your days. I have worked with my head, and now I will teach you, too."

Iván marvelled.

"Teach us," he said, "for now and then the hands get tired, and it would be nice to use the head instead."

The devil promised to teach him.

And Iván proclaimed throughout his kingdom that a clean-looking man had appeared who would teach people how to work with their heads, that they could work more with their heads than with their hands, and that they should come and learn.

In Iván's kingdom there was a high tower, and a straight staircase led up to it, and at the top there was a spy-room. Iván took the gentleman there so that he might see better.

The gentleman stood up on the tower and began to speak from it. The fools gathered around to look at him. The fools thought that he would show them in fact how to work with the head instead of the hands. But the old devil taught them only in words how to live without working.

The fools did not understand a word. They looked and looked and went away, each to his work.

The old devil stood on the tower a day, and a second day, and kept talking. He wanted to eat; but the fools did not have enough sense to send some bread up to the tower. They thought that if he could work better with his head than with his hands, he would somehow earn bread for himself with his head. The old devil stood another day in the tower-room, and kept talking all the time. And the people came up and looked, and looked and went away.

Then Iván asked:

"Well, has the gentleman begun to work with his head?"

"Not yet," people said, "he is still babbling."

[Pg 519]

The old devil stood another day on the tower and began to weaken; he tottered and struck his head against a post. One of the fools saw that, and told Iván's wife about it, and she ran to her husband in the field.

"Come, let us go and see," she said. "The gentleman is beginning to work with his head."

Iván was surprised.

"Indeed?" he said. He turned in the horse, and went to the tower. When he came up to it, the old devil was weakened from hunger and tottering from side to side and knocking his head against the posts. Just as Iván came up, the devil stumbled and fell and rattled down the stairs, head foremost: he counted all the steps.

"Well," said Iván, "the clean-looking gentleman told the truth when he said that at times the head bursts. This is worse than calluses: such works will leave bumps on the head."

The old devil came down the whole staircase and struck his head against the ground. Iván wanted to go and see how much work he had done, but suddenly the earth gave way, and the old devil went through the earth, and nothing but a hole was left.

Iván scratched himself.

"I declare," he said, "it is a nasty thing! It is again he. He must be the father of those others. What a big fellow he is!"

Iván is still living, and people are all the time rushing to his kingdom, and his brothers, too, came to him, and he is feeding them all. If any one comes and says: "Feed me!" he replies:

"All right, stay here, we have plenty of everything."

They have but one custom in his country, and that is, if one has calluses on his hands, he may sit down at the table, and if he has not, he gets the remnants.

Made in the USA
Columbia, SC
31 July 2017